D1052482

The Wicked Day

MARY STEWART

FAWCETT CREST • NEW YORK

To Geordie Haddington
with deep affection

Contents

Prologue

Merlin is dead."

It was no more than a whisper, and the man who breathed
was barely at arm's length from the woman, his wife, but
he walls of the cottage's single room seemed to catch and
hrow the sentence on like a whispering gallery. And on the
voman the effect was as startling as if he had shouted. Her
and, which had been rocking the big cradle beside the turf
re, jerked sharply, so that the child curled under the blan-
ets woke, and whimpered.

For once she ignored him. Her blue eyes, incongruously
ale and bright in a face as brown and withered as dried
eaweed, showed a shifting mixture of hope, doubt and fear.
here was no need to ask her man where he had got the
ews. Earlier that day she had seen the sail of the trading
hip standing in towards the bay where, above the cluster
f dwellings that formed the only township on the island,
he queen's new house stood, commanding the main har-
our. The fishermen at their nets beyond the headland were
vont to pull close in to an incomer's course and shout for
ews.

Her mouth opened as if a hundred questions trembled
here, but she asked only one. "Can it really be true?"

"Aye, this time it's true. They swore it."

One of the woman's hands went to her breast, making
he sign against enchantment. But she still looked doubtful.

1

"Well, but they said the same last autumn, when—" she hesitated, then gave the pronoun a weight that seemed to make a title of it, "—when She was still down in Dunpeldyr with the little prince, and expecting the twin babies. I mind it well. You'd gone down to the harbour when the trader put in from Lothian, and when you brought the pay home you told me what the captain said. There'd been a feast made at the palace there, even before the news came in of Merlin's death. She must have 'seen' it with her magic, he said. But in the end it wasn't true. It was only a vanishing, like he'd done before, many a time."

"Aye, that's true. He did vanish away, all through the winter, no one knows where. And a bad winter it was, too, the same as here, but his magic kept him alive, because they found him in the end, in the Wild Forest, as crazy as a hare, and they took him up to Galava to nurse him. Now they say he took sick and died there, before ever the High King got back from the wars. It's true enough this time, wife, and we've got it first, direct. The ship picked it up when they put in for water at Glannaventa, with Merlin lying dead in his bed not forty miles off. There was a lot else, news about some more fighting down south of the Forest, and another victory for the High King, but the wind was too strong to catch all they said, and I couldn't get the boat in any nearer. I'll go up to the town now and get the rest." He dropped his voice still further, a thread of hoarse sound. "It isn't everyone in the kingdom will go into mourning for this news, not even those that were tied in blood. You mark my words, Sula, there'll be another feast at the palace tonight." As he spoke he gave a half-glance over his shoulder towards the cottage door, as if afraid that someone might be listening there.

He was a small, stocky man, with the blue eyes and weather-beaten face of a sailor. He was a fisherman, who all his life had plied his trade from this lonely bay on the biggest island of the Orkney group, the one they called Mainland. Though rough-seeming and slow-witted, he was an honest man, and good at his trade. His name was Brude, and he was thirty-seven years old. His wife, Sula, was four years younger, but so stiff with rheumatism and so bent by heavy toil that she already looked an old woman. It seemed impossible that the child in the cradle could have been borne by her. And indeed, there was no resemblance. The child, a boy some two years old, was dark-eyed and dark-haired, with none of the Nordic colouring that appeared so often among the folk of the Orkney Islands. The hand that clutched the blankets of the cradle was fine-boned and narrow, the dark hair thick and silky, and there was a slant to the brows and the long-lashed eyes that might even indicate some strain of foreign blood.

Nor was the child the only incongruous thing about the place. The cottage itself was very small, little more than a hovel. It was set on a flat patch of salty turf a little way back from the shore, protected to either side by the rise of the land towards the cliffs that enclosed the bay, and from the tides by the rocky ridge that bordered the shore and held back the piled boulders of the storm beach. Inland lay the moors, from which a tiny stream came trickling, to splash in a miniature waterfall down past the cottage to the beach. Some way in from the tide-line it had been dammed to form a makeshift reservoir.

The cottage walls were built of stones gathered from the storm beach. These were flat slabs of sandstone, broken from the cliffs by wind and sea, and weathered naturally, making a simple kind of dry-stone walling, easy to do, and reasonably close against the weather. No mortar was used, but the cracks were caulked with mud. Each storm that came washed some of the mud away, and then more had to be added, so that from a distance the cottage looked like nothing more than a crude box of smoothed mud, with a thatch of rough heather-stems capping it. The thatch was held down by old, patched fishing nets, the ends of which were weighted with stones. There were no windows. The doorway was low and squat, so that a man had to bend double to enter. It was covered only with a curtain of deerskin, roughly tanned and as stiff as wood. The smoke from the fire within came seeping in sullen wisps round the edges of the skin.

But inside, this poorest of poor dwellings showed some glimpses of simple comfort. Though the child's cradle was of old, warped wood, the blankets were soft and brightly dyed, and the pillow was stuffed with feathers. On the stone shelf that served the couple for a bed was a thick, almost luxurious coverlet of sealskin, spotted and deep-piled, a quality of skin which would normally go by right to the

3

house of one of the warriors, or even the queen herself.
And on the table—a worm-ridden slab of sea-wrack propped
on stones, for wood was scarce in the Orkneys—stood the
remains of a good meal: not red meat, indeed, but a couple
of gnawed wings of chicken and a pot of goose-grease to
go with the black bread.

The cottagers themselves were poorly enough dressed.
Brude had on a short, much-mended tunic, with over it the
sleeveless coat of sheepskin which, in summer and winter
protected him from the weather at sea. His legs and feet
were thickly wrapped in rags. Sula's gown was a shapeless
affair of moss-dyed homespun, girdled with a length of rope
such as she wove for her husband's nets. Her feet, too, were
bound up in rags. But outside the cottage, beached above
the tidemark of black weed and smashed shells, lay a good
boat, as good as any in the islands, and the nets spread to
dry over the boulders were far better than Brude could have
made. They were a foreign import, made of materials unob-
tainable in the northern isles, and would normally be beyond
the means of such a household. Brude's own lines, hand
twisted from reeds and dried wrack, stretched from the cottage's thatch to heavy anchor-stones on the turf. On the lines
hung the split carcasses of drying fish, and a couple of big
seabirds, gannets, Sula's namesake. These, dried and stored
and eked out with shellfish and seaweeds, would be winter
food. The promise of better fare, however, was there with
the half-dozen hens foraging along the tidemark, and the
heavy-uddered she-goat tethered on the salt grass.

It was a bright day of early summer. May, in the islands,
can be as cruel as any other month, but this was a day of
sunshine and mild breezes. The stones of the beach looked
grey and turquoise and rosy-red, the sea creamed against
them peacefully, and the turf of the ridge behind was thick
with sea-pink and primrose and red campion. Every ledge
of the cliffs that bounded the bay was crowded with seabirds
claiming and disputing their nesting territory, and nearer, on
shingle or turf, the pied oystercatchers brooded their eggs
or flew, screaming, to and fro along the tide. The air was
loud with their cries. Even had there been a listener outside
the cottage doorway, he could have heard nothing for the
noise of the sea and the birds, but inside the room the furtive
hush persisted. The woman said nothing, but apprehension

4

still showed in her face, and she put up a sleeve to dab at her eyes.

Her husband spoke impatiently.

"What is it, woman? You're never grieving for the old enchanter? Whatever Merlin was to King Arthur and to the mainland folks with his magic, he's been nought to us here. He was old, besides, and even though men said he'd never die, it seems he was mortal after all. What's there to weep for in that?"

"I'm not weeping for him, why should I? But I'm afeared, Brude, I'm afeared."

"For what?"

"Not for us. For him." She gave a half-glance towards the cradle where the boy, awake but still drowsy from his afternoon's sleep, lay quietly, curled small under the blankets.

"For him?" asked her husband, surprised. "Why? Surely all's well for us now, and for him, too. With Merlin gone, that was enemy to our King Lot, and by all accounts to this boy of his as well, who's to harm him now, or us for keeping him? Maybe we can stop watching now in case other folks see him and start asking questions. Maybe he can run out now and play like other children, not hang on your skirts all day, and be babied like you've had him. You'd not keep him in much longer, anyway. He's long since grown beyond that cradle."

"I know, I know. That's what I'm feared of, don't you see? Losing him. When the time comes for Her to take him back from us—"

"Why should it? If she didn't take him away when the news came of King Lot's death, why should she do it now? Look, wife. When the king her husband went, you'd have thought that was when she'd see to it that his bastard went, too, quietly-like. That was when I was afeared, myself. When all's said, it's the little prince, Gawain, that's king of the Orkneys now, by right, but with this boy, bastard or not, nearly—what?—nearly a year older, there's some might say—"

"Some might say too much." Sula spoke sharply, and with such patent fear that Brude, startled, took a stride to the doorway, jerked the curtain aside, and peered out.

"What ails you? There's no one there. And if there were,

they'd hear nothing. The wind's getting up, and the tide's well in. Listen."

She shook her head. She was staring at the child. Her tears had dried. When she spoke, it was barely above a whisper.

"Not outside. There's no folk could get near enough without we heard the sea-pies screaming. It's here in the house we need to watch. Look at him. He's not a baby now. He listens, and sometimes you'd swear he understood every word."

The man trod to the cradle's side and looked down. His face softened. "Well, if he doesn't, he soon will. The gods know he's forward enough. We've done what we've been paid for—and more, seeing what a sickly wean he was when we took him first. Now look at him. Any man might be proud of a son like him." He turned away, reaching for the staff that stood propped beside the doorway. "Look you, Sula, if any ill had been coming, it would have come before this. If harm was meant to him, the payments would have stopped, wouldn't they? So stop your fretting. You've no call now to be fearful."

She nodded, but without looking at him. "Yes. It was simple of me. You're right, I dare say."

"It's a few years yet before young Gawain will be troubling his head about kingdoms, and king's bastards, and by that time this one might well be forgotten. And if that means they stop the payments, who cares for that? A man needs a son to help him, in my trade."

She looked up at him then, and smiled. "You're a good man, Brude."

"Well," he said gruffly, pushing aside the curtain, "let's have an end to this. I'm going up to the town now, to hear what other news the sailors brought."

Left alone with the child, the woman sat for a while without moving, the fear still in her face. Then the boy's hand reached towards her, and she smiled suddenly, a smile that brought youth back, bright and pretty, to her cheeks and eyes. She leaned to lift him from the cradle, and set him on her knee. She picked up a crust of the black bread from the table, sopped it in a beaker of goat's milk, and held it to his lips. The boy took the bread and began to eat it, his dark

ead cuddled into her shoulder. She laid her cheek against
is hair, and put a hand up to stroke it.

"Men are fools, so they are," she said softly. "They never
ee what's staring them in the eye. You'll be no fool, though,
ny bonny, not with the blood that's in you, and the way
hose eyes look and see right through to the back of things,
and you only a baby still. . . ." She gave a little laugh, her mouth
against the child's hair, and the boy smiled at the sound.

"King Lot's bastard, is it? Well, so they say, and better
so. But if they saw what I see, and knew what I guessed at,
ah, these many months past . . ."

She rocked the child closer, calming herself, sending her
mind back to those summer nights two years ago when Brude,
with a gift of gold ensuring his silence, had put out, not to
his accustomed fishing ground, but farther west, into deeper
water. For four nights he had waited there, grumbling at the
oss of his catch, but kept faithful and silent by the gift of
gold and the queen's promise. Then on the fifth night, a
calm, twilit night of the Orkney summer, the ship from Dun-
eldyr had stolen into the sound and dropped anchor, and
a boat put out from her side with three men, queen's soldiers,
owing it. Brude answered their soft hail, and presently the
thwarts of the two craft rubbed together. A bundle passed.
The larger boat dipped away and vanished. Brude turned his
own boat landward, and made all speed to the cottage where
Sula waited by the empty cradle, holding on her lap the shawl
that she had woven for her own dead child.

A bastard, that was all they had been told. A royal bastard. And as such a danger, somewhere, to someone. But
some day, perhaps, to be useful. So keep silent, and nurture
him, and your reward may one day be great. . . .

The reward had long since ceased to matter to Sula. She
lived with the only reward she needed, the child himself.
But she lived, too, with the constant fear that some day,
when it became expedient to one or the other remote and
royal personage, her boy would be taken from her.

She had long ago formed her own guesses as to the identity
of these personages, though she knew better than to speak
of them, even to her husband. Not King Lot; of that she
was certain. She had seen his other children by the queen;
they had Morgause's red-gold hair and their father's high
colour and sturdy build. No such signs identified her foster

7

child. The dark hair and eyes might, indeed, have been Lot's, but their setting, with the line of brow and cheek-bone, was quite different. And something in the mouth, the hands, the slender build and warm, clear skin, some elusive way of moving and looking, marked him, to Sula's constantly watching eyes, as the queen's child, but not the king's.

And, this once granted, other things became clear: the queen's men who had hurried the child out of Dunpeldyr before King Lot arrived home there from the wars; the subsequent massacre of all the town's infants in an attempt to catch and destroy that one child, a massacre attributed by Lot and his queen to King Arthur and his adviser Merlin, but instigated in fact (it was whispered) by King Lot himself; and the regular payments, in cash and kind, that came secretly from the palace, where, during the child's lifetime, King Lot had rarely set foot. From the queen, then. And even now that King Lot was dead, she paid still, and still the child was safe. This, to Sula, was all the proof that was needed. Queen Morgause, a lady not renowned for gentleness, would hardly so have nurtured her husband's bastard; a bastard, moreover, older than the eldest legitimate prince, and as such, arguably, with a prior claim to the kingdom.

Queen's bastard, then. By whom? To Sula's mind there was no doubt there, either. She had never laid eyes on Queen Morgause's half-brother, Arthur the High King of Britain, but like everyone else she had heard many tales of that wonder-working young man. And the first of those tales was that of the great battle of Luguvallium, where the boy Arthur, appearing suddenly at King Uther's side, had led his troops to victory. Afterwards—so the tale went, told with pride and indulgence—he had gone, still ignorant of his true parentage, to lie with Morgause, who was Uther's bastard daughter, and so Arthur's own half-sister.

The timing was right. The child's age, and looks, and ways were right. And those rumours about the massacre at Dunpeldyr, whether ordered by Lot or by Merlin, were accounted for, and even—such were the ways of the great—justified.

Now Lot was dead, and Merlin, too. King Arthur had other and greater matters on his mind, and besides—if all the tales that reached the taverns were true—by this time e had other bastards by the score, and had shut this shame-ul begetting from his mind, or else forgotten it. As for Mor-ause, she would not kill her own son. Never that. But with King Lot gone, and Merlin gone, and the High King far away, why should she leave him here any longer? Why any more need to keep him secret in this lonely place?

She clutched the child closer, her fear cold and heavy in her. "The Goddess keep you safe, make her forget you. Make her forget you. Leave you here. My bonny, my Mordred, my boy from the sea." The child, roused by the sudden movement, tightened his arms round her and said something. It was inaudible, muffled against her neck, but she caught her breath and fell silent, rocking, staring over the child's head at the cottage wall.

After a while the small, ordinary sounds of the room, and the long *hush* of the sea outside, seemed to calm her. The child drowsed in her arms. Softly, she began to sing him back to sleep.

> From the sea you came, my prince, my Mordred.
> You escaped the fay with the long hair that
>   tosses on the waves.
> You came from her sister, the sea-queen
> Who eats drowned sailors, who draws the boats
> Down into deep waters.
> You came to the land, to be prince of the land,
> And you will grow, grow, grow . . .

Queen Morgause did not make a feast that night.

When the fresh news was brought of the hated enchanter's death she sat for a long time very still, then, taking a lamp in her hand, she left the bright hall where the talk was still going noisily round, and made her way to the sealed chambers underground where she worked her dark magic, and waited for such glimmers of Sight as came to her.

In the first chamber, her stillroom, a half-empty flask stood on the table. In it was the remains of the poison she had mixed for Merlin. Smiling, she passed through another door, and knelt by the pool of seeing.

Nothing came clearly. A bedchamber, with a curved wall; a tower room, then? The bed with a man in it, still as death. And he looked like death: a very old man, gaunt as a skeleton, with grey hair straggling on the pillow, and a matted grey beard. She did not recognize him.

He opened his eyes, and it was Merlin. The dark, terrifying eyes, set in that grey skull, looked straight across the miles, across the seas, into hers where she knelt by the secret pool.

Morgause, crouching there with her hands to her belly as if she would guard Lot's last, unborn child, knew then that once more the reports were false. Merlin lived still, and prematurely aged as he was, with his health wrecked by the poison, he still had power enough to bring her and her plans to nothing.

Kneeling there, she began a frantic, frightened spell that in the old man's weakened state, might serve to protect herself and her brood of sons from Arthur's vengeance.

BOOK I

The Boy from the Sea

I

The boy was alone in the summer world with the singing of the honey bees.

He lay flat on his back in the heather at the head of the cliff. Not far from him was the straight-cut line of dark turf where he had been working. The squared peats, stacked like slices of black bread along the ditched gash, were drying in the hot sun. He had been working since daybreak, and the line was a long one. Now the mattock lay idle against the peats while the boy drowsed after his midday meal. One hand, outflung on the heather, still held the remains of a barley bannock. His mother's two hives—crude skeps of barley straw—stood fifty paces in from the brink of the cliff. The heather smelled sweet and heady, like the mead that would be made from the honey. To and fro, sometimes within a finger's breadth of his face, the bees hurtled like slingshot. The only other sound in the drowsy afternoon was the crying, remote below him, of the seabirds at their nests along the cliff.

Something changed in the note of that crying.

The boy opened his eyes, and lay still, listening. Underneath the new, disturbed screaming of kittiwakes and razorbills, he heard the deeper, four-fold alarm note of the big gulls. He himself had not moved for half an hour or more, and in any case they were used to him. He turned his head,

to see a flock of wheeling wings rise like blown snow above
the cliff's edge some hundred paces away. There was a cove
there, a deep inlet with no beach below. Hundreds of sea
birds nested there, guillemots, shags, kittiwakes, and with
them the big falcon. He could see her now, flying with the
gulls that screamed to and fro.

The boy sat up. He could see no boat in the bay, but then
a boat would hardly have caused such a disturbance among
the high-nesting colonies on the cliff. An eagle? He could
see none. At the most, he thought, it might be a predator
raven after the young ones, but any change in the monotony
of the day's work was to be welcomed. He scrambled to his
feet. Finding the remains of the bannock still in his hand,
he made as if to eat it, then saw a beetle on it, and threw it
away with a look of disgust. He ran across the heather towards the cove where the disturbance was.

He reached the edge and peered down. The birds flung
themselves higher, screaming. Puffins hurtled from the rock
below him in clumsy glide, legs wide and wings held stiffly.
The big black-backed gulls vented their harsh cries. The
whitened ledges where the kittiwakes sat in rows on their
nests were empty of adult birds, which were weaving and
screaming in the air.

He lay down, inching forward to peer directly down the
cliff. The birds were diving in past a buttress of rock where
wild thyme and sea-pink made a thick carpet splashed with
white. Clumps of rose-root stirred in the wind of their wings.
Then, among all the commotion, he heard a new sound, a
cry like the cry of a gull, but somehow subtly different. A
human cry. It came from somewhere well down the cliff
out of sight beyond the rocky buttress where the birds wheeled
most thickly.

He moved carefully back from the edge, and got slowly
to his feet. There was no beach at the foot of the cliff,
nowhere to leave a boat, nothing but the steadily beating,
echoing sea. The climber had gone down and there could
only be one reason for trying to climb down here.

"The fool," he said with contempt. "Doesn't he know that
the eggs will all be hatched now?" Half reluctantly he picked
his way along the cliff top to a point from which he could
see, stranded on a ledge beyond the buttress, another boy.

It was no one he knew. Out in this lonely corner of the

land there were few families, and with the sons of the other fishermen Brude's son had never felt in tune. And oddly enough his parents had never encouraged him to mix with them, even as a child. Now, at ten years old, well grown and full of a wiry strength, he had helped his father with the man's jobs already for several years. It was a long time since, in his rare days off, he had troubled with children's ploys. Not that, for such as he, birds'-nesting was a child's game; till, each spring, he made his way down these very cliffs to collect the freshly laid eggs for food. And later he and his father, armed with nets, would come to catch the young ones for Sula to skin and dry against the winter's hardships.

So he knew the ways down the cliff well enough. He also knew how dangerous they were, and the thought of being burdened with someone clumsy enough to strand himself, and probably by now thoroughly scared, was not pleasant.

The boy had seen him. His face was upturned, and he waved and called again.

Mordred made a face, then cupped his hands to his mouth. "What is it? Can't you get back?"

A vivid pantomime from below. It seemed unlikely that the climber could hear what was said, but the question was obvious, and so, too, was his answer. He had hurt his leg, otherwise—and somehow his gestures conveyed this clearly —he would not have dreamed of calling for help.

This bravado had little or no effect on the boy at the head of the cliff. With a shrug that indicated more boredom than anything else, the fisherman's son began the climb down.

It was difficult, and in two or three places dangerous, so Mordred went slowly, taking his time. At length he landed on the ledge beside the climber.

The boys studied one another. The fisherman's son saw a boy of much his own age, with a shock of bright red-gold hair and hazel-green eyes. His complexion was clear and ruddy, his teeth good. And though his clothes were torn and stained with the dirt of the cliff, they were well made of good cloth, and brightly dyed in what looked like expensive colours. On one wrist he wore a copper bracelet no brighter than his hair. He sat with one leg over the other, gripping the hurt ankle tightly in both hands. He was obviously in pain, but when Mordred, with the working man's contempt for his idle betters, looked for signs of tears, he saw none.

15

"You've hurt your ankle?"

"Twisted it. I slipped."

"Is it broken?"

"I don't think so, just sprained. It hurts if I try to sta▮ on it. I must say I'm glad to see you! I seem to have be▮ here for ages. I didn't think anyone would be near enou▮ to hear me, specially through all that noise."

"I didn't hear you. I saw the gulls."

"Well, thank the gods for that. You're a pretty goo▮ climber, aren't you?"

"I know these cliffs. I live near here. All right, we'll hav▮ to try it. Get up and let's see how you manage. Can't y▮ put that foot down at all?"

The red-haired boy hesitated, looking faintly surprise▮ as if the other's tone was strange to him. But all he said wa▮ "I can try. I did try before, and it made me feel sick. I dor▮ think—some of those places were pretty bad, weren't the▮ Hadn't you better go and get help? Tell them to bring a rope▮

"There's no one within miles." Mordred spoke imp▮ tiently. "My father's away with the boat. There's only Moth▮ and she'd be no use. I can get a rope, though. I've got o▮ up at the peats. We'll manage all right with that."

"Fine." There was some attempt at a gay smile. "I'll wa▮ for you, don't fret! But don't be too long, will you? They▮ be worried at home."

At Brude's cottage, thought Mordred, his absence wou▮ never have been noticed. Boys such as he would have ▮ break a leg and be away for a working day before anyon▮ would start to trouble. No, that was not quite fair. Brud▮ and Sula sometimes were as anxious over him as fowls wi▮ a single chicken. He had never seen why; he had ailed noth▮ ing in all his life.

As he turned to go he caught sight of a small lidded bask▮ on the ledge beside the other boy. "I'll take that basket u▮ now. Save trouble later."

"No, thanks. I'd sooner bring it up myself. It'll be a▮ right, it hooks on to my belt."

So, maybe he had found some eggs, thought Mordre▮ then forgot all about it as he turned himself back to the cli▮ climb.

Beside the peat cuttings was the crude sled of driftwoo▮ that was used to drag the cut sods down to the stack besid▮

16

e cottage. Fastened to the sled was a length of reasonably ood rope. Mordred slipped this from its rings as quickly as e could, then ran back to the cliff, and once again made ie slow climb down.

The injured boy looked composed and cheerful. He caught ie rope's end and, with Mordred's help, made it fast to his elt. This was a good one, strongly made of polished leather, ith what looked like silver studs and buckle. The basket /as already clipped there.

Then began the struggle to the top. This took a very long me, with frequent pauses for rest, or for working out how est the injured boy might be helped up each section of the limb. He was obviously in pain, but made no complaint, nd obeyed Mordred's sometimes peremptory instructions /ithout hesitation or any show of fear. Sometimes Mordred /ould climb ahead and make the rope fast where he could, hen descend to help the other boy with the support of arm r shoulder. In places they crawled, or edged along, belly) rock, while all the time the seabirds screamed and wheeled, he wind of their wings stirring the grasses on the very cliff, nd their cries echoed and re-echoed to and fro over the .eeper thud and wash of the waves.

At last it was over. The two boys reached the top safely, nd pulled themselves over the last few feet onto the heather. 'hey sat there, panting and sweating, and eyeing one an- ther, this time with satisfaction and mutual respect.

"You have my thanks." The red-haired boy spoke with a ind of formality that gave the words a weight of genuine eriousness. "And I'm sorry to have given you that trouble.)nce down that cliff would be enough for anyone, but you vere up and down it as spry as a goat."

"I'm used to it. We take eggs in the spring, and then the oung birds later. But it's a bad bit of rock. It looks so easy, vith the stone weathered into slabs like that, but it's not afe, not safe at all."

"You don't need to tell me now. That was what happened. t looked like a safe step, but it broke. I was lucky to get off with just a sprained ankle. And lucky that you were there, oo. I hadn't seen anyone all day. You said you lived near iere?"

"Yes. In a bay about half a mile over yonder. Seals' Bay, 's called. My father's a fisherman."

"What's your name?"

"Mordred. What's yours?"

That faint look of surprise again, as if Mordred shoul have known. "Gawain."

It obviously meant nothing to the fisherman's son. H touched the basket which Gawain had set on the grass be tween them. From it came curious hissing sounds. "What' in there? I thought it couldn't be eggs."

"A couple of young peregrines. Didn't you see the falcon I was half afraid she'd come and knock me off the ledge but she contented herself with screaming. I left two other anyway." He grinned. "Of course I got the best ones."

Mordred was startled. "Peregrines? But that's not a lowed! Only for the palace people, that is. You'll be in rea trouble if anyone sees them. And how on earth did you ge near the nest? I know where it is, it's under that overhan with the yellow flowers on, but that's another fifteen fee lower than the ledge where you were."

"It's easy enough, but a bit tricky. Look." Gawain opene the basket a little way. In it Mordred could see the two youn birds, fully fledged but still obviously juveniles. They hisse and bounced in their prison, floundering, with their claw fast in a tangle of thread.

"The falconer taught me." Gawain shut the lid again. "Yo lower a ball of wool to the nest, and they strike at it. A often as not they'll tangle themselves, and once they're fas in it, you can draw them up. You get the best ones that way too, the bravest. But you have to watch for the mother bird.

"You got those from that ledge where you fell? After yo were hurt, then?"

"Well, there wasn't much else to do while I was stuc there, and besides, that was what I'd gone for," said Gawai simply.

This was something Mordred could understand. Out c his new respect for the other, he spoke impulsively. "Bu you really could be in trouble, you know. Look, give me th basket. If we could get them free of the wool, I'll take ther down again and see if I can get them back to the nest."

Gawain laughed and shook his head. "You couldn't. Don' worry. It's all right. I thought you didn't know me. I ar from the palace, as it happens. I'm the queen's son, th eldest."

"You're *Prince* Gawain?" Mordred's eyes took in the boy's clothes again, the silver at his belt, the air of good living, the self-confidence. Suddenly, at a word, his own was gone, with the easy equality, even the superiority that the cliff climb had given him. This was no longer a silly boy whom he had rescued from danger. This was a prince; the prince, moreover, who was heir to the throne of Orkney; who would be King of the Orkneys, if ever Morgause saw fit—or could be forced—to step down. And he himself was a peasant. For the first time in his life he felt suddenly very conscious of how he looked. His single garment was a short tunic of coarse cloth, woven by Sula from the waste wool gathered from bramble and whin where the sheep had left it. His belt was a length of cord made from bere stalks. His bare legs and feet were stained brown with peat, and were now scratched and grimy from the cliff climb.

He said, hesitating: "Well, but oughtn't you to be attended? I thought—I didn't think princes ever got out alone."

"They don't. I gave them all the slip."

"Won't the queen be angry?" asked Mordred doubtfully.

A flaw at last in that self-assurance. "Probably." The word, brought out carelessly, and rather too loudly, sounded to Mordred a distinct note of apprehension. But this, again, he understood, could even share. It was well known among the islanders that their queen was a witch and to be feared. They were proud of the fact, as they would have been proud of, and resigned to, a brutal but efficient warrior king. Anyone, even her own sons, might without shame be afraid of Morgause.

"But perhaps she won't have me beaten this time," said Orkney's young king, hopefully. "Not when she knows I've hurt my foot. And I did get the peregrines." He hesitated. "Look, I don't think I can get home without help. Will *you* be punished, for leaving your work? I'd see that your father didn't lose by it. Perhaps, if you want to go and tell them where you are—"

"That doesn't matter." Mordred spoke with sudden, renewed confidence. There were after all other differences between him and this wealthy heir to the islands. The prince was afraid of his mother, and would soon have to account for himself, and bribe his way back to favour with his looted hawks. Whereas he, Mordred—

19

He said easily: "I'm my own master. I'll help you back. Wait while I get the peat sled, and I'll pull you home. I think the rope's strong enough."

"Well, if you're sure—" Gawain took the offered hand, and was hauled to his feet. "You're strong enough, anyway. How old are you, Mordred?"

"Ten. Well, nearly eleven."

If Gawain felt any satisfaction about the answer, he concealed it. As they faced one another, eye to eye, Mordred was seen to be the taller by at least two fingers' breadth. "Oh, a year older than me. You probably won't have to take me far," added Gawain. "They'll have missed me by now, and someone'll be sent to look for me. In fact, there they are."

It was true. From the head of the next inland rise, where the heather lifted to meet the sky, came a shout. Three men came hurrying. Two of them, royal guards by their dress, bore spears and shields. The third led a horse.

"Well, that's all right," said Mordred. "And you won't need the sled." He picked up the rope. "I'll get back to the peats, then."

"Well, thanks again." Gawain hesitated. It was he, now, who suddenly seemed to feel something awkward in the situation. "Wait a minute, Mordred. Don't go yet. I said you wouldn't lose by this, that's only fair. I've no coin on me, but they'll send something. . . . You said you lived over that way. What's your father's name?"

"Brude the fisherman."

"Mordred, Brude's son," said Gawain, nodding. "I'm sure she'll send something. If she does send money, or a gift, you'd take it, wouldn't you?"

From a prince to a fisherman's son, it was an odd question, though neither boy seemed to find it so.

Mordred smiled, a small, close-lipped smile that Gawain found curiously familiar. "Of course. Why shouldn't I? Only a fool refuses gifts, particularly when he deserves them. And I don't think I'm a fool," added Mordred.

2

The message from the palace came next day. It was brought by two men, queen's guards by their dress and weapons, and it was not coin, or any sort of gift; it was a summons to the royal presence. The queen, it seemed, wanted to thank her son's rescuer in person.

Mordred, straightening from the peat digging, stared at them, trying to control, or at least conceal, the sudden spurt of excitement within him.

"Now? Go with you now, you mean?"

"Those were the orders," said the elder of the guards, cheerfully. "That's what she said, bring you back with us now."

The other man added, with rough kindliness: "No need to be afraid, youngster. You did well, by all accounts, and there should be something in it for you."

"I'm not afraid." The boy spoke with the disconcerting self-possession that had surprised Gawain. "But I'm too dirty. I can't go to the queen like this. I'll have to go home first, and get myself decent."

The men glanced at one another, then the elder nodded. "Well, that's fair enough. How far is home from here?"

"It's only over there, you can see where the path runs along the cliff top, and then down. Only a few minutes." He stopped as he spoke, to pick up the rope of the sled. This

21

was already half loaded. He threw the mattock on top of the load, and set off, dragging the sled. The grass of the track worn and dry, was slippery, easy for the whalebone runners He went quickly, the two men following. At the head of the slope the men paused, waiting, while the boy, with the ease bred by the daily task, swung the sled round to run downhill in front of him, himself leaning back against the rope to act as brake. He let the load run into the stacked peat on the grass behind the cottage, then dropped the rope and ran indoors. Sula was pounding grain in the quern. Two of the hens had come indoors and were clucking round her feet She looked up, surprised.

"You're early! What is it?"

"Mother, get me my good tunic, will you? Quickly." He snatched up the cloth that did duty as a towel, and made again for the door. "Oh, and do you know where my necklet is, the thong with the purple shells?"

"Necklet? Washing, in the middle of the day?" Bewildered, Sula got up to do as he asked. "What's this, Mordred? What has happened?"

For some reason, probably one he did not know himself the boy had told her nothing about his encounter with Gawain on the cliff. It is possible that his parents' intense interest in everything he did set him instinctively to guard parts of his life from them. In keeping his encounter with the prince a secret, he had hugged to himself the thought of Sula's pleasure when the queen, as he confidently expected, gave him some reward.

His pleased sense of importance, even glee, sounded in his voice. "It's messengers from Queen Morgause, Mother They've come to bid me to the court. They're waiting for me out there. I have to go straight away. The queen want to see me herself."

The effect of his announcement startled even him. His mother, on her way to the bedplace, stopped as if struck then turned slowly, one hand out to the table's top, as if she would have fallen without its support. The pestle fell from her fingers and rolled to the floor, where the hens ran to it clucking. She seemed not to notice. In the smoky light of the room her face had gone sallow. "Queen Morgause? Sent for you? Already?"

Mordred stared. "'Already?' What do you mean, Mother? Did somebody tell you what happened yesterday?"

Sula, her voice shaking, tried to recover herself. "No, no. I meant nothing. What did happen yesterday?"

"It was nothing much. I was out at the peats and I heard a cry from the cliff over yonder, and it was the young prince, Gawain. You know, the oldest of the queen's sons. He was half down the cliff after young falcons. He'd hurt his leg, and I had to take the rope down from the sled, and help him climb back. That's all. I didn't know who he was till afterwards. He told me his mother would reward me, but I didn't think it would happen like this, not so quickly, anyway. I didn't tell you yesterday, because I wanted it to be a surprise. I thought you'd be pleased."

"Pleased, of course I'm pleased!" She took a great breath, steadying herself by the table. Her fists, clenched on the wood, were trembling. She saw the boy staring, and tried to smile. "It's great news, son. You father will be glad. She—he'll give you silver, I shouldn't wonder. She's a lovely lady, Queen Morgause, and generous where it pleases her."

"You don't look pleased. You look frightened." He came slowly back into the room. "You look ill, Mother. Look, you've dropped your stick. Here it is. Sit down now. Don't worry, I'll find the tunic. The necklet's in the cupboard with it, isn't it? I'll get it. Come, sit down."

He took hold of her gently, and set her back on the stool. Standing in front of her, he was taller than she. She seemed to come to herself sharply. Her back straightened. She gripped his arms above the elbows in her two hands and held him tightly. Her eyes, red-rimmed with working near the smoke of the peat fire, stared up at him with an intensity that made him want to fidget and move away. She spoke in a low, urgent whisper:

"Look, my son. This is a great day for you, a great chance. Who knows what may come of it? A queen's favour is a fine thing to come by. . . . But it can be a hard thing, forby. You're young yet, what would you know of great folk and their ways? I don't know much myself, but I know something about life, and there's one thing I can tell you, Mordred. Always keep your own counsel. Never repeat what you hear." In spite of herself, her hands tightened. "And never, never tell anyone anything that's said here, in your home."

"Well, of course not! When do I ever see anyone to tal[k] to, anyway? And why should the queen or anyone at th[e] palace be interested in what goes on here?" He shifted un[-]comfortably, and her grip loosened. "Don't worry, Mothe[r]. There's nothing to be afraid of. I've done the queen a favour, and if she's such a lovely lady, then I don't see what els[e] can come of this except good, do you? Look, I must go now. Tell Father I'll finish the peats tomorrow. And keep som[e] supper for me, won't you? I'll be back as soon as I can."

To those who knew Camelot, the High King's court, an[d] even to people who remembered the state Queen Morgaus[e] had kept in her castle of Dunpeldyr, the "palace" of Orkne[y] must have seemed a primitive place indeed. But to the bo[y] from the fisherman's hut it appeared splendid beyond ima[g-] ination.

The palace stood behind and above the cluster of sma[ll] houses that made up the principal township of the island[s]. Below the town lay the harbour, its twin piers protecting [a] good deep anchorage where the biggest of ships could tie u[p] in safety. Piers, houses, palace, all were built of the sam[e] flat weathered slabs of sandstone. The roofs, too, were [of] great flagstones hauled somehow into place and then hidde[n] by a thick thatching of turf or heather-stems, with deep eave[s] that helped to throw the winter's rains away from walls an[d] doors. Between the houses ran narrow streets, steep gut[s] also paved with the flagstones so lavishly supplied by th[e] local cliffs.

The main building of the palace was the great central hal[l]. This was the "public" hall, where the court gathered, whe[n] feasts were held, petitions were heard, and where many [of] the courtiers—nobles, officers, royal functionaries—sle[pt] at night. It comprised a big oblong room, with other, smalle[r] chambers opening from it.

Outside was a walled courtyard where the queen's so[l-] diers and servants lived, sleeping in the outbuildings, an[d] eating round their cooking fires in the yard itself. The onl[y] entrance was the main gateway, a massive affair flanked t[o] either side by a guardhouse.

At a short distance from the main palace buildings, an[d] connected with them by a long covered passage, stood th[e] comparatively new building that was known as "the queen'[s]

24

ouse." This had been built by Morgause's orders when she first came to settle in Orkney. It was a smaller yet no less grandly built complex of buildings set very near the edge of the cliff that here rimmed the shore. Its walls looked almost like an extension of the layered cliffs below. Not many of the court—only the queen's own women, her advisers, and her favourites—had seen the interior of the house, but its modern splendours were spoken of with awe, and the townspeople gazed up in wonder at the big windows—an unheard-of innovation—which had been built even into the seaward walls.

Inland from palace and township stretched an open piece of land, turf grazed close by sheep, and used by the soldiers and young men for practice with horses and arms. Some of the stabling, with the kennels, and the byres for cattle and goats, was outside the palace walls, for in those islands there was little need of more defense than that provided by the sea, and to the south by the iron walls of Arthur's peace. But some way along the coast, beyond the exercise ground, stood the remains of a primitive round tower, built before men's memory by the Old People, and splendidly adaptable as both watchtower and embattled refuge. This Morgause, with the memory of Saxon incursions on the mainland kingdom, had had repaired after a fashion, and there a watch and ward was kept. This, with the guard kept constantly on the palace gate, was part of the royal state that fitted the queen's idea of her own dignity. If it did nothing else, said Morgause, it would keep the men alert, and provide some sort of military duty for the soldiers, as a change from exercises that all too readily became sport, or from idling round the palace courtyard.

When Mordred with his escort arrived at the gate the courtyard was crowded. A chamberlain was waiting to escort him to the queen.

Feeling awkward and strange in his seldom-worn best tunic, stiff as it had come from the cupboard, and smelling faintly musty, Mordred followed his guide. He was taut with nerves, and looked at nobody, keeping his head high and his eyes fixed on the chamberlain's shoulder-blades, but he felt the stares, and heard mutterings. He took them to be natural curiosity, probably mingled with contempt; he cannot have

known that the figure he cut was curiously courtier-like, hi
stiffness very like the dignified formality of the great hall.

"A fisherman's brat?" the whispers went. "Oh, aye? We'v
heard that one before. Just look at him....So who's hi
mother? Sula? I remember her. Pretty. She used to work a
the palace here. In King Lot's time, that was. How long ag
now since he visited the islands? Twelve years? Eleven
How the time does go by, to be sure....And he must b
just about that age, wouldn't you say?"

So the whispers went. They would have pleased Mor
gause, had she heard them, and Mordred, whom they woul
have enraged, did not hear them. But he heard the muttering
and felt the eyes. He stiffened his spine further, and wishe
the ordeal safely over, and himself home again.

Then they had reached the door of the hall, and as th
servants pushed it open, Mordred forgot the whispers, hi
own strangeness, everything except the splendid scene i
front of him.

When Morgause, suffering under Arthur's displeasure
had finally left Dunpeldyr for her other kingdom of Orkney
some stray glimmer in her magic glass must have warne
her that her stay in the north would be a long one. She ha
managed to bring many of the treasures from Lot's souther
capital. The king who reigned there now at Arthur's behest
Tydwal, must have found his stronghold stripped of most o
its comforts. He was a stark lord, so cannot have care
overmuch. But Morgause, that lady of luxury, would hav
thought herself ill used had she been denied any of the ap
purtenances of royalty, and she had managed, with her spoils
to make herself a bower of comfort and colour to cushio
her exile and enhance her once famous beauty. On all side
the stone walls of the hall were hung with brilliantly dye
cloths. The smooth flagstones of the floor were not, as migh
have been expected, strewn with rushes and heather, bu
had been made luxurious with islands of deerskin, brow
and fawn and dappled. The heavy benches along the side
walls were made of stone, but the chairs and stools standing
on the platform at the hall's end were of fine wood carefull
carved and painted, and bright with coloured cushions, whil
the doors were of strong oak, handsomely ornamented, an
smelling of oil and wax.

The fisherman's boy had no eyes for any of this. His gaze

was fixed on the woman who sat in the great chair at the center of the platform.

Morgause of Lothian and Orkney was still a very beautiful woman. Light from a slit window caught the glimmer of her hair, darkened from its young rose-gold to a rich copper. Her eyes, long-lidded, showed green as emerald, and her skin had the same smooth, creamy pallor as of old. The lovely hair was dressed with gold, and there were emeralds at her ears and at her throat. She wore a copper-coloured gown, and in her lap her slender white hands glinted with jewelled rings.

Behind her her five women—the queen's ladies—looked, for all their elegant clothing, plain and elderly. Those who knew Morgause had no doubt that this was an appearance as carefully contrived as her own. Some score of people stood below the dais, about the hall. To the boy Mordred it seemed crowded, and fuller of eyes even than the outer courtyard. He looked for Gawain, or for the other princes, but could not see them. When he entered, pausing rather nervously just inside the doorway, the queen was sitting half turned away, talking with one of her counsellors, a smallish, stout greybeard who bent humbly to listen as she spoke.

Then she saw Mordred. She straightened in her tall chair, and the long lids came down to conceal the sudden flash of interest in her eyes. Someone prodded the boy from behind, whispering: "Go on. Go up and then kneel."

Mordred obeyed. He approached the queen, but when he would have knelt, a movement of one of her hands bade him stand still. He waited, very straight, and apparently self-contained, but making no attempt to conceal the wonder and admiration he felt at this, his first sight of royalty enthroned. He simply stood and stared. If the onlookers expected him to be abashed, or the queen to rebuke him for impertinence, they were disappointed. The silence that held the hall was one of avid interest, coupled with amusement. Queen and fisherman's boy, islanded by that silence, measured one another eye to eye.

If Mordred had been half-a-dozen years older, men might more readily have understood the indulgence, even the apparent pleasure with which she regarded him. Morgause had made no secret of her predilection for handsome youths, a fancy which had been allowed a relatively free reign since

27

the death of her husband. And indeed Mordred was personable enough, with his slender, straight body, fine bones, and the look of eager yet contained intelligence in the eyes under their wing-tipped brows. She studied him, stiff but far from awkward in his "best" tunic, the only one he had, apart from the rags of every day. She remembered the stuff she had sent for it, years ago, a length of homespun patchily dyed that not even the palace slaves would have worn. Anything better, missed from the coffers, might have caused curiosity. Round his neck hung a string of shells, unevenly threaded with some sort of wooden charm obviously carved by the boy himself from a piece of sea-wrack. His feet, though dusty from the moorland road, were finely shaped.

Morgause saw all this with satisfaction, but she saw more besides: the dark eyes, an inheritance from the Spanish blood of the Ambrosii, were Arthur's; the fine bones, the folded subtle mouth, came from Morgause herself.

At length she spoke. "Your name is Mordred, they tell me?"

"Yes." The boy's voice was hoarse with nervousness. He cleared his throat. "Yes, madam."

"Mordred," she said, consideringly. Her accent, even after her years in the north, was still that of the southern mainland kingdoms, but she spoke clearly and slowly in her pretty voice, and he understood her very well. She gave his name the island pronunciation. "Medraut, the sea-boy. So you are a fisherman like your father?"

"Yes, madam."

"Is that why they gave you your name?"

He hesitated. He could not see where this was leading. "I suppose so, madam."

"You suppose so." She spoke lightly, her attention apparently on smoothing a fold of her gown. Only her chief counsellor, and Gabran her current lover, knowing her well, guessed that the next question mattered. "You never asked them?"

"No, madam. But I can do other things besides fish. I dig the peats, and I can turf a roof, and build a wall, and mend the boat, and—and milk the goat, even—" He paused uncertainly. A faint ripple of amusement had gone round the hall, and the queen herself was smiling.

"And climb cliffs as if you were a goat yourself. For which," she added, "we should all be grateful."

"That was nothing," said Mordred. His confidence returned. There was really no need to be afraid. The queen was a lovely lady, as Sula had told him, not at all as he had imagined a witch to be, and surprisingly easy to talk to. He smiled up at her. "Is Gawain's ankle badly sprained?" he asked.

A new rustle went round the hall. "Gawain," indeed! And a fisher-boy did not hold conversation with the queen, standing as straight as one of the young princes, and looking her in the eye. But Morgause apparently noticed nothing unusual. She ignored the murmurs. She had not ceased to watch the boy closely.

"Not very. Now that it has been bathed and bound up he can walk well enough. He will be back at the exercise of arms tomorrow. And for this he has you to thank, Mordred, and so have I. I repeat, we are grateful."

"The men would have found him very soon, and I could have lent them the rope."

"But they did not, and you climbed down twice yourself. Gawain tells me that it is a dangerous place. He should be whipped for climbing there, even though he did bring me two such splendid birds. But you..." The pretty teeth nibbled at the red underlip as she considered him. "You must have some proof of my gratitude. What would you like?"

Really taken aback now, he stared, swallowed, and began to stammer something about his parents, their poverty, the coming winter and the nets that had been patched twice too often, but she interrupted him. "No, no. That is for your parents, not for you. I have already found gifts for them. Show him, Gabran."

A young man, blond and handsome, who stood near her, stooped and lifted a box from behind her chair. He opened it. In it Mordred glimpsed coloured wools, woven cloth, a net purse glinting with silver, a stoppered wine flask. He went scarlet, then pale. Suddenly, the scene had become somehow unreal, like a dream. The chance encounter at the cliff, Gawain's talk of reward, the summons to the queen's house—all this had been exciting, with its promise of some change in the monotonous drudgery of his life. He had come here expecting at most a silver coin, a word from the queen, some delicacy, perhaps, that could be begged from the palace kitchens before he ran home. But this—Morgause's beauty and kindness, the unaccustomed splendours of the hall, the magnificence of the gifts for his parents, and the promise apparently, of more for himself... Dimly, through the heart-beating confusion, he felt that it was all too much. There was something more here. Something in the looks the courtiers were exchanging, in the speculative amusement in Gabran's eyes. Something he did not understand, but that made him uneasy.

Gabran shut the lid of the box with a snap, but when Mordred reached to lift it Morgause stopped him.

"No, Mordred. Not now. We shall see that they have it before today's dusk. But you and I still have something to talk about, have we not? What is fitting for the young man to whom the future king of these islands owes a dear debt? Come with me now. We will talk of this in private."

She stood up. Gabran moved quickly to her side, his arm ready for her hand, but ignoring him, she stepped down from the dais and reached a hand towards the boy. He took it awkwardly, but somehow she made a graceful gesture of it, her jewelled fingers touching his wrist as if he were a courtier handing her from the hall. When she stood beside him she was very little taller than he. She smelled of honeysuckle and the rich days of summer. Mordred's head swam.

"Come," she said again, softly.

The courtiers stood back, bowing, to make a way for them. Her slave drew back a curtain to show a door in the side wall. Guards stood there to either side, their spears held stiffly. Mordred was no longer conscious of the stares and the whispering. His heart was thudding. What was to come now he could not guess, but it could only, surely, be more wonders. Something was hanging in the clouds for him; fortune was in the queen's smile and in her touch.

Without knowing it, he tossed the dark hair back from his brow in a gesture that was Arthur's own, and with head high he escorted Morgause royally out of her hall.

3

The corridor between the palace and the queen's house was a long one, without windows, but lit by torches hung on the walls. There were two doors in its length, both on the left. One must be the guardroom; the door stood ajar, and beyond it Mordred could hear men's voices and the click of gaming-stones. The other gave on the courtyard; he remembered seeing guards there. It was shut now, but at the end of the corridor a third door stood open, held wide by a servant for the passage of the queen and her attendants.

Beyond was a square chamber, which acted apparently as an anteroom to the queen's private apartments. It was unfurnished. To the right a slit window showed a narrow strip of sky, and let in the noise of the sea. Opposite, on the landward side, was another door, at which Mordred looked with interest, and then with awe.

This doorway was curiously low and squat—the same primitive shape as the door of his parents' cottage. It was set deep under a massive stone lintel, and flanked by jambs almost as thick. He had seen such entrance-ways before; they led down to the ancient underground chambers that could be found here and there through the islands. Some said they had been built, like the tall brochs, by the Old People, who had housed their dead there in stone chambers beneath the ground. But the simpler folk regarded them as magical places, the *sidhe* or hollow hills that guarded the gates of the Otherworld; and the skeletons that were found there, of men and beasts, were the remains of unwary creatures who had ventured too far within those dark precincts. When mist shrouded the islands—which was rare in those windy seas—it was said that gods and spirits could be seen riding out on their gold-decked horses, with the sad ghosts of the dead drifting round them. Whatever the truth, the islanders avoided the mounds that hid these underground chambers, but it seemed that the queen's house had been built beside one of them, perhaps only discovering it when the foundations were dug. Now the entrance was sealed off by a heavy door of oak, with big iron hasps, and a massive lock to keep it fast against whatever lurked behind it in the dark.

Then Mordred forgot it, as the tall door ahead of them opened between its two armed guards, and beyond was a blaze of sunlight, and the warmth and scent and colour of the queen's house.

The room they entered was a copy of Morgause's chamber at Dunpeldyr; a smaller copy, but still, to Mordred's eyes, magnificent. The sun streamed in through a big square window, under which a bench made a window-seat, gay with blue cushions. Near it, full in the sunlight, stood a gilded chair with its footstool and a cross-legged table nearby. Morgause sat down, and pointed to the windowseat. Mordred took his place obediently, and sat waiting in silence, with thumping heart, while the women, at a word from the queen, betook themselves with their stitchery to the far end of the room, in the light from another window. A servant came hurrying to the queen's side with wine in a silver goblet, and then, at her command, brought a cup of the sweet honey drink for Mordred. He took a sip of it, then set the cup down on the window sill. Though his mouth and throat were dry, he could not drink.

The queen finished her wine, then handed the goblet to Gabran, who must already have had his orders. He took it straight to the servant at the door, shut the door behind the man, then went to join the women at the other end of the room. He lifted a small knee harp from its shroud in the corner, and, settling himself on a stool, began to play.

Only then did the queen speak again, and she spoke softly

...o that only Mordred, close beside her, would be able to hear.

"Well, Mordred, so now let us talk. How old are you? No, don't answer, let me see.... You will soon pass your eleventh birthday. Am I not right?"

"Y—yes," stammered the boy, amazed. "How did—oh, of course, Gawain told you."

She smiled. "I would have known without being told. I know more about your birth than you do yourself, Mordred. Can you guess how?"

"Why, no, madam. About my birth? That's before you came to live here, isn't it?"

"Yes. I and the king my husband still held Dunpeldyr in Lothian. Have you never heard what happened in Dunpeldyr, the year before Prince Gawain was born?"

He shook his head. He could not have spoken. He still had no inkling of why the queen had brought him here and was speaking to him like this, secretly, in her private chamber, but every instinct pricked him to the alert. It was coming now, surely, the future he had dreaded, and yet longed for, with the strange, restless and sometimes violent feelings of rebellion he had had against the life to which he had been born, and to which he had believed himself sentenced till death, like all his parents' kin.

Morgause, still watching him closely, smiled again. "Then listen now. It is time you knew. You will soon see why...."

She settled a fold of her gown, and spoke lightly, as if talking of some trifling matter far back in the past, some story to tell a child at lamp-lighting.

"You know that the High King Arthur is my half-brother by the same father, King Uther Pendragon. Long ago King Uther planned my marriage to King Lot, and though he died before it could take place, and though my brother Arthur was never Lot's friend, we were married. We hoped that through the marriage a friendship, or at least an alliance, might be formed. But, whether through jealousy of Lot's prowess as a soldier, or (as I am persuaded) because of lies told to him by Merlin, the enchanter, who hates all women, and who fancies himself wronged by me, King Arthur has always acted more as an enemy than as a brother and a just lord."

She paused. The boy's eyes were fixed, enormous, his

33

lips slightly parted. She smoothed her gown again, and her voice took on a deeper, graver note.

"Soon after King Arthur had assumed the throne of Britain, he was told, by the evil man Merlin, that a child had been born somewhere in Dunpeldyr, a son of its king, who would prove to be Arthur's bane. The High King never hesitated. He sent men north to Dunpeldyr to seek out and kill the king's sons. Oh, no"—a smile of great sweetness—"not mine. Mine were not yet born. But to make sure that any bastard, perhaps unknown, of King Lot's should die, he ordered that all the children in the town, under a certain age, should die." Sorrow throbbed in her voice. "So, Mordred, on that dreadful night some score of children were taken by the soldiers. They were put out to sea in a small boat, which was driven by wind and waves until at last it drove onto a rock and foundered, and the children were all drowned. All but one."

He was as still as if held by a spell. "Me?" It was a whisper, barely audible.

"Yes, you. The boy from the sea. Now do you understand why you were given that name? It was true."

She seemed to be waiting for an answer. He said, huskily, "I thought it was because of being a fisherman, like my father. A lot of the boys that help with the nets are called Mordred, or Medraut. I thought it was a sort of charm to keep me safe from the sea-goddess. She used to sing a song about it. My mother, I mean."

The green-gilt eyes opened a little wider. "So? A song? What sort of song?"

Mordred, meeting that look, recollected himself. He had forgotten Sula's warning. Now it came back to him, but there was no harm, surely, in the truth? "A sleeping song. When I was small. I don't really remember it, except the tune."

Morgause, with a flick of her fingers, dismissed the tune. "But you never heard this tale before? Did your parents ever speak of Dunpeldyr?"

"No, never. That is"—he spoke with patent honesty—"only as all the folk speak of it. I knew that it was part of your kingdom once, and that you had dwelt there with the king, and that the three oldest princes were born there. My —my father gets news from the ships that come in, of all the kingdoms beyond the sea, the wonderful lands. He has

34

old me so much that I—" He bit his lip, then burst out irresistibly with the question that burned him. "Madam, how did my father and mother save me from that boat and bring me here?"

"They did not save you from the boat. You were saved by the King of Lothian. When he knew what had happened to the children he sent a ship to save them, but it came too late for all but you. The captain saw some wreckage floating still, the boat's ribs, with what looked like a bundle of cloth still there. It was you. An end of your shawl had caught on a splintered spar, and held you safe. The captain took you up. By the garment you wore, and the shawl that saved your life, he knew which of the children you were. So he sailed with you to Orkney, where you might be reared in safety." She paused. "Have you guessed why, Mordred?"

She could see, from the boy's eyes, that he had guessed why long since. But he lowered his lids and answered, as meekly as a girl:

"No, madam."

The voice, the folded mouth, the maiden-like demureness, was so much Morgause's own that she laughed aloud, and Gabran, who had been her lover now for more than a year, looked up from his harp and allowed himself to smile with her. "Then I will tell you. Two of the bastards of the King of Lothian were killed in that massacre. But there were known to be three in the boat. The third was saved by the mercy of the sea-goddess, who kept him afloat in the wreckage. You are a king's bastard, Mordred, my boy from the sea."

He had seen it coming, of course. She looked to see some spark of joy, or pride, or even speculation. There was none. He was biting his lip, fighting with some trouble that he wanted to, but dared not, express.

"Well?" she asked at length.

"Madam—" Another pause.

"Well?" A touch of impatience. Having laid a royal gift in the boy's hand, albeit a false one, the lady looked for worship, not for doubts which she could not understand. Never having herself been moved by love, it did not occur to her that her son's feelings for his foster parents needed to be weighed against pleasure and ambition.

He blurted it out then. "Madam, was my mother ever in Dunpeldyr?"

Morgause, who liked to play with people as if they wer creatures caged for her whims, smiled at him and told, fo the first time in the interview, the simple truth. "Of course Where else? You were born there. Did I not say so?"

"But she said she had lived in Orkney all her life! Mordred's voice rose, so that the chatter at the room's othe end hushed for a moment before a glance from the quee sent the women back, heads bent, to their work. The bo added, more softly, looking wretched: "And my father. H can't know, surely, that she—that I . . . ?"

"Foolish boy, you have not understood me." Her voic was indulgent. "Brude and Sula are your foster parents, wh took you at the king's behest, and kept the secret for him Sula had lost a son, and she took you to nurse. No doub she has given you the love and care she would have give her own child. As for your real mother"—quickly, she fore stalled the question that in fact he was too dazed to ask— "I cannot tell you that. For very fear she said nothing, no made any claim, and for fear of the High King, nothing ha ever been said. She may have been only too thankful t forget the matter herself. I asked no questions, though I knew one of the boys had been saved from the boat. Then whe King Lot died, and I came to Orkney to bear my younges son and care for the other three in safety, I was content t let the matter rest. As you must, Mordred."

Not knowing what to say, he was silent.

"For all I know your own mother may be dead. To drear of some day seeking her out would be folly—and what woul be the profit? A girl of the town, the pleasure of a night? She studied his down-dropped lids, his expressionless face "Now Dunpeldyr is in the hands of a king who is Arthur' creature. There would be no profit in such a search, Mordred and there might well be much danger. Do you understan me?"

"Yes, madam."

"What you do when you are a man grown is your affair but you will do well to remember that King Arthur is you enemy."

"Then—I am the one? I am to be—his bane?"

"Who knows? That is with the gods. But he is a hard man and his adviser Merlin is both clever and cruel. Do you thin

36

hey would take any chances? But while you remain in these slands—and while you keep silent—you are safe."

Another pause. He asked, almost whispering it: "But why have you told me, then? I will be secret, yes, I promise, but why did you want me to know?"

"Because of the debt I owe you for Gawain. Had you not helped him, he might have tried to climb himself, and fallen o his death. I was curious to see you, so I sent for you on that excuse. It might have been better to leave you there all your life, knowing nothing. Your foster parents would never have dared to speak. But after what happened yesterday—" A pretty, half-deprecating gesture. "Not every woman wishes o nurture her husband's bastards, but I and my family owe you something, and I pay my debts. And now that I have seen you, and spoken with you, I have decided how to make that payment."

The boy said nothing. He seemed to have stopped breathing. From the far end of the room came the murmur of music, and the soft voices of the women.

"You are ten years old," said Morgause. "You are well grown and healthy, and I think that you could do me some service. There are not so many in these islands with the blood and the promise that might make a leader. In you I think I see that promise. It is time you left your foster home, and took your place here with the other princes. Well, what do you say?"

"I—I will do as you wish, madam," stammered the boy. It was all he could say, above the words that went on and on in his brain, like the music of the harp. *The other princes. It is time you took your place here with the other princes.*... Later, perhaps, he would think of his foster parents with affection and with regret, but now all he had room for was the vague but dazzling vision of such a future as he had barely dared even to dream of. And this woman, this lovely royal lady, would in her graciousness offer him, her husband's bastard, a place beside her own true-born sons. Mordred, moved by an impulse he had never felt before, slipped from the window-seat and knelt at Morgause's feet. With a gesture at once graceful and touchingly unpracticed, he lifted a fold of the copper-coloured velvet and kissed it. He sent a look of worship up at her and whispered: "I will serve you with my life, madam. Only ask me. It is yours."

His mother smiled down at him, well satisfied with th conquest she had made. She touched his hair, a gesture tha brought the blood up under his skin, then sat back agains the cushions, a pretty, fragile queen looking for strong arm and ready swords to protect her.

"It may be a hard service, Mordred. A lonely queen need all the love and protection that her fighting men can giv her. For that you will be trained alongside your brothers and live with them here in my palace. Now you will go dow to Seals' Bay to take leave of your parents, then bring you things back here."

"Today? Now?"

"Why not? When decisions are taken they should be acte upon. Gabran will go with you, and a slave to carry you goods. Go now."

Mordred, still too awed and confused to point out that h could carry all his worldly goods himself, and in one hand got to his feet, then stooped to kiss the hand she held ou to him. It was noticeable that this time the courtly mov came almost naturally. Then the queen turned away, dis missing him, and Gabran was at his elbow, hurrying hin from the room, along the corridor, and out into the courtyar where the coloured sky of sunset was already fading int dusk, and the air smelled of the smoke of fires where supper were being cooked.

A man, a groom by his dress, came up with a horse read bridled. It was one of the sturdy island ponies, cream-col oured and as shaggy as a sheep.

"Come," said Gabran, "we'll be late for supper as it is You don't ride, I suppose? No? Well, get up behind me. Th man can follow."

Mordred hung back. "There's no need, I've nothing t carry, really. And you don't need to come either, sir. If yo stay and get your supper now, I can run home and—"

"You'll soon learn that when the queen says I have to g with you, then I have to go." Gabran did not trouble t explain that his orders had been even more explicit. "He i not to have speech alone with Sula," Morgause had said "Whatever she has guessed, she has told him nothing yet it seems. But now that she is going to lose him, who know what she may come out with? The man does not matter: H is too stupid to guess at the truth, but even he may give th boy the true tale of how he was brought, by arrangement, from Dunpeldyr. So take him, and stay with them, and bring him back quickly. I shall see to it that he does not go back there again."

So Gabran said, crisply: "Come, your hand," and with Mordred behind him on the cob, and clinging to him like a young peregrine to its ball of fleece, he cantered off along the track that led to Seals' Bay.

4

Sula had been sitting outside the cottage door in the last of the daylight, gutting and splitting a catch of fish ready for drying. When the horse appeared at the head of the cliff path she had just carried the bucket of offal down to throw it onto the shingle, where the hens wrangled with the seabirds for their share of the stinking pile. The noise was deafening as the big gulls swooped and fought and chased one another, and the smell rose sickeningly on the wind.

Mordred slipped off the cob's rump as Gabran drew rein. "If you wait here, sir, I'll run down with this, and get my things. I'll be back in just a moment. It—it won't take long. I think my mother was expecting this, or something like it. I'll be as quick as I can. Maybe I can come back tomorrow, if they want me to? Just for a talk?"

Gabran, without even troubling to reply, slid off the horse's back and looped the rein over his wrist. When Mordred, holding the box carefully, started down the slope, the man followed.

Sula, turning back towards the cottage, saw them. She had been watching the cliff top for Mordred's return, and now, seeing how he was accompanied, she stood for a few moments very still, unconsciously clutching the slimy bucket close to her body. Then, coming to herself, she threw the bucket down by the doorway, and went quickly into the cottage. A dim yellow glow showed round the curtain's edge as she lighted the lamp.

The boy pushed the curtain aside and went in eagerly, carrying the box.

For once the room was free of smoke. On good summer days Sula cooked their food in the clay oven outside, over a fire built up of dried kelp and dung. But the stink of fish pervaded the whole cove, and inside the cottage the smell of the fish-oil in the lamp caught at the throat. Though he had been used to it all his life, Mordred—with the scents and colours of the queen's room bright in his memory—noticed it now, with a mixture of pity, shame and what he was too young to recognize as self-dislike; shame because Gabran so obviously intended to come in with him, and guilt because he was ashamed for him to do so.

To his immediate relief, Sula was alone. She was wiping her hands on a rag. Blood from a grazed finger mingled on the rag with the slime and scales from the fish. The flint knife lying on the table showed a rim of blood, too.

"Your hand, Mother, you've cut it!"

"It's nothing. They kept you a long time."

"I know. The queen herself wanted to talk to me. Wait till I tell you! The palace, it's a wonderful place, and I went right into the queen's own house.... But look here first, Mother! She gave me presents."

He set the box on the table, and opened it.

"Mother, look! The silver is for you and Father, and the cloth, see, isn't it fine? Thick, too, good for winter. And a flask of good wine, with a capon from the palace kitchen. All this is for you...."

His voice trailed away uneasily. Sula had not even glanced at the treasures; she was still wiping her hands, over and over again, on the greasy rag.

Suddenly, Mordred was impatient. He took the rag from her and threw it down, shoving the box nearer. "Aren't you even going to look at them? Don't you even want to know what the queen said to me?"

"I can see she was generous. We all know she can be generous when it takes her. What was there for you?"

"Promises." Gabran spoke from the doorway as he stooped to enter. When he straightened his head was only a finger's breadth from the stones of the roof. He was dressed in a

41

knee-length robe of yellow, with a deep tagged border of green. Yellow stones winked at his belt, and he wore a collar of worked copper. He was a fair man, with a crisp mane as blond as barley straw falling to his shoulders, and the blue eyes of the north. His presence filled the room and made the cottage seem more poverty-stricken and dingy even than before.

If Mordred was conscious of this, Sula was not. Unimpressed, she faced Gabran squarely, as she would have faced an enemy. "What sort of promises?"

Gabran smiled. "Only what every man should have, and Mordred has proved himself a man now—or at least the queen thinks so. A cup and a platter for his meat, and tools for his work."

She stared at him, her lips working. She did not ask what he meant. Nor did she make any of the gestures of hospitality that came naturally to the folk of the islands.

She said harshly: "These he has."

"But not such as he should have," said Gabran, gently. "You know as well as I, woman, that there should be silver on his cup, and that his tools are not mattocks and fish hooks, but a sword and a spear."

To expect and dread a thing for a lifetime does not prepare one for the thing itself. It was as if he had set the very spear to her breast. She threw up her hands, hiding her face with her apron, and sank onto the stool beside the table.

"Mother, don't!" cried Mordred. "The queen—she told me—you must know what she told me!" Then, to Gabran, distressed: "I thought she knew. I thought she would understand."

"She does understand. Do you not, Sula?"

A nod. She had begun to rock herself, as if in grief, but she made no sound.

Mordred hesitated. Among the rough folk of the islands, affectionate gestures were rarely made. He went to her, but contented himself with a touch on the shoulder. "Mother, the queen told me the whole story. How you and my father took me from the sea-captain who had found me, and reared me for your own. She told me who I am . . . at least, who my real father is. So now she thinks I should go up to the palace with the other—King Lot's other sons, and the nobles, and train as a fighting man."

Still she said nothing. Gabran, watching by the door, never moved.

Mordred tried again. "Mother, you must have known I would be told some day. And now that I know . . . you mustn't be sorry. *I* can't be sorry, you must see that. It doesn't change anything here, this is still my home, and you and Father are still . . ." He swallowed. "You'll always be my folk, you will, believe me! Some day—"

"Aye, some day," she interrupted him, harshly. The apron came down. In the wavering light of the lamp her face was sickly pale, smeared with dirt from the apron. She did not look at Gabran, elegant in the doorway. Mordred watched her appealingly; there was love in his face, and distress, but there was also something she recognized, a high look of excitement, ambition, the iron-hard will to go his way. She had never set eyes on Arthur, High King of Britain, but looking at Mordred, she recognized his son.

She said, heavily: "Aye, some day. Some day you'll come back, grown and grand, and carrying gold to give the poor folk who nursed you. But now you try to tell me that nothing's changed. For all you say it makes no difference who you are—"

"I didn't say that! Of course it makes a difference! Who wouldn't be glad to know he was a king's son? Who wouldn't be glad to have the chance to bear arms, and maybe some day to travel abroad and see the mainland kingdoms, where things are happening that matter to the world? When I said nothing would change, I mean the way I feel—the way I feel about you and my father. But I can't help wanting to go! Please try to understand. I can't pretend, not all the way, that I'm sorry."

At the distress in his face and voice she softened suddenly. "Of course you can't, boy. You must forgive an old woman who's dreaded this moment for so long. Yes, you must go. But do you have to go now? Is yon fine gentleman waiting to take you back with him?"

"Yes. They said I had just to get my things and go straight back."

"Then get them. Your father won't be back till the dawn tide. You can come and see him as soon as they let you." A glimmer of something that was almost a smile. "Don't you worry, boy, I'll tell him what's happened."

"He knows all about it, too, doesn't he?"

"Of course he does. And he'll see that it had to come. He's made himself forget it, I think, though I've seen it coming this past year or so. Yes, in you, Mordred. Blood tells. Still, you've been a good son to us, for all there's been something in you fretting after a different way.... We took pay for you, you know that.... Where did you think we got the money for the good boat, and the foreign nets? I'd have nursed you for nothing, in place of the one I lost, and then you were as good as our own, and better. Aye, we'll miss you sorely. It's a hard trade for a man as he gets older, and you've pulled your weight on the rope, that you have."

Something was working in the boy's face. He burst out: "I won't go! I won't leave you, Mother! They can't make me!"

She looked sadly at him. "You will, lad. Now you've had a sight of it, and a taste of it, you will. So get your things. Yon gentleman's on the fidget to be gone."

Mordred glanced from her to Gabran. The latter nodded and said, not unkindly: "We should hurry. The gates will soon be shut."

The boy went across to his bedplace. This was a stone shelf, with a bag stuffed full of dried bracken for a mattress, and a blue blanket spread across. From a recess in the wall below the shelf he took his possessions. A sling, some fish hooks, a knife, his old working tunic. He had no shoes. He laid the fish hooks back on the bed, and the working tunic with them. He hesitated over the sling. He felt the smooth wood that fitted so readily into his hand, and fingered the bag of pebbles, rounded and glossy, gathered so carefully from the beach. Then these, too, he laid aside. Sula watched him, saying nothing. Between them the words hung, unspoken: *the tools for his work; a sword and a spear...*

He turned back. "I'm ready now." He was empty-handed, but for his knife.

If any of the three noticed the symbolism of the moment, nothing was said. Gabran reached for the door curtain. Before he could touch it it was pushed aside, as the goat shouldered her way into the room. Sula got up from her stool, and reached for the bowl to hold the milk. "You'd best go, then. Come back when they let you, and tell us what it's like up there at the palace."

44

Gabran held the curtain wide. Mordred went slowly towards the door. What was there to say? Thanks were not enough, and yet were more than enough. He said awkwardly: "Goodbye then, Mother," and went out. Gabran let the curtain fall behind them.

Outside, the tide was on the turn, and the wind had freshened, dispersing the smell of fish. The sweet air met him. It was like plunging into a different stream.

Gabran was untying the horse. In the growing darkness the knots were awkward, and he fumbled over them. Mordred hesitated, then ran back into the stink of the hut. Sula was milking the goat. She did not look up. He could see a track of moisture in the dirt on her cheek like the track of a snail. He stopped in the doorway, clutching the curtain, and said hoarsely and rapidly: "I'll come back whenever they let me, truly I will. I—I'll see you're all right, you and he. Some day . . . some day I promise I'll be somebody, and I'll look after you both."

She made no sign.

"Mother."

She did not look up. Her hands never stopped.

"I hope," said Mordred, "that I never do find out who my real mother is." He turned and ran out again into the dusk.

"Well?" asked Morgause.

It was well past dawn. She and Gabran were alone together in her bedchamber.

In the outer room her women slept, and in the chamber beyond that the five boys—Lot's four and her son by Arthur—had been asleep long since. But the queen and her lover were not abed. She sat beside a glowing bank of peat. She wore a long night robe of creamy white, and furred slippers made from the winter skin of the blue hare that runs on the High Island. Her hair was loose over her shoulders, glimmering in the peat fire's glow. In that soft light she looked little more than twenty years old, and very beautiful.

Though, as ever, she stirred his senses, the young man knew that this was not the moment to show it. Still fully dressed, his damp cloak over his arm, he kept his distance and answered her, subject to monarch:

"All is very well, madam. It's done, just as you wished it done."

"No trace of violence?"

"None. They were asleep—either that, or they had drunk too much of the wine you sent them."

A small smile, that innocence would have thought innocent, hung on her pretty mouth. "If they only sipped it, Gabran, it was enough." She lifted the lovely eyes to his, saw nothing there but dazzled admiration, and added: "Did you think I would take chances? You should know better. So, it was easy?"

"Very easy. All that will appear is that they drank too deeply, and were careless, and that the lamp fell and the oil spilled on the bedding, and—" A gesture finished it for him.

She drew a breath of satisfaction, but something in his voice gave her pause. Though Morgause valued, and was even fond of, her handsome young lover, she would have got rid of him in a moment if it had suited her to do so; but as yet she had need of him, and must keep him faithful. She said gently: "Too easy, I think you mean, Gabran? I know, my dear. Men like you don't like an easy killing, and killing these folk is like slaughtering beasts—no work for a fighting man. But it was necessary. You know that."

"I suppose so."

"You told me that you thought the woman knew something."

"Or guessed. It was hard to tell. These folk all look like weathered kelp. I couldn't be certain. There was something in the way she spoke to him, and the way she looked when he said you had told him the whole story." He hesitated. "If so, then she—both of them—have kept silence all these years."

"So?" said the queen. She held a hand out to the fire's warmth. "That is not to say they would have gone on keeping it. With the boy gone, they might begin to feel they had a grievance, and folk with a grievance are dangerous."

"Would they have dared speak? And to whom?"

"Why, to the boy himself. You told me that Sula urged him to go back there, and naturally—at first—he would have been eager to go. One word, one hint, would have been enough. You know whose son he is; and you have seen him. Do you think it needs more than a breath to kindle a blaze of ambition that could destroy all my plans for the future? Take my word for it, it was necessary. Gabran, dear boy, you may be the best lover a woman ever took to her bed, but you could never rule any kingdom wider than that same bed."

"Why should I ever want to?"

She threw him a smile, part affection, part mockery. Emboldened, he took half a step towards her, but she stopped him. "Wait. Consider. This time I'll tell you why. And don't pretend you've never made a guess at my plans concerning this bastard." She turned her hand this way and that, apparently admiring the glitter of her rings. Then she looked up, confidingly. "You may be right in part. I may have flown my hawk too early and too fast, but the chance came to take the boy from his foster home and bring him here without too much questioning. Besides, he is ten years old, high time he should be trained in the skills and manners of a prince. And once I had taken that step, the other had to follow. Until the right moment comes, my brother Arthur must hear no hint of his whereabouts. Nor must that arch-mage Merlin, and in his heyday he could have heard the very rushes whispering on the Holy Isle. Old and foolish as he is, we can risk nothing. I have not kept my son and Arthur's a secret all these years, to have him taken from me now. He is my pass to the mainland. When he is ready to go there, I shall go with him."

He was hers again, she noted. Pleased, flattered by her confidence, eager. "Back to Dunpeldyr, do you mean?"

"Not Dunpeldyr, no. To Camelot itself."

"To the High King?"

"Why not? He has no legitimate son, and from all accounts is unlikely to get one. Mordred is my pass to Arthur's court. . . . And after that, we shall see."

"You sound very sure," he said.

"I am sure. I have seen it." At the look in his eyes she smiled again. "Yes, my dear, in the pool. It was clear as crystal—a witch's crystal. I and my sons, all of them, at Camelot, dressed as for a feast, and bearing gifts."

"Then surely—not that I'm questioning it, but—couldn't that mean you would have been safe, even without what was done tonight?"

"Possibly." Her voice was indifferent. "We cannot always

read the signs aright, and it may be that the Goddess knew already what would be done tonight. Now I am sure that I am safe. All I have to do is wait for Merlin's death. Already more than once, we have heard rumours of his disappearance, or death, and each time I have rejoiced, only to find that the rumour was false, and the old fool lived still. But the day must soon come when the report will be true. I have seen to that, Gabran. And when it is, when he is no longer at Arthur's side, then I may go in safety, and Mordred with me. I can deal with my brother.... If not as I dealt with him before, then as a sister deals who has some power, and a little beauty still."

"Madam—Morgause—"

She laughed gently, and stretched a hand to him. "Come, Gabran, no need for jealousy! And no need to fear me, either. All the witchcraft I ever use against you, you know well how to deal with. The rest of this night's work will be more to your taste than what is past. Come to bed now. All is safe, thanks to you. You have served me more than faithfully."

And so did they. But Gabran did not voice the thought aloud. And soon, stripped of his damp clothing, and lying in the great bed beside Morgause, he forgot it, and forgot, too, the two dead bodies he had left in the smoking shell of the cottage on the shore.

5

Mordred woke early, at his usual time.

The other boys still slept, but this was the hour when his foster father had always roused him for work. For a few moments he lay, unsure of his surroundings, then he remembered. He was in the royal palace. He was a king's son, and the king's other sons were here, sleeping in the same room. The eldest of them, Prince Gawain, lay beside him, in the same bed. In the other bed slept the three younger princes, the twins, and the baby, Gareth.

He had had no speech with them yet. Last evening after Gabran had brought him to the palace, he had been taken in charge by an old woman who had been nurse to the royal boys; she was still, she told him, nurse to Gareth, and looked after the boys' clothes and to some extent their welfare. She led Mordred to a room full of chests and boxes, where she fitted him out with new clothing. No weapons yet; he would get those tomorrow, she told him sourly, soon enough, and then no doubt he would be about his killing and murdering like the rest of them. Men! Boys were bad enough, but at least they could be controlled, and let him mark her words, she might be an old woman, but she could still punish where punishment was due... . Mordred listened, and was silent, fingering the good new clothes, and trying not to yawn as the old woman fussed about him. From her chatter—and she was never silent—he learned that Queen Morgause was, to say the least, an erratic parent. One day she would take the boys riding, showing them mainland customs of hunting with hawk and hound; they would ride all day, and she would feast them late into the night, then the next day the boys would find themselves apparently forgotten, and be forbidden even to go to her rooms, only to be summoned again at night to hear a minstrel, or to entertain a bored and restless queen with talk of their own day. Nor were the boys treated alike. Possibly the only Roman principle held to by Morgause was the one of "divide and rule." Gawain, as the eldest and the heir, was given extra freedom and some privileges forbidden to the others; Gareth, the posthumous youngest, was the favourite. Which left the twins, and they, Mordred gathered from old Ailsa's pinched lips and headshakings, were difficult enough without the constant rubbings of jealousy and frustrated energies.

When at length, with his new clothes carefully folded over his arm, Mordred followed her to the boys' bedchamber, he was thankful to find that all four were there before him, and already sound asleep. Ailsa lifted Gareth out of Gawain's bed, then pushed the twins over and tucked the younger boy in beside them. None of them so much as stirred. She pulled the coverlets up close round them, and pointed Mordred silently to the place beside Gawain. He stripped, and slipped into the warmth of the bed. The old woman tut-tutted round the room for a few more minutes, picking up discarded clothing and laying it on the chest between the beds, then went out, shutting the door gently behind her. Mordred was asleep before she even left the room.

And now it was daylight, a new day, and he was wide awake. He stretched luxuriously, with excitement running through his body. He could feel it in his very bones. The bed was soft and warm, and smelled only slightly of the dressed furs that covered it. The room was big, and to his eyes very well furnished, with the two wide beds and the clothes-chest and a thick woven rug hanging over the door to keep out the worst of the draughts. Floor and walls alike were made with the flat, local stone slabs. At this early hour, even in summer, the room was very cold, but it was cleaner than Sula's hut could ever be, and something in the boy recognized and welcomed this as desirable. Between the beds, above the clothes-chest, was a narrow window through which the early morning air poured, cool and clean and smelling of the salt wind.

He could lie still no longer. Gawain, beside him, still slept, curled like a puppy in the welter of furs. In the other bed little could be seen of the twins save the tops of their heads; Gareth had been pushed to the bed's edge, and lay sprawling half out of it, but still deeply asleep.

Mordred slid out of bed. He padded to the clothes-chest, and, kneeling upon it, looked out of the window. This faced away from the sea; from it, by craning, he could see the courtyard and the main outer gateway of the palace. The sound of the sea came muted, a murmur under the incessant calling and mewing of the gulls. He looked the other way, beyond the palace walls, where a track ran green through the heather towards the summit of a gentle hill. Beyond that curved horizon lay his foster home. His father would be breaking his fast now, and soon would be gone about his work. If Mordred wanted to see him (to get it over with, said a small voice, quickly stifled in the dark and barely heeded rearward of his mind) he must go now.

On the chest lay the good tunic that he had been given last night, with a cloak, a brooch, and a leather belt with a buckle of copper. But in the very moment of reaching for the prized new clothing he changed his mind, and with something like a shrug picked up his old garment from the corner where he had thrown it, and slipped it on. Then, ducking past the door curtain, he let himself out of the room, and padded barefooted along the chill stone corridors to the hall.

The hall was still full of sleepers, but guards were changing duty for the morning shift, and servants were already moving. No one stopped him or spoke to him as he picked his way across the cluttered floor and out into the courtyard. The outer gate was open, and a cart of turfs was being dragged in by a couple of peasants. The two guards stood watching, at ease, eating their breakfast bannocks and taking turn and turn about to drink from a horn of ale.

As Mordred approached the gate one of the men saw him, nudged the other, and said something inaudible. The boy hesitated, half expecting to be stopped, or at any rate questioned, but neither of the men made a move to do so. Instead, the nearest one lifted a hand up in a half-salute, and then stood back to let the boy go by.

Perhaps no other moment of royal ceremony in Prince Mordred's life was ever to equal that one. His heart gave a great bound right into his throat, and he felt the colour rush into his cheeks. But he managed a calm enough "Good morning," then ran out through the palace gate and up the green track into the moor.

He ran along the track, his heart still beating high. The sun came up, and long shadows streamed away ahead of him. The night's dew shivered and steamed on the fine grasses, on the rushes smoothed by the light wind, till the whole landscape thrilled and shimmered with light, a softer repetition of the endless, achingly bright shimmer of the sea. Overhead, the clouds wisped back, and the air filled with singing as the larks launched themselves from their nests in the heather. The air rippled with song as the land with light. Soon he reached the summit of the moor, and before him stretched the long, gentle slope towards the cliffs, and beyond them again the endless, shining sea.

From this point he could see, clear across the sea in the early light, the hills of the High Island. Beyond them lay the mainland—the real mainland, the great and wonderful land that the islanders called, half in jest, half in ignorance, "the next island." Many times, from his father's boat, he had seen its northern cliffs, and had tried to imagine the rest; its vastness, its forests, its roads and ports and cities. Today, though hidden from view, it had ceased to be a dream. It was the High Kingdom, to which he would one day travel, and where he would one day matter. If his new status was to mean anything, it would mean that. He would see to it.

He laughed aloud with joy, and ran on.

He came to the turf cutting. He paused, deliberately lingering by the ditch he had dug only yesterday. How long ago, already, it seemed. Brude would have to finish it now—alone, too, though lately he had been complaining about pains in his back. Perhaps, thought the boy, since they were apparently going to leave him free to come and go from the palace, he could come down early each day for an hour before the other boys were up, and finish the digging. And if he were given real princely status, with servants, he could maybe set them to the task, or to the collecting of the lichens for his mother's dyestuffs. The basket was still standing there by the diggings, where he had left it yesterday, forgotten. He snatched it up, and ran on down the track.

The gulls were up, and screaming. The sound met him, raw on the wind from the sea. Something else was on that wind, a strange smell, and in the gulls' screaming a high shiver of panic that touched him like the edge of a knife. Smoke? There was usually smoke from the cottage, but this was a different smoke, a sour, chilled and sullen emanation, carrying with it a smell that mocked the good scent of roasting meat on the rare days when Sula had meat in the pot. This was not a good smell; it was sickening, an ugly mockery, making the morning foul.

Mordred's breeding, perverse though it was, had made him the child of one fighting king, and the grandson, twice over, of another. This combined with his hard peasant upbringing to make fear, for him, something to be faced immediately, and found out. He flung the basket of lichens down and ran full tilt along the cliff path, to where he could see down into the bay that had been his home.

Had been. The familiar cottage, with its clay oven, its lines of pegged fish, the hanging festoons of drying nets—all had vanished. Only the four walls of his home still stood, blackened and smoking with the sluggish, stinking smoke that befouled the sea-wind. Most of the outer roof slabs still lay in place, held as they were by stone supports built into the walls, but those in the center were thinner, and here and there had been pegged into place by driftwood. The thatch of the roof, dry with summer, had burned fiercely, and, with the pegs destroyed, the slabs had sagged, tilted, and then cracked, sliding down with their blazing load of thatch into the room below, making a pyre of what had been his home.

It must be, in very truth, a pyre. For now, retchingly, he recognized the smell that had reminded him of Sula's cooking pots. Sula herself, with Brude, must be inside—underneath that pile of burned rubble. The roof had fallen directly over their bedplace. To Mordred, groping, dazed, for the cause of disaster, there was only one explanation. His parents must have been asleep when some stray spark from the unwatched embers, blown by the draught, had lodged in the wind-dried turfs of the roof, and smouldered to a blaze. It was to be

53

hoped that they had never woken, had perhaps been ren
dered unconscious by the smoke, to be killed by the falling
roof before the fire even touched them.

He stood there so long, staring, unbelieving, sick, that
only the sharp wind, piercing the shabby tunic to the skin,
made him shiver suddenly and move. He squeezed his eyes
shut, as if in some silly hope that when he opened them the
place would be whole again, the horror only a nightmare
dream. But the horror remained. His eyes, wide again, showed
wild like a nervous pony's. He started slowly down the path,
then suddenly, as if some invisible rider had applied whip
and spur, he began to run.

Some two hours later Gawain, sent from the palace, found
him there.

Mordred was sitting on a boulder at some distance from
the cottage, staring out to sea. Nearby lay Brude's upturned
boat, unharmed. Gawain, pale and shocked, called his name,
but when Mordred gave no sign of having heard him, he
reluctantly approached to touch the unheeding boy on the
arm.

"Mordred. They sent me to find you. What on earth's
happened?"

No reply.

"Are they—your folk—are they—*in* there?"

"Yes."

"What happened?"

"How do I know? It was like that when I came down."

"Ought we to—is there anything—?"

Mordred moved at that. "Don't go near. You are not to
go. Let them."

He spoke sharply, authoritatively. It was the tone of an
elder brother. Gawain, held by horrified curiosity, obeyed
without thinking. The men who had come with him were
already at the cottage, peering about them with subdued
exclamations, whether of horror or simple disgust it was hard
to tell.

The two boys watched, Gawain half sickened, half fascinated, Mordred pale, and stiff in every muscle.

"Did you go in?" asked Gawain.

"Of course. I had to, hadn't I?"

Gawain swallowed. "Well, I think you should come back

ow, with me. The queen must be told." Then, when Mordred made no move: "I'm sorry, Mordred. It's a dreadful thing o happen. I'm sorry. But there's nothing you can do now, ou must see that. Leave it to them. Let's go now, shall we? ou look ill."

"I'm all right. I was sick, that's all." He slid down off the oulder, stooped to a rock pool, and dashed a handful of the alt water into his face. He straightened, rubbing his eyes s if coming out of sleep. "I'll come now. Where have the en gone?" Then, angrily: "Have they gone inside? What's to them?"

"They have to," said Gawain quickly. "Don't you see, he queen will have to know.... It isn't as if they—your olk—as if they had just been ordinary folk, is it?" Then, as Mordred turned to stare at him, half blindly: "Don't forget ho you are now, and they were the king's servants, themelves, in a way. She has to know what happened, Mordred."

"It was an accident. What else?"

"I know. But she has to have a report. And they'll do hatever's decent. Come on, we don't have to stay. There's othing we can do, nothing at all."

"Yes, there is." Mordred pointed to the cottage door, here the milch goat, bleating, pattered to and fro, to and ro, frightened by the unaccustomed movement, the smells, he chaos, but driven by the pain of her swollen udders. "We an milk the goat. Have you ever milked a goat, Gawain?"

"No, I haven't. Is it easy? Are you going to milk it now? ere?"

Mordred laughed, the brittle, light laugh of tensions reeased. "No. We'll take her with us. And the hens, too. If ou get that net that's drying on the boat's keel, I'll see if I an catch them."

He dived for the nearest, secured it in an expert grip, then wooped on another as it wrestled with some tidbit in the eaweed. The simple anticlimax to tragedy did its work as rief and shock exploded thankfully into action. Gawain, rince and king-designate of Orkney, stood irresolutely for few moments, then did as he was bidden, and ran to strip he net off the upturned boat.

When the men at length emerged from the cottage and tood, in a close-talking huddle, near the doorway, they saw he two boys toiling up the path. Gawain led the goat, and

Mordred carried, slung over his shoulder, an improvised ba of netting filled with protesting hens.

Neither boy looked back.

They were met at the palace gate by Gabran, who listene in silence to the story Gawain poured out, and thereafter having spoken gently to Mordred, called up servants to ri the boys of their livestock ("And she is to be milked straigh away!" insisted Mordred) and then hurried them straight int the palace.

"The queen must be told. I shall go to her now. Mordred go in and change and make yourself decent. She will war to see you. Gawain, go with him."

He hurried off. Gawain, looking after him with narrowe eyes, as if seeing something far away and bright, said unde his breath: "And one day, my fine Gabran, you will no command princes as if they were your dogs. We know whose dog *you* are! Who are you to take news to my mother in m place?" He flashed a sudden grin at Mordred. "All the same I'd sooner he did today! Come on, we'd better get clean."

The twins were in the boys' room, ostensibly busy, bu obviously waiting with some impatience for their first sigh of their new half-brother. Agravain was sitting on the be sharpening his dagger on a whetstone, while Gaheris, on th floor, rubbed a leather belt with grease to flex it. Gareth wa not there.

The twins were stocky, well-built boys, with the rudd hair and high colour that marked Morgause's sons by Lo and, at the moment, sullen expressions that were somethin less than welcoming. But it had apparently been made clea to them that Mordred must be welcomed, for they gave hi a civil enough greeting, and thereafter sat staring at hin much as cattle do at something strange and perhaps dan gerous that has strayed into their pasture.

A servant hurried in with a bowl of water and a napkin which he set on the floor. Gawain ran to the clothes-ches and threw Mordred's things off onto his bed. He burrowe inside the chest for his own things, while Mordred began t strip.

"What are you changing for?" asked Agravain.

"Our mother wants us," said Gawain, muffled.

"Why?" asked Gaheris.

Gawain shot a look at Mordred that meant, plainly, Not word. Not yet. Aloud, he said: "That's our business. You'll hear later."

"Him, too?" Agravain pointed at Mordred.

"Yes."

Agravain was silent, watching as Mordred slipped into one of the new tunics, and reached for the worked leather belt with its sheath for a dagger, and the hanger for a drinking horn. He fastened the buckle, and looked about him for the silver-mounted horn Ailsa had given him.

"It's there, on the window sill," said Gaheris.

"Did she really give you that one? You're lucky. It's a beauty. It's the one I asked for," said Agravain. The words were not angry or sullen, in fact they contained no expression at all, but Mordred's eyes flicked to him and then away again, as he clipped the horn to his belt.

"There was only one." Gawain spoke over his shoulder. "And you and Gaheris always have to have the same."

"Gareth's to get the golden one," said Gaheris. He spoke in the same flat, unboylike tone. Again Mordred glanced, and again the lids dropped over his eyes. Something had registered in that cool brain, and was stored away for the future.

Gawain wiped his face and dried it, then threw the napkin to Mordred, who caught it. "Be quick, then we've got to do our feet. She's fussy about the rugs." He glanced round. "Where's Gareth, anyway?"

"With her, of course," said Gaheris.

"Did you expect a full council of welcome, then, brother?" asked Agravain.

Conversing with the twins, thought Mordred, drying his feet, was like talking with a boy and his reflection. Gawain said sharply: "It'll keep. I'll see you later. Come on, Mordred, we'd better go."

Mordred stood up, smoothing down the soft folds of the new tunic, and followed Gawain to the doorway. The servant, coming in at that moment for the bowl, held the door wide. Gawain paused without thinking, the natural gesture of a host letting the guest precede him through the doorway. Then, as if remembering something, he went quickly through himself, leaving Mordred to follow.

The queen's door was guarded as before. The spears came

57

down as the boys approached. "Not you, Prince Gawain," said one of the men. "Orders. Just the other one."

Gawain stopped short, then stood to one side, his face stony. When Mordred glanced at him, with a word of half anxious apology ready, he turned quickly away without speaking, and strode off down the corridor. His voice rang out, calling for a servant, peremptory, self-consciously royal.

All three of them, thought Mordred to himself. Well, Gawain's still generous because of the cliffside rescue, but the other two are angry. I'll have to go carefully. The quick brain behind the smooth brow added it all together, and found a total that did not displease him. So they saw him as a threat, did they? Why? Because he was, in fact, King Lot's eldest son? Somewhere deep inside him that tiny spark of emulation, of longing, of desire for high doing, kindled and glowed as something new: ambition. Disjointed but clear, his thoughts spun. Bastard or not, I am the king's eldest son, and they don't like it. Does this mean that I really am a threat? I must find out. Perhaps he married her, my mother, whoever she was . . . ? Or perhaps a bastard can inherit . . . ? Arthur himself was begotten out of wedlock, and so was Merlin, that found the King's sword of Britain. . . . Bastardy, what need it matter after all? What a man is, is all that counts. . . .

The spears lifted. The queen's door was open. He pushed the confused and mounting thoughts aside, and came to the core of the matter. I shall have to be careful, he thought. More than careful. There is no reason at all why she should favour me, but as she does, I must take care. Not just of them. Of her. Most of all, of her.

He went in.

6

Mordred, during the lonely vigil on the beach, and then the long, silent trudge back to the palace and the bracing exchange with the twins in the boys' room, had had ample time to regain something like his normal—and formidably adult—self-command. Morgause, scanning him closely as he approached her, did not guess at it. The delayed effects of shock still showed, and the disgust and horror of what he had seen had drained the blood from his face and the life from his movements. The boy who walked forward and stood in front of the queen was silent and white-faced and kept his downcast eyes on the floor, while his hands, tucked into the new leather belt, gripped themselves into fists which apparently fought to control his emotion.

So Morgause interpreted it. She sat in her chair by the window where the sun poured in and made a pool of warmth. Gabran had gone out again, taking Gareth with him, but the queen's women were there, at the far end of the room, three of them at their stitchery, a fourth sorting a basketful of newly spun wool. The distaff, polished from much use, lay beside her on the floor. Mordred was reminded, sharply, at a moment when he least wanted it, of Sula's long days spent in the cottage doorway, spinning, a task which of late had been increasingly painful to her knotted fingers. He looked away, staring at the floor, and hoping, with violence, that the queen's condolences and kindness would not overset his control.

He need have had no fear. Morgause set her chin on her fist, regarding him. In the new clothes he looked princely, and enough like Arthur to make her eyes narrow and her mouth tighten as she said, in a light pretty voice as emotionless as a bird's: "Gabran told me what has happened. I am sorry."

She sounded completely indifferent. He glanced up, then down again, and said nothing. Why, indeed, should she care? For her it was a relief not to have to pay any more. But for Mordred...In spite of all the trappings of princedom, he saw his position. With no other place to go to, he was completely at the mercy of a queen who, apart from the trivial debt of the cliff climb, had no cause to wish him well. He did not speak.

Morgause proceeded to make the situation plain. "It seems that, nonetheless, the Goddess watches over you, Mordred. Had you not been brought to our notice, what would have become of you now, without a home, or any way to make a livelihood? Indeed, you might well have perished with your foster parents in the flames. Even had you escaped, you would have had nothing. You would have become a servant to any peasant who needed a skilled hand with his boat and net. A serfdom, Mordred, as hard to break out of as slavery."

He neither moved nor glanced up, but she saw the faint tremor of bracing muscles, and smiled to herself.

"Mordred. Look at me."

The boy's eyes lifted, expressionless.

She spoke crisply. "You have had a sad shock, but you must fight to put it behind you. You know now that you are a king's bastard, and that all you have owed to your foster home is your food and lodging—and even that by the king's orders many years ago. I also had my orders, and have obeyed them. I might never have chosen to take you from your foster home, but chance and fate willed it otherwise. The very day before you met Prince Gawain on the cliff, I saw something in the crystal that warned me."

She paused on the lie. There had been a brief flash in the boy's eyes. She interpreted it as the half-frightened, half-fascinated interest that the poor folk accorded her pretensions to magic power. She was satisfied. He would be her reature, as were the other palace folk. Without magic, and he terror she took care that it invoked, a woman could hardly have held this stark and violent kingdom, so far from the protecting swords of the kings whose task it was to keep Britain as one. She went on: "Don't misunderstand me. I had no warning of last night's disaster. If I had looked into the pool—well, perhaps. But the Goddess works in strange ways, Mordred. She told me you would come to me, and see, you have come. So now it is doubly right that you should forget all that is past, and try your best to become a fighting man who has a place here in the court." She eyed him, then added, in a softer tone: "And indeed, you are welcome. We shall see that you are made so. But, king's bastard or not, Mordred, you must earn your place."

"I will, madam."

"Then go now, and begin."

So Mordred was absorbed into the life of the palace, a life in its own way as harsh and uncompromising as his previous peasant existence, and rather less free.

The Orkney stronghold boasted nothing that a mainland king would have recognized as a military training-ground. Outside the palace walls the moor sloped up gently to landward, and this wild stretch, flat enough, and in good weather dry enough for soldiers to maneuver on, served as parade ground, practice ground, and playground, too, for the boys when they were allowed the freedom of it. Which was almost daily, for the princes of Orkney had to suffer no such formal lessons in the arts of war as disciplined the sons of the greater, mainland chiefs. Had King Lot still lived, and kept his state at Dunpeldyr in his mainland kingdom of Lothian, he would no doubt have seen to it that his elder sons, at least, went out daily with sword or spear or even the bow, to learn the bounds of their home country, and to see something of the lands that marched with theirs, from which threats or help might come in time of war. But in the islands there was no need for this kind of vigilance. All winter long—and winter lasted from October until April, and sometimes May— the seas kept the shores, and often even the neighbouring isles were seen only as clouds floating behind the other clouds that scudded, laden with rain or snow, across the sea. In some ways the boys liked winter best. Then Queen Morgause, snugged down in her palace against the incessant winds, spent her days by the fireside, and they were free even of her spasmodic interest. They were free to join the hunts for deer or boar—no wolves were to be found on the island—and enjoyed the breakneck rides when, armed with spears, they followed the shaggy hounds over wild and difficult country. There were sealhunts, too, bloody, exciting forays over the slippery rocks, where a false step could mean a broken leg, or worse. Their bows they were soon expert with; the island abounded in birds, which could be hunted at any time. As for swordplay and the arts of war, the queen's officers saw to the first, and the second could be picked up any evening round the supper fires of the soldiers in the courtyard. Of formal learning there was none. It is possible that, in the whole of the kingdom, Queen Morgause herself was the only one who knew how to read. She kept a box full of books in her room, and sometimes, by the winter fire, she would unroll one of these, while her women looked on, awed, and begged her to read to them. This she did only rarely, because the books were for the most part collections of the old lores that men called magic, and the queen guarded her skills with jealousy. About these the boys knew nothing, and would have cared less. Whatever the power—and it was genuine enough—that had come down through some trick of the blood to Morgause, and to Morgan her half-sister, it had quite passed by every one of her five sons. Indeed, they would have despised it. Magic, to them, was something for women; they were men; their power would be that of men; and they pursued it eagerly.

Mordred, perhaps, more eagerly than any. He had not expected to be received easily and at once into the brotherhood of the princes, and indeed, there were difficulties. The twins were always together, and Gawain kept young Gareth close by him, protecting him against the rough fists and feet of the twins, and at the same time trying to stiffen him against the over-indulgence of his mother.

It was through this that, in the end, Mordred broke into the charmed square of Morgause's legitimate children. One night Gawain woke to hear Gareth sobbing on the floor. The twins had thrown him out of bed onto the cold stone, and then laughingly fought off the child's attempts to clamber back into the warmth. Gawain, too sleepy to take drastic action, simply pulled Gareth into his own bed, which meant that Mordred had to move out and bed down with the twins. They, wide awake and spoiling for trouble, did not move to make way for him, but, each to his edge of the wide bed, set themselves to defend it.

Mordred stood in the cold for a few minutes, watching them, while Gawain, unaware of what was going on, comforted the youngest boy, paying no heed to the stifled giggles of the twins. Then, without attempting to get into bed, Mordred reached suddenly forward, and, with a swift tug, dragged the thick furred coverlet away from the boys' naked bodies, and prepared to bed down with it himself, on the floor.

Their yells of fury roused Gawain, but he merely laughed, his arm round Gareth, and watched. Agravain and Gaheris, goosefleshed with cold, hurled themselves, all fists and teeth, at Mordred. But he was quicker, heavier, and completely ruthless. He flung Agravain back across the bed with a blow in the belly that left him retching for breath, then Gaheris's teeth met in his arm. He whipped up his leather belt from the chest where it lay, and lashed the other boy over back and buttocks till he let go and, howling, ran to protect himself behind the bed.

Mordred did not follow them. He threw the coverlet back on the bed, dropped the belt on the chest, then climbed into bed, covering himself against the brisk draught from the window.

"All right. Now that's settled. Come in. I won't touch you again, unless you make me."

Agravain, sulky and swallowing, waited only a minute or two before obeying. Gaheris, hands to his buttocks, spat furiously: "Bastard! Fisher-brat!"

"Both," said Mordred equably. "The bastard makes me older than you, and the fisher-brat stronger. So get in and shut up."

Gaheris looked at Gawain, got no help there, and, shivering, obeyed. The twins turned their backs to Mordred, and apparently went straight to sleep.

From the other side of the chamber Gawain, smiling, held up a hand in the gesture that meant "victory." Gareth, the tears drying on his face, was grinning hugely.

Mordred answered the gesture, then pulled the coverlet

closer and lay down. Soon, but not before he was certain that the twins were genuinely asleep, he allowed himself to relax into the warmth of the furs, and drifted off himself into a slumber where, as ever, the dreams of desire and the nightmares were about equally mingled.

After that there was no real trouble. Agravain, in fact, conceived some kind of reluctant admiration for Mordred, and Gaheris, though in this he would not follow his twin, accorded him a sullen neutrality. Gareth was never a problem. His sunny nature, and the drastically swift revenge that Mordred had taken on his tormentors, ensured that he was Mordred's friend. But the latter took good care not to come between the little boy and the object of his first worship. Gawain was the one who mattered most, and Gawain, having in his nature something of the Pendragon that superseded the dark blood of Lothian and the perverse powers of his mother, would be quick to resent any usurper. As far as Gawain was concerned, Mordred himself stayed neutral, and waited. Gawain must make the pace.

So autumn went by, and winter, and by the time summer came round again, Seals' Bay was only a memory. Mordred, in bearing, dress, and knowledge of the arts necessary to a prince of Orkney, could not be distinguished from his half-brothers. The eldest by almost a year, he was necessarily matched with Gawain rather than with the younger ones, and though at first Gawain had the advantage of training, in time there was little to choose between them. Mordred had subtlety, call it cunning, and a cool head; Gawain had the flashing brilliance that on his worse days became rashness and sometimes savagery. On the whole they met equal to equal with their weapons, and respected one another with liking, though not with love. Gawain's love was still and always for Gareth, and, in a strained and often unhappy way, for his mother. The twins lived for each other. Mordred, though accepted and seemingly at home in his new surroundings, stood always outside the family, self-contained, and apparently content to be so. He saw little of the queen, and was unaware of how closely she watched him.

One day, after autumn had come again, he went down to Seals' Bay. He came to the head of the cliff path and stood as he had so often stood, looking down into the green dip of the bay. It was October, and the wind blew strongly. The heather was black and dead-looking, and here and there in the damp places the sphagnum moss grew golden green and deep. Most of the seabirds had gone south, but still out over the grey water the white gannets hovered and splashed like sea-spirits. Down in the bay the weather had so worked on the ruined cottage that the walls, washed clear of the mud that had bound their stones together, looked more like piles of rock thrown there by the tide than like part of a human dwelling. The burned and blackened debris had been long since dispersed by wind and sea.

Mordred walked down the slope and trod deliberately over the rain-washed grass to the door of his foster home. Standing on the sill, he looked about him. It had rained hard during the past week, and pools of fresh water stood here and there. In one of them, something white showed. He stooped to it, and his hand met bone.

For a shrinking second he paused, then with a sudden movement grasped the thing, and lifted it. A fragment of bone, but whether animal or human he could not tell. He stood with it in his hand, trying deliberately to let it conjure up emotion or memory. But time and weather had done their work; it was cleansed, sterile, indifferent as the stones on the storm beach. Whatever those people, that life, had been, it was over. He dropped the bone back in the flooded crevice, and turned away.

Before he climbed the path again he stood looking out to sea. Free he was now, in one sense; but what his whole being longed for was the freedom that lay beyond that barrier of water. Still something in his spirit beat itself against the space of air that lay between the Orkneys and the mainland kingdoms that were the High Kingdom.

"I'll go there," he said to the wind. "Why else did it all happen as it did? I'll go there, and see what can be made of a bastard prince from Orkney. She can't stop me. I'll take the next ship."

Then he turned his back on the cove, and went home to the palace.

7

It was not with the next ship, or even in the next year, that the chance came. In the event Mordred, true to his nature, was content to watch and bide his time. He would go, but not until something was assured for him. He well knew how little chance there was in the world beyond the islands for an untried and untrained boy; such a one would end—king's bastard or no—in penniless servitude or slavery. Life in Orkney was better than that. Then, in his third summer in the palace, a certain ship from the mainland put into harbour, and it became, suddenly, interesting.

The *Meridaun* was a small trader newly come from Caer y n'a Von, as people now called the old Roman garrison town of Segontium in Wales. She carried pottery goods and ores and smelted iron and even weapons for an illegal market run by the small smithies back of the barracks in the fortified port.

She also carried passengers, and to the islanders who crowded to the wharf to meet her, these were of more interest even than the much-needed goods. Ships brought news, and the *Meridaun*, with her mixed cargo of travellers, brought the biggest news for many years.

"Merlin is dead!" shouted the first man off the gangplank, big with the news, but before the crowd, pressing eagerly nearer, could ask him for details, the next asserted loudly:

"Not so, good folk, not so! Not when we left port, that is, but it's true he's very sick, and not expected to see the month out...."

Gradually, in response to the crowd's clamour for details, more news emerged. The old enchanter was certainly very ill. There had been a recurrence of the falling sickness, and he had been in a coma—"a sleep like death itself"—and had neither moved nor spoken for many days. The sleep might even now have passed into death.

The boys, with the townsfolk, had gone down to the wharf for news. The younger princes, eager and excited at the commotion and the sight of the ship, pressed forward with the crowd. But Mordred hung back. He heard the buzz of talk, the shouted questions, the self-important answers; noise surrounded him, but he might have been alone. He was back in a kind of dream. Once before, dimly in shadows somewhere, he had heard the same news, told in a frightened whisper. He had forgotten it till now. All his life he had heard tales of Merlin, the King's enchanter, along with tales of the High King himself and the court at Camelot; why, then, somewhere deep in a dream, had he already heard the news of Merlin's death? It had certainly not been true then. Perhaps it was not true now....

"It's not true."

"What's that?"

He came to himself with a start. He must, he realized, have spoken aloud. Gawain, beside him, was staring.

"What do you mean, it's not true?"

"Did I say that?"

"You know you did. What were you talking about? This news of old Merlin? So how do you know? And what's it to us, anyway? You look as if you were seeing ghosts."

"Maybe I am. I—I don't know what I meant."

He spoke lamely, and this was so unlike him that Gawain stared still harder. Then both boys were shoved aside as a man pushed roughly through the press. The boys reacted angrily, then drew aside as they saw that the man was Gabran. The queen's lover called peremptorily over the heads of the crowd:

"You, there! Yes, you, and you, too...Come with me! Bring what tidings you have straight to the palace. The queen must hear them first."

The crowd stood back a trifle sullenly, and let the news-bringers through. They went willingly with Gabran, important and obviously hopeful of reward. The people watched them out of sight, then turned back to the wharf, fastening on the next people to disembark.

These were traders, apparently; the first, by the look of the traps his man carried, was a goldsmith, then came a worker in leather, and last of all a travelling physician, whose slave followed him, laden with his impedimenta of boxes and bags and vials. To him the folk crowded eagerly. There was no doctor in these northern islands, and one went for ailments to the wise-women or—in extreme cases—to the holy man on Papa Westray, so this was an opportunity not to be missed. The doctor, in fact, lost no time in starting business. He stood on the sunny wharfside and started his rattling spiel, while his slave began to unpack the cures for every ill that might be expected to afflict the Orcadians. His voice was loud and confident, and pitched to overbear any rival attempt at business, but the goldsmith, who had preceded him off the ship, made no attempt to set up his stall. He was an old man, stooped and grey, whose own clothes boasted examples of a refined and lovely work. He paused at the edge of the crowd, peering about him, and addressed Mordred, who was standing near.

"You, boy, can you tell me—ah, now, I beg your pardon, young sir. You must forgive an old man whose sight is bad. Now I can see that you're quality, and so I'll beg you again of your kindness to tell me which is the way to the queen's house?"

Mordred pointed. "Straight up that street, and turn west at the black altar stone. The track will carry you right to the palace. It's the big building you can see—but you said your sight was poor? Well, if you follow the crowd, I think most people will be going there now, to get more news."

Gawain took a step forward. "Perhaps you know more yourself? Those fellows with their news from court—where were they from? Camelot? Where are you from yourself, goldsmith?"

"I am from Lindum, young sir, in the south-east, but I travel, I travel."

"Then tell us the news yourself. You must have heard, on the voyage, all that those men had to tell."

"Why, as to that, I heard very little. I'm a poor sailor, you see, so I spent my time below. But there's something those fellows there didn't mention. I suppose they wanted to be first with the news. There's a royal courier on board. He was as sick as I, poor fellow, but even without that, I doubt if he'd have shared his tidings with ordinary folk like us."

"A king's courier? When did he come aboard?"

"At Glannaventa."

"That's in Rheged?"

"That is so, young sir. He hasn't disembarked yet, has he, Casso?"

This to the tall slave who stood behind him carrying his baggage. The man shook his head. "Well, he'll be going straight up to the palace, too, you can be sure of that. If you want hot news, young sirs, you'd best follow. As for me, I'm an old man, and as long as I can follow my trade, the world can pass me by. Come, Casso, you heard? Up that path yonder as far as the black altar stone. Then turn east."

"It's west," said Mordred, quickly, to the slave. The man nodded, smiling, then took his master's arm and guided him up the rough steps towards the road. The pair trudged off and were lost to sight behind the hut where the harbour master lived.

Gawain was laughing. "Well, the palace ram has made a mistake this time! To escort a couple of tale-bearers up to the queen and not even wait to hear that there was a king's courier on board! I wonder—"

He did not finish the sentence. Some shouts and a fuss on deck indicated the approach of someone important. Presently a man came up from below, well dressed and smoothly barbered, but still pallid with sea-sickness. At his belt was a messenger's pouch, with its lock and seal. He trod importantly down the gangplank. Distracted from the physician, some of the crowd moved towards him, the boys with them, but they were disappointed. The courier, ignoring everyone, and refusing to answer any questions, climbed the steps and headed at a fast pace for the palace. As he cleared the last huts of the township he was met by Gabran, hurrying, this time with a royal escort of men-at-arms.

"Well, she knows now," said Gawain. "Come on, hurry," and the boys trotted uphill in the messenger's wake.

The letter that the courier bore came from the queen's sister Morgan, Queen of Rheged.

There was little love lost between the two ladies, but a stronger bond than love united them: hatred of their brother Arthur the King. Morgause hated him because she knew that Arthur loathed and feared the memory of the sin she had led him to commit with her; Morgan because, though married to a great and warlike king, Urbgen, she wanted at the same time a younger man and a greater kingdom. It is human to hate those whom, blameless, we hope to destroy, and Morgan was prepared to betray both brother and husband to achieve her desires.

It was of the first of these desires that she wrote to her sister. "You remember Accolon? I have him now. He would die for me. And needs must, perchance, should Arthur or that devil Merlin come to hear of my plans. But rest easy, sister; I have it on authority that the enchanter is sick. You will know that he has taken a pupil into his house, a girl, daughter of Dyonas of the River Islands, who was one of the Ladies of the Lake convent at Ynys Witrin. Now they say she is his mistress, and that in his weakness she strives to learn his power from him, and is in a fair way to steal it all, and suck him dry and leave him bound for ever. I know that men say the enchanter cannot die, but if this tale be true, then once Merlin is helpless, and only the girl Nimuë stands in his place, who is to say what power we true witches cannot grasp for ourselves?"

Morgause, reading by her window, made a mouth of impatience and contempt. "We true witches." If Morgan thought that she could even touch the edges of Morgause's art, she was an over-ambitious fool. Morgause, who had guided her half-sister's first steps in magic, could never be brought to admit, even to herself, that Morgan's aptitude for sorcery had already led her to surpass the witch of Orkney, with her sex potions and poisonous spells, by almost as much as Merlin in his day had surpassed them both.

There was not much more to the letter. "For the rest," Morgan had written, "the country is quiet, and this means I fear, that my lord King Urbgen will soon be home for the winter. There is talk of Arthur's going to Brittany, in peace to visit with Hoel. For the present he stays at Camelot in wedded bliss, though there is still no sign of an heir."

This time Morgause, reading, smiled. So the Goddess had heard her invocations, and savoured her sacrifices. The rumours were true. Queen Guinevere was barren, and the High King, who would not put her away, must remain without an heir of his body. She glanced out of the window. There he was, the one who was supposed, all those years ago, to have been drowned. He was standing with the other boys on the flat turf outside the walls, where the goldsmith's servant had set up his master's sleeping tent and stove, and the old man chatted with the boys as he laid out his implements.

Morgause turned abruptly from the window, and at her call a page came running.

"That man outside the walls, he's a goldsmith? Just come with the ship? I see. Then bid him bring some work to show me. If he is skilled, then there will be work for him here, and he will lodge within the palace. But the work must be good, fit for a queen's court. Tell him that, or he need not trouble me."

The boy ran. The queen, the letter lying in her lap, looked out beyond the moorland, beyond the green horizon where the sky reflected the endless shining of the sea, and smiled, seeing again the vision she had had, shrined in the crystal, of Camelot's high towers, and herself, with her sons beside her, carrying to Arthur the rich gifts that would be her pass to power and favour. And the richest gift of all stood there below her window: Mordred, the High King's son.

Though as yet only the queen knew it, it was to be the boys' last summer together in the islands, and it was a lovely one. The sun shone, the winds were warm and moderate, the fishing and hunting good. The boys spent their days out in the air. For some time now, under Mordred's tuition, they had even taken to the sea, something that the islanders did not readily do for sport, since the currents, at that meeting-place of two great seas, were fickle and dangerous. To begin with, Gaheris was seasick, but was ashamed to let the "fisher-brat" get the better of him, so persisted, and in time became a passable sailor. The other three took to sailing like gulls to the wave-tops, and a new respect grew up between the "real princes" and the elder boy, when they saw how well and with what authority he handled a boat in those difficult waters. His seamanship, it is true, was never tried in rough weather; the queen's indulgence would have come to a speedy end if there had been any evidence of real risk; so the five of them held their tongues about the moments of excitement, and did their exploring of the coastlines unrebuked. If Morgause's counsellors knew better than she what risks were run even in summer weather, they said nothing to Morgause; Gawain would be king one of these days, and his favour was already courted. Morgause, in fact, took little interest in anything beyond her palace walls, and "Witches don't like sailing," said Gareth, in all innocence of what his words implied. Indeed, the princes were proud, if anything, of their mother's reputation as a witch.

This showed itself in certain ways through that summer. Beltane the goldsmith and his slave Casso were housed in one of the palace outbuildings, and were seen daily working at their trade in the courtyard. This by the queen's commission; she gave them silver, and some small store of precious stones salvaged years ago from Dunpeldyr, and set them to fashioning torques and arm-rings and other jewels "fit for a king." She told no one why, but word got about that the queen had had a magical vision concerning things of such beauty and price, and that the goldsmith had come —by chance, magic, what you would—to make reality catch up with the dream.

Beautiful the things certainly were. The old man was a superb craftsman, and more than that, an artist of rare taste, who had been taught—as he never tired of telling—by the best of masters. He could work both in the Celtic mode, those lovely patterns of strongly angled but fluid lines, and also in ways learned, so he said, from the Saxons in the south, with enamel and niello and metals finely worked as filigree. The finer work he did himself; he was so shortsighted as to be, for normal purposes, almost blind, but he could do close work with a marvellous precision. The larger work, and all the routine, was done by the man Casso, who was also permitted to take in repairs and other local commissions from time to time. Casso was as silent as Beltane was garrulous, and it was some time before the boys—who spent long hours hanging around the stove when anything interesting was being done—discovered that Casso was in fact dumb. So all their questions were fired at Beltane, who talked and worked happily and without ceasing; but Mordred, watching almost as silently as the slave, saw that the latter missed very little, and gave, when those downcast eyes lifted now and again, an impression of intelligence far quicker than his master's. The impression was momentary, and soon forgotten; a prince had little thought to spare for a dumb slave, and Mordred, these days, was completely the prince, accepted by his half-brothers and—still to his puzzlement—high in the queen's favour.

So the summer wore through, and at the end of it the queen's magical prevision was justified. On a fine day of September another ship docked. And the news came that changed life for all of them.

8

It was a royal ship. The boys saw it first. They had their
boat out that day, and were fishing some way out in the firth.
The ship came scudding with a fair wind, her sails set full,
and the gilded mast flying a pennant that, though none of
them had seen it before, they recognized immediately, with
excitement. A red dragon on a background of yellow gold.

"The High King's standard!" Mordred, at the steering-
oar, saw it first.

Gaheris, never one to control himself, gave a yell of ex-
ultation, as savage as a war-cry. "He's sent for us! We are
to go to Camelot! Our uncle the High King has remembered,
and sent for us!"

Gawain said, slowly: "So she saw it truly. The silver gifts
are for King Arthur. But if she is his sister, why should she
need such gifts as those?"

His brothers paid no heed. "Camelot!" said Gareth, wide-
eyed.

"He won't want *you*." That was Agravain, sharply.
"You're far too young. She wouldn't let you go, anyway.
But if our uncle the High King sends for *us*, how can she
stop us?"

"You'd go?" That was Mordred, dryly.

"What do you mean? I'd have to. If the High King—"

"Yes, I know. I meant, would you want to go?"

Agravain stared. "Are you mad? Not want to go? Why on earth not?"

"Because the High King was never a friend to our father, that's what he means," put in Gaheris. He added, nastily: "Well, we can see why Mordred might not dare go, but the High King's our mother's brother, after all, and why should he be our enemy, even if he was our father's?" He glanced at Gawain. "And that's what you meant, too? That she's taking all that treasure to buy herself back in?"

Gawain, busy with a rope, did not reply. Gareth, understanding only half of what was said, put in eagerly: "If she goes, too, then she will take me, I know she will!"

"Buy herself back in!" Agravain repeated it explosively. "Why, that's folly! It's easy to see what's happened. It was that wicked old man Merlin who poisoned the High King's mind against us, and now he's dead at last, because you can bet anything you like, that's the news the ship brings, and now we can go to court at Camelot, and lead the High King's Companions!"

"Better and better." Mordred spoke more dryly than ever. "When I asked if you would want to go, I was remembering that you didn't approve of his policies."

"Oh, his policies," said Agravain, impatiently. "This is different. This may be a chance to get away from here, and into the middle of things. Just let me get there, to Camelot, I mean, and get half a chance to see some life and some fighting, and to hell with his policies!"

"But what fighting will there be? That's the whole point, isn't it? That's what you were so angry about. If he is really set on making a lasting peace with Cerdic the Saxon, you won't see any fighting."

"He's right," said Gaheris, but Agravain laughed.

"We'll see. For one thing, I don't think even Arthur will get a Saxon king to agree to terms and keep them, and for another, once I get there, and within reach of any Saxon, treaty or not, there'll be fighting!"

"Fine talking," said Gaheris, with scorn.

"But if there's a treaty—" began Gareth indignantly. Gawain interrupted. His voice was tense and even, overlying excitement. "Hold your tongues, the lot of you. Let's get back home and find out. At the very least it's news. Mordred, may we put about now?" For Mordred, by consent, was always captain of their sea-going expeditions, as Gawain was of their forays by land.

Mordred nodded, and gave the orders for trimming the sail. That he allotted the hardest tasks to Agravain may not have been coincidence, but the latter said nothing, hung on to the bucking rope, and helped to bring the lively boat about and send it skimming landwards, rocking in the spreading wake of the King's ship.

Whether or not the ship carried any message concerning the boys, a royal envoy had certainly been on board, and had gone ashore before the ship was barely trimmed to the quay. Though he spoke to no one save for a brief acknowledgment of the courtesy meeting accorded him by the queen's chief men, part of his news was already known to the crew, and by the time the boys beached their craft and scrambled ashore, the words were passing from mouth to mouth with a knell of awe and dread, mingled with the poor folks' furtive excitement at the thought of such a momentous change in high places.

The boys crowded in, listening where they could, questioning those of the crew who were on the wharfside.

It was as they had guessed. The old magician was dead at last. He had been entombed, with splendid mourning, in his own cave of Bryn Myrddin, near Maridunum, where he had been born. One of the soldiers accompanying the King's messenger had been there on duty, and told vivid tales of the ceremony, the King's grief, of fires the length and breadth of the land, and finally of the court's return to Camelot and the dispatch of the royal ship to the Orkneys. About its business there the sailors were vague, but the rumour went, they told the boys, that Queen Morgause's family were to be taken back forthwith to the mainland.

"I told you so!" said Gaheris to his brothers, in triumph. They began to run along the road that led to the palace. Mordred, after a second's hesitation, followed. Suddenly, it seemed, things had changed. He was on the outside again, and Lot's four sons, united in the golden prospect opening before them, seemed hardly to notice him. They were talking busily as they ran.

"—And it was Merlin who advised the High King to make the Saxon peace," panted Agravain.

"So perhaps now we'll see our uncle taking the sword again," said Gaheris happily. "And he'll want us—"

"And break his own sworn oath?" asked Gawain, sharply.

"Perhaps it isn't only us he wants," said Gareth. "Perhaps he's sent for our mother, too, now that Merlin's gone. He was a wicked man, I've heard her say so, and he hated her because he was jealous of her magic. She told me that. Perhaps, now he's dead, our mother will work magic for the King instead."

"The King's enchantress? He's got one already," said Gawain, dryly. "Didn't you hear? The lady Nimuë has Merlin's power, and the King turns to her for everything. So they were saying."

They were near the gate now. They dropped to a walk. Gareth turned to his half-brother.

"Mordred, when we go to Camelot, you'll be the only one left here. What will you do?"

The only one left here. . . . The firstborn of the King of Orkney, left, alone of the princes, in Orkney? Mordred saw the same thought strike Gawain at the same moment. He said, shortly: "I haven't thought about it. Come on, let's get in and find out what the man has to say."

He ran in through the gate. Gawain hung on his heel for a moment, then followed, and the rest with him.

The palace was buzzing, but no one knew anything except the larger rumours that the boys had already heard. The envoy was still closeted with the queen. People crowded in the corridors and in the hall, but made way for the princes when in a short time, clean and changed, they pushed their way through to the doors that led to the queen's private chambers.

Time went by. The light began to fade, and servants went about kindling the torches. It was time to eat. Cooking smells crept through the rooms, making the boys remember their hunger. In their excitement they had not eaten the barley cakes they had had in the boat. But still the queen's door did not open. Once they heard her voice, raised sharply, but whether in anger or excitement it was impossible to tell. The boys shifted uneasily, looking at one another.

"It *must* be true that we are to go," said Agravain. "What other message would our uncle the High King send with one of the royal ships?"

"Even if it isn't," said Gawain, "we can surely send a message back by the ship to our uncle the High King, at least to remind him that we exist."

(And if any of them says "our uncle the High King" again, thought Mordred, with savage irritation, I shall start shouting about "my father the King of Lothian and Orkney," and see what they say to that!)

"Hush!" he said aloud. "He's coming out. Now we shall know."

But they were to learn nothing yet. The queen's door opened, and the envoy came out between the guards, his face set and uninformative, as such men are trained to be. He walked forward without a look to right or left, and the people made way for him. No one spoke to him, the princes themselves moving aside without asking any of the eager questions that burned on their lips. Even here, in the islands at the back of the north wind, they knew that one did not question a King's envoy any more than one questioned the King. He brushed past them as if they did not exist—as if a mere messenger of the High King were of more account than all the princes of the islands.

A chamberlain came forward to take him in charge, and he was escorted to the quarters set aside for him in the palace. The queen's door stayed all the while firmly closed.

"I want my supper," said Gareth earnestly.

"It looks as if we'll get it," said Agravain, "long before she's decided to tell us what's going on."

This proved to be the case. It was late that night, verging indeed on the hour when normally the boys were sent to bed, when the queen sent for them at last.

"All five?" repeated Gawain, when the message came.

"All five," said Gabran. He could not help looking curiously at Mordred, and the other four pairs of eyes followed his. Mordred, tensing himself against the sudden upsurge of excitement, hope and apprehension, looked, as was his habit, detached and expressionless.

"And hurry," said Gabran, holding the door.

They hurried.

They filed into Morgause's chamber, silent, expectant and nervously awed by what they saw there. The queen had used the long interval since the messenger's dismissal to sup-

talk with her counsellors, and have a stormy but satisfactory little interlude with Gabran, then she had had her women bathe and dress her in a robe of state, and arrange, for the interview with her sons, a royal setting.

Her tall gilded chair had been carried in from the hall, and she sat there beside a glowing fire of peats with her feet on a crimson footstool. On a table at her elbow stood a golden goblet, still holding wine, and beside this lay the scroll that the King's messenger had given her, the royal seal of the Dragon splashed across it like a bloodstain.

Gabran, leading the boys into the room, crossed the floor to stand behind the queen's chair. No one else was there; the women had long since been dismissed. Beyond the window the midnight moon, at the full, had cooled from marigold to silver, and a sharp-edged blade of light cut across Morgause's chair, sparking on gold and drowning in the folds of her gown. She had had herself dressed in one of her finest robes, a sweeping shimmer of bronze-coloured velvet. Her girdle was set with gold and emeralds, her hair was braided with gold, and on it she had set one of her royal coronets, a thin circlet of red Celtic gold that had been King Lot's, and that the boys had seen before only when they had been allowed to sit in on the formal royal councils.

The torches had been put out, and no lamps were lit. She sat between firelight and moonlight, looking queenly and very beautiful. Mordred, possibly alone of the five, noticed how pale she was beneath the unwonted flush in her cheeks. She has been weeping, he thought, then, more accurately, and with that touch of ice that was all Arthur's: She has been drinking. Gawain is right. They are going away. Then what of me? Why send for me? Because they are afraid to leave me here alone, King Lot's firstborn? Here alone, and royal, what of me? His face gave no sign of his racing thoughts; he held himself still, beside Gawain, and half a head taller, and waited, to all appearances the least concerned person in the room. Then he saw that, of them all, the queen was looking only at him, Mordred, and his heart gave a jump, then settled to a fast, hard beat.

Morgause looked away from him at last, and surveyed them all for a while in silence. Then she spoke.

"You all know that the ship which lies in the harbour

comes from my brother the High King Arthur, and that it has brought his ambassador with messages for me."

No reply. She expected none. She looked along the row of boys, at the lifted faces, the eyes that were beginning to sparkle with joyful expectation. "I see that you have been making guesses, and I imagine they are the right ones. Yes, it has come at last, the summons that I know you have longed for. I, too, though it has come in a way I cannot welcome.... You are to go to Camelot, to the court of the High King your uncle."

She paused. Gawain, the privileged, said quickly: "Madam, Mother, if this distresses you I am truly sorry. But we've always known this would happen, haven't we? Just as we know that training and fortune, for those of our blood, must be found one day on the mainland, and in the press of affairs, rather than here in these islands?"

"Certainly." One hand was tapping on the table where the King's letter lay half unrolled. What, Mordred wondered, could the terms of that letter have been, to send Morgause to the wine flask, and to string her up until every nerve was, visibly, vibrating like an overtuned lute string?

Gawain, encouraged by her brief answer, asked impulsively: "Then why don't you welcome the summons? It isn't as if you would be losing—"

"Not the summons itself. The way it has come. We all knew it would happen one day, when—when my chief enemy was gone from the King's side. I have foretold it, and I had my own plans. I would have had you, Gawain, stay here; you are to be king, and your place is here, in my presence or without it. But he has asked for you, so you must go. And this man he has sent, this 'ambassador,' as he styles himself"—her voice was full of scorn—"is to stay here in your stead as 'regent.' And who knows where that will lead? I will tell you frankly what I fear. I fear that once you and your brothers are out of the Orkneys, Arthur will cause this creature of his to take from you the only land that still remains yours, as he took Lothian, and leave this man here in your stead."

Gawain, flushed with excitement, was disposed to argue. "But, Mother—madam—surely not? Whatever he did in Dunpeldyr out of enmity to our father King Lot, you are his sister, and we his close kin, all he has. Why should he want to shame and dispossess us?" He added, ingenuously: "He would not do it! Everyone I've talked to—sailors and travellers and the traders who come here from all over the world—they all say that Arthur is a great king, and deals only in justice. You will see, madam Mother, that there's nothing to fear!"

"You talk like a green boy," said Morgause sharply. "But this much is certain, there is nothing to be done here, nothing to be gained by disobeying the King's summons. All we can do is trust in the safe conduct he has sent, but once in Arthur's presence we can take our voices to his council—to the Round Hall if we have to—and see then if, in the face of me, his sister, and you, his nephews, he can refuse us our rights in Dunpeldyr."

Us? We? No one spoke the words, but the thought went from boy to boy with the sourness of disappointment. None of them had admitted to himself that this longed-for enlargement of their world held also the promise of a release from a capricious maternal rule. But each, now, felt a cast-down sense of loss.

Morgause, mother and witch, read it perfectly. Her lip curled. "Yes, I said 'we.' The orders are clear. I am to present myself at the court of Camelot as soon as the High King returns from Brittany. No reason is given. But I am to take with me—" Her hand touched Arthur's letter again. She seemed to be quoting. "'—All five of the princes.'"

"*He* said 'all five'?" This time the question burst from the twins, speaking as one. Gawain said nothing, but turned to stare at Mordred.

Mordred himself could not have spoken. A confused sense gripped him of elation, of disappointment, of plans made and abandoned, of pride and the anticipation of humiliation. And with these, fear. He was to go to Camelot, by order of the High King himself. He, the bastard of that king's erstwhile enemy. Could it be that all five of Lot's sons were summoned to some doom only held from them till now by the old enchanter's presence? He rejected that immediately. No, the legitimate princes were also the sons of the High King's sister; but what claim had he, Mordred, on any favour from Arthur? None: a memory, only, of enmity, and a tale of a past attempt to murder him by drowning. Perhaps Arthur's memory was as long as this, and now he would finish the work botched in that midnight massacre of long ago. . . .

This was folly. With the hard control that he had trained in himself, Mordred put speculation aside and concentrated on what was certain. He was going; that at least. And if the King had tried to murder him once, that had been when Merlin was alive, so presumably with Merlin's advice. Now, with Merlin dead, Mordred was at least as safe as his brothers. So he would take what the world of the mainland offered; and at the very least, once out of this island fastness, he could find out, by stealth if need be, or by mere precedent from the King's own advisers, what was due to the eldest born of a king, even when others were born later to supersede him. . . .

He dragged his attention back to what the queen was saying. They would take their own ship, it seemed, the *Orc*, which through Morgause's magical prevision was ready, new-rigged and painted and furnished with the luxury she craved. . . . And the gifts that they would take with them were all but ready. . . . Clothes for the boys, robes and jewels for their mother . . . Gabran to go with them, and men of the royal guard . . . A Council of four to be left in charge of affairs under the High King's ambassador . . . And since the High King himself would not be back in Camelot before October's end, their journey could be leisurely, and would give them time to visit Queen Morgan in Rheged. . . .

"Mordred!"

He jumped. "Madam?"

"Stay. The others go. Ailsa!"

The old woman appeared at the bedchamber door.

"Attend the princes to their chamber, and wait on them there. See that they do not linger to talk, but get straight to their beds. Gabran, leave me! No, this way. Wait for me."

Gabran turned on his heel and went into the bedchamber. Gawain, scowling after him, met his mother's eye, wiped the scowl from his face and led his brothers forward to kiss her hand. Ailsa swept them out, beginning to fuss and cluck before the door was well shut.

Mordred, alone with the queen, felt his skin tighten as he braced himself to hear what was to come.

9

As the door shut behind the other boys, Morgause rose abruptly from her chair, and went to the window.

The move took her out of the firelight and into the waxing silver of the moon. The cold light, behind her shoulder, threw her face and form into darkness, but lit the edges of hair and robe so that she seemed a creature of shadow rimmed with light, half visible and wholly unreal. Mordred felt again that pricking of the skin, as a beast's flesh furs up at the approach of danger. She was a witch, and like everyone else in those islands he feared her powers, which to him were as real and as natural as the dark that follows daylight.

He was too inexperienced, and too much in awe of the queen, to realize that she was at a loss, and was also, in spite of herself, deeply uneasy. The High King's envoy had been cool and curt; the letter he bore had been no more than a brief royal command, officially couched, demanding her presence and that of the five boys; no reason given, no excuse allowed, and an escort of soldiers on the ship to enforce it. Morgause's questions had got nothing more from the ambassador, whose cold demeanour was in itself a kind of threat.

It was not certain, but seemed probable, from the terms of the order, that Arthur had discovered where Mordred was; he obviously suspected, if he did not know, that the fifth boy at the Orkney court was his son. How he knew, she could not imagine. It had been common gossip all those years ago, that she had lain with her half-brother Arthur just before her marriage to Lot, and had been in due time brought to bed of a son, but it was also generally believed that the son, among the other babies of Dunpeldyr, had been murdered. She was sure that no one here in Orkney knew or suspected who Mordred was; the whispers at court were all of "Lot's bastard," the likely boy that the queen favoured. There were, of course, other, lewder whispers, but these only amused the queen.

But somehow Arthur knew. And this letter left no doubt. The soldiers would escort her to Camelot, and all her sons with her.

Morgause, facing the son who was to be her passport to Arthur's favour, to a renewal of power and position in the center of affairs, was trying to decide whether to tell him here and now whose son he was.

Through the years he had been in the palace, living and being taught with his half-brothers, she had never really considered telling him the truth. The time would come, she had told herself, the chance to reveal him and then to use him; either time, or her magic, would show her the moment.

The truth was that Morgause, like many women who work chiefly through their influence on men, was subtle rather than clever, and she was also by temperament lazy. So the years had gone by, and Mordred remained in ignorance, his secret known only to his mother and to Gabran.

But now, somehow, to Arthur, who, hard on Merlin's death, was sending for his son. And though Morgause had for years vilified Merlin through hatred and fear, she knew that it was he who had originally protected both Mordred and herself from Arthur's impetuous fury. So what did Arthur want now? To kill Mordred? To make sure at last? She could not guess. What would happen to Mordred did not concern her except as it would affect herself, but for herself she was apprehensive. Since the night she had lain with her half-brother to engender the boy, she had never seen Arthur; the tales of the powerful and fiercely brilliant king could not altogether be squared with her own memory of the eager boy whom she had entrapped deliberately to her bed.

She stood with her back to the bright moon. Her face was

hidden from her son, and when she spoke, her voice sounded coolly normal.

"Have you, like Gawain, been talking to the sailors and the traders who come ashore here?"

"Why, yes, madam. We usually go down to the wharf, along with the folk, to hear the news."

"Have any of them...I want you to think back carefully...have any of them during the past weeks or months singled you out to talk to, and have they questioned you?"

"I don't think—about what, please, madam?"

"About yourself. Who you are, what you are doing here with the princes in the palace." She made it sound reasonable. "Most people here know by this time that you are a bastard of King Lot's, who was farmed out to foster, and who came here on your foster parents' death. What they do not know is that you were saved from the Dunpeldyr massacre, and came here by sea. Have you spoken of this to anyone?"

"No, madam. You told me not to."

Searching that schooled face, those dark eyes, she was convinced. She was used to the guileless stare of the liar—the twins lied frequently for the sheer pleasure of doing it—and was sure this was the truth. Was sure, too, that Mordred was still too much in awe of her to disobey.

She made certain. "That is as well for you." She saw the flicker in the boy's eyes, and was satisfied. "But has anyone questioned you? Anyone at all? Think carefully. Has anyone seemed to know, or to guess about it?"

He shook his head. "I can't remember anything like that. People do say things like 'You're from the palace, aren't you? Five sons, then, the queen has? A fortunate lady!' And I tell them that I am the king's son, but not the queen's. But usually," he added, "they ask someone else about me. Not me."

The words were ingenuous, the tone was not. It meant: "They would not dare question me, *me*, but they are curious, so they ask. I am not interested in what is said."

He caught, against the moonlight, the shadow of a smile. Her eyes were blank and dark, gaps of nothingness. Even her jewels were quenched. She seemed to grow taller. Her shadow, thrown by the moon, grew monstrous, engulfing him. The air felt cold. In spite of himself, he began to shiver.

She watched him, still smiling, as she put out the first dark feelers of her magic. She had made her decision. She would tell him nothing; the long journey south should not be clouded and made difficult by her own sons' reaction to the news of Mordred's real status as son of the High King. Or by the knowledge that must go with it, of their mother's incest with her half-brother. It might be common talk on the mainland, but no one in the islands would have dared repeat it. Her four sons had heard nothing. Even to herself Morgause would not admit how the fact might be received.

For all her powers she had no idea why the King had sent for them. It was possible that he had sent for Mordred only to kill him. In which case, thought Morgause, coolly eyeing her eldest son, there would be no need for him to know anything—or her other sons either. If not, what was needed now was to shackle this boy to her, to ensure his obedience, and for this she had a well-tried pattern. Fear and then gratitude, complicity and then devotion; with these she had proved and held her lovers, and would now hold her son.

She said: "You have been loyal. I am glad. I knew it, but I wanted to hear it from you. I need not have asked you, you realize that, don't you?"

"Yes, madam." He was puzzled by the weight she seemed to be putting on the question, but he answered simply. "Everyone knows that you know everything, because you are—" he had been going to say "a witch" but swallowed the word and said instead, "—that you have powers of magic. That you can see what is hidden from other men by distance and by time."

Now it was certain that she was smiling. "A witch, Mordred. Indeed, yes, I am a witch. I have powers. Go on, say it."

He repeated it obediently. "You are a witch, madam, and you have powers."

She inclined her head, and her shadow dipped and grew again. The cold air eddied past him. "And you do well to be afraid of them. Remember them always. And when men come to question you, as they will do, in Camelot, remember the duty you owe to me, as my subject and my—step-son."

"I will. But what will they—why should they—?" He stopped, confused.

"What is going to happen when we reach Camelot? Is that

it? Well, Mordred, I will be frank with you; I have had visions, but all is not clear. Something clouds the crystal. We can guess what will come to my sons, his nephews, but to you? Are you wondering what will come to such as you?"

He nodded merely, not trusting his voice. It would have taken a stronger spirit than the island-bred boy's to outface a witch by moonlight. She seemed to gather magic round her, like the moonlight growing on the folds of velvet and in the streaming silk of her hair.

"Listen to me. If you do as I bid you, now and always, you will come to no harm. There is power in the stars, Mordred, and some of it is for you. That much I have seen. Ah, I see that you like that?"

"Madam?" Had she guessed, with her witch's powers, at his dreams, at his ignorant plotting? He held himself in, quivering. She saw his head go up and his fists clench again on the belt at his waist. Watching out of her enveloping darkness, she felt interest and a kind of perverted pride. He had courage. He was her son, after all. . . . The thought brought another in its wake.

"Mordred."

His eyes sought her in the shadows. She held them for a few moments, letting the silence draw out. He was her son, yes, and who knew what fragment of her power had gone down to him while she held him in her body? None of Lot's sons, those sturdy earthmen, had inherited so much as a flicker of it; but Mordred could be heir not only to the powers she had drawn from her Breton mother, but to some sidelong glimmer of the greater power of the archmage, Merlin. The dark eyes raised to hers and held steady there were Arthur's, but they were, too, like the enchanter's hated eyes that had held her own and beaten them down not once but many times before the last.

She asked suddenly: "Have you never wondered who your own mother was?"

"Why, yes. Yes, of course. But—"

"I ask only because there were, in Dunpeldyr, many women who boasted of having the Sight. Was your dam, I wonder, one of those? Do you have dreams, Mordred?"

He was shivering. Through his brain went all the dreams, dreams of power and nightmares of the past: the burned cottage, the whispers in the gloom, fear, suspicion, ambition. He tried to close his mind against her probing magic.

"Madam, lady, I have never—that is—"

"Never known the Sight? Never had a dream of fore-knowledge?" Her voice changed. "When the news came before of Merlin's death, with the *Meridaun*, you knew it was not yet true. You were heard to say so. And events proved you right. How did you know?"

"I—I didn't know, madam. I—that is—" He bit his lip, thinking back confusedly to the wharfside crowd, the shouting, the jostling. Had Gawain told her? No, Gabran must have overheard him. He licked his lips and tried again, patiently struggling for the truth. "I didn't even know I had spoken aloud. It meant nothing. It's not the Sight, or—or what you said. It might have been a dream, but I think it was something I'd heard a long time ago, and it turned out then that it wasn't true, either. It makes me think of darkness, and someone whispering, and—" He stopped.

"And?" she demanded sharply. "Well? Answer me?"

"And a smell of fish," Mordred muttered, to the floor. He was not looking at her, or he would have seen the flash of relief, rather than mockery, in her face. She drew a long breath. So, no prevision there; merely a cradle memory, a half-dream from babyhood when those stupid peasants discussed the news that came from Rheged. But it would be better to make sure.

"A strange dream, indeed," she said, smiling. "And certainly this time the messengers are right. Well, let us make sure. Come with me." Then, when he did not move, with a touch of impatience: "Come when I bid you. We shall look into the crystal together now, and maybe we shall find what the future holds for you."

She left the moonlit window and went by him with a brush of velvet on his bare arm, and a faint breath of scent like night-flowers. The boy drew an unsteady breath and followed her, like someone drugged. Outside the doorway the guards stood motionless. At the queen's gesture Mordred lifted a lamp down from the wall, then followed her as she led the way through the silent rooms and into the antechamber, where she paused before the sealed doorway.

During his years at the palace the boy had heard many tales about what lay beyond the ancient door. It was a dumb

88

geon, a torture chamber, a place where spells were woven, the shrine where the witch-queen spoke with the Goddess herself. No one knew for sure. If anyone but the queen had ever passed through that doorway, it was certain that only the queen had ever come out again. He began to tremble again, and the flame shook in the lamp.

Morgause did not speak. She lifted a key that hung on a chain from her girdle, and unlocked the door. It opened in silence on its greased hinges. At a gesture from her, Mordred held the lamp high. Before them a flight of stone steps led steeply downwards into a passageway. The walls glimmered in the lamplight, sweating with damp. Walls and steps alike were of rough rock, unchiselled, the living rock into which the Old People had burrowed for their burial chambers. The place smelled fresh and damp, and salty from the sea.

Morgause pulled the door shut behind them. The lamp guttered in the draught and then burned strongly. She pointed, in silence, then led the way down the steps and along a passageway, straight and smoothly floored, but so low that they had to stoop to avoid striking their heads on the roof. The air of the place was dead, and one would have said still, but all the while there was a sound that seemed to come from the rock itself: a murmur, a hum, a throb, which Mordred suddenly recognized. It was the sound of the sea, echoing through the passageway more like a memory of waters that had once washed there, than like the sound of the living sea without. The two of them seemed to be walking into the corridors of a vast sea-shell whose swirling echo, straight from the depths, was breathed now by the air. It was a sound he had heard many a time, as a child, playing with shells on the beach of Seals' Bay. Momentarily, the memory dispelled the darkness and the drug of fear. Soon, surely, thought the boy, they would come out into a cave on the open shore?

The passage twisted to the left, and there, instead, was another low door. This, too, was locked, but answered to the same key. The queen led the way in, leaving the door open. Mordred followed her.

It was no cave, but a small room, its walls squared and smoothed by masons, its floor made of the familiar polished slabs. There was a lamp hanging from the rocky ceiling. Against one wall stood a table, on which were boxes and bowls and sealed jars with spoons and pestles and other instruments of ivory and bone, or of bronze bright with use. Stone slabs had been set into the walls to make shelves, and on them stood more boxes and jars, and bags of leather tied with lead wire and stamped with some seal he did not recognize, of circles and knotted snakes. A high stool stood by the table, and against another wall was a small stove, with beside it a skep of charcoal. A fissure in the roof apparently served to lead the fumes away. The stove must be lit frequently, or had been very recently. The room was dry.

On a high shelf glimmered a row of what Mordred took to be globes or jars made of a strange, pale pottery. Then he saw what they were: human skulls. For a sickening moment he imagined Morgause distilling her drugs, here in her secret stillroom, and making her magic from human sacrifices, the dark Goddess herself shut away in her subterranean kingdom. Then he saw that she had merely tidied away the original owners of the place, when the grave-chamber had been converted to her use.

It was bad enough. The lamp quivered in his hand again, so that the sheen on the bronze knives trembled, and Morgause said, half smiling:

"Yes. You do well to be afraid. But they do not come in here."

"They?"

"The ghosts. No, hold the lamp steady, Mordred. If you are to see ghosts, then be sure to be as well armed against them as I."

"I don't understand."

"No? Well, we shall see. Come, give me the light."

She took the lamp from him and walked towards the corner beyond the stove. Now he saw that there, too, was a door. This one, of rough driftwood planks, was narrow and high, shaped irregularly like a wedge; it had been made to fit another natural fissure in the rock walls. It came open with the creak of warped wood, and the queen beckoned the boy through.

This at last was the sea-cave, or rather, some inner chamber of it. The sea itself drove and thundered somewhere near at hand, but with the hollow boom and suck of a spent force whose power has been broken elsewhere.

This cavern must be above all but the highest tides; the floor was flat, and dry, its slabs tilted only slightly towards

90

he pool that stood at the cavern's seaward side. The only utlet must be deep under the water. No other was visible.

Morgause set the lamp down at the very edge of the water. ts light, still in the draughtless air, glowed steadily, down nd down into the inky depths of the water. It must be some ime since the pool had been disturbed by any stray pulse f the tides. It lay still and black, and deep beyond imagi- ation or sight. No light could penetrate that black liquid; he lamplight merely threw back, sharp and small, the re- lection of the rock that overhung the water.

The queen sank to her knees at the pool's edge, drawing Mordred down beside her. She felt him trembling.

"Are you still afraid?"

Mordred said, through shut teeth: "I am cold, madam."

Morgause, who knew that he was lying, smiled to herself. Soon you will forget that. Kneel there, pray to the Goddess, nd watch the water. Do not speak again until I bid you. Now, son of the sea, let us learn what the pool has to tell us."

She fell silent herself at that, and bent her gaze on the nky depths of the pool. The boy stayed as still as he could, taring down at the water. His mind still swam in confusion; e did not know whether he hoped more, or dreaded more, o see anything in that dead crystal. But he need not have eared. For him, the water was only water.

Once he stole a glance sideways at the queen. He could ot see her face. She was bowed over the water, and her air, unbound, flowed down to make a tent of silk that reached nd touched the surface of the pool. She was so still, so ranced, that even her breathing did not stir the surface where er hair trailed like seaweed. He shivered suddenly, then urned back and stared fiercely down into the water. But if he ghosts of Brude and Sula and of the score of murdered babies that lay to Morgause's account were present in that cave, Mordred saw no hint of them, felt no cold breath. He only knew that he hated the darkness, the tomb-like stillness, he held breath of expectation and dread, the slight but un- mistakable emanations of magic that breathed from Mor- gause's trance-held body. He was Arthur's son, and though he woman, with all her magic, could not know it, this short hour when he was made privy to her secrets was to sever him from her more completely than banishment. Mordred himself was not aware of this; he only knew that the distant suck and thunder of the sea spoke of the open air, and wind and light on the tide's foam, and drew him irresistibly away in spirit from the dead pool and its drowned mysteries.

The queen moved at last. She drew a long, shuddering breath, then pushed back her hair, and stood up. Mordred jumped thankfully to his feet and hurried to the door, pulling it open for her and following her through the wedgeshaped gap with a sense of relief and escape. Even the stillroom, with its gruesome watchers, seemed, after the silence of the cave, the tranced breathings of the witch, as normal as the palace kitchens. Now he could catch the smell of the oil that Morgause blended to make her heavy perfumes. He latched the door thankfully, and turned to see her setting the lamp down on the table.

It seemed that she already knew the answer to her question, because she spoke lightly.

"Well, Mordred, now you have looked into my crystal. What did you see?"

He did not trust himself to speak. He shook his head.

"Nothing? Are you telling me that you saw nothing?"

He found his voice. It came hoarsely. "I saw a pool of sea-water. And I heard the sea."

"Only that? With the pool so full of magic?" She smiled, and he was surprised. Foolishly, he had expected her to be disappointed.

"Only water, and rock. Reflections of rock. I—I did think once that I saw something move, but I thought it was an eel."

"The fisherman's son." She laughed, but this time the epithet held no mockery. "Yes, there is an eel. He was washed in last year. Well, Mordred, boy from the sea, you are no prophet. Whatever power your true mother may have had, it has passed you by."

"Yes, madam." Mordred spoke with patent thankfulness. He had forgotten what message she had bidden him look for in the crystal. He was wishing violently that the interview was over. The acrid smell of lamp oil mingling with the heavy scents of the queen's unguents oppressed him. His head swam. Even the sound of the sea seemed a whole world away. He was trapped in this shutaway silence, this ancient and airless tomb, with this sorceress of a queen who puzzled im with her questions, and confused him with her strange nd shifting moods.

She was watching him now, a strange look that made him hift his shoulders as if all at once he felt himself a stranger o the body inside his clothes. He said, more to break the ilence than because he wanted to know:

"Did you see anything in the pool, madam?"

"Indeed, yes. It was still there, the vision that I saw yesterday, and before that, before Arthur's messenger ever came ere." Her voice went deep and level, but found no echo in hat deadened air.

"I saw a crystal cave, and in it my enemy, dead and on is bier between the candles, and no doubt rotting away into he forgetfulness I once cursed him with. And I saw the Dragon himself, my dear brother Arthur, sitting among his ilded towers, beside his barren queen, waiting for his ship o come back to Ynys Witrin. And then myself, with my ons, and with you, Mordred, all of us together, bearing gifts or the King and within the gates of Camelot at last... at ast.... And there the vision faded, but not before I saw him oming, Mordred, the Dragon himself... a dragon wingless ow, and ready to listen to other voices, try other magic, ie down with other counsellors."

She laughed then, but the sound was as discomforting as er look. "As he did once before. Come here, Mordred. No, eave the lamp alone. We will go up in a minute. Come here. Nearer."

He approached and stood in front of her. She had to look p to meet his eyes. She put up her hands and took him by he arms. "As he did once before," she repeated, smiling.

"Madam?" said the boy hoarsely.

Her hands tightened on his arms. Then suddenly she drew im to her, and before he could guess at what she purposed he reached up and kissed him, lingeringly, upon the mouth.

Bewildered, half-excited, aroused by her scent and the nexpectedly sensual kiss, he stood in her grip, trembling, ut not this time with either cold or fear. She kissed him gain, and her voice was honey-sweet against his lips. "You ave your father's mouth, Mordred."

Lot's mouth? Her husband's, who had betrayed her by ying with his mother? And she kissed him? Wanted him, erhaps? Why not? She was a lovely woman still, and he

93

was young, and as experienced sexually as any boy of his age. There was a certain lady of the court who had taken pleasure in teaching him pleasure, and there was also a girl a shepherd's daughter who lived a few miles from the palace who watched for him when he rode that way across the heather, with the evening wind blowing in from the sea. ... Mordred, brought up in islands as yet untouched either by Roman civilization or Christian ethic, had no more sense of sin than a young animal, or one of the ancient Celtic gods who haunted the cairns and rode by like rainbows on sunny days. Why, then, should his body recoil, rather than respond to hers? Why feel as if, clingingly, something evil had brushed him by?

She pushed him away suddenly, and reached for the lamp. She lifted it, then paused, looking him over slowly with that same discomforting look. "Trees can grow tall, it seems, Mordred, and still be saplings. Too much, perhaps, yet not enough your father's son.... Well, let us go. I to where my patient Gabran waits for me, and you to your child's bed with the other children. Do I need to remind you to say nothing about anything that has befallen this night, or anything I have said?"

She waited for a reply. He managed to say: "About this, madam? No. No."

"'This'? What is 'this'? About anything that you have seen, or not seen. Maybe you have seen enough to know that I am to be obeyed. Yes? Well then, do as I bid you and you will come to no harm."

She led the way in silence, and he followed her up the passageway and out into the antechamber. The key shot behind them in the well-greased wards. She neither spoke again nor looked at him. He turned and ran from her along the cold corridors and through the dark palace to his bed chamber.

During the days that followed, Mordred tried, along with the other boys, and half the Orcadians besides, to come near enough to the King's envoy to have speech with him. In the case of the islanders, and the younger princes, it was a matter of curiosity. What was the mainland like? The fabled castle of Camelot? The King himself, hero of a dozen stark battles, and his lovely Queen? Bedwyr his friend, and others of the companion knights?

But all, princes and commoners alike, found it impossible to come near the man. After that first night he slept on board the royal ship, and disembarked daily to be escorted, ostensibly for a word of courtesy with Queen Morgause, but really, rumour had it, to make sure that her preparations went forward fast enough to catch the good autumn weather.

The queen was not to be hurried. Her ship, the *Orc*, lay by the wharf, ready in all but the last touches. Workmen busied themselves with the final gilding and painting, while their women stitched at the great decorated sail. In the palace itself Morgause's own women busied themselves with the finishing, tending and packing of the sumptuous clothes that the queen planned for her reception at Camelot. Morgause herself spent many hours in her secret room below the rock. She was not, as whispers went, consulting her dark Goddess, but in fact concocting unguents and lotions and perfumes, and certain subtle drugs that had the reputation of restoring beauty and the energy of youth.

In his corner of the courtyard, Beltane the goldsmith still sat at his work. The gifts for Arthur were finished, packed in wool in the box made to receive them; the old man was busy now with jewels for Morgause herself. Casso, the dumb slave who helped him, had been set to fashioning buckles and brooches for the princes; though he was not an artist like his master, he made a good job of the designs given him by Beltane, and seemed to enjoy the time the boys spent watching him and talking round the smelting-stove. Mordred, alone of them all, tried some sort of communication with him, asking questions that needed no more than a nod or a shake of the head for answer, but he got no further than a few facts about Casso himself. He had been a slave all his life. He had not always been dumb, but had had his tongue cut out by a cruel master, and considered himself the most fortunate of men to have been taken in by Beltane and taught a trade. A dull life indeed, thought Mordred, and wondered—though only idly—at the air of contentment that the man visibly wore; the air, if the boy had recognized it, of a man who has come to terms with his limitations, and who has made a place for himself in life, which he fills with integrity. Mordred, who had had small reason during his life to think the best of any man, assumed merely that the slave had some sort of satisfactory private life which he managed independently of his master. Women, possibly? He could certainly afford them. When (his master safely abed) the slave joined in the soldiers' dice game, he always had coin in plenty, and easily stood his share of the wine. Mordred knew where the money came from. Not from Beltane, that was sure; who—apart from the odd gift—ever paid his own slaves? But there had been a day a month or so back when Mordred took a small boat out alone and went fishing, coming back late in the half-light that was all the night the islands knew in summer. There was a small trading ship lying moored at the royal wharf; most of her men were on shore for the night, but some officers were apparently still aboard; he heard a man's voice, and then a chink that might have been the sound of coins passing. As he tied his boat to the wharf in the shadow of the trader he saw a man walk quickly down the gangplank and up through the town towards the palace gate. He recognized Casso. So, the man took commissions privately, did he? Legitimate trading would hardly need to be done at midnight. Well, a man had to fend for himself, thought Mordred, with a shrug, and forgot all about it.

The day came at last. On a bright sunny morning of October the queen with her women, followed by the five boys, Gabran, and her chief chamberlain, headed the stately procession to the wharf. Behind them a man carried the box of treasure destined for Arthur, and another bore gifts for the King of Rheged and his wife, Morgause's sister. A page-boy struggled with the leashes of two tall island-bred hounds destined for King Urbgen, while another boy, looking scared, carried at arm's length a stout wicker cage in which spat and snarled a half-grown wildcat intended as a curious addition to Queen Morgan's collection of strange birds and beasts and reptiles. With them went an escort of Morgause's own men-at-arms, and last of all—ostensibly to honour her but looking suspiciously like a guard—marched a detachment of the King's soldiers from the *Sea Dragon*.

Even in the merciless light of morning the queen looked lovely. Her hair, washed with sweet essences and dressed with gold, sparkled and shone. Her eyes were bright under their tinted lids. Normally she favoured rich colours, but today she wore black, and the somber dress gave her figure, thickened with child-bearing, almost the old lissome slenderness of her girlhood, and set off the jewels and the creamy skin. Her head was high and her look confident. To either side of the way the islanders crowded, calling greetings and blessings. Their comfort-loving queen had not granted them many such glimpses of her since her banishment to these shores, but now she had given them a sight indeed, a royal procession, queen and princes and their armed and jewelled escort, with, to top all, a sight of King Arthur's own ship with its dragon standard waiting to shepherd the *Orc* to the mainland kingdom.

The *Orc* took sail at last, curving out into the strait between the royal island and its neighbour. Astern of her, at the edge of her creaming wake, rode the *Sea Dragon*, a hound herding the hind and her five young steadily southward into the net spread for them by the High King Arthur.

* * *

Once away from the Orkneys with the queen and her family safely embarked, the captain of the *Sea Dragon* was not too much concerned with speed; the High King was still in Brittany, and Morgause's presence would suffice when he was once more at Camelot. But he had wisely allowed extra time for the voyage in case the ships struck bad weather, and this, very soon, they did. During their passage of the Muir Orc—that strait of the Orcadian Sea that lies between the mainland and the outer isles—they met winds of almost gale force, that drove the two ships apart, and sent even the hardiest of the passengers below. At length, after some days of stormy weather, the gales abated, and the Orcadian ship beat into the sheltered waters of the Ituna Estuary and dropped anchor there. The *Sea Dragon* struggled into the same wharf a few hours later, to find the Orkney party still on board, but making preparations to go ashore and travel to Luguvallium, the capital of Rheged, to visit King Urbgen and Morgan his queen.

The captain of the *Sea Dragon*, though perfectly aware that he was prisoners' escort rather than guard of honour, saw no reason to prevent the journey. King Urbgen of Rheged, though his queen had transgressed notably against her brother Arthur, had always been a faithful servant of the High King; he would certainly see to it that Morgause and her precious brood were kept safe and close while the ships were repaired after the gale.

Morgause, who saw no need to ask permission for the journey, had already dispatched a letter to her sister, bidding her expect them. Now a courier was sent ahead, and at length the party, as carefully escorted as before, set out for King Urbgen's castle.

For Mordred, the ride was all too short. Once the party left the shore and struck inland through the hills he was passing through very different country from any that he had seen or even been able to imagine before.

What impressed him first was the abundance of trees. In Orkney the only trees were the few stunted alders and birches and wind-bitten thorns that huddled along the meager shelter of the glens. Here there were trees everywhere, huge can-opied growths, each with its island of shadow and its de-pendent colony of bushes and ferns and trailing plants. Great forests of oak clothed the lower hillsides, giving way on higher ground to pines that grew right up to the foot of the tallest cliffs. Down every gully in those cliffs crowded more trees, rowan and holly and birch, the thickly wooded clefts seeming to hang from the silver mountain-crests like the ropes that held down the thatch of his parents' cottage. Willow and alder lined every smallest stream, and along the roadways, on the slopes, bordering the moorland stretches and sheltering every cottage and sheep-cote, were trees and more trees, all in the russet and gold and rich red of autumn, backed with the black glint of holly and the dark accent of the pines. Along the track where they rode the hazel-nuts dropped ripe from their fringed calyxes, and under the silver webs of autumn late blackberries glinted like garnets. Gareth pointed excitedly to a burnished slow-worm pouring itself away into the bracken, and Mordred saw small deer watching them from the ferns at the edge of the forest, as still and dappled as the forest floor where they stood.

Once, when their road led them over a high pass, and between the crests of the hills the country opened on a blue distance, Mordred checked his horse, staring. It was the first time he had seen so far with no sea visible. For miles and miles the only water was the small tarns that winked in the hanging valleys, and the white of streams running down through the grey rock to feed them. Hill after blue hill rose into the distance where a great chain of mountains lifted to one square-topped and white. Mountain or cloud? It was the same. This was the mainland, the kingdom of the kingdoms, the stuff of dreams.

One of the guard closed in then, with a smile and a word, and Mordred moved back into the troop.

Afterwards he was to have only the haziest recollections of his first sojourn in Rheged. The castle was huge, crowded, grand and troubled. The boys were handed straight to the king's sons; in fact the sharp impression was of being bundled out of the way while some crisis, never fully explained to them, was sorted out. King Urbgen, perfectly courteous, was abstracted and brief; Queen Morgan did not appear at all. It seemed that recently she had been kept in a seclusion that almost amounted to imprisonment.

"Something about a sword," said Gawain, who had managed to overhear a conversation in the guardroom. "The

High King's sword. She took it from Camelot while he was abroad, and put a substitute in its place."

"Not just the sword," said Gaheris. "She took a lover, and gave the sword to him. But the High King killed him just the same, and now King Urbgen wants to put her away."

"Who told you that? Surely our uncle would never let him use his sister so, whatever she had done."

"Oh, yes. Because of the sword, which was treachery. So the High King will let him put her away," said Gaheris eagerly. "As for the lover—"

But at this point Gabran came across the courtyard to them, with a summons to the stables, and even Gaheris, not famed for his tact, thought it better to postpone the discussion for the time being.

They found out a little more, but only a little, from Urbgen's two sons. They were grown men, sons by the king's first marriage, seasoned fighters who had at first taken pride in their father's alliance with Arthur's young sister, but now wished her gone, and were ready to support Urbgen's petition to have the marriage set aside.

The truth, it appeared, was this. Morgan, tied by marriage to a man many years her senior, had taken as lover one of Arthur's Companions, a man called Accolon, brave, ambitious and high-spirited. Him she had persuaded, while Arthur was abroad from Camelot, to steal his great sword Caliburn, that men called the sword of Britain, and carry it to Rheged, leaving in its place a substitute fashioned secretly by some creature of Morgan's in the north.

What the queen intended was never satisfactorily explained. She cannot have thought that young Accolon, even with Urbgen out of the way, the sword of Britain in his hand, and Morgan married to him, could ever have been able to supplant Arthur as High King. It was more probable that she had used her lover to further her own ambition, and that the tale she eventually told to Urbgen was truthful in the main. She had had dreams, she said, which had led her to expect Arthur's sudden death abroad. So, to forestall the chaos following on this, she had taken it upon herself to secure the symbolic sword of Britain for King Urbgen, that tried and brilliant veteran of a dozen battles, and husband of Arthur's only legitimate sister. True, Arthur himself had declared the Duke of Cornwall to be his heir, but Duke Cador was dead, and his son Constantine still a child....

So went the tale. As for the substitution of a worthless copy for the royal sword, that, she alleged, had only been a device to help the theft. The sword hung habitually above the King's chair in the Round Hall at Camelot, and nowadays was taken down only for ceremony, or for battle. The copy had been hung there only to deceive the eye. But from it might have come tragedy. Arthur had returned unharmed from his travels, and Accolon, afraid for himself and Morgan should the theft be discovered, challenged the King to fight, and with his own good sword attacked Arthur armed only with the brittle copy of Caliburn. The outcome of that fight was already part of the growing legend of the King. In spite of his treacherous advantage Accolon had been killed, and Morgan, afraid now of the vengeance of both brother and husband, declared to all who would listen that the fight was none of her making, but only Accolon's, and since he was dead, no one could contradict her. If she mourned her dead lover, she did so in secret. To those who would listen she deplored his folly, and protested her devotion—mistaken, she admitted, but real and deep—to her brother Arthur and to her own lord.

Hence the turmoil in the castle. No decisions had been made as yet. The lady Nimuë, successor to Merlin as Arthur's adviser, and (it was said) to Merlin's power, had come north to recover the sword. Her message was uncompromising. Arthur was not prepared to forgive his sister for what he saw as treachery; and should Urbgen wish to avenge the betrayal of his bed, he had the King's leave to use his faithless queen as he saw fit.

As yet the King of Rheged had barely trusted himself to talk with his wife, let alone judge her. The lady Nimuë was still housed in Luguvallium, though not in the castle itself; somewhat to Urbgen's relief she had declined his offer of hospitality, and was lodged in the town. Urbgen had had enough (as he confided to his sons) of women and their dabblings in dreams and sorcery. He would have liked to refuse Morgause's visit, but there were no grounds on which he could do so, and besides, he was curious to see "the witch of Orkney" and her sons. So the great King Urbgen steered his way cautiously between Nimuë and Morgause, allowing the latter to visit and talk with her sister at will, and praying that the former, now that her business in the north was concluded, would leave Luguvallium without too embarrassing a confrontation with her old enemy Morgause.

After supper on the third night of their visit, Mordred, avoiding the other boys, walked back alone from the hall to the rooms where the princes were housed. His way took him through a strip of land which lay between the main block of the castle buildings and the river.

Here lay a garden, planted and tended for Queen Morgan's pleasure; her windows looked out over beds of roses and flowering shrubs, and lawns that edged the water. Now the stalks of dead lilies stood up in a tangle of sweetbriar and leafless honeysuckle, and fungus rings showed dark green on the grass. Marks on the walls beside the queen's windows showed where the cages of her singing birds had hung before being carried indoors for the winter. Swans idled at the river's edge, no doubt waiting for the food the queen had brought them in less troubled days, and a pair of snow-white peacocks had flown to roost, like great ghosts, in a tall pine tree. In summer no doubt the place was pretty and full of scent and colour and the songs of birds, but now, in the chill damp of an autumn evening, it looked deserted and sad, and smelled of unswept leaves and river-mud.

But Mordred lingered, fascinated by this new example of mainland luxury. He had never seen a garden before, never even imagined that a piece of land could be carefully designed and planted simply for beauty, and its owner's pleasure. Earlier he had caught a glimpse, from a window, of a statue looking like a ghost against a dark tangle of leaves. He set himself to explore.

The statue was strange, too. A girl, airily draped, stooped as if to pour water from a foreign-looking shell into a stone basin below her. The only statues he had seen before were the crude gods of the islands, stones with watching eyes. This girl was lovely, and almost real. The dusk made gentle shadows of the grey lichen that patched her arms and gown. The fountain was dry now, the shell empty, but the stone bowl was still filled with water and the remains of the summer's water-lilies. Below the blackened leaves he could just see, dimly, the sluggish movement of fish.

He left the dead fountain, and trod softly across the lawn towards the river bank and the floating swans. There, facing the river and hidden from the palace windows by a brick wall thick with vines, was an arbour, a charming place, paved with mosaic work and furnished with a curved stone bench whose ends were richly carved with grapes and cupids.

Something was lying on the bench. He went across to look. It was an embroidery frame, holding its square of linen half worked with a pretty design of strawberries twined in their leaves and flowers. He picked it up curiously, to find that the linen was sodden, and marked by the stone where it had lain. It must have been there for some time, forgotten. He was not to know that Queen Morgan herself had dropped it when, here in their usual trysting-place, the news had been brought to her of her lover's death. She had not been in the garden since that day.

Mordred laid the spoiled linen back on the seat, and re-crossed the lawn to the path below the windows. As he did so a light was kindled in one of them, and voices came clearly. One of these, raised in distress or anger, was unfamiliar, but the other, answering it, was the voice of Morgause. He caught the words "ship" and "Camelot," and then "the princes," and at that, without even pausing to think about it, he left the path and stepped up close to the wall under the window, listening.

The windows were unglazed, but set high in the wall, a few spans above his head. He could hear only in snatches, as the women raised their voices or moved nearer the window. Morgan—for the first voice proved to be hers—seemed to be pacing the chamber, restless, and half-distraught.

She was speaking. "If he puts me away ... if he dares! I, the High King's own sister! Whose only fault is that she was led astray by care for her brother's kingdom and love of her lord! Could I help it if Accolon was mad for love of me? Could I help it if he attacked Arthur? All that I did—"

"Yes, yes, you have told me that tale already." Morgause was unsympathetic and impatient. "Spare me, I beg you! But have you managed to make Urbgen believe it?"

"He will not speak with me. If I could only come to him—"

Morgause interrupted again, amusement veiling contempt. "Why wait? You are Queen of Rheged, and you keep telling whoever will listen that you deserve nothing of your lord but gratitude and a little forgiveness for folly. So why hide away here? If I were you, sister, I would put on my finest gown, and the queen's crown of Rheged, and go into the hall, attended, when he is at meat, or in council. He will have to listen to you then. If he is still undecided about it, he won't risk slighting Arthur's sister in open court."

"With Nimuë there?" asked Morgan bitterly.

"Nimuë?" Morgause sounded considerably startled. "Merlin's trollop? Is she still here?"

"Yes, she's still here. And she's a queen now, too, sister, so watch your tongue! She married Pelleas since the old enchanter died, didn't you know? She sent the sword south, but she stayed on, lodging somewhere in the town. I suppose he didn't tell you that? Just holds his tongue and hopes you won't meet!" A shrill, edged laugh as Morgan turned away again. "Men! By Hecate, how I despise them! They have all the power, and none of the courage. He's afraid of her ... and of me ... and of you, too, I don't doubt! Like a big dog among spitting cats.... Oh, well, perhaps you're right. Perhaps—"

The rest was lost. Mordred waited, though the subject held small interest for him. The outcome of the queen's trespass and the king's anger concerned him not at all. But he was intrigued by what he had heard of Morgan's reputation, and by the easy mention of great names that until now had only been the stuff of lamplight tales.

In a minute or so, when he could distinguish words again, he did hear something that made him prick up his ears.

Morgause was speaking. "When Arthur gets home will you go to see him?"

"Yes. I have no choice. He has sent for me, and they tell me that Urbgen is making arrangements for my escort."

"Guard, do you mean?"

"And if I do, why should *you* smile, Morgause? What do you call *your* escort of king's soldiers that is taking you south at Arthur's orders?"

There was spite in her voice. Morgause reacted to it swiftly.

"That is rather different. *I* never played my lord false—"

"Ha! Not after he married you, at any rate!"

"—nor proved traitor to Arthur—"

"No?" Morgan's laugh was wild. "Traitor, well, no! Traitor isn't quite the word, is it? And he wasn't your king at the time, I grant you that!"

"I prefer not to understand you, sister. You can hardly mean to accuse me—"

"Oh, come, Morgause! Everyone knows about that now! And here, in this very castle! Well, all right, it's a long time ago. But you surely don't think he's sent for you now for old times' sake? You can't be deluding yourself that he'll want *you* near him? Even with Merlin gone, Arthur won't want you back at court. Depend on it, all he wants is the children, and once he has them—"

"He won't touch Lot's children." Morgause's voice was raised for the first time, edged and sharp. "Even he would not dare! And why should he? Whatever quarrel lay between him and Lot in the past, Lot died fighting under the Dragon banner, and Arthur will honour his sons in consequence. He must support Gawain's claims, he can do no other. He will not dare let it be said that he is finishing the murder of the children."

Morgan was right beside the window. Her voice, pitched low, and rather breathless, was nevertheless quite clear. "Finishing? He never began it. Oh, don't look like that. Everyone knows that, too. It was not Arthur who had the babies massacred. No, nor Merlin, either. Don't pretend to me, Morgause."

There was a slight pause, then Morgause spoke with her old indifference. "Past history, like the other thing. And for what you said just now, if all he wanted was the boys, he need not have sent for me at all, only for them. But no, I am ordered to bring them myself to him at Camelot. And call it what you like, the escort is a royal one. . . . You will see, sister, that I shall take my rightful place again, and my sons with me."

"And the bastard? What do you imagine will happen to him? Or should I say, what do you plan to do with him?"

"Plan?"

Morgan's voice rose in sudden triumph. "Ah, yes, that's different, isn't it? That hit the center. There's danger there, Morgause, and you know it. You may tell what tale you like, but you only have to look at him to guess the truth. . . . . So, the murder's out, and what happens now? Merlin foretold what would come of it if you let him live. The massacre may be past history, but who's to say what Arthur will do, now that he's found him at last?"

The sentence broke off as somewhere a door opened and shut. Footsteps sounded, and a servant's voice with some message, then the two queens moved away from the window. Someone else, the servant probably, came to the window and leaned out. Mordred kept close by the wall, in the deep shadow. He waited, perfectly still, till the oblong cast by the lighted window showed empty and bright on the lawn, then ran silently to the sleeping-chamber he shared with the other boys.

His pallet—he slept alone here—lay nearest the door, separated from the others by a stone buttress. Beyond the buttress Gawain lay with Gareth. Both were already asleep. From the far side of the chamber Agravain said something in a whisper, and Gaheris grunted and turned over. Mordred muttered a "Good night," then, without disrobing, drew a coverlet over himself and lay down to wait.

He lay rigid in the darkness, trying to school his racing thoughts and calm his breathing. He had been right, then. The chance that had taken him through the garden had proved it. He was not being taken south in honour, as a prince, but for some purpose he could not guess at, but which would almost certainly be dangerous. Imprisonment, perhaps, or even—the shrill malice of Morgan's voice made this seem possible—death at the hands of the High King. Morgause's patronage, for which until the night in the stillroom he had been grateful, seemed likely to prove useless. She would be powerless to protect him, and had in fact sounded indifferent.

He turned his head on the hard pillow, listening. No sound from the others except the soft regular breathing of slumber. Outside, the castle was still awake. The gates would still be open, but would soon be shut and guarded for the night. Tomorrow would see him back under escort with the Orkney party, bound for the ship, and Camelot, and whatever awaited him there. The *Orc* might not even dock again before putting in to Ynys Witrin, where Arthur's ally King Melwas held the island for the King. If he was to escape, it must be now.

He was hardly aware of the moment when the decision was made. It seemed to be there ready, inevitable, awaiting only the moment. He sat up cautiously, pushing the coverlet back. He found his hands were shaking, and was angry. He was used to running alone, wasn't he? He had in a sense been alone all his life, and he would shift alone for himself again. There were no ties to break. The only tie of affection he had ever known had been swallowed by the flames on that night so many years ago. Now he was the wolf outside the pack; he was Mordred, and Mordred depended on Mordred, and on no man else, nor—and it was a relief to be rid of a half-suspicious gratitude at last—on any woman.

He slid off the bed, and in a minute or two had gathered his things together. A cloak of thick russet wool, his belt and weapon, the precious drinking horn, the kidskin pouch with the coins carefully saved over the years. He was in his best clothes; the rest were still on board the *Orc*, but that could not be helped. He piled the bedding so that, at a glance, it looked as if a sleeper was there, then let himself softly out of the room, and, heart beating high, found his way through the maze of empty corridors to the courtyard. All unknowing he passed the very room where the young Arthur had begotten him on his half-sister Morgause.

The courtyard, though well lighted at all times, was usually fairly empty at this time of night, when supper was done and men had gone to bed, or to the dice games round the fires. The guards would be there, and a foraging hound or two, but Mordred thought he could depend on slipping out through the shadows when the men's attention was elsewhere.

Tonight, though, late as the hour was, there was still a good deal of activity. A few men in servants' livery were standing around near the steps that led down from the main door of the castle. Among them were two whom Mordred recognized as the king's chief chamberlains. One of these, with a gesture, sent a couple of servants running with torches to the main gateway. This stood wide open, and the men ran through it to wait outside, lighting the way to the bridge. A light in one of the stables, and the sound of trampling hoofs and men's voices, indicated that horses were being saddled there.

Mordred drew back into the shadow of a deep doorway. The first shock of dismay gave way to hope. If guests were leaving the castle as late as this, he might be able, in the general coming and going, to slip out unremarked among their servants.

A stir and bustle at the head of the castle steps heralded the king's appearance there. He came out with his two sons, all three still dressed as they had been in the hall at supper time. There was a lady with them. Mordred, who had not yet seen Queen Morgan, wondered for a moment if this could be she, but this lady was dressed for travel, and her manner was by no means that of an erring wife who doubted her lord's forgiveness. She was young, and apparently unescorted save for a couple of armed servants, but she bore herself as if she was accustomed to deference, and it seemed to the watching boy that King Urbgen, as he spoke to her, inclined himself with a kind of respect. He was protesting something, perhaps asking her to defer her departure until a better time, but not (thought Mordred shrewdly) pressing it too hard. She thanked him with charm and decision, gave her hand to the two princes, then came swiftly down the steps as the horses were brought from the stable.

She passed quite close to Mordred's doorway, and he caught a glimpse of her face. She was young, and beautiful, but with a force and edge to her that, even in repose, was chilling. The veil that covered her dark hair was held in place by a narrow coronet of gold. A queen, yes. But more than that. Mordred knew straight away who this must be: Nimuë, lover and successor to Merlin the King's enchanter; Nimuë, the "other Merlin," the witch whom, for all their angry spite, he guessed that both Arthur's sisters feared.

Urbgen himself put her up on her horse. The two armed attendants mounted. She spoke again, smiling now, and apparently reassuring him about something. She reached her hand down to him, and he kissed it and stood back. She wheeled her horse towards the gate, but even as it started forward she reined in. Her head went up, and she looked around her. She did not see Mordred; he had pressed himself well back out of sight; but she said sharply, to the king:

"King Urbgen, these two men leave with me, and no one else. See the gates shut after me, and set guards on your guest-chambers. Yes, I see you understand me. Keep an eye to the hen harrier and her brood. I have had a dream that one of them was fledged already, and flying. If you value Arthur's love, keep the cage locked, and see that they come safely to his hand."

She gave Urbgen no time to reply. Her heel moved, and her horse sprang forward. The two servants followed her. The king, staring after her, pulled himself out of some unpleasant abstraction, and snapped an order. The torch-bearers came running in, and the gates creaked shut. Bars went down with a crash. The guards, with their lord's eye on them, stayed watchfully at attention. He spoke a few words with the captain on duty, then with his sons went back into the castle. The chamberlains and servants followed.

Mordred waited no longer. He dodged back through the shadows and made for the nearest door that would take him to the boys' side of the castle. This was a door giving on a corridor lined with workshops and storerooms. Here, at this hour, no one was about. He slipped through, and then ran.

His first thought was only to get back to his bedchamber before the guard was set on it, but as he ran up the corridor and saw the rows of doors, some locked, some latched only, some standing wide, he realized that here might be another way of escape. The windows. The rooms on his left looked straight out over the river bank. The windows would be high, but not too high for an active boy to jump from, and as for the river, it would not be a pleasant crossing at this season, but it could be made. He might even be lucky, and find the bridge unwatched.

He checked, glancing in through the nearest open door. Useless, the window was barred. The next door was pad-

110

locked. The third was shut, but not locked. He pushed it open and went cautiously inside.

It was a storeroom of sorts, but with a strange smell to it, and full of strange sounds, small uneasy stirrings and twitterings and the occasional cheep and flutter. Of course. The queen's birds. The cages were housed here. He gave them barely a glance. The window was unbarred, but narrow. Too narrow? He ran to it. One of the cages stood on the wedge-shaped sill. He seized it in both hands to lift it to the floor.

Something hissed like a viper, spat, and slashed. The boy dropped the cage and jumped back, the back of his hand laid open. He clapped it to his mouth and tasted the spurt of salt blood. From the cage two blazing lamps glared green, and a low, threatening snarl began to rise towards a shriek.

The wildcat. It crouched at the very back of the cage, terrifying, terrified. The small, flattened ears were laid back, invisible in the bristling fur. Every fang showed. A paw was still raised, armed and ready.

Mordred, furious at the fright and the pain, reacted as he had been trained. His knife whipped out. At the sight of the blade the wildcat—instinct or recognition, it was the same —sprang immediately, furiously, and the armed paw raked out through the bars. Again and again it slashed, pressed against the cage wall, staying at the attack. Its paws and breast were bloody, but not with the boy's blood; someone had jammed a dead rat between the bars; the cat had eaten none of it, but the blood had splashed and congealed, and the cage stank.

Mordred slowly lowered his knife. He knew—what Orkney peasant did not?—a good deal about wildcats, and he knew how this one had been caught, after the dam and the rest of the brood were slaughtered. So here it was—it was little more than a kitten—so small, so fierce, so brave, caged and stinking for a queen's pleasure. And what pleasure? They could never tame it, he knew. It would be teased and made to fight, matched maybe with dogs that it would blind and then maul before they killed it. Or it would simply refuse food, and die. The rat had not been touched.

The window was far too narrow to let him through. For a moment he stood, sucking the blood from his hand, fighting down the disappointment that threatened to turn too shamefully to fear. Then with an effort he took command of himself. There would be another chance. It was a long way to Camelot. Once outside the castle, let them see if they could keep him prisoner. Let them try to harm him. Like the cat, he was no tame beast to wait caged for death to come to him. He could fight.

The cat slashed again, but could not reach him. Mordred looked around him, saw a forked pole, the sort the harvesters used for catching vipers, and with that lifted the cage and turned it with the door-hatch towards the window. The cage filled almost the whole space. He pushed the pole into the loop, and carefully raised the wicker hatch. The carcass of the rat rose with it, and the cat struck again, spitting, at this new moving danger. It found itself striking into air. For two long minutes it stayed perfectly still, no movement but the ripple of fur and the twitch of a tail, then slowly, stalking freedom as it would stalk its prey, it crept to the edge of the basket, to the edge of the sill, and looked down.

He did not see it go. One moment it was there, a prisoner, the next gone into the free night.

The other prisoner dragged the cage back from the window that was too small for him, threw it to the floor, and put the pole carefully back where he had found it.

There was already a guard on the bedchamber door. He moved his weapon to the ready, then, seeing who approached him, shifted uncertainly and grounded the spear again.

Mordred, expecting this, had slung the russet cloak round him, and underneath it clutched his effects close to him, hiding his injured hand. The guard could see nothing in his face except cool surprise.

"A guard? What's this, has something happened?"

"King's orders, sir." The man was wooden.

"Orders to keep me out? Or in?"

"Oh, in—well, that is, I mean to say, to look after you, like, sir." The man cleared his throat, ill at ease, and tried again. "I thought you was all in there, asleep. You been with your lady queen, then, maybe?"

"Ah. King's orders to report on our movements, too?" Mordred let a moment of silence hang, while the man fidgeted, then he smiled. "No, I was not with Queen Morgause. Do you always ask the king's guests where they spend their nights?"

The man's mouth opened slowly. Mordred read it all easily: surprise, amusement, complicity. He slipped his free hand into the pouch at his belt and took out a coin. They had been speaking softly, but he lowered his voice still further. "You won't tell anyone?"

The man's face relaxed into something like a grin. "Indeed, no, sir. Excuse me, I'm sure. Thank you, sir. Good night, sir."

Mordred slipped past him and let himself quietly into the bedchamber.

For all his caution, he found Gawain awake, up on an elbow, and reaching for his dagger.

"Who's that?"

"Mordred. Keep your voice down. It's all right."

"Where've you been? I thought you were in bed and asleep."

Mordred did not reply. He had a habit of quenching silences. He had discovered that if you failed to answer an awkward question, people rarely asked it twice. He did not know that this was a discovery normally only made in later life, and by some weaker natures not at all. He crossed to his bedplace, and, once hidden by the buttress, dropped his bundle on the bed, and his cloak after it. Gawain was not to know that under the cloak he had been fully dressed.

"I thought I heard voices," whispered Gawain.

"They've set a guard on the door. I was talking to him."

"Oh." Gawain, as Mordred calculated, did not sound particularly interested. He probably did not realize that it was the first time in Rheged that such a guard had been set. He would be assuming, too, that Mordred had merely been out to the privy. He lay back. "That must have been what woke me. What's the time?"

"Must be well after midnight." Mordred, winding a kerchief round his injured hand, said softly: "And we have to make an early start in the morning. Best get some sleep now. Good night."

After a while Mordred slept, too. Half a league away, in

113

the edge of the vast tract of woodland that was called the Wild Forest, a young wildcat settled into the crotch of an enormous pine tree and began washing its fur clean of the smell of captivity.

12

In the morning it was apparent that Nimuë's warning had been extended to their escort. The soldiers saw to it that the Orkney party stayed together, and, with the greatest possible tact, made the close guardianship seem an honour. Morgause took it as such, and so did the four younger princes, who rode at ease, talking gaily with the guard and laughing, but Mordred, with a good horse under him and the open stretches of mainland moor beckoning from either side of the road, fretted and was silent.

All too soon they reached the harbour. The first thing to be noticed was that the *Orc* rode alone at the wharfside. The *Sea Dragon*, explained the escort's captain, had suffered only slight storm damage, so had held on her way south; he and the armed escort were to sail with the party in the *Orc*. Morgause, annoyed, but beginning to be apprehensive and so not daring to show it, acquiesced perforce, and they boarded the ship. This was now a little too crowded for comfort, but the winds had abated, and the passage out of the Ituna Estuary and southward along the coast of Rheged was smooth and even enjoyable.

The boys spent their time on deck, watching the hilly land slide past. Gulls slanted and cried behind the ship. Once they threaded a fleet of fishing boats, and once saw, in a small inlet of the hilly coast, some men on ponies herding cattle

("Probably stolen," said Agravain, sounding approving rather than otherwise), but apart from that, no sign of life. Morgause did not appear. The sailors taught the boys to tie knots, and Gareth tried to play on a little flute one of them had made from reeds. They all improvised fishing lines, and had some success, and in consequence ate good meals of fresh-baked fish. The princes were in wild spirits at the adventure, and at the dazzling prospect, as they saw it, in store for them. Even Mordred managed at times to forget the cloud of fear. The only fly in the ointment was the silence of the escort. The boys questioned the soldiers —the princes with innocent curiosity, Mordred with careful guile—but the men and their officers were as uncommunicative as the royal envoy had been. About the High King's orders or plans for their future they learned nothing.

So for three days. Then, with the ship's master cocking a worried eye aloft at the suddenly moody canvas, the *Orc* put into Segontium, on the coast of Wales just across from Mona's Isle.

This was a much bigger place than the little Rheged port. Caer y n'a Von, or Segontium, as it had been in Roman times, was a big military garrison, recently rebuilt to at least half its old strength. The fortress lay on the stony hillside above the town, and beyond that again rose the foothills and then the cloud-holding heights of Y Wyddfa, the Snow Hill. To seaward, across a narrow channel as blue in the sunshine as sapphire, lay the golden fields and magic stones of Mona, isle of druids.

The boys lined the ship's rail, staring and eager. At length Morgause came out of her cabin. She looked pale and ill, even after such a smooth and easy voyage. ("Because she's a witch, you see," said Gareth, proudly, to the escort's captain.) When the ship's master told her that they must wait in harbour for a change of wind, she said thankfully that she would not sleep on board, and her chamberlain was sent across to engage rooms at the wharfside inn. This was a prosperous, comfortable place, and good rooms were forthcoming. The party went cheerfully on shore.

They were there for four days. The queen kept to her rooms with the women. The boys were allowed to explore the town, or, still carefully watched, to go down to the shore to hunt for crabs and shellfish. The second time they set out,

Mordred, as if on an impulse of boredom, turned back. Though he did not say so within his brothers' hearing, he let the two guards see that crab-hunting offered no amusement to a boy who had done it for a living only a few years ago. He left them to it, and went alone into the town, then, hiding his eagerness, sauntered at an easy pace along the track that climbed away from the houses and led past the fortress walls towards the distant heights of Y Wyddfa.

The air was dazzlingly clear after the night's frost. The stones were already warm. He sat down. To any watcher he would appear to be enjoying the view and the sunshine. In fact he was looking carefully about him at the prospect of escape.

Above him, in the distance, a boy tended a flock of sheep. Their tracks seamed the face of the hill. Higher, beyond the slopes of stony pasture, lay a wood, the outskirts of the forest that swept up to clothe the flanks of the Snow Hill. A gap in the trees showed where a road led eastward.

There lay the way. The road would surely join the famous Sarn Elen, the causeway that led down to Deva and the inland kingdoms. He could lose himself there, easily. He had all his money on him, and, with last night's frost as an excuse, had brought his cloak.

A pebble rattled on the path. He looked round, to see, barely a dozen paces away, the two guards standing, at ease, ostensibly gazing idly into the distance towards the beach below the town. But their pose was alert, and from time to time their glances came his way.

It was the same two men who had accompanied the princes to the shore. Now, small in the distance, he could see his brothers, easily recognizable among the other crabcatchers on the beach. He looked for their escort, and saw none.

The men had left the other boys to their pastime, and had followed him quietly up the hillside. The conclusion was inescapable. The guards were for him alone.

An emotion that the caged wildcat would have recognized swelled burstingly in Mordred's breast, and into his throat. He wanted to shout, to lash out, to run.

To run. He jumped to his feet. Instantly the men were moving, casually, towards him. They were young and fit. He could never outdistance them. He stood still.

"Time to be going back, young sir," said one of them pleasantly. "Nearly dinner time, I reckon."

"Your brothers are going in," said the other, pointing. "Look, sir, you can see them from here. Shall we go down now?"

Mordred's face was still as stone. His eyes betrayed nothing of the emotion that filled him. Something that no wild animal—and few men—would have understood kept him silent and apparently indifferent. In two deep and steadying breaths he willed the fear and with it the furious disappointment to spill from him. He could almost feel it draining from his finger-tips like blood. In its place came the faintest tremor of released tension, and then, into the emptiness, the calm of his habitual control.

He nodded to the men, said something distant and polite, and walked back to the inn between them.

He tried again next day.

The princes, tired of the shore and the town, were avid to visit the great fortress on the hillside, but this their mother would not consider. Indeed, the escort's captain said flatly that even princes of Orkney would not be allowed within the gates. The place was fortified and always held in readiness.

"For what?" asked Gawain.

The man nodded at the sea.

"Irish?"

"Picts, Irish, Saxons. Anyone."

"Is King Maelgon here himself?"

"No."

"Which is Macsen's Tower?" The idle-sounding question came from Mordred.

"Whose tower?" demanded Agravain.

"Macsen's. Someone spoke of it yesterday." The someone had been one of his guards, who had remarked that the site of the tower was well up on the hillside, not far below the wood.

The captain pointed. "It's up there. You can't see it now, though, it's a ruin."

"Who was Macsen?" asked Gareth.

"Do they teach you nothing in Orkney?" The man was indulgent. "He was Emperor of Britain, Magnus Maximus, a Spaniard by birth—"

118

"Of course we know that," interrupted Gawain. "We are related to him. He was Emperor of Rome, and it was his sword that Merlin raised for the High King: Caliburn, the King's sword of Britain. Everyone knows that! Our mother is descended from him, through King Uther."

"Then should we not visit the tower?" asked Mordred. "It's not inside the fortress, so surely anyone can go? Even if it's ruined—"

"Sorry." The captain shook his head. "Too far. Against orders."

"Orders?" Gawain was beginning to bristle, but Agravain spoke across him, rudely, to Mordred.

"Anyway, why should *you* want to go? You're not Macsen's kin! We are! *We* are royal through our mother as well."

"Then if I am bastard Lothian, you can count yourselves bastard Macsen," snapped Mordred, fear and tension breaking suddenly into fury, and careless for once of his tongue.

He was safe enough. The twins, loyal to their boyhood rule of silence where their mother was concerned, would never have thought of repeating the insult to Morgause. Their methods were more direct. After a startled pause of sheer surprise, they yelled with rage and fell on Mordred, and the pent-up energies of seaboard suddenly exploded in a very pretty dog-fight all round the inn yard. After they had been pulled apart and then beaten for fighting, the queen was so angry at the disturbance that she forbade any more excursions from the inn. So no one got to Macsen's Tower, and the boys had to content themselves with knucklebones and mock fights and story-telling; children's ploys, said Mordred, this time with open contempt, still smarting, and stayed away.

The next day, quite suddenly in the evening, the wind changed, and blew strongly again from the north. Under the watchful eye of the escort the party re-embarked, and the *Orc* made quickly south with a steady wind until she could turn in from the open weather to the quiet waters of the Severn Sea. The water was like glass. "Right to the Glass Isle," said the master, "I do assure you." And the shallow-draughted *Orc* did indeed sail in on an estuary mirror-smooth, with the oars out for the last stretch to take the little ship clear up to the wharf of Ynys Witrin, the Isle of Glass, almost in the shadow of the palace walls of Melwas, its king.

* * *

119

Melwas's palace was little more than a large house set in the flat meadowland rimming the largest of the three sister islands called Ynys Witrin. Two of the islands were hills, low and green, that rose gently from the encircling water. The third was the Tor, a high, cone-shaped hill symmetrical as an artifact, and girdled at its base with apple orchards where wisps of smoke proclaimed the cottages of the village that was Melwas's capital. It towered above the surrounding water-logged flatland of the Summer Country like a great beacon. This, in fact, was one of its functions; a beacon turret stood at the very top of the Tor, the nearest signal point to Camelot itself. From that summit, the boys were told, those walls and shining towers might be seen quite close and clearly, across the glassy reaches of the Lake.

King Melwas's own fortress lay just below the Tor's summit. The approach to it was a winding road, steeply cut from the gravel of the hill. In winter, men said, the mud made it all but impossible to get to the top. But then in winter there was no fighting. The king and his company stayed in the comfort of the lakeside mansion, and their days were filled with hunting, which was mostly, in that sodden Summer Country, wild-fowling in the marshes. These stretched away to southward, with their glinting waters only occasionally broken by the willow islands and the alder-set reedbeds where the marsh-dwellers had built their raised hovels.

King Melwas received the party kindly. He was a big, brown-bearded man, with a high colour and a red, full-lipped mouth. His attitude to Morgause was one of open admiration. He greeted her with the ceremonial kiss of welcome, and if this was a shade too prolonged, Morgause made no objection. When she presented her sons the king was warm in his welcome of them, and rather warmer in his praise of the woman who had borne so handsome a tribe. Mordred, as always, was presented last. If, during the formal greetings, the king's look came back rather too often to the tall boy standing behind the other princes, no one but the boy himself seemed to notice. Then Melwas, with another lingering look, turned back to Morgause, with the news that a courier awaited her from the High King.

"A courier?" Morgause was sharp. "To me, the King's sister? You must mean one of his knights? With an escort for us?"

But no; it seemed that the go-between was merely one of the royal couriers, who, waiting duly on Morgause, gave Arthur's message briefly and with little ceremony. Morgause and her party were to remain on Ynys Witrin until the following day, when they were to ride, with an escort sent by Arthur, to Camelot. There the King would receive them in the Round Hall.

The younger boys, excited and barely controllable, noticed nothing amiss, but Gawain and Mordred could see how anger fought with growing apprehension in her as she questioned the man sharply.

"He said nothing more, madam," repeated the courier. "Only that he desired your presence tomorrow in the Round Hall. Until then, you will stay here. The Lady Nimuë, madam? No, she has not yet returned from the north. That is all I know."

He bowed and went. Gawain, puzzled and inclined to be angry, started to speak, but his mother waved him to silence, and stood for a while biting her lip and thinking. Then she turned quickly to Gabran.

"Have them call my women. They are to unpack our clothes, and lay out the white robe for me, and the scarlet cloak. Now, yes, now, man! Do you think I will stay here tamely overnight, and go at his bidding to the Round Hall tomorrow? Do you not know what that is? It's Arthur's council chamber, where judgments are given. Oh, yes, I have heard of that hall, with its 'Perilous Chair' for the wrongdoers and those with grievances against the High King!"

"But what peril can there be for you? You have done him no wrong," said Gabran quickly.

"Of course not!" snapped Morgause. "Which is why I will not go like a suppliant or a wrong-doer, to be received in front of the Council by my own brother! I will go now, tonight, while he is in hall at supper with the Queen and all the court. Let us see then if he intends to deny her state to the mother of—" She stopped, and apparently changed what she had been going to say. "—To his sister and his sister's sons."

"Madam, will they let you go?"

"I am not a prisoner. How can they stop me, without letting people see that I am ill used? Besides, the King's troop has gone back to Camelot, has it not?"

"Yes, madam, but King Melwas—"

"After I am dressed, you may ask King Melwas to come and see me.

Gabran turned rather reluctantly to go.

"Gabran." He stopped and turned. "Take the boys with you. Tell the women to get them ready. Their court clothes. I will see to it that Melwas gives us horses and an escort." Her lips thinned. "As long as we are guarded, Arthur cannot hold him accountable. In any case, that is Melwas's danger, not ours. Now go. You will not ride with us. You will follow with the rest tomorrow."

Gabran hesitated, then, catching her eye, bowed his head and went from the room.

It was not hard to guess what sort of persuasion she used with Melwas. In the event, she got her way. By the brief autumnal sunset the little party was riding across the causeway that led eastwards across the Lake. Morgause rode a pretty grey mare, richly harnessed with green and scarlet, and chiming with bells. Mordred, to his great surprise, was given a handsome black horse, well matched with the one Gawain rode. The armed escort sent by Melwas clattered along, strung out alongside them on the narrow causeway. At their backs the sun set in a furnace of molten brass that died slowly to burnt green and purple. There was a chill to the air, a touch of frost coming with the blue shadows of twilight.

The horses' hoofs scrunched up to a ridge of gravel, and then the road lay ahead, a pale strip leading through the watery wilderness of reeds and alders. Duck and wading birds fled upwards with a clatter, the water rippling back from their wakes like melted metal. Mordred's horse shook its head and the bridle rang with silver. In spite of himself he felt his heart lift suddenly with excitement. Then all at once someone exclaimed and pointed.

Ahead, at the summit of a thickly rising forest, their bannered pinnacles catching the last of the sunset and flaming up into the evening sky like torches, rose the towers of Camelot.

13

It was a city set on a hill. Caer Camel was flat-topped and very wide, but it stood up as conspicuously as the Tor in the midst of that level or low-rolling countryside. Its steep sides were ridged, horizontally, as if a gigantic plough had been driven round the hill. These ridges were revetments and ditches, designed to hinder attackers. At the crest of the ringed hillside the fortress walls circled the summit like the crown on a king's head. At two points, north-east and south-west, the massive defense works were pierced by gates.

Morgause's party approached from the south-west, towards the entrance called the King's Gate. They crossed a small winding river, then followed the road as it curved steeply upwards through thick trees. At the top, set in the corner of Camelot's outer walls, stood the massive double gate, open still but guarded. They halted while the escort's captain rode forward to exchange words with the officer of the watch.

Presently both men came back together to where Morgause waited.

"Madam." The officer made her a courteous inclination. "You were not looked for until tomorrow. I have no orders concerning your party. If you will wait here, I will send a message up—"

"The King is in hall?"

"Madam, yes, he is at supper."

"Then take me to him."

"Madam, I cannot. If you—"

"You know who I am?" The icy question was meant to intimidate.

"Of course, madam—"

"I am the High King's sister, daughter of Uther Pendragon. Am I to be kept here at the gate like a suppliant or a courier?"

A faint film of sweat showed on the man's forehead, but he was not noticeably discomposed. "Of course not, madam, not here, outside the gates. Please ride within. The men are coming now to close them. But I'm afraid you must wait here while a message goes up to the hall. I have my orders."

"Very well. I won't make it hard for you. My chamberlain will go to him." Morgause spoke firmly, flatly, as if even now she had no doubt that her command would be obeyed. She softened it with one of her prettiest smiles. Mordred saw that she was nervous. Her mare, reading its rider's mood, fidgeted and tossed its head till the golden tassels swung in a tangle.

The officer, with apparent relief, agreed to this, and after a word with his mistress the chamberlain went off between two of the guards. Morgause's party rode up through the deep, fortified archway of the King's Gate, and were halted just inside it to wait.

Behind them the great gates swung shut. The bars clanged down into place. Overhead, along the battlemented walls, went the tramp and stamp of sentries. Ironically enough these sounds, which should have reminded Mordred forcibly that he was a prisoner, still constrained to meet an unknown and doubtful fate, hardly got through to him. He was too busy looking about him. This was Camelot.

Inside the gate a roadway led uphill towards the walls of the palace. Poles were set at intervals along this road, with torches hung in brackets to light the way. Midway up a considerable slope the road forked, the left-hand way leading to a gateway in the palace walls beyond which could be seen the tops of trees, now bare. Another garden? Another prison made for a queen's pleasure? The other branch of the road curled round under the palace walls to another, bigger gate which must lead into the township. Above the wall could be discerned the roofs and turrets of houses, shops and workshops grouped around the market-place, with, beyond these again to the north, the barracks and stables. The town gates were shut, and no people were about except the sentries.

"Mordred!"

Mordred, startled out of his thoughts, looked up. Morgause was beckoning.

"Here, beside me."

He urged his horse forward to her right. Gawain started to move to her other side, but him she waved back. "Stay with the others."

Gawain, who, since the dog-fight in the inn yard, had held aloof from Mordred, scowled as he reined back, but he said nothing. None of the others spoke. Something of Morgause's tension had communicated itself even to Gareth. She did not speak again, but sat straight and still, staring at her horse's ears. Her hood was back, her face expressionless and rather pale.

Then it changed. Mordred, looking where she looked, saw the chamberlain hurrying back with the two guards, and, some way behind them, alone, a man coming down the road towards them.

From the sharp reaction of the gate guards he knew who this must be, and that his coming was totally unexpected. Against all precedent, Arthur the High King had come out alone, to receive them at the outer gate of his fortress.

The King stopped a few paces away and said shortly to the guards: "Let them come."

No ceremony of welcome. No offer of the kiss and the handclasp and the smile. He stood by one of the torch-poles, its light flickering on a face as cold and indifferent as that of a judge.

The chamberlain hurried to Morgause's side, but she waved him back. "Mordred. Your hand, please."

No more time for surprise. No more time for anything except the one, overmastering apprehension. He slid from his horse, threw the rein to a servant and helped the queen dismount. She held his arm for a moment, tightly, looking up at him as if she would have said something, then she let him go, but kept him close beside her. Gawain, still scowling, pushed forward uninvited, and this time was ignored. The other boys fell in behind, nervously. Servants led the horses back. Arthur had still made no move. Morgause, with a boy to either side of her, and the three younger ones behind, went forward to meet the King.

Mordred could never afterwards say what made the first sight of the High King so impressive. No ceremony, no attendants, none of the trappings of majesty and power; the man was not even armed. He stood alone, cold, silent and formidable. The boy stared. Here was a solitary man, dressed in a brown robe trimmed with marten, dwarfed by the range of lighted buildings behind him, by the trees that lined the roadway, by the spears of the armed guards. But in fact, in all that ringing, frosty, dusk-lit space, none of the party had eyes for anything but that one man.

Morgause went down on the frosty ground in front of him, not in the deep reverence customary in the presence of the High King, but kneeling. She lifted a hand, caught Mordred by the arm, and pulled him down, too, to his knees. He felt a slight tremor in her grip. Gawain, with the other boys, stayed standing. Arthur had not even glanced at them. His attention was all for the kneeling boy, the bastard, his son, brought to his feet like a suppliant, and staying there, head up and eyes darting every way, like a wild thing wondering which way to run.

Morgause was speaking:

"My lord Arthur, brother—you may imagine what a joy it was to myself and my family when word came, after all these years, that we might once more have sight of you, and visit your court on the mainland. Who has not heard of the splendours of Camelot, and marvelled at the tales of your victories, and of your greatness as king of these lands? Greatness which, from that first great fight at Luguvallium, I, and my lord King Lot, predicted for you..."

She stole a look up at Arthur's unresponsive face. She had deliberately moved straight onto dangerous ground. At Luguvallium, Lot had tried first to betray Arthur, and then to overthrow him, but it was then that he had lain with Morgause to beget Mordred. Mordred, eyes cast down now and studying the frost patterns on the ground in front of him, caught the moment of uncertainty before she drew a quick breath and spoke again.

"Perhaps between us—between you and Lot, and even between you and myself, my brother—there have been things that were better not recalled. But Lot was slain in your service, and since then I have lived alone, quietly, in exile, but uncomplaining, devoting myself to the care and rearing of my sons...." The faintest emphasis here, and another quick glance upward. "Now, my lord Arthur, I have come at your command, and pray you for clemency towards us all."

Still no reply from the King, nor any movement of welcome. The light, pretty voice went on, the words like pebbles striking against the silence. Mordred, his eyes still downcast, felt something as strong as a touch, and looked up suddenly, to find the King's eyes fixed on him. He met them for the first time, eyes which were at the same time curiously familiar, and yet strange, charged with a look that sent a thrill through him, not of fear, but as if something had struck him below the heart and left him gasping. With the touch his fear was gone. Suddenly, and for the first time since Morgause had veiled logic with threats and sorcery, he saw clearly how foolish his fears had been. Why should this man, this king, trouble to pursue the bastard of an enemy dead these many years? It was beneath him. It was absurd. For Mordred the air cleared at last, as if a foul mist, magic-crammed, had blown aside.

He was here in the fabled city, the center of the mainland kingdoms. Long ago he had planned for this, dreamed of it, schemed for it. He had tried, in the fear and distrust engendered by Morgause, to escape from it, but here he had been brought, like something destined for sacrifice to her Goddess of the black altar. Now no thought of flight remained. All his old ambitions, his boyhood dreams, flew back, lodged, crystallized. He wanted this, to be part of this. Whatever it took to win a place in this king's kingdoms, he would do it, be it....

Morgause was still speaking, with an unaccustomed note of humility. Mordred, with the new cold light illumining his brain, listened and thought: Every word she says is a lie. No, not a lie, the facts are true enough, but everything she is, everything she is trying to do...all is false. How does he bear it? Surely he cannot be deceived? Not this king. Not Arthur.

"...So I pray you do not hold me to blame, brother, for coming now, instead of waiting for the morrow. How could I wait, with the lights of Camelot so near across the Lake?

I had to come, and to make sure that in your heart you still bore me no malice. And see, I have obeyed you. I am here with all the boys. This on my left is Gawain, eldest of Orkney, my son and your servant. His brothers, too. And this on my right...this is Mordred." She looked up. "Brother, he knows nothing. Nothing. He will be—"

Arthur moved at last. He stopped her with a gesture, then stepped forward and held out a hand. Morgause, on a sudden intake of breath, fell silent and laid hers in it. The King raised her. Among the boys, and the servants watching from the gate, there was a movement of relief. They had been received. All would be well. Mordred, rising to his feet, felt something of the same lightening of tension. Even Gawain was smiling, and Mordred found himself responding. But instead of the ritual kiss of welcome, the embrace and the words of greeting, the King said merely:

"I have something to say to you that cannot be said before these children." He turned to the boys. "Be welcome here. Now go back to the gatehouse, and wait."

They obeyed. "The gifts," said the chamberlain, "the gifts, quickly. All is not well yet, it seems." He seized the box from a servant, and hurried forward to lay it at the King's feet, then retreated hastily, disconcerted. Arthur did not even glance at the treasure. He was speaking to Morgause, and, though the people at the gate could neither hear what was said nor see her face, they watched how her pose stiffened to defiance, then passed again to supplication and even to fear, and how through it all the King stood like stone, and with a face of stone. Only Mordred, with his new clear sight, saw grief there, and weariness.

There was an interruption. From beyond the gates came a sound, growing rapidly louder. Hoofbeats, a horse approaching at a stumbling gallop up the chariotway. A man's voice called out hoarsely. One of the gate guards said, under his breath: "The courier from Glevum! By the thunder, he's made good time! He must bring hot news!"

The challenge, another shout, the creak and crash of the gates opening. A tired horse clattered through. They smelled the reek of exhausted sweat. A breathless word from the courier, and the horse held on its way without pausing, straight up to where the King stood with Morgause.

The rider half fell from the saddle, and went down on one

knee. The King looked angry at the interruption, but the courier spoke urgently, and after a pause Arthur beckoned to the guards. Two of them went forward, halting one on either side of Morgause. Then the King turned, with a sign to the courier, and walked back up the roadway with the man following him. At the foot of the palace steps he stopped. For a few minutes the two, King and courier, stood talking, but from the gatehouse the boys could see and hear nothing. Then, suddenly, the King swung round, and shouted.

In a moment, it seemed, the frozen tensions of the night were shattered; from uneasy peace the place sprang to something very like battle orders. A huge grey war-stallion was brought by two grooms, who clung to the bit as it plunged and screamed. Servants came running with the King's cloak and sword. The gates swung open. Arthur was in the saddle. The grey stallion screamed again and climbed the torchlit air, then leaped forward under the spur, and was past the boys and out of the gates with the speed of a thrown spear. The grooms led the courier's exhausted horse away, and the courier himself, walking like a lame man, followed.

In the gatehouse all was bustle and snapped orders. Melwas's men-at-arms withdrew, and the boys, with the chamberlain and the queen's servants, found themselves being hurried up the road towards the palace, past the place where Morgause still stood stiffly between her guards. Just as they reached the palace gate, a troop of armed riders burst out of it and went streaming past at a gallop to vanish downhill in the King's wake.

The gallop died. The outer gates crashed shut once more. The echoes faded into quiet. The place seemed to edge back, quivering, towards a kind of peace. The boys, waiting at the palace gates with the servants and guards, crowded together, wondering, confused and beginning to be scared. Gareth was crying. The twins muttered together, with glances at Mordred that were far from friendly. Avoiding them, and Gawain's puzzled scowl, Mordred felt, more than ever before, isolated from them. His thoughts darted like trapped birds. They all had time, now, to feel the cold.

At length someone—a big man with a red face and a high manner—came to them. He spoke straight to Mordred.

"I am Cei, the King's seneschal. You are to come with me."

"I?"

"All of you."

Gawain elbowed Mordred aside, stepped forward and spoke. He was curt to the point of arrogance. "I am Gawain of Orkney. Where are you taking us, and what has happened to my mother?"

"King's orders," said Cei, briefly, but hardly reassuringly. "She's to wait till he gets back." He spoke more gently, to Gareth. "Don't be afraid. No harm will come to you. You heard him say you would be made welcome."

"Where's he gone?" demanded Gawain.

"Didn't you hear?" asked Cei. "It seems that Merlin's still alive, after all. The courier saw him on the road. The King's gone to meet him. Now, will you come with me?"

14

The boys had only a brief stay at Camelot before orders came that the court would remove to Caerleon for Christmas. Meanwhile they were lodged apart from the other boys and young men, under the special care of Cei, who was Arthur's foster brother, and privy to all his counsels. He saw to it that none of the rumours that went flying about among the people of Camelot came to the boys' ears. Until Arthur himself had spoken with Mordred, Mordred was to learn nothing. Cei guessed, and rightly, that the King would want to consult with Merlin before he decided what was to be done with the boy, or with Morgause herself. The boys did not see Morgause; she was lodged somewhere apart, not as a prisoner, they were told, but allowed to communicate with no one, until the King returned.

In fact he did not return. The story of his wild ride to greet his old friend was brought back to a city agog for news.

It was true that Merlin the enchanter was alive. An attack of his old sickness, a trance-like state like death, had been taken for death itself, but he had recovered, and at length escaped from the sealed tomb where he had been left for dead. Now he had ridden with the King for Caerleon, and Arthur's Companions—the picked group of knights who were his friends—had gone with them. The court would follow.

So for the time remaining at Camelot before the court's

removal to Wales, the boys were kept busy with pursuits that exhausted them, but that were much to their taste.

They were taken in hand straight away by the master-at-arms, and what training they had had in the islands was commented on with a sarcasm that even Gawain did not care in this place to resent, and augmented with a rigorous course of work. There were long hours spent, too, on horseback, and here none of them pretended that the Orkney training had been adequate. The High King's horses were as far removed from the rough ponies of the islands as Morgause's men-at-arms were from Arthur's chosen Companions.

It was not all work. Play, too, there was in plenty, but consisting entirely of war games, hours spent over maps drawn in sand, or modelled—this to the boys' wide-eyed wonder—in clay relief. Hours, too, at mock fights or competing at archery. In this last they excelled, and of all of them Mordred had the steadiest draw and the best eye. And there was hunting. In winter the wild-fowling in the marshes was varied and exciting, but there was hunting to be had as well, deer and boar, in the rolling country to the eastward, or among the wooded slopes that rose towards the downlands in the south.

The court removed itself to Caerleon in the first week of December, and the Orkney boys with it. But not their mother. Morgause was taken on Arthur's orders to Amesbury, where she was lodged in the convent. It was a nominal imprisonment only, and a gentle one, but imprisonment nonetheless. Her rooms were guarded by King's troops, and the holy women replaced her own waiting-women. Amesbury, birthplace of Ambrosius, belonged to the High King, and would see his orders carried out to the letter. When the spring weather came, and the roads opened, she would be taken north to Caer Eidyn, where her half-sister Queen Morgan was already immured.

"But what has she done?" demanded Gaheris furiously. "We know what Queen Morgan did, and she is rightly punished. But our mother? Why, she came to Orkney soon after our father was killed. The King must know that—it would be the spring after Queen Morgan's wedding in Rheged. Years ago! She's never been out of the islands since. Why should he imprison her now?"

"Because at that same wedding she tried to murder Merlin." The answer, uncompromising, came from Cei, who, alone among the nobles, spent time with the boys during their hours of leisure.

They stared at him. "But that was years ago!" cried Gawain. "I was there—I know, because she's told me—but I don't remember it at all. I was only a baby. Why send for her now to account for something that happened then?"

"And what did happen?" This from Gaheris, red-faced and with jaw outthrust.

"He says she tried to murder Merlin," said Agravain. "Well, she didn't succeed, did she? So why—?"

"How?" asked Mordred quietly.

"Woman's way. Witch's way, if you like." Cei was unmoved by the younger boys' angry questions. "It happened at that very wedding feast. Merlin was there, representing the King. She drugged his wine, and saw to it that he would drink a deadlier poison later, when she was not there to be blamed. And so it fell. He did recover, but it left him with the sickness that recently struck him down and caused him to be left for dead—and will kill him in the end. When Arthur sent for her, and for you, Merlin was believed dead, and in his tomb. So he sent for her to answer for the murder."

"It's not true!" shouted Gaheris.

"And if it were," said Gawain, cold now, and with that aggressive arrogance he had adopted since they came to Camelot, "what of it? Where is the law that says a queen may not destroy her enemy in her own way?"

"That's so," said Agravain quickly. "She always said he was her enemy. And what other way had she? Women cannot fight."

"He must have been too strong for her spells," said Gareth. "They didn't work." The only emotion in his voice was regret.

Cei surveyed them. "There was a spell, certainly, and one tried many times, but in the end it was cold poisoning. This is known to be true." He added, kindly: "There's nothing to be gained in talking further about this until you see the King. What can you know of these matters? In your outland kingdom you were reared to think of Merlin, and maybe even the King himself, as your enemies."

He paused, looking at them again. The boys were silent. "Yes, I see that you were. Well, until he talks with Merlin,

133

and with Queen Morgause, we will leave the matter. She can count herself fortunate that Merlin is not dead. And as for you, you must content yourselves with the King's assurance that he will not harm you. There are things to settle, old scores to resolve that you know nothing about. Believe me, the King is a just man, and Merlin's counsels are wise, and harsh only when it is needful."

When he left them, the boys burst out into angry talk and speculation. It seemed to Mordred, listening, that their anger was more on their own account than on their mother's. It was a matter of pride. None of them would have wanted to be, once again, under Morgause's rule. This new freedom, this world of men and men's actions, suited them all, and even Gareth, who in Orkney had run the risk of effeminacy, was hardening up to become one of them. He, like the rest, saw no reason for a prince to stop at murder if it suited his plans.

Mordred said nothing, and the others did not find this strange. What claim after all had the bastard on the queen? But Mordred did not even hear them. He was back in the darkness, with the smoke and the smell of fish and the frightened whispering. "Merlin is dead. They made a feast at the palace, and then" —*and then*—"the news came." And the queen's words in the stillroom, with the potions and the scent and the indefinable smell of evil, and the feel of her mouth on his.

He shook himself free of the memories. So Morgause had poisoned the enchanter. She had gone north to the islands knowing that she had already sown the seeds of death. And why not? The old man had been her enemy: was his, Mordred's, enemy. And now the enemy was alive, and would be at Caerleon for Christmas along with the rest.

Caerleon, City of Legions, was very different from Camelot. The Romans had built a strong fortress there, on the river they called the Isca Silurum; this fortress, strategically placed on the curve of the river near its confluence with a smaller stream, had been restored first by Ambrosius, then later enlarged to something like its original proportions by Arthur. A city had grown up outside the walls, with marketplace and church and palace near the Roman bridge which—

patched here and there, and with new lamp-posts—spanned the river.

The King, with most of the court, lived in the palace outside the fortress walls. Many of his knights had lodgings within the fort, and so, to begin with, had the Orkney boys. They were still lodged apart, with some of Arthur's servants doing duty alongside the people brought from Orkney. Gabran, to his own obvious discomfort, had had perforce to remain with the boys; there had naturally been no question of his being allowed to follow Morgause to Amesbury. Gawain, still smarting from the painful mixture of shame on his mother's behalf and jealousy on his own, lost no opportunity of letting the man see that now he had no standing at all. Gaheris followed suit, but more openly, as was his habit, adding insults where he could to contempt for his mother's displaced lover. The other two, less conscious perhaps of Morgause's sexual vagaries, scarcely noticed him. Mordred had other things on his mind.

But days passed, and nothing happened. If Merlin, back from the dead, was indeed planning to spur Arthur to revenge on Morgause and her family, he was in no hurry to do so. The old man, weakened by the events of the summer and autumn, kept mainly to the rooms allotted to him in the King's house. Arthur spent a good deal of time with him, and it was known that Merlin had attended one or two of the meetings of the privy council, but the Orkney boys saw nothing of him.

It was said that Merlin himself had advised against a public homecoming. There was no announcement, no scene of public rejoicing. As time went on, people came simply to accept his presence among them again, as if the "death" of the King's cousin and chief adviser, and the country-wide mourning, had been another and more elaborate example of the enchanter's habit of vanishing and reappearing at will. They had always known, men said wisely, that the great enchanter could not die. If he had chosen to lie in a death-like trance while his spirit visited the halls of the dead, why, then, he had come back wiser and more powerful than ever. Soon he would go back to his hollow hill again, the sacred Bryn Myrddin, and there he would remain, invisible at times maybe, but nevertheless present and powerful for those to call on who needed him.

Meantime, if Arthur had yet found time to discuss the Orkney boys—that Mordred was by far the most important of these none of them of course guessed—nothing was said. The truth was that Arthur, for once unsure of his ground, was procrastinating. Then his hand was forced, quite inadvertently, by Mordred himself.

It was on the evening before Christmas. All day a snowstorm had prevented the boys from riding out, or exercising with their weapons. With the feast days, both of Christmas and the King's birthday, so near, no one troubled to give them the usual tuition, so the five of them spent an idle day kicking their heels in the big room where they slept with some of the servants. They ate too much, drank more than they were accustomed to of the strong Welsh metheglin, quarrelled, fought, and eventually subsided to watch a game of tables that had been going on for some time at the other end of the room. The final bout was in progress, watched, with advice and encouragement, by a crowd of onlookers. The players were Gabran and one of the local men, whose name was Llyr.

It was late, and the lamps burned low. The fire filled the room with smoke. A cold draught from the windows sent a gentle drift of snow to pile unheeded on the floor.

The dice rattled and fell, the counters clicked. The games went evenly enough, the piled coins being pushed from player to player as the luck changed. Slowly the piles grew to handfuls. There was silver in them, and even the glint of gold. Gradually the watchers fell silent; no more jesting, no more advice where so much was at stake. The boys crowded in, fascinated. Gawain, his hostility forgotten, peered closely over Gabran's shoulder. His brothers were as eager as he. The contest, in fact, showed signs of becoming Orkney against the rest, and for once even Gaheris found himself on Gabran's side. Mordred, no gambler himself, stood across the board from them, by chance in the opposing camp, and watched idly.

Gabran threw. A one and a two. The moves were negligible. Llyr, with a pair of fives, brought his last counter off and said exultantly: "A game! A game! That equals your last two hits! So, one more for the decider. And they are running for me, friend, so spit on your hands and pray to your outland gods."

Gabran was flushed with drinking, but still looked sober enough, and elegant enough, to obey neither of these exhortations. He pushed the stake across, saying doubtfully: "I think I'm cleaned out. Sorry, but we'll have to call that the decider. You've won, and I'm for bed."

"Oh, come on." Llyr shook the dice temptingly in his fist. "Your turn's coming. It's time the luck changed. Come on, give it a try. You can owe me. Don't break it up now."

"But I really am cleaned out." Gabran pulled his pouch from its hangers and dug into the depths. "Nothing, see? And where am I to get more if I lose again?" He thrust his fingers deep into the pouch, then pulled it inside out and shook it over the board. "There. Nothing." No coins fell, but something else dropped with a rattle and lay winking in the lamplight.

It was a charm, a circular amulet of wood bleached to silver by the sea, and carved crudely with eyes and a mouth. In the eye-holes were gummed a pair of blue river-pearls, and the curve of the grinning mouth had been filled with red clay. A goddess-charm of Orkney, crude and childishly made, but, to an Orcadian, a potent symbol.

Llyr poked at it with a finger. "Pearls, eh? Well, what's wrong with that for a stake? If she brings you luck you'll win her back and plenty else besides. Throw you for starters?"

The dice shook, fell, rattled to either side of the charm. Before they came to rest they were rudely disturbed. Mordred, suddenly cold sober, leaned forward, shot out a hand and grabbed the thing.

"Where did you get this?"

Gabran looked up, surprised. "I don't know. I've had it for years. Can't remember where I picked it up. Perhaps the—"

He stopped. His mouth stayed half open. Still staring at Mordred, he slowly went white. If he had announced it aloud, he could not have confessed more openly that he remembered now where the charm had come from.

"What is it?" asked someone. No one answered him. Mordred was as white as Gabran.

"I made it myself." He spoke in a flat voice that those who did not know him would have thought empty of any

137

emotion at all. "I made it for my mother. She wore it always. Always."

His eyes locked on Gabran's. He said nothing more, but the phrase finished itself in the silence. *Till she died.* And now, completely, as if it had been confessed aloud, he knew how she had died. Who had killed her, and who had ordered the killing.

He did not know how the knife came into his hand. Forgotten now were all the arguments about a queen's right to kill where she chose. But a prince could, and would. He kicked the board aside, and the pieces went flying. Gabran's own knife lay to hand. He grabbed it and started up. The others, slowed with drink and not yet seeing more than a sudden sharp wrangle over the game, reacted too slowly. Llyr was protesting good-naturedly: "Well, all right. So take it, if it's yours." Another man made a grab for the boy's knife-hand, but Mordred, eluding him, jumped for Gabran, knife held low and expertly, pointing upwards to the heart. Gabran, as sober now as he, saw that the threat was real and deadly, and struck out. The blades touched, but Mordred's blow went home. The knife went deep, in below the ribs, and lodged there.

Gabran's knife fell with a clatter. Both his hands went to clasp the hilt that lodged under his ribs. He bent, folded forward. Hands caught at him and lowered him. There was very little blood.

There was complete silence now in the room, broken only by the short, exhausted breathing of the wounded man. Mordred, standing over him, flung round the shocked company a look that could have been Arthur's own.

"He deserved it. He killed my parents. That charm was my mother's. I made it for her and she wore it always. He must have taken it when he killed them. He burned them."

There was not a man present who had not killed or seen killing done. But at that there were sick looks exchanged. "Burned them?" repeated Llyr.

"Burned them alive in their home. I saw it afterwards."

"Not alive."

The whisper was Gabran's. He lay half on his side, his body curled round the knife, his hands on the hilt, but shrinkingly, as if he would have withdrawn it, but feared the pain. The silver chasing quivered with his harsh, small breaths.

"I saw it, too." Gawain came to Mordred's side, looking down. "It was horrible. They were poor people, and old. They had nothing. If this is true, Gabran . . . Did you burn Mordred's home?"

Gabran drew a deep breath as if his lungs were running out of air. His face was pale as parchment and the gilt curls were dark with sweat.

"Yes."

"Then you deserve to die," said Gawain, shoulder to shoulder with Mordred.

"But they were dead," whispered Gabran. "I swear it. Burned . . . afterwards. To hide it."

"How did they die?" demanded Mordred.

Gabran did not reply. Mordred knelt by him quickly, and put a hand to the dagger's hilt. The man's hands twitched, but fell away, strengthless. Mordred said, still with that deceptive calm: "You will die anyway, Gabran. So tell me now. How did they die?"

"Poison."

The word sent a shiver through the company. Men repeated it to each other, so that the whisper ran through the air like a hissing. Poison. The woman's weapon. The witch's weapon.

Mordred, unmoving, felt Gawain stiffen beside him. "You took them poison?"

"Yes. Yes. With the gifts. A present of wine."

None of the local people spoke. And none of those from Orkney needed to. Mordred said softly, a statement, rather than a question: "From the queen."

Gabran said, on another long, gasping breath: "Yes."

"Why?"

"In case the woman knew . . . guessed . . . something about you."

"What about me?"

"I don't know."

"You are dying, Gabran. What about me?"

Gabran, queen's minion, queen's dupe, told his last lie for the queen. "I do not know. I . . . swear it."

"Then die now," said Mordred, and pulled the knife out.

They took him straight away to the High King.

15

Arthur was doing nothing more alarming than choosing a hound puppy out of a litter of six. A boy from the kennels had brought them in, with the bitch in anxious attendance, and the six pups, white and brindled, rolled yapping and wrestling with one another round the King's feet. The bitch, restless and uneasy, darted in repeatedly to pick up a pup and restore it to the basket, but before she had grabbed another, the first would clamber straight out and re-join the tumble on the floor.

The King was laughing, but when his guards brought Mordred in, the laughter went out of his face as if a light had been quenched. He looked startled, then recovered himself.

"What is this? Arrian?"

The man addressed said stolidly: "Murder, sir. A stabbing. One of the Orkney men. This young man did it. I didn't get the rights of it, sir. There's others outside that saw it. Do you want them brought in as well, sir?"

"Later, perhaps. I'll talk to the boy first. I'll send when I want them. Let them go now."

The man saluted and withdrew. The hound-boy began to gather up the pups. One of them, a white one, eluded him, and, squeaking like an angry mouse, charged back to the King's feet. It seized a dangling lace in its teeth and, growling, worried it furiously. Arthur glanced down as the hound-boy pulled the pup away. "Yes. That's the one. To be named Cabal again. Thank you." The boy scuttled out with the basket, the bitch at his heels.

Mordred stayed where the men had left him, just inside the door. He could hear the guard outside being mounted again. The King left his chair by the leaping fire, and crossed to where a big table stood, littered with papers and tablets. He seated himself behind this, and pointed to the floor across the table from him. Mordred advanced and stood. He was shaking, and it took all his will-power to control this, the reaction from his first kill, from the hideous memory of the burned cottage and the feel of that weather-washed bone in his hand, and now the dreaded confrontation with the man he had been taught was a ferocious enemy. Gone, now, was the cool conviction that the High King would not trouble with such as he; Mordred had himself provided a just excuse. That he would be killed now, he had no doubt at all. He had brawled in a king's house, and, though the man he had killed was one of the Orkney household, and was justly punished for a foul murder, Mordred, even as a prince of Orkney, could hardly hope to escape punishment himself. And though Gawain had supported him, he would hardly go on doing so now that Gabran's confession had branded Morgause, too, with the murder.

None of this showed in the boy's face. He stood, pale-faced and still, with his hands gripped together behind his back where the King could not see their trembling. His eyes were lowered, his mouth compressed. His face looked sullen and obstinate, but Arthur knew men, and he saw the telltale quiver under the eyes, and the quick rise and fall of the boy's breathing.

The King's first words were hardly alarming.

"Supposing you tell me what happened."

Mordred's eyes came up to find the King watching him steadily but not with the look that had brought Morgause to her knees in the roadway at Camelot. He had, indeed, a fleeting but powerful impression that the King's main attention was on something quite other than Mordred's recent crime. This gave him courage, and soon he found himself talking, freely for him, without noticing how Arthur's apparently half-absent questioning led him through all the details, not just of the killing of Gabran, but of his own story from the beginning. Too highly wrought to wonder why the King should want to hear it, the boy told it all: the life with Brude and Sula, the meeting with Gawain, the queen's summons and subsequent kindness, the ride to Seals' Bay with Gabran, the final hideous discovery of the burned-out cottage. It was the first time since Sula's death, and the end of his own childhood, that he had found himself talking—confiding, even—in someone with whom communication was easy. Easy? With the High King? Mordred did not even notice the absurdity. He went on. He was talking now about the killing of Gabran. At some point in the tale he took a step forward to the table's edge, and laid the wooden charm in front of the King. Arthur picked it up and studied it, his face expressionless. On his hand a great carved ruby glimmered, making the pathetic thing the crude toy that it was. He laid it down again.

Mordred came to an end at last. In the silence that followed, the flames in the big fireplace flapped like flags in the wind.

Again the King's words were unexpected. He spoke as if the question came straight from some long-held thought, that seemed, to the matter in hand, quite irrelevant.

"Why did she call you Mordred?"

With all the familiar talk behind him, the boy hardly paused to think as he replied, with a directness that only an hour ago would have been unthinkable:

"It means the boy from the sea. That's where they got me from, after I was saved from the boat that you had the children put in to drown."

"I?"

"I heard since that it wasn't you, lord. I don't know the truth of it, but that is what I was told first."

"Of course. That is what she would tell you."

"She?"

"Your mother."

"Oh, no!" said Mordred quickly. "Sula never told me anything, not about the boat, or about the killings. It was Queen Morgause who told me, much later. As for my name, half the boys in the islands are called Mordred, Medraut. . . . The sea is everywhere."

"So I understand. Which is why it has taken so long for

142

me to locate you, even knowing where your mother was. No, I am not talking about Sula. I mean your real mother, the woman who bore you."

Mordred's voice came strangled. "You know that? You were—you mean you were *looking* for me? You actually know who my mother is—who I really am?"

"I should." The words came heavily, as if loaded with meaning, but Arthur seemed to change direction, and added merely: "Your mother is my half-sister."

"*Queen Morgause*?" The boy gaped, thunderstruck.

"Herself."

Arthur left it there for the moment. One thing at a time. Mordred's eyes blinked rapidly, his brain taking in this astounding new fact, thinking back, thinking ahead....

He looked up at last. Fear was forgotten now; the past, even the recent past, forgotten also. There was a blaze behind his eyes that told of an almost overmastering excitement.

"I see it now! She did tell me a little. Only hints—hints that I couldn't understand, because the truth never occurred to me. Her own son... Really her own son!" A deep breath. "Then *that* is why she sought me out! Gawain was only the excuse. I did think it strange that she should want to nurture one of her husband's bastards by some girl from the town. And even to show me favour! When all the time I was her own, and only a bastard because I was born before time! Oh, yes, I know that now! They had been wed barely eight months when I was born. And then King Lot came back from Linnuis and—"

A sudden complete stop. The excited comprehension vanished as if a shutter had dropped across his eyes.

More things were coming together. He said, slowly: "*It was King Lot* who ordered the massacre of the babies? Because his eldest son had a doubtful birth? And my mother saved me, and sent me to Brude and Sula in the Orkneys?"

"It was King Lot who ordered the massacre. Yes."

"To kill me?"

"Yes. And to blame me for it."

"Why that?"

"For fear of the people. The other parents whose children did die. Also because, even though in the end he fought

143

under my command, Lot was always my enemy. And for other reasons."

The last sentence came slowly. Arthur, still feeling his way towards the moment when the most important truth might be told, lent it a weight that might have been expected to set Mordred asking the question that had been fed to him. But Mordred was not to be steered. He was busy with his own long obsession. He took a step forward, to lean with both hands flat on the table and say, with intensity:

"Yes, other reasons! I know them! I was his eldest born, but because I was begotten out of wedlock he was afraid that in days to come men might doubt my birth, and make trouble in the kingdom! It was better to be rid of me, and get another prince in wedlock, who might in due time take the kingdom without question!"

"Mordred, you are running too far ahead. You must listen."

It is doubtful if Mordred noticed that the High King was speaking with less than his usual assurance. Was looking, indeed, if one could use such a word of the great duke of battles, embarrassed. But Mordred was past listening. The full implications of what he had learned in the past few minutes swept over him in a bewildering cloud, but brought with them a new confidence, a lifting of caution, the driving satisfaction of at last being able to say it all, and to say it to the man who could make it come true.

He swept on, stammering a little. "Am I not, then, in sober fact, heir to Dunpeldyr? Or, if Tydwal is to hold that stronghold for Gawain, then of the Orkneys? Sir, the two kingdoms, so far apart, are hard for one man to hold, and this, surely, could be the time to divide them? You have said you will not let Queen Morgause go back. Let me go back instead!"

"You have not understood me," said the King. "You have no right to either one of Lot's kingdoms."

"No right!" It could have been the young Arthur himself who said it, springing upright like a bow when the arrow flies. "When you yourself were begotten out of wedlock by Uther Pendragon, on the lady who was still Duchess of Cornwall, and who could not wed him before a month was out?"

No sooner was it said than he would, if he could, have swallowed the words back. The King said nothing, nor did

144

his look change, but recollection struck Mordred silent, and with it his fear returned. Twice in one evening he had lost his temper, he, Mordred, who for years now had fought his nature down to achieve, as armour against the displacement, the insecurity of his life, that sea-cold shell of control.

Stumblingly, he tried to unsay it. "My lord, I'm sorry. I didn't mean to insult you or . . . or your lady mother. I only meant—I've thought about this for so long, thought every way whether it could be legal for me to have a place, a place to rule. . . . I know I could. One does. . . . And I thought about you, and how you came to it. Of course I did. Everyone knows—that is—men do say—"

"That I am technically a bastard?"

Amazingly, the King did not sound angry. Mordred's courage crept back. His fists pressed into the table, striving for steadiness. He said carefully: "Yes, sir. I wondered about the law, you see. The mainland law. I was going to find out, and then ask you. My lord, if Gawain goes to Dunpeldyr, then, by the Goddess herself, I promise you that I am fitter than Gaheris or Agravain to rule the Orkneys! And who knows what trouble and moil there could be if twins were named successors?"

Arthur did not answer at once. Mordred, his plea made, the words said, subsided into silence. The King came out of his thoughts, and spoke.

"I have listened to you because I was curious to know what kind of man you had grown to be, with your strange upbringing, so like my own." A slight smile. "As 'everyone knows,' I, too, was begotten out of wedlock, then hidden for many years. With me it was fourteen years, but I was in a household where from the start I was taught the skills of knighthood. You have had less than four years of such teaching, but they tell me you have made much of them. You will come into your own, believe me, but not as you have planned or imagined. Now you will listen to me. And sit down, please."

Wondering, the boy pulled up a stool and sat. The King himself stood up, and paced the length of the room and back before speaking.

"First of all, whatever the law, whatever the precedent, there is no question of your taking the kingdom of the Orkneys. That will be for Gawain. My intention is to keep Gawain and his brothers here among my fighting knights, and then, when the time is right, and if he wishes it, let him take back his island kingdom from my hand. And in the meantime, Tydwal will stay in Dunpeldyr."

He stopped his pacing, and sat down again.

"This is not injustice, Mordred. You can have no claim to either Lothian or the Orkneys. You are not Lot's son." He gave it emphasis. "King Lot of Lothian was not your father."

A pause. The flames roared in the chimney. Outside in a corridor somewhere, someone called out and was answered. The boy asked, in a flattened, neutral voice: "Do you know who is?"

"I should," said the King, for the second time.

Now comprehension was instant. The boy went upright on the stool. It brought his eyes almost on a level with the King's.

"*You?*"

"I," said Arthur, and waited.

This time it took a moment or two, and then, not the sick disgust he expected, but merely wonder and a slow assessment of this new fact.

"With Queen Morgause? But that—that—"

"Is incest. Yes." He left it there. No excuse, no protestation of his own ignorance of the relationship when Morgause seduced her young half-brother to her bed. In the end the boy said merely:

"I see."

It was Arthur's turn to be startled. Held so in his own consciousness of sin, of disgust at the memory of that night with Morgause, who had since become for him a symbol of all that was evil and unclean, he had not taken into account the peasant-reared boy's reaction to a sin far from uncommon in the inbred islands of his homeland. In that homeland, indeed, it would hardly be counted as a sin. Roman law had not stretched so far, and it was not to be supposed that Mordred's Goddess—who was also Morgause's—had implanted much sense of sin in her followers.

Mordred, indeed, was already wholly occupied in other considerations. "So that means I am—I am—"

"Yes," said Arthur, and watched the wonder, and through it the excitement, kindle in the eyes so like his own. No affection—how could there be?—but a shift of the powerful

146

and inborn ambition. And why not? thought the King. Guinevere will have no child by me. This boy is twice Pendragon, and from all reports as well-liking as any boy will ever be. Just now he is feeling as I felt when Merlin told me the same thing, and put the sword of Britain into my hand. Let him feel it. The rest, as the gods will it, will come.

Of the prophecy of Merlin, that the boy would cause his downfall and death, he never thought at all. The moment was for him one of joy, unspoiled.

Unspoiled, too, miraculously, by Mordred's indifference to the long-past sin. Because of this very lack of reaction he found that he could speak of it himself.

"It was after the battle at Luguvallium. My first fight. Your mother, Morgause, came north to tend her father, King Uther, who was sick, and though we did not know it, dying. I did not know then that I, too, was a child of Uther Pendragon's. I believed Merlin to be my father, and, indeed, loved him as such. I had never seen Morgause before. You will be able to guess how lovely she was, at twenty....I went to her bed that night. It was not until afterwards that Merlin told me Uther Pendragon was my father, and I myself heir to the High Kingdom."

"But she knew?" Mordred, quick as ever, had fastened on the thing unsaid.

"So I believe. But even my ignorance cannot excuse my share of the sin. I know that. In doing what I did, I wronged you, Mordred. So the wrong persists."

"How? You looked for me, and brought me here. You need not have done so. Why did you?"

"When I ordered Morgause here," said Arthur, "I thought her guilty of Merlin's death, that was—is—the best man in all this realm, and the one dearest to me. She is still guilty. Merlin is old before his time, and carries in him the germ of the poison she fed to him. He knew that she had poisoned him, but for the sake of her sons he never told me. He judged that she ought to live, so long as she stayed harmless in exile, to rear them against the day when they could serve me. I only learned of the poison when he lay, as we thought, dying, and in his delirium spoke of it, and of Morgause's repeated attempts to kill him by poison or by sorcery. So after his entombment I sent for her to answer for her crime,

147

judging, too, that it was time her sons left her care and came into my charge."

"All five. That surprised everyone. You said you had had reports, sir. Who told you about me?"

Arthur smiled. "I had a spy in your palace. The goldsmith's man, Casso. He wrote to me."

"The slave? He could write? He gave no hint of it. He's dumb, and we thought there was no way he could communicate."

The King nodded. "That's why he is valuable. People talk freely in front of a slave, especially a dumb one. It was Merlin who had him taught to write. Sometimes I think that even his smallest acts were dictated by prevision. Well, Casso saw and heard plenty while he was in Morgause's household. He wrote to me that the 'Mordred' now in the palace must be the one."

Mordred was thinking back. "I think I saw him send the message. There was a trading ship tied up at the wharf; it had been unloading wood. I saw him go on board, and someone gave him money. I thought he must be doing work on his own, that the goldsmith didn't know about. That would be it?"

"Very possibly."

The memory brought back others: Morgause and her private smiling when he spoke of his "mother." Her test to see if she had passed on the Sight to her son. And Sula; Sula must have known that one day he would be taken from her. She had been afraid. Had she suspected, then, what might one day happen?

He asked abruptly: "Did she really have Gabran kill them?"

"If he said so, knowing he was dying, you may be sure of it," said the King. "She would think no more of it than of flying her hawk at a hare. She had your first nurse, Macha, murdered in Dunpeldyr, and herself goaded Lot into killing Macha's child, who had taken your place in the royal cradle. And, though Lot gave the order, it was Morgause who instigated the massacre of the children. This we know for truth. There was a witness. There have been many killings, Mordred, and none of them clean."

"So many killings, and all for me. But why?" The one clue he had been given, all those years ago, he had, like Arthur, forgotten in the excitement and heady promise of

148

this meeting. "Why did she keep me alive? Why trouble to have me kept in secret all those years?"

"To use as a tool, a pawn, what you will." If the King remembered the prophecy now, he did not burden the boy with it. "Maybe as a hostage in case I found out she had murdered Merlin. It was after she reckoned herself safe that she took you out of hiding, and even then the disguise she chose for you—Lot's bastard son—was sufficient to conceal you. But I can't guess further than that about her motives. I have not got her kind of subtlety." He added, in answer to some kind of appeal in the boy's intense gaze: "It does not come from the blood we share with her, Mordred. I have killed many men in my time, but not in such ways, or for such motives. Morgause's mother was a Breton girl, a wise-woman, so I have heard. These things go from mother to daughter. You must not fear these dark powers in yourself."

"I don't fear them," said Mordred quickly. "I have nothing of the Sight, no magic, she told me so. She did once try to find out about it. I think now that she was afraid I might 'see' what had happened to my foster parents. So she took me down with her to the underground chamber where there is a magic pool, and told me to look there for visions."

"And what visions did you see?"

"Nothing. I saw an eel in the pool. But the queen said there were visions. She saw them."

Arthur smiled. "I told you that you were of my blood rather than hers. To me, water is only water, though I have seen the mage-fire that Merlin can call from the air, and other marvels, but they were all marvels of the light. Did Morgause show you any magic of her own?"

"No, sir. She took me to the chamber where she made her spells and mixed her magic potions—"

"Go on. What's the matter?"

"Nothing. It was nothing, really. Just something that happened there." He looked away, towards the fire, reliving the moments in the stillroom, the clasp, the kiss, the queen's words. He added, slowly, to himself, making the discovery: "And all the time she knew I was her own son."

Arthur, watching him, made a guess that was a certainty. The rush of anger that he felt shook him. Over it he said, very gently: "You, too, Mordred?"

"It was nothing," said the boy again, rapidly, as if to brush it aside. "Nothing, really. But now I know why I felt the way I did." A quick glance across the table. "Oh, it happens, everyone knows it does. But not like that. Brother and sister, that's one thing...but mother and son? Not that, ever. At least, I never heard of it. And she knew, didn't she? She knew. I wonder why she would want—?"

He let it die and was silent, looking down at the hands held fast now between his knees. He was not asking for a reply. He and the King already knew the answer. There was no emotion in his voice but puzzled distaste, such as one might accord some perverted appetite. The flush had died from his cheeks, and he looked pale and strained.

The King was thinking, with growing relief and thankfulness, that here there would be no tie to break. Violent emotions create their own ties, but what remained between Morgause and Mordred could surely be broken here and now.

He spoke at length in a carefully low key, equal to equal, prince to prince.

"I shall not put her to death. Merlin is alive, and her other killings are not my concern to punish here and now. Moreover, you will see that I cannot keep you near me—here in my court where so many people know the story, and suspect that you are my son—and forthwith put your mother to death. So Morgause lives. But she will not be released."

He paused, leaning back in the great chair, and regarding the boy kindly. "Well, Mordred, we are here, at the start of a new road. We cannot see where it will lead us. I promised to do right by you, and I meant it. You will stay here in my court, with the other Orkney princes, and you, like them, will have royal status as my nephew. Where men guess at your parentage, you will find that you have more respect, not less. But you must see that, because of what happened at Luguvallium, and because of the presence of Queen Guinevere, I cannot openly call you son."

Mordred looked down at his hands. "And when you have others by the Queen?"

"I shall not. She is barren. Mordred, leave this now. The future will come. Take what life offers you here in my household. All the princes of Orkney will have the honour due to royal orphans, and you—I believe you will in the end have more." He saw something leap again behind the boy's eyes.

150

"I do not speak of kingdoms, Mordred. But perhaps that, too, if you are sufficiently my son."

All at once the boy's composure shattered. He began to shake. His hands went up to cover his face. He said, muffled: "It's nothing. I thought I would be punished for Gabran. Killed, even. And now all this. What will happen? What will happen, sir?"

"About Gabran, nothing," said the King. "He was to be pitied, but his death, in its way, was just. And about you, for the moment, very little, except that tonight you will not go to your bedchamber with the other boys. You will need time alone, to come to terms with all you have just learned. No one will wonder at this; they will think merely that you are being held apart because of Gabran's death."

"Gawain, the others? Are they to know?"

"I shall talk to Gawain. The others need know nothing more yet than that you are Morgause's son, and eldest of the High King's nephews. That will be sufficient to explain your standing here. But I shall tell Gawain the truth. He needs to know that you are not a rival for Lothian or the Orkneys." He turned his head. "Listen, there is the guard changing outside. Tomorrow is the feast of Mithras, and the Christmas of the Christians, and for you, I expect, some winter festival of your outland Orkney gods. For us all, a new beginning. So be welcome here, Mordred. Go now, and try to sleep."

BOOK II

The
Witch's Sons

I

Snow fell thickly soon after Christmas, and the ways were blocked. It was almost a month before the regular service of royal couriers could be resumed. Not that it mattered; there was little of any moment to report. In the depths of winter men—even the most dedicated warriors—stayed at home hugging the fire and looking to their houses and the needs of their families. Saxons and Celts alike kept close to their hearthstones, and if they sat whetting their weapons by the light of the winter fires, all knew that there would be no need of them until the coming of spring.

For the Orkney boys life at Caerleon, though restricted by the weather, was still lively and full enough to banish thoughts of their island home, which in any case had been, in midwinter, a place of doubtful comfort. The exercise grounds by the fortress were cleared, and work went on almost daily, in spite of snow and ice. Already a difference could be seen. Lot's four sons—the twins especially—were still wild to the point of recklessness, but as their skills improved, so also did their sense of discipline, which brought with it a certain pride. The quartet still tended to divide naturally into two pairs, the twins on the one hand and Gawain with young Gareth on the other, but there were fewer quarrels. The main difference could be discerned in their bearing towards Mordred.

Arthur had duly spoken with Gawain, a long interview which must have held, with the truth about Mordred's birth, some weighty kind of warning. Gawain's attitude to his half-brother had perceptibly altered. It was a mixture of reserve and relief. There was relief in the knowledge that his own status as Lot's eldest son would never be challenged, and that his title to the Orkney kingdom was to be upheld by the High King himself. Behind this there could be seen something of his former reserve, perhaps a resentment that Mordred's status as bastard of the High King put him higher than Gawain; but with this went caution, bred of the knowledge of what the future might hold. It was known that Queen Guinevere was barren; hence there was, Gawain knew, every possibility that Mordred might some day be presented as Arthur's heir. Arthur himself had been begotten out of wedlock and acknowledged only when grown; Mordred's turn might come. The High King was, indeed, rumoured to have other bastards—two, at least, were spoken of—but they were not at court, or seen to have his favour as Mordred had. And Queen Guinevere herself liked the boy and kept him near her. So Gawain, the only one of Lot's sons who knew the truth, bided his time, and edged his way back towards the guarded friendship that he and the older boy had originally shared.

Mordred noticed the change, recognized and understood its motives, and accepted the other boy's overtures without surprise. What did surprise him, though, was the change in the attitude of the twins. They knew nothing of Mordred's parentage, believing only that Arthur had accepted him as King Lot's bastard, and, so to speak, an outrider of the Orkney family. But the killing of Gabran had impressed them both. Agravain because a killing—any killing—was to his mind proof of what he called "manhood." Gaheris because for him it was that, and more; it was a fully justified act that avenged all of them. Though outwardly as indifferent as his twin to his mother's rare moments of fondness, Gaheris had nursed through his childhood a sore and jealous heart. Now Mordred had killed his mother's lover, and for that he was prepared to accord him homage as well as admiration. As for Gareth, the act of violence had impressed even him with respect. During the last months in Orkney Gabran had grown too self-assured, and with it arrogant, so that even the gentle youngest son had bitterly resented him. Mordred, in avenging the woman he had called mother, had in a way acted for them all. So all five of the Orkney boys settled down to work together, and in the comradeship of the training fields and the knights' hall, some kind of seedling loyalty to the High King began to grow.

News got through from Camelot with the February thaw. The boys were given tidings of their mother, who was still in Amesbury. She was to be sent north to the convent at Caer Eidyn soon after the court moved to Camelot, and her sons would be allowed to see her before she went. They accepted this almost with indifference. Perhaps Gaheris, ironically, was the only one of them who still missed his mother; Gaheris, the one she had ignored. He dreamed about her still, fantasies of rescue and return to Orkney's throne, with her grateful, and himself triumphant. But with daylight the dreams faded; even for her, he would not have abandoned the new, exciting life of the High King's court, or the hopes of preferment eventually into the ranks of the favoured Companions.

At the end of April, when the court had settled itself again for the summer in Camelot, the King sent the boys to make their farewells to their mother. This, it was rumoured, against the advice of Nimuë, who rode over from her home in Applegarth to greet the King. Merlin was no longer with the court: since his last illness he had lived in seclusion, and when the King removed from Caerleon the old enchanter retired to his hilltop home in Wales, leaving Nimuë to take his place as Arthur's adviser. But this time her advice was overruled, and the boys were duly sent up to Amesbury, with a sufficient escort led by Cei himself, with Lamorak, one of the knights.

They lodged on the way at Sarum, where the headman gave them shelter, making much of the High King's nephews, and rode next morning for Amesbury, which lies at the edge of the Great Plain.

It was a bright morning, and Lot's sons were in high spirits. They had good horses, were royally equipped, and looked forward almost without reservation to seeing Morgause again and showing off their new-found splendour before her. Any fears they might have had for her had long since been laid to rest. They had Arthur's word for it that she was not to be put to death, and though she was a prisoner, the kind of confinement that a convent would offer was not (so thought her sons in their youthful ignorance) so very different from the life she had led at home, where she had lived secluded for the most part among the women of her own household. Great ladies, indeed, they assured each other, often sought the life freely for themselves; it allowed no power of decision or rule, of course, but to the eager arrogance of youth this seemed hardly to be the woman's part. Morgause had acted as queen for her dead husband and her young son and heir, but such power could have been temporary only, and now (Gawain said it openly) was no longer necessary. There could be no more lovers, either; and this, to Gawain and Gaheris, the only ones who had really noticed or cared, was much to the good. Long might the convent keep her mewed up; in comfort, naturally, but prevented from interfering in their new lives, or bringing shame on them through lovers little older than themselves.

So they rode gaily. Gawain was already years away from her in spirit, and Gareth was concerned only with the adventure of the moment. Agravain thought about little but the horse he was riding, and the new tunic and weapons he sported ("really fit for a prince, at last!") and about all he would have to tell Morgause of his prowess at arms. Gaheris looked forward with a kind of guilty pleasure to the meeting; this time, surely, after so long an absence, she must show her delight in her sons, must give and receive caresses and loving words; and she would be alone, with no wary lover beside her chair, watching them, whispering against them.

Mordred alone rode in silence, once again apart, outside the pack. He noticed, with a stir of satisfaction, the attention, which was almost deference, paid him by Lamorak, and the careful eye that Cei kept on him. Rumour had run ahead of truth at court, and neither King nor Queen had made any attempt to scotch it. It was allowed to be seen that, of the five, Mordred was the one who mattered most. He was also the only one of the boys who felt some sort of dread of the coming interview. He did not know how much Morgause had been told, but surely she must know about her lover's death. And that death was on his hands.

So they came towards Amesbury on a fine sunny morning, with the dew splashing in glittering showers from their horses' hoofs, and met Morgause and her escort out riding in the woods.

It was a ride for exercise, not for pleasure. This much was immediately apparent. Though the queen was richly dressed, in her favourite amber cloth with a short furred mantle against the cool spring breezes, her mount was an indifferent-seeming mare, and to either side of her rode men in the uniform of Arthur's troops. From the hand of the man on her right a leading rein ran looping to the ring of the mare's bridle. A woman, plainly cloaked and hooded, rode a few paces in the rear, flanked in her turn by another pair of troopers.

It was Gareth who first recognized his mother in the little group of distant riders. He called out, stretching high in the saddle and waving. Then Gaheris spurred past him at a gallop, and the others, like a charge of cavalry, went racing across the space of wooded ground, with laughter and hunting calls and a clamour of welcome.

Morgause received the rush of young horsemen with smiling pleasure. To Gaheris, who pressed first to the mare's side, she gave a hand, and leaned a cheek to his eager kiss. Her other hand she reached towards Cei, who dutifully raised it to his lips, then, relinquishing it to Gawain, reined back to let the boys crowd in.

Morgause leaned forward, both arms reaching for her sons, her face glowing.

"See, they lead my horse, so I may ride without hands! I was told I might hope to see you soon, but we did not look for you yet! You must have longed for me, as I for you. . . . Gawain, Agravain, Gareth, my darling, come, kiss your mother, who has hungered all these long winter months for a sight of you. . . . There, there, now, that's enough. . . . Let me go, Gaheris, let me look at you all. Oh, my darling boys, it has been so long, so long. . . ."

The turn towards pathos went unnoticed. Still too excited, too full of their new importance, the young horsemen caracoled around her. The scene took on the liveliness of a pleasure party.

"See, Mother, this is a stallion from the High King's own stable!"

"Look, lady, at this sword! And I've used it, too! The

159

master-at-arms says that I promise as well as any man of my age."

"You are well, lady queen? They treat you well?" This was Gaheris.

"I am to be one of the Companions," Gawain put in, gruffly proud, "and if there is fighting in the coming summer, he has promised I shall be there."

"Will you be in Camelot for Pentecost?" asked Gareth.

Mordred had not spurred forward with the rest. She did not seem to notice. She had not even glanced his way, where he rode between Cei and Lamorak as the party turned back towards Amesbury. She laughed with her sons, and talked gaily, and let them shout and boast, and asked questions about Camelot and Caerleon, listening to their eager praises with flattering attention. From time to time she threw a gentle look, or a charming word, to Lamorak, the knight riding nearest, or even to the men of the escort. She was concerned, one might have guessed, with the report that would eventually go back to Arthur. Her looks were mild and sweet, her words innocent of anything but a mother's interest in her sons' progress, and a mother's gratitude for what the High King and his deputies were doing for them. When she spoke of Arthur—this was to Cei, across the heads of Gareth and Gaheris—it was with praise of his generosity towards her children ("my orphaned boys, who would otherwise be robbed of all protection") and for the King's grace, as she called it, towards herself. It was to be noticed that in a while she assumed a further, and complete, act of grace. She turned her lovely eyes full on Cei and asked, with sweet humility:

"And did the King my brother send you to take me back to court?"

When Cei, flushing and looking away, told her no, she said nothing, but bowed her head and let a hand steal to her eyes. Mordred, who rode to that side of her and a little in the rear, saw that she was tearless, but Gaheris pushed forward to her other side and laid a hand on her arm.

"Soon, though, lady! It will surely be soon! As soon as we get back we will petition him! By Pentecost, surely!"

She made no reply. She gave a little shiver, pulled her cloak closer, and glanced up at the sky, then, with an effort that was patent, straightened her shoulders. "Look, the day is clouding over. Let us not loiter here. Let us get back."

Her smile was bright with bravery. "Today, at least, Amesbury will cease to seem a prison."

By the time the party neared the village of Amesbury, Cei, at her left hand, was visibly unbending, Lamorak stared with open admiration, and Lot's sons had forgotten that they had ever wanted to be free of her. The spell was woven again. Nimuë had been right. The links so recently forged in Caerleon were wearing thin already. The Orkney brothers would take a less than perfect loyalty back to their uncle the High King.

2

The convent gate was open, and the porter watching for them. He stared in surprise at the sight of the Camelot party, and shouted to a sack-clad youth—a novice—who was grubbing among lettuces in a weedy bed beside a wall. The novice went running, and by the time the party rode into the yard the abbot himself, slightly out of breath but with unimpaired dignity, appeared at the doorway of his house and stood waiting at the head of the steps to receive them.

Even here, under the abbot's eye, Morgause's spell held good. Cei, moving with stolid courtesy to help her dismount, was beaten to it by Lamorak, with Gawain and Gaheris close behind. Morgause, with a smile at her sons, slid gracefully into Lamorak's arms, and then held to him a moment, letting it be seen that the ride, and the excitement of the meeting, had taxed her frail strength. She thanked the knight prettily, then turned to the boys again. She would rest awhile in her own rooms, she told them, while Abbot Luke made them welcome, then later, when they were fed and changed and rested, she would receive them.

So, to the abbot's barely concealed irritation, Morgause, having turned her status as prisoner into that of a queen granting audience, moved off towards the women's side of the convent, supported on the arm of her waiting-woman, and followed, as if by a royal escort, by her four guards.

In the years since Arthur's crowning, and more especially since Morgause had come as his prisoner, the High King had sent gifts and money to the foundation at Amesbury, so the place was larger and better kept than when the young King had first ridden south to see his father buried in the Giants' Dance.

Where there had been fields behind the chapel, there was now a walled garden, with its orchard and fishpond, and beyond this a second courtyard had been built, so that the quarters of men and women could be separate. The abbot's house had been enlarged, and there was no longer any need for him to vacate his quarters for royal guests; a well-built wing of guest rooms faced south onto the garden. To this the travellers were escorted by the two young novices appointed to see to their comfort. The boys were shown into the guests' dorter, a long, sunny room with half-a-dozen beds, and with no convent-like austerity about it. The beds were new and good, with painted headboards, the floor was of stone, scrubbed white and covered with brightly woven rugs, and wax candles stood ready in silver sconces. Mordred, glancing around him, and out of the broad windows where the sun shone warmly on lawn and fishpond and blossoming apple trees, reflected dryly that no doubt Morgause could take all the privileges she wanted, and welcome: she must be, in a quite literal sense, the most paying of guests.

The meal was good, too. The boys were served in the small refectory attached to the guest house, and afterwards made free of the convent grounds and the town—it was little more than a village—outside the walls. Their mother, they were told, would receive them after evening chapel. Cei did not appear; he was closeted with Abbot Luke; but Lamorak stayed with the boys, and in response to their pleading took them riding out on the Great Plain, where, two miles or so from Amesbury, stood the great circle of stones called the Giants' Dance.

"Where our kinsman the great Ambrosius is buried, and our grandfather Uther Pendragon beside him," said Agravain to Mordred, with a touch of his old arrogance. Mordred said nothing, but caught Gawain's quick look, and smiled to himself. From Lamorak's sidelong glance it could be guessed that he, too, knew the truth about Arthur's eldest "nephew."

As befitted the convent's guests, they all went to the

evening service. A little to Mordred's surprise, Morgause attended, too. As Lamorak and the boys approached the chapel door, the nuns went by two by two, with slow steps and downcast eyes. At the rear of the little procession walked Morgause, dressed simply in black, her face veiled. Two women attended her; one was the waiting-woman who had been riding with her, the other looked younger, with the ageless face of extreme stupidity, and the heavy pale look of ill-health. Last came the abbess, a slightly built, sweet-faced woman, with an air of gentle innocence which was perhaps not the best quality for the ruler of such a community. She had been appointed head of the women's side of the convent by the abbot, who was not the man to brook any rival in authority. Since Morgause's coming Abbot Luke had had cause to regret his choice; Mother Mary was not the woman to control her royal prisoner. On the other hand the convent, since that prisoner's coming, had flourished exceedingly, so, as long as the Queen of Orkney was safely held, Abbot Luke could see no need to interfere with the too-gentle rule of the abbess. He himself was not entirely immune to the flattering respect Morgause showed him, or to the fragile charm she exhibited in his presence, and besides, there was always the possibility that some day she would be reinstated, if not in her own kingdom, then at court, where she was, after all, the High King's half-sister....

The younger of Morgause's women brought the queen's message soon after chapel. The four younger princes were to sup with their mother. She would send for them later. She would see Prince Mordred now.

Across the barrage of objections and questions that this provoked Mordred met Gawain's eyes. Alone of the four, he looked commiserating rather than resentful.

"Well, good luck," he said, and Mordred thanked him, smoothing his hair and settling his belt and the hanger at his hip, while the woman stood waiting by the door, staring with pale eyes out of that lard-like face and repeating, as if she could only speak by rote:

"The young princes are to take supper with Madam, but now she will see Prince Mordred, alone."

Mordred, as he followed her, heard Gawain say in a low quick aside to Gaheris: "Don't be a fool, it's hardly a privilege. She never even looked at him this morning, did she?

And you must know why. You can't surely have forgotten Gabran? Poor Mordred, don't envy him this!"

He followed the woman across the lawn. Blackbirds hopped about on the grass, pecking for worms, and a thrush sang somewhere among the apple trees. The sun was still warm, and the place full of the scent of apple blossom and primroses and the yellow wallflowers beside the path.

He was aware of none of it. All his being was turned inward, centered on the coming interview, wishing now that he had had the hardihood to disagree when the King had said to him: "I have refused to see her, ever again, but you are her son, and I think you owe her this, if only as a courtesy. You need never go back. But this time, this one time, you must. I have taken her kingdom from her, and her sons; let it not be said that I did so with brutality."

And in his head, over this voice of memory, two other voices persisted, of the boy Mordred, the fisherman's son, and of Mordred the prince, son of the High King Arthur, and a man grown.

Why should you fear her? She can do nothing. She is a prisoner and helpless.

That was the prince, tall and brave in his silver-trimmed tunic and new green mantle.

She is a witch, said the fisher-boy.

She is a prisoner of the High King, and he is my father. My father, said the prince.

She is my mother, and a witch.

She is no longer a queen. She has no power.

She is a witch, and she murdered my mother.

You are afraid of her? The prince was contemptuous.

Yes.

Why? What can she do? She cannot even cast a spell. Not here. You are not alone with her now in an underground tomb.

I know. I don't know why. She is a woman alone, and a prisoner, and without help, and I am afraid.

A side door stood open under the arcade of the nuns' courtyard. The woman beckoned, and he followed her in, along a short passage which ended in another door.

His heart was hammering now, his hands damp. He

clenched them at his sides, then loosed them deliberately, fighting back towards calmness.

I am Mordred. I am my own man, beholden neither to her nor to the High King. I shalt listen to her, and then go. I need never see her again. Whatever she is, whatever she says, it cannot matter. I am my own man, and I do my own will.

The woman opened the door without knocking, and stood aside for him to enter.

The room was large, but chilly and sparsely furnished. The walls were of daubed wattle, roughly plastered and painted, the floor of stone, bare of any rugs or coverings. To one side, looking out on the arcade, was a window, un glazed and open to the evening breeze. Opposite this was another door. Against the long wall of the room stood a heavy table and bench of carved and polished wood. At one end of the table was the room's single chair, high-backed and ornately carved, but without cushions. A couple of wooden stools flanked it. The table was set as if for the evening meal, with platters and cups of pewter and red clay and even wood. One part of Mordred's brain—the part that stayed coolly observant in spite of moist skin and rushing heart—noted with a twist of amusement that his half-brothers looked to be in for a meal frugal even by monkish standards. Then the far door opened, and Morgause came into the room.

Once before, when for the first time the ragged fisher boy had been brought, among the lights and colours of the palace, face to face with the queen, he had had eyes for nothing else; now in this bare and chilly room he forgot it all, and stared at her.

She was still dressed in her chapel-going black, without colour or ornament except a silver cross (*a cross?*) which hung on her breast. Her hair was plainly braided in two long plaits. She was no longer veiled. She moved forward to stand beside the chair, one hand on its tall back, the other holding a fold of her gown. She waited there in unmoving silence while the waiting-woman latched the door and went with her heavy, deliberate tread across the room to leave by the inner door. As it opened and shut behind her, Mordred caught a glimpse of stacked chairs and the gleam of silver hidden by a pile of coloured stuffs. Someone spoke quickly and was hushed. Then the door shut quietly and he was alone with the queen.

He stood still, waiting. She turned her head on its poised neck and let the silence hang longer. Light from the window moved in the heavy folds of her skirt, and the silver cross on her breast quivered. Suddenly, like a diver coming up into air, he saw two things clearly: the whitened knuckles of the fist that gripped the black cloth at her side, and the movement of her breast with her quickened breathing. She, too, faced this interview with something less than equanimity. She was as tense as he.

He saw more. The marks against the plaster where hangings had been hastily removed; the lighter patches on the floor where rugs had lain; scratches where chairs and lamps and tables—all the furnishings light enough for the women to handle—had been dragged out and stacked in the inner room, along with the cushions and silver and all the luxuries without which Morgause would have felt herself sadly ill-used. And this was the point. Once more, as had been her habit, Morgause had set the scene. The plain black clothes, the bare chilly chamber, the lack of attendants—the Queen of Orkney was concerned still with the report that would go back to Arthur, and with what her sons would find. They were to see her as a lonely and oppressed prisoner, kept in sad confinement.

It was enough. Mordred's fear faded. He gave a courtly bow and thereafter stood easily, waiting, apparently quite unperturbed by the silence and the scrutiny of the queen.

She let her hand fall from the chair-back, and taking up a fold of the heavy skirt on the other side, swept to the front of the chair, and sat. She smoothed the black cloth over her knees, folded her hands, white against black, lifted her head, and looked him slowly up and down from head to foot. He saw then that she was wearing the royal circlet of Lothian and Orkney. Its pearls and citrines, set in white gold, glimmered in the red gold of her hair.

When it was apparent that he was neither awed nor disconcerted, she spoke.

"Come nearer. Here, where I can see you. Hm. Yes, very fine. 'Prince Mordred,' it is now, they tell me. One of the ornaments of Camelot, and a hopeful sword at Arthur's service."

He bowed again, and said nothing. Her lips thinned.

"So he told you, did he?"

"Yes, madam."

"The truth? Did he dare?" Her voice was sharp with scorn.

"It seems like the truth. No one would invent such a tale to boast of it."

"Ah, so the young serpent can hiss. I thought you were my devoted servant, Mordred the fisher-boy?"

"I was, madam. What I owe you, I owe you. But what I owe him, I owe likewise."

"A moment's lust." She spoke contemptuously. "A boy after his first battle. An untried young pup that came running to the first woman that whistled him."

Silence. Her voice rose a fraction. "Did he tell you that?"

Mordred spoke steadily, in a voice almost devoid of expression. "He told me that I am his son, begotten by him in ignorance on his half-sister, after the battle at Luguvallium. That immediately afterwards you contrived to marry King Lot, who should have been your sister's lord, and with him went as his queen to Dunpeldyr, where I was born. That King Lot, hearing of the birth too soon after the marriage, and fearful of nurturing what he suspected to be a bastard of the High King's, tried to have me killed, and to that end drowned all the young children in Dunpeldyr, putting the blame for this upon the King. That you, madam, helped him in this, knowing that you had already sent me to safety in the islands, where Brude and Sula had been paid to care for me."

She leaned forward. Her hands moved to the chair-arms, gripping. "And did Arthur tell you that he, too, wanted you dead? Did he tell you that, Mordred?"

"He did not need to. I would have known it, anyway."

"What do you mean?" she asked sharply.

Mordred shrugged. "It would have been reasonable. The High King looked then to have other sons, by his queen. Why should he wish to keep me, a bastard out of his enemy?" His look challenged her. "You cannot deny that you are his enemy, nor that Lot was. And that is why you kept me, isn't it? I used to wonder why you paid Brude to keep me, Lot's son. And I was right to wonder. You would never have kept Lot's son by another woman. There was one called Macha,

168

was there not? A woman whose baby son was put in my cradle, to draw Lot's sword and let your son escape?"

For a moment she made no answer. She had lost colour. Then she said, ignoring his last statement: "So, I kept you from Lot's vengeance. You know that. You admit it. What did you say a moment ago? That what you owe me, you owe me. Your life, then. Twice, Mordred, twice." She leaned forward. Her voice throbbed. "Mordred, I am your mother. Don't forget that. I bore you. For you I suffered——"

His look stopped her. She had a moment to consider that any of her four sons by Lot would have already been at her knees. But not this one. Not Arthur's son.

He was speaking, coldly. "You gave me life, yes, for a moment's lust. You said that, not I. But it was true, was it not, madam? A woman whistling up a boy to her bed. A boy she knew to be her half-brother, but who she also knew would one day be a great king. I owe you nothing for that."

She flared suddenly, shrilly, into anger. "How dare you? You, a bastard spawn, hatched in a hovel by a pair of filthy peasants, to speak to me——"

He moved. Suddenly he was as angry as she. His eyes blazed. "They say, don't they, that the sun begets spawn on the reptiles as they lie in the mud?"

Silence. Then she drew in a hissing breath. She sat back in her chair, and her hands clasped again in her lap. With his momentary loss of control, she had regained hers. She said, softly: "Do you remember going with me once into a cave?"

Again silence. He moistened his lips, but said nothing.

She nodded. "I thought you had forgotten. Then let me remind you. Let me remind you to fear me, my son Mordred. I am a witch. I shall remind you of that, and of a curse I once laid on Merlin, who also took it upon himself to berate me for that unguarded night of love. He, like you, forgot that it takes two to make a child."

He stirred. "A night of love and a birthing does not make a mother, madam. I owed Sula more, and Brude. I said I owed you nothing. It's not true. I owe you their deaths. Their hideous deaths. You killed them."

"I? What folly is this?"

"Would you deny it? I should have suspected it long ago. But now I know. Gabran confessed before he died."

That shook her. To his surprise, he realized that she had not known. The colour came to her cheeks and faded again. She was very pale. "Gabran dead?"

"Yes."

"How?"

Mordred said, with satisfaction: "I killed him."

"You? For that?"

"Why else? If it grieves you—but I see that it does not. If you had even asked for him, or looked for him, someone would have told you, you would have known. Do you not even care about his death?"

"You talk like a green fool. What use was Gabran to me here? Oh, he was a good lover, but Arthur would never have let him come to me here. Is that all he told you?"

"That is all he was asked. Why, did he do other murders for you? Was it he who served Merlin the poison?"

"That was years ago. Tell me, has the old wizard been talking to you? Is it he who has put you under his spell as Arthur's man?"

"I have not spoken with him," said Mordred. "I've barely seen him. He has gone back into Wales."

"Then did your father the High King"—the words spat —"who has been so open with you, did he tell you what Merlin promised? For you?"

He answered, dry-mouthed: "You told me. I remember it. But all that you told me then was lies. You said he was my enemy. That was a lie. All of it, lies! Neither is Merlin my enemy! All this talk of a promise—"

"Is the truth. Ask him. Or ask the King. Better still, ask yourself, Mordred, why I should have kept you alive. Yes, I see that you understand it now. I kept you alive because by so doing I shall in the end have my revenge on Merlin, and on Arthur who despised me. Listen. Merlin foresaw that you would bring doom on Arthur. From dread of it he drove me from court, and poisoned Arthur's mind against me. So since that day, my son, I have done my utmost to bring that doom nearer. Not only by bearing you, and keeping you safe from Lot's murdering sword, but with a curse renewed at the dark of every moon since the day I was banished from my father's court, to spend my young life in the far, cold corners of the realm; I, the daughter of Uther Pendragon, reared in the wealth and gaiety—"

170

He interrupted her. He had only heard the one thing. "I, the doom of Arthur? How?"

At the note in his voice she began to smile. "If I knew, I would hardly tell you. But I don't know. Nor did Merlin."

"Why did he not have me destroyed, if this is true?"

Her lip curled. "He had scruples. You were the son of the High King. Merlin used to say that the gods do their own work in their own way."

Another silence, then Mordred said, slowly: "But in this matter, it seems they will have to work through men's hands. Mine. And I can tell you now, Queen Morgause, that I shall bring no doom on the King!"

"How can you avoid it when not you, nor I, nor even Merlin, know how it will strike?"

"Except that it will strike through me! You think I shall wait passively for that? I shall find a way!"

She was contemptuous. "Why pretend to be so loyal? Are you telling me that you love him, all in a moment? You have neither love nor loyalty in you. Look how you have turned against me, and you were to serve me all your days."

"One cannot build on rotten rock!" he said, furiously.

She was smiling now. "If I am rotten, you are my blood, Mordred. My blood."

"And his!"

"A son is his mother's stamp," she said.

"Not always! The others are yours, and their sire's, you have only to look at them. But I, no one would know me for your son!"

"But you are like me. They are not. They are bold, handsome fighters, with the minds of wild cattle. You are a witch's son, Mordred, with a smooth and subtle tongue and a serpent's tooth and a mind that works in silence. My tongue. My bite. My mind." She smiled a slow, rich smile. "They may keep me shut up till my life's end, but now my brother Arthur has taken to himself another such: a son with his mother's mind."

The cold had crept into his very bones. He said huskily: "This is not true. You cannot come at him through me. I am my own man. I will not harm him."

She leaned forward. She spoke softly, still smiling. "Mordred, listen to me. You are young, and you do not know the world. I hated Merlin, but he was never wrong. If Merlin saw it written in the stars that you would be Arthur's doom, then how can you escape it? There will come a day, the wicked day of destiny, when all will come to pass as he foretold. And I, too, have seen something, not in the heavens, but in the pool below the earth."

"What?" he asked, hoarsely.

She still spoke softly. There was colour in her face now, and her eyes shone. She looked beautiful. "I have seen a queen for you, Mordred, and a throne if you have the strength to take it. A fair queen and a high throne. And I see a snake striking at the kingdom's heel."

The words seemed to echo round the room, deep in note like a bell. Mordred spoke quickly, trying to kill the magic. "If I turned on him, then indeed I would be a snake."

"If you are," rejoined Morgause smoothly, "it is a role you share with the brightest of the angels, and the one who was closest to his lord."

"What are you talking about?"

"Oh, stories the nuns tell."

He said, very angrily: "You are talking nonsense to frighten me! I am not Lot or Gabran, a besotted tool to do your murders for you. You said I was like you. Very well. Now that I am warned, I shall know what to do. If I have to leave court and stay away from him, I shall do it. No power on earth can make me lift a hand to kill *unless I wish it*, and this death I swear to you I shall never undertake. I swear it by the Goddess herself."

No echo. The magic was gone. The shouted words fell into dead air. He stood panting, a hand clenched on his sword hilt.

"Brave words," said Morgause, very lightly, and laughed aloud.

He turned and ran from the room, slamming the door to shut off the laughter which followed him like a curse.

3

Once back in Camelot the memory of Amesbury and its imprisoned queen began to fade as the boys were plunged again into the life and excitement of the capital.

At first Gaheris complained loudly to whoever would listen about the hardships his mother was obviously suffering. Mordred, who might have enlightened him, said nothing. Nor did he mention his own interview with the queen. The younger boys probed now and then, but were met with silence, so soon stopped asking, and lost interest. Gawain, who must have guessed what the tenor of that interview might be, was perhaps unwilling to risk a snub, so showed no curiosity, and was told nothing. Arthur did ask Mordred how he had fared, then, accepting his son's "Well enough, sir, but not well enough to crave another meeting," merely nodded and turned the subject. It was observed that the King was angry, bored or impatient if his sisters were spoken of, so mention of them was avoided, and in time they were almost forgotten.

Queen Morgause was not after all sent north to join her sister Morgan. The latter, in fact, came south.

When King Urbgen, after a grim and lengthy interview with the High King, had finally put Queen Morgan aside, and given her back into Arthur's jurisdiction, she was held for some time at Caer Eidyn, but eventually won her brother's grudging permission to travel south to her own castle—

one that Arthur himself had granted her in happier days— among the hills to the north of Caerleon. Once settled there, with a guard of Arthur's soldiers and such of her women as were willing to remain in captivity with her, she settled down to a small approximation of a royal court, and proceeded (so rumour said, and for once rumour was right) to hatch little plots of hatred against her brother and her husband, as busily and almost as cozily as a hen hatches her eggs.

She also besieged the King from time to time, through the royal couriers, for various favours. One repeated request was for her "dear sister" to be allowed to join her at Castell Aur. It was well known that the two royal ladies had little fondness for one another, and Arthur, when he brought himself to think about it at all, suspected that Morgan's desire to join forces with Morgause was literally that: a wish to double the baneful power of such magic as she had. Here rumour spoke again, in whispers: It was being said that Queen Morgan far surpassed Morgause in power, and that none of it was used for good. So Morgan's requests were shrugged off, the High King tending, like any lesser man beset by a nagging woman, to shut his ears and turn the other way. He simply referred the matter to his chief adviser, and had the sense to let a woman deal with the women.

Nimuë's advice was clear and simple: keep them guarded, and keep them apart. So the two queens remained under guard, one in Wales, the other still in Amesbury, but—again on Nimuë's advice—not too strictly prisoned.

"Leave them their state and their titles, their fine clothing and their lovers," she said, and when the King raised his brows, "Men soon forget what has happened, and a fair woman under duress is a center for plotting and disaffection. Don't make martyrs. In a few years' time the younger men won't know or care that Morgause poisoned Merlin, or did murder here and there. They have already forgotten that she and Lot massacred the babies at Dunpeldyr. Give any evil-doer a year or two of punishment, and there will be some fool willing to wave a banner and shout, 'Cruelty, let them go.' Let them have the things that don't matter, but keep them close, and watch them always."

So Queen Morgan held her small court at Castell Aur, and sent her frequent letters along the couriers' road to Camelot, and Queen Morgause remained in the convent at Amesbury. She was permitted to increase the state in which she lived, but even so her captivity was possibly not so easy as her sister's, involving as it did a certain degree of lip-service to the monastic rule. But Morgause had her methods. To the abbot she presented herself as one who, long shut away from the true faith in the pagan darkness of the Orkneys, was eager and willing to learn all she could about the "new religion" of the Christians. The women who served her attended the devotions of the good sisters, and spent many long hours helping with the nuns' sewing and other, more menial tasks. It might have been noted that the queen herself was content to delegate this side of her devotions, but she was civility itself to the abbess, and that elderly and innocent lady was easily deceived by the attentions of one who was half-sister to the High King himself, whatever the supposed crimes she had committed.

"Supposed crimes." Nimuë was right. As time went by, the memory of Morgause's alleged crimes grew fainter, and the impression, carefully fostered by the lady herself, of a sweet sad captive, devoted to her royal brother, reft from her beloved sons, and far from her own land, grew, spreading far beyond the convent walls. And though it was common knowledge that the High King's eldest "nephew" bore in fact a closer and somewhat scandalous relationship to the throne— well, it had happened a long time ago, in dark and troubled times, when Arthur and Morgause were very young, and even now you could see how lovely she must have been . . . still was. . . .

So the years passed, and the boys became young men, and took their places at court, and Morgause's dark deeds became a legend rather than a true memory, and Morgause herself lived on comfortably at Amesbury; rather more comfortably, in fact, than she had lived either in her chilly fortress of Dunpeldyr or the windy fastness of the Orkneys. What she lacked, and fretted for, was power, something more than she exercised over her small and private court. As time went by and it became obvious that she would never leave Amesbury, was, in fact, almost forgotten, she turned back secretly to her magic arts, convincing herself that here lay the seeds of influence and real power. One skill certainly remained with her; whether it was the plants carefully watched over in the nunnery gardens, or the spells with which they were gathered and prepared. Morgause's unguents and perfumes still worked their strong magic. Her beauty stayed with her, and with it her power over men.

She had lovers. There was the young gardener who tended the herbs and simples for her brewing, a handsome youth who had once had hopes of joining the brotherhood. It might be said that the queen did him a favour. Four months as her lover taught him that the world outside the walls held delights that at sixteen he could not bear to renounce; when she dismissed him eventually with a gift of gold, he left the convent and went to Aquae Sulis, where he met the daughter of a wealthy merchant, and thereafter prospered exceedingly. After him came others, and it was easier still when a garrison established itself on the Great Plain for exercises, and the officers tended to ride into Amesbury after work to sample what the local tavern had to offer in the way of wine and entertainment. Simpler yet when Lamorak, who had brought the boys on that long-ago visit to see their mother, was appointed garrison commander, and took it upon himself to call at the convent to ask after the health of the captive queen. She received him herself, charmingly. He called again, with gifts. Within the month they were lovers, Lamorak vowing that it had been love at first sight, and lamenting that so many wasted years had passed since their first meeting in the woodland ride.

Twice, during these years, Arthur lodged nearby, the first time with the garrison, the second time in Amesbury itself, at the house of the headman.

On the first occasion, despite Morgause's efforts, he refused to see her, contenting himself with sending to the abbess and asking formally after the prisoner's health and wellbeing, and sending deputies—Bedwyr and, ironically, Lamorak—to talk with the queen. The second time occurred some two years later. He would have preferred to sleep again at garrison headquarters, but this might have seemed slighting to the headman's hospitality, so he lodged in the town. He gave orders that while he was in the township Morgause should not be permitted outside the convent walls, and he was obeyed. But one evening when he and half a dozen of his Companions sat at supper with the abbot and the head citizens of the township, two of Morgause's women came to the door with a tale of the captive queen's sickness, and pathetic pleas for the King's presence at her bedside. She longed only, they said, for the King's forgiveness before she died. Or if he was still set against her, she begged—and it could be seen, from the messengers' faces, with what pathos—that he should grant at least one dying wish. This was that she should see her sons once more.

Lot's sons were not in Amesbury with the King. Gaheris was with the garrison on the Plain; Gawain with the other two brothers was still in Camelot. The only one of the five in Amesbury was Mordred, who, as always now, was at his father's side.

To him Arthur, waving the women back out of earshot, said softly: "Dying? Do you suppose this is true?"

"She was out riding three days ago."

"Oh? Who says so?"

"The swineherd in the beech wood. I stopped and spoke with him. She gave him a coin once, so he watches for her. He calls her 'the pretty queen.'"

Arthur frowned, tapping the table. "There's been a cold wind all the week. I suppose she could have taken a chill. Even so—" He paused. "Well, I'll send someone tomorrow. Then, if this tale is true, I suppose I must go myself."

"And by tomorrow everything will be suitably arranged."

The King looked at him sharply. "What do you mean by that?"

Mordred said dryly: "When she sent for me before, she was alone in a cold room with no comforts. I saw them through the door, hastily stacked in the next room."

Arthur's frown deepened. "So you suspect trickery here? Still? But how? What could she do?"

Mordred shifted his shoulders as if he felt cold. "Who knows? As she reminded me, more than once, she is a witch. Keep away from her, sir. Or—let me go and see for myself if this tale of mortal sickness is true."

"You are not afraid of her witchcraft?"

"She has asked to see her sons," said Mordred, "and I am the only one here in Amesbury." He did not add that though his spirit, fed with fear by Morgause herself, shrank from her, he knew himself to be safe. He was to be—he could still hear the angry spitting voice—his father's bane.

To that end she would preserve him, as she had done through those early years.

He said: "If you send now, sir, to say you will see her in the morning, that is when—if this is indeed a trick—she will make her preparations. I myself will go now, tonight."

After a little more discussion the King agreed, and, returning gratefully to his guests, sent one of his Companions to inform Queen Morgause that he would see her on the morrow.

As before, he sent Lamorak.

There was a horse tied up outside the orchard wall. Here the coping was low, and a bough of an old apple tree had forced the bricks outwards until they bulged, then broke and fell, making a place that could, with agility and the help of a horse's saddle, be climbed.

The night was moonless, but the sky glistened with stars as thick and numerous as daisies on a lawn. Mordred paused to look at the horse. Something about its white blaze and the stocking on its near fore was familiar. He looked closer, and saw on the breastband the silver boar of Orkney, and recognized Gaheris's roan. He ran a hand over its shoulder. It was damp and hot.

He stood for a moment, thinking. If the news of Morgause's illness had sped, as such news will, on the wings of gossip, to garrison headquarters, Gaheris must have ridden out immediately to visit the queen. Or he might, having been refused permission to accompany Arthur with Mordred to Amesbury, have ridden out secretly, determined to see his mother. In either case the visit was surreptitious, or he would have gone to the gate.

Mordred thought, with a touch of amusement, that in any case Morgause had not expected the visit, so would probably not yet, on this chilly night, have stripped herself of her comforts. Gaheris, whatever his loyalties, would have to share witness to his mother's health and circumstances when Mordred reported on them to Arthur.

He walked soft-footed round to the convent gate, was inspected under the lamp by the guards, showed the King's pass, and was admitted.

Within the convent walls no guards were appointed, and all was silent and deserted. Morgause now had one wing of the convent—the buildings between the orchard and the women's arcade—to herself and her attendants. Mordred walked quietly past the chapel and let himself into the arcade. Here a nun nodded beside a brazier in a little lodge. Again he showed the King's pass, was recognized and allowed through.

The arches of the arcade showed black and empty. The grass in the center of the court was grey in the starlight, its own starred daisies shut for the night, invisible. An owl flew silently across the roof tops and into the orchard boughs. The only light was the glow from the brazier in the lodge.

Mordred paused, undecided. It was late, but not yet midnight. Morgause, like most witches, was a night-time creature; surely one of her windows should be showing a light? And certainly, if the deathbed story were true, her women would be wakeful, watching by her bedside. Perhaps a lover? He had heard that she took her pleasures still. But if Gaheris was here . . . *Gaheris*?

Mordred swore aloud, sickened at himself for the thought, and then again for the knowledge that the suspicion was justified.

He tried the door under the arcade, found it unlocked, then let himself into the building and went swiftly up the well-remembered corridor. Here was the door to the queen's apartments. After a moment's hesitation, he pushed it open and went in without knocking.

This room was not as he remembered it, but as he would have seen it had Morgause not stripped it of its furnishings. Starlight fell softly through the window to light the hangings, the waxed surfaces of furniture, the gleam of gold and silver vessels. Thick rugs muffled his tread. He crossed the room to the inner door, which gave on the antechamber to the queen's bedroom. Here he paused. Her women, or surely one of them, would be awake? He bent his head and knocked softly on the panel.

There was a sound from inside the room, a hurried movement, followed by stillness, as if his knock had startled someone who did not want to be found there. Mordred hesitated again, then set his mouth and reached for the latch, but before he could lay hand on it the door was pulled open, and Gaheris stood there, sword in hand.

The antechamber was lit by a single candle. Even in its

faint, diffused light it could be seen that Gaheris was as white as a ghost. When he saw Mordred he went, if possible, whiter still. His mouth slowly opened to a black 0, and he said, on a gasping breath: "*You?*"

"Whom did you expect?" Mordred spoke very softly, his eye going beyond Gaheris to the door of the queen's bed-chamber. This was shut, and a heavy curtain was drawn across it to keep out the chill draughts of night. Two women were there, on couches to either side of the queen's door. One was Morgause's own waiting-woman, the other a nun, presumably excused the night offices, and set to share the watch on behalf of the convent. Both slept soundly, the nun, indeed, snoring in a slumber that seemed rather too heavy. On a table by the wall stood two cups, and the room smelled of spiced wine.

Gaheris's sword moved, but indecisively, then he saw that Mordred was not even looking at him, and lowered it again. Mordred said, on a whisper that was the merest thread of sound: "Put that up, you fool. I came on the King's orders, why do you think?"

"At this time of night? To do what?"

"Not to harm her, or would I have knocked on her door, or come naked as I am?"

The word, between soldiers, meant "unarmed," and to a knight was as good as a shield. He spread his empty hands wide. Gaheris, slowly, began to slide his blade back into its housing.

"Then what—" he was beginning, when Mordred, with a swift gesture commanding silence, stepped past him into the room, and, crossing to the table, picked up one of the cups and sniffed at it. "And the woman in the lodge could hardly keep awake long enough to see me through."

He met Gaheris's stare, and smiled, setting the cup down again. "The King sent me because a message came that she was ill, and failing. He would have come himself tomorrow. But now I think he need not." He lifted a hand quickly. "No, have no fear. It cannot be true. These women have been drugged, and it is easy to guess—"

"Drugged?" Gaheris seemed to take it in slowly, then his head moved, his eyes searching the dark corners of the room like an animal scenting an enemy, and his hand flew back to his hilt. He said, hoarsely: "Then it *is* danger!"

"No. *No.*" Mordred moved quickly, to take his half-brother lightly by the arm, turning him away from the queen's door. "The drug is one of the queen's potions. I know that smell. So put your fears at rest, and come away. It's certain that she is neither ill nor in any other kind of danger. The King need not come in the morning, but no doubt you will be permitted to see her then. He has sent for the others already, in case the story is true."

"But how do you know—?"

"And keep your voice down. Come, we'll go. I want to show you some beautiful tapestries in the outer room." He smiled, shaking the other's unresponsive arm. "Oh, for the gods' sake, man, can't you see? She's got a lover with her, that's all! So neither you nor I can visit her tonight!"

Gaheris stood for a moment, rigid against Mordred's hand, then with a wild gesture he shook himself free and leaped for the bedchamber door. He ripped the curtain aside and flung the door back with a crash against the wall.

4

In the endless, stupefied moment before anyone moved, they
saw it all.

Lamorak naked, mounted, light slipping over the sweating
muscles of his back. Morgause beneath him, hidden by shadows, except for the restless, eager hands, and the long hair
spread across the pillows. Her night robe lay in a huddle on
the floor, beside Lamorak's discarded clothing. His sword
belt, with sword and dagger sheathed, was carefully laid
across a stool at the other side of the room.

Gaheris made a sound hardly recognizable as human, and
jerked wildly at his sword.

Mordred, two paces behind him, shouted a warning.
"Lamorak!" and grabbed again at his half-brother's arm.

Morgause screamed. Lamorak gasped, turned his head,
saw, flung himself off the woman's body and ran for his
sword. The move left her exposed to the merciless starlight:
the sprawled flesh, the marks of love, the gaping mouth, the
hands still weaving in air over the space where her lover's
body had been.

The hands dropped. She recognized Gaheris in the doorway, with Mordred struggling to hold him, and the scream
checked in a gasp as she hurriedly pushed herself up from
the pillows and grabbed for the tumbled coverlet.

Gaheris, cursing, jerked the dagger from his belt and cut

down at Mordred's restraining hand. The blade bit, and Mordred's grip loosened. Gaheris wrenched himself free.

Lamorak had reached the stool and snatched up his sword belt. Clumsily, still perhaps numb with shock, he wrenched at the hilt in the half-darkness, but the loose belt wrapped itself round his arm, and the hilt jammed. Wrenching at it, naked as he was, he turned to face the other sword.

Mordred, blood dripping from his cut hand, pushed past Gaheris, getting himself between the two men, then thrust the flat of both hands hard against his half-brother's chest.

"Gaheris! Wait! You can't kill an unarmed man. And not this, not here. Wait, you fool! He's a Companion; leave this to the King."

It is doubtful if Gaheris even heard him, or felt his hands. He was crying, on hard, sobbing breaths, and looked more than half mad. Nor did he make any attempt to push past Mordred to attack Lamorak. He swung suddenly round, away from both men, and raced for the queen's bed, his sword held high.

Clutching the coverlet to her, blinded by her hair, she tried to roll away and dodge him. She screamed again. Before the other men had even realized his purpose Gaheris, at the bedside, swung his sword up, and brought it down with all his strength across his mother's neck. And again. And yet again.

The only sound was the soft and dreadful hacking of metal into flesh and feathered bedding. Morgause died at the first blow. The coverlet dragged from her clutching hands, and the naked body fell back into the merciful shadows. Less mercifully the head, half severed, lolled into starlight on its blood-drenched pillows. Gaheris, himself drenched in the first dreadful fountain of blood, lifted the red sword for another blow, then, with a howl like a hurt dog, threw it aside with a clatter, and, flinging himself to his knees in the pool of blood, put his head down beside his mother's on the pillow and wept.

Mordred found that he was holding Lamorak with a grip that hurt them both. The killing had been so swift, so unlooked-for, that neither man had made any conscious move at all. Then Lamorak came to himself with a jerk and a gasping curse, and tried to arm Mordred aside. But Morgause was dead and beyond help, and her son knelt unheeding,

183

uncaring, his unprotected back to them both, his sword ten paces away on the floor. Lamorak's blade wavered, and sank. Even here, even in this moment, the rigid training held. There had been a dreadful slaying done in hot blood. But now the blood was cold, the room was cold, and there was nothing to be done. Lamorak stood still in Mordred's grasp, his teeth beginning to chatter now with reaction, horror and the icy chill of shock.

Mordred let him go. He picked the knight's clothing up, and bundled it into his arms.

"Here, get these on, and go. There's nothing to be gained by staying. Even if he was fit to fight you now, it cannot be here, you know that." He stooped quickly for Gaheris's abandoned sword, then, taking Lamorak by the arm, urged him towards the bedroom door. "Into the other room now, before he comes to. The thing's done, and all we can do is prevent that madman from making it worse."

In the antechamber the women still slept. As Mordred shut and latched the door the nun stirred in her sleep and muttered something that could have been "Madam?" then slept again. The two men stood rigid, listening. No sound, no movement. Morgause's screaming, brief as it had been, had not been heard through the thick walls and closed doors.

Lamorak had hold of himself now. He was still very pale, and looked sick and haunted, but he made no attempt to argue with Mordred, and set himself to dress quickly, with only a glance or two at the shut door of the dreadful room.

"I shall kill him, of course," he said thickly.

"But not here." Mordred was cool. "So far you've done nothing that any man would blame you for. The King will be angry enough at the mess, without your adding to it. So take my advice and go now, quickly. What you do later is up to you."

Lamorak looked up from fastening his tunic. "What are you going to do?"

"Get you out of here, Gaheris away, and then report to the King. I was sent to do that anyway. Not that it matters now, but I suppose her tale of being ill, dying even, was pure invention?"

"Yes. She wanted to see the King and plead with him herself for release." He added, very softly: "I was going to marry her. I loved her, and she me. I had promised to talk

184

with him myself tomorrow...today. If she were my wife, surely Arthur would have let her leave here, and live once more in freedom?"

Mordred did not reply. Another tool, he was thinking. I was once her pass to power, and now this man, poor gullible fool, was to be her pass to liberty. Well, she is gone, and the King will hardly be sorry, but in death, as in life, she will wreck the peace of all those near her.

He said: "You knew that the King had sent for Gawain and the other two already?"

"Yes. What will they—what will happen there?" A glance towards the door.

"Gaheris? Who knows? As for you...I said you were to be blamed for nothing. But they will blame you, be sure of that. It is even likely that, being the men they are, they will try to kill Gaheris, too. They like to keep sex and murder right in the family."

This, dry as spice-dust, made Lamorak, even through the grief and rage of the moment, look sharply at the younger man. He said, slowly, as if making a totally new discovery: "You—why, you're one of them. Her own son. And you talk as if...as if..."

"I am different," said Mordred, shortly. "Here, your cloak. No, that bloodstain's mine, you needn't mind it. Gaheris stabbed my hand. Now, for the Goddess' sake, man, go, and leave him to me."

"What will you do?"

"Lock the room so that the women don't screech the place down when they wake, and get Gaheris out the way he came in. You came in through the main gate, of course? Do the guards know you're still here?"

"No. I left in due course, and then...I have a way in. She used to leave a window open when she knew..."

"Yes, of course. But then, why trouble—?" He was going to ask, Why trouble to drug the women? but then he saw that Morgause's sexual affairs would necessarily have to be hidden from the abbess. The holy women could hardly be expected to connive at them.

"I'll have to leave court, of course," said Lamorak. "You will tell the King—?"

"I'll report exactly what happened. I don't imagine the King will blame you. But you'd do well to get away until

Gawain and the others have been settled. Good luck and good speed."

Lamorak, with one last look towards the silent bedroom door, went from the room. Mordred glanced once again at the sleeping women, propped Gaheris's blood-stained sword in a shadowed corner where a faldstool hid it from view, then went back into the queen's bedchamber and shut the door behind him.

He found Gaheris on his feet, swaying like a drunken man and looking vaguely round him as if for something he had forgotten.

Mordred took him by the shoulder and drew him, unresisting, away from the bedside. Stooping, he twitched the stained coverlet across to cover the dead body. Gaheris, rigid as a sleepwalker, let himself be led from the room.

Once in the antechamber, and with the door shut, he spoke for the first time, thickly. "Mordred. It was right. It was right to kill her. She was my mother, but she was a queen, and to do thus...to bring shame on us and on all our line...No one can gainsay my right, not even Gawain. And when I kill Lamorak—that was Lamorak, wasn't it? Her—the man?"

"I didn't see who it was. He snatched up his clothes and went."

"You didn't try to hold him? You should have killed him."

"For the love of Hecate," said Mordred, "save all that for later. Listen, I thought I heard footsteps. It could be time for the night office. Anyone could come by."

This was not true, but it served to rouse Gaheris. He gave a startled glance around, as if just waking to a perilous situation, and said sharply: "My sword?"

Mordred lifted it from the corner and showed it. "When we are outside the walls. Come. I saw where you left your horse. Quickly."

They were crossing the orchard before Gaheris spoke again. He was still on the treadmill of agonized guilt.

"That man. Lamorak, I know it was, and you know, too. You called his name. Don't try to shield him. Arthur's man, one of the Companions. He should be killed, too, and I shall do it. But she, she to lie with such a one...It must have happened before, you know. Those women were drugged.

186

They must have been lovers—" He choked on the word, then went on: "She spoke of him once to me. Of Lamorak. She told me that he had killed our father King Lot, and that she hated him. She lied. To me. To me."

Mordred said, quietly: "Don't you see, Gaheris? She lied to blind you, and she lied twice. Lamorak never killed Lot, how could he? Lot died of the wounds he got at Caledon, and they fought on the same side there. So unless Lamorak stabbed King Lot in the back, and that was not his way, he could not be his killer. Did you never think of that?"

But Gaheris had no thoughts but the same trapped and torturing ones. "She took him as her lover, and lied to me. We were all deceived, even Gawain. Mordred, the others will say that what I did was right, will they not?"

"You know as well as I how likely Gawain is to forgive you this. Or Gareth. Even your twin may not support you. And though the King isn't likely to grieve for your mother, he'll have to listen if the Orkney princes demand what they will call justice."

"They will ask it on Lamorak!"

"For what?" said Mordred, coolly. "He would have married her."

That silenced Gaheris for a moment. They had reached the orchard wall, and he paused under the apple tree and turned. The moon was rising now behind a drift of cloud, and the bloodstains on his breast showed black.

"If they do not kill him, I shall," he said.

"You can try," said Mordred dryly. "And he will kill you, make no mistake. And then your brothers will try to kill him. So you see what this night's work has done?"

"And you? You seem to care nothing for what has happened. You speak as if it hardly touched you."

"Oh, it touches me," said Mordred briefly. "Now, we are wasting time. What's done is done. You will have to leave court, you know that. You will be well advised to get away before your brothers get here. Get over the wall now, Gaheris; your horse is there."

Gaheris swung himself over, and Mordred, climbing after him, stayed astride the wall while his brother untied the horse and checked the girths. Then he handed Gaheris's sword down into his hand.

"Where will you go?" he asked him.

"North. Not to the islands, and Dunpeldyr is held for Arthur as well. What is not? But I shall find a place where I can sell my sword."

"Meantime take my purse. Here."

"My thanks, brother." Gaheris caught it. He swung himself to the saddle. It brought him almost to Mordred's level. He hung on the rein for a moment while the roan horse danced, eager to move. "When you see Gawain and the others—"

"Tell them the truth and plead your cause for you? I'll do what I can. Farewell."

Gaheris pulled the horse's head round. Soon there was no sign of him except the fast soft thud of retreating hoofs. Mordred jumped down from the wall and walked back across the orchard.

5

So died Morgause, witch-queen of Lothian and Orkney, leaving by her death and its manner another hellbrew of trouble for her hated brother.

The trouble was far-reaching. Gaheris suffered banishment, and Lamorak, riding white-faced and silent into headquarters to surrender his sword, was relieved of his command and bidden to absent himself until the dust should have time to settle.

This would not be soon. Gawain, savage with outraged pride rather than grief, swore on all the wild gods of the north to be avenged both on Lamorak and on his brother, and ignored all that Arthur could say to him, pleas and threats alike.

It was pointed out that Lamorak had offered marriage to Morgause, and that her acceptance gave him the betrothed's claim to her bed, and with it the right to avenge her murder himself. This right Lamorak, one of Arthur's first and most loyal Companions, had waived. Gaheris, he had sworn, was safe from him. But none of this appeased Gawain, whose anger had in it a large measure of sheer sexual jealousy.

Just as violent was Gawain's railing against Gaheris, but there he got no support from his brothers. Agravain, who had always been the leader of the twins, seemed lost without Gaheris; he tended to turn to Mordred, who, for reasons of his own, suffered him willingly enough. Gareth said little throughout, but withdrew into silence. In her death as in her life his mother had wronged him deeply: bitter as was the story of her dreadful death to her youngest son, the tales of her impurity, which were common knowledge now, wounded him more.

But all the shouts for vengeance had to die. Lamorak had gone, no one knew where. Gaheris had vanished northward into the mists, Morgause was buried in the convent grave-yard, and Arthur went with his followers back to Camelot. Gradually, for sheer lack of fuel, the blaze kindled by the murder died down. Arthur, fond of his nephews, and secretly relieved at the news of Morgause's death, steered as carefully as he could between the shoals, kept the princes as busy as he might, gave Gawain as much authority as he dared, and waited with weary apprehension for the storm to break again. About Gaheris he could not bring himself to care overmuch, but Lamorak, who was innocent of all but folly, was almost certainly doomed. Some day Arthur's valued Companion would come against one of the Orkney princes, and be killed, fair or foul. Nor would it stop there. Lamorak, too, had a brother, at present serving in Dumnonia with one Drustan, a knight whom Arthur hoped to attract into his service. It was possible that he, or even Drustan himself—who was a close friend to both brothers—would in turn swear and require vengeance.

So Morgause, in her death, did what she had planned to do with her life. She had planted a canker in the blossoming chivalry of Arthur's court: not, ironically, the bastard she had reared to be his bane, but her three legitimate oldest, her wild, unpredictable and now almost ungovernable sons.

Outside it all stood Mordred. He had shown himself re-sourceful and cool, had prevented further bloodshed on that murderous night, and had gained time for good counsel. That the Orkney princes would not—some said could not—re-spond to good counsel was hardly his fault. It was noticeable that less and less did the court count him as one of the "Orkney brood." Subtly, the distance between him and his half-brothers increased. And with Morgause dead, men hardly troubled any longer with the fiction of "the High King's nephew." He was simply "Prince Mordred," and known to be close to the King and Queen in love and favour.

Some time after Arthur's return to Camelot he called a council in the Round Hall.

It was the first such council that the two younger Orkney brothers had been entitled, as Companions, to attend. Even Mordred, who with Gawain had been given that status some years ago, met with a change: instead of sitting at the King's left, as had been his privilege over the past two years, he was led by the royal usher to the chair on Arthur's right, where Bedwyr usually sat. Bedwyr took the seat to the left. If he felt demoted he did not show it; he gave Mordred a smile that seemed genuine, and a ceremonious little bow that acknowledged his new status to the younger man.

Bedwyr, the King's friend of boyhood days, and constant companion in the closest sense, was a quiet man with the eyes of a poet, and, after the King's, the most deadly sword in the kingdoms. He had fought at Arthur's side through all the great campaigns, and with him shared the glory of wiping the Saxon Terror from Britain's boundaries. Possibly alone of the warrior lords, he showed no impatience with the long-drawn peace, and when Arthur had had to travel abroad at the request of allies or kinsmen, and take his fighting men with him, Bedwyr never seemed to resent the necessity of staying behind as regent for his king. Rumour, as Mordred well knew, gave reasons for this: Bedwyr had not married, and in the close company as he was of both King and Queen, it was whispered that he and Queen Guinevere were lovers. But Mordred, also constantly with them, had never caught a look or gesture that bore this out. Guinevere was as gay and kind to him as he had ever seen her with Bedwyr, and, perhaps with a little of the inbred jealousy taught by Morgause, he would have denied, even with his sword, any overt hint of such a connection.

So he returned Bedwyr's smile, and sat down in the new place of honour. He saw Gawain, leaning close to his brother, whisper something, and Agravain nodding, then the King spoke, opening the Council, and they fell silent. The meeting droned on. Mordred noticed with amusement how Agravain and Gareth, at first rigid with importance and attentive to every word, soon grew bored and impatient, and sat in their seats as if on thorns. Gawain, like the greybeard beside him, was frankly dozing in a shaft of sunshine from a window. The King, patient and painstaking as ever, seemed to throw off preoccupations with an effort. The round table in the middle of the hall was loaded heavily with papers and tablets, and by it the secretaries scribbled without ceasing.

As usual at the Round Hall councils, routine matters were dealt with first. Petitions were heard, complaints tabled, judgments given. King's messengers brought what information was fitted for the public ear, and later, those of the King's knights-errant who had returned home would report on their adventures to the Council.

These were the travelling knights who acted at once as Arthur's eyes and as his deputies. Years ago, once the Saxon wars were over and the country settled, Arthur had looked around for means to occupy what Merlin had called "the idle swords and the unfed spirits." He knew that the long and prosperous peace which contented most men was not to the liking of some of his knights, not the young men only, but the war veterans, men who knew no other life but that of fighting. There was no longer any need for the picked body of Companions, the knights who under Arthur had led the force of cavalry which had been used as such a swift and deadly weapon during the Saxon campaigns. The Companions remained his personal friends, but their status as commanders was changed. They were appointed personal representatives of the King himself, and, as deputies armed with royal warrants, and each in command of his own men, they travelled the kingdoms, answering the call of the petty kings or leaders who needed help or guidance, and taking with them the High King's justice and the High King's peace wherever they went. They also policed the roads. Robbers still lurked in the wilder parts of the country, haunting fords and crossways where traders or rich travellers might be ambushed. These they sought out and killed, or brought them back for the King's justice. One other and most important task was the protection of monasteries. Arthur, though not himself a Christian, recognized the growing importance of these foundations as centers of learning and as an influence for peace. Their hospitality, moreover, was a vital part of the peaceful commerce of the roads.

Three of these knights presented themselves now. As the first of them came forward there was a stir of interest in the hall, and even the sleepers roused themselves to attention. Sometimes the reports were of fighting; occasionally prisoners were brought in, or tales told of strange happenings in remote and wild parts of the country. This had given rise to the belief held by the ignorant, that Arthur never sat down to supper until he had heard some tale of marvels.

But there were no marvels to be presented. One man came from North Wales, one from Northumbria, the third —one of the knights deputed to watch the Saxon boundaries—from the upper Thames valley. This man reported some activity, though peaceful, in Suthrige, that region south of the Thames occupied by Middle Saxon settlers; some kind of official visit, he thought, from a party of Cerdic's West Saxons. The man from North Wales told of a new monastic foundation where the Christian grail, or cup of ceremonial, would be raised on the next feast day. The man from Northumbria had nothing to report.

Mordred, watching from his place beside the King, noticed with quickened interest that Agravain, waiting with obvious impatience through the speeches of the first two knights, went still and attentive while the last one spoke. When the man had done, and been dismissed with the King's thanks, Agravain visibly relaxed and went back to his yawning.

Northumbria? thought Mordred, then filed the thought away and turned his attention to the King.

At last the hall was cleared of all but councillors and Companions. Arthur sat back in the royal chair, and spoke.

He came straight to the news that had caused him to call the Council.

A courier from the Continent had arrived on the previous evening with grave tidings. Two of the three young sons of Clodomir, the Frankish king, had been murdered, and their brother had fled for sanctuary to a monastery, from which it was thought that he would not dare emerge. The murderers, the boys' uncles, would no doubt proceed to divide King Clodomir's kingdom between them.

The news carried grave implications. Clodomir (who had been killed a year ago in battle with the Burgundians) had been one of the four sons of Clovis, King of the Salian Franks, who had led his people out of their northerly lands down into what had once been the prosperous country of Roman Gaul, and had made it his own. Savage and ruthless, like all of the Merwing dynasty, he had nevertheless created a powerful and stable kingdom. At his death that kingdom had been divided, as was the custom, among his four sons. Clodomir and Childebert, the eldest legitimate sons, held the central part of Gaul: Clodomir to the east, his lands bordering on those of the hostile Burgundians; and Childebert to the west, in that part of Gaul which bordered and contained the peninsula of Brittany.

And here lay the rub.

Brittany, called Less Britain in the common tongue, was in fact almost a province of the High Kingdom. Over a century ago it had been populated by men from Greater Britain, and the tie remained strong; communication was easy and trade brisk, and the tongue, with slight regional variations, was the same. Brittany's king, Hoel, was cousin to Arthur, and the two kings were bound to one another, not only through kinship and treaties of alliance, but because Brittany was still as much part of the federation of lands known as the High Kingdom as was Cornwall, or the Summer Country round Camelot itself.

"The matter," said the King, "is not desperate; indeed, it may turn out for the best, since infants never make safe rulers. But you see the situation. Clodomir was killed at Vézeronce last year by the Burgundians. They are still hostile, and wait only for a chance to attack again. So we have the vital central province of the Franks, with the Burgundians to the east, and on the west the land ruled by King Childebert, which contains our own Celtic province of Brittany. Now Clodomir's kingdom will be divided yet again, in which case King Childebert will extend his lands eastward, while his brothers move in from north and south. Which means that, as long as we retain the friendship of these kings, we have them as a barrier between ourselves and the Germanic peoples to the east."

He paused, then, looking around, repeated: "As long as we have the friendship of these kings. I said the matter was not yet desperate. But in time it may be. We must prepare for it. Not yet, as some of you wish, by raising armies. That will come. But by forming alliances, bonds of friendship, cemented by offers of help and fair trading. If the kingdoms of Britain are to remain secure against the destroyers from the east, then all the kingdoms within our sea-girt coasts must join together in their defense. I repeat, all."

"The Saxons!" said someone. It was Cian, a young Celt from Gwynedd.

"Saxons or English," said Arthur, "they own, by agreement, a good proportion of the eastern and south-eastern coastal lands, those which were the territories of the old Saxon Shore, with what other settlements were granted them by Ambrosius, and by myself after Badon Hill. These Saxon Shore lands lie like a wall along the Narrow Sea. They can be our bulwark, or they can betray." He paused. There was no need to gather eyes. All were fixed on him. "Now this is what I have to say to the Council. I have called a meeting with the chief of their kings, Cerdic of the West Saxons, to talk to him about defense. At our next Council I shall be prepared to tell you the result of that meeting."

He sat down then, and the ushers were on their feet, preventing uproar and trying to sort into order the men who wanted to speak. Under cover of the noise Arthur grinned at Bedwyr. "You were right. A hornets' nest. But let them talk it out, and have their say, and when I go it will be, nominally at least, with their support."

He was right. By supper time all who wanted to had said their say. Next day a courier rode to the village which the West Saxon king called his capital, and the meeting was arranged.

Mordred was to go with the King. He used the interval before Cerdic's reply came to ride over to Applegarth to see Nimuë.

6

Since the day when Nimuë had visited King Urbgen of Rheged, and prevented Mordred's escape, he had never seen her. She was married to Pelleas, king of the islands to the west of the Summer Country, where the River Brue meets the Severn Sea. Nimuë herself had been born a princess of the River Isles, and had known her husband since childhood. Their castle stood almost within sight of the Tor, and when Pelleas, who was one of Arthur's Companions, was with the King, Nimuë would take her place as Lady of the Lake maidens in the convent on Ynys Witrin, or else retire alone to Applegarth, the house that Merlin had built near Camelot, and which he had left to her, along with his title, and—men whispered—how much more. It was fabled that during the long illness that had weakened the old enchanter towards his seeming death, he had made over all his knowledge to his pupil Nimuë, implanting in her brain even his own childhood's memories.

Mordred had heard the stories, and though with manhood and security he had grown more skeptical, he remembered the impression he had received in Luguvallium of the enchantress's power, so he approached Applegarth with something that might even have been called nervousness.

It was a grey stone house, four-square round a small courtyard. An old tower jutted at one corner. The house stood cupped in rolling upland pastures, and was surrounded by orchards. A stream ran downhill past the walls.

Mordred turned his horse off the road and into the track that led uphill beside the stream. He was halfway towards the house when another horseman approached him. To his surprise he saw that it was the King, riding alone on his grey mare.

Arthur drew rein beside him. "Were you looking for me?"

"No, sir. I had no idea you were here."

"Ah, so Nimuë sent for you? She told me you were coming, but she did not tell me when, or why."

Mordred stared. "She said I was coming? How could she? I hardly knew it myself. I—there was something I wanted to ask her, so I rode here, you might say on impulse."

"Ah," said Arthur. He regarded Mordred with what looked like amusement.

"Why do you smile, sir?" Mordred was thinking, with thankfulness: He cannot begin to guess what was in my mind. Surely he cannot guess. But Nimuë . . . ?

"If you have never met Nimuë, then gird your loins and put up your shield," said Arthur, laughing. "There's no mystery, at least not the kind ordinary mortals such as you and I can understand. She would know you were coming because she knows everything. As simple as that. She will even know why."

"That must save a world of words," said Mordred dryly.

"I used to say that. To Merlin." A shadow touched the King's face, and was gone. The amusement came back. "Well, good luck to you, Mordred. It is time you met the ruler of your ruler." And still laughing, he rode down the hill to the road.

Mordred left his horse at the archway that led into the courtyard, and went in. The place was full of flowers, and the scent of herbs and lavender, and doves crooned on the wall. There was an old man by the well, a gardener by his clothes, drawing water. He glanced up, touched a hand to his brow, and pointed the way to the tower door.

Well, thought Mordred, she is expecting me, isn't she?

He mounted the stone steps and pushed open the door.

The room was small and square, with one large window opening to the south, and beneath it a table. The only other furnishings were a cupboard, a heavy chair, and a couple of stools. A box stood on the table with books, neatly rolled, inside it. By the table, with her back to it and facing the door, stood a woman.

She neither spoke nor made any movement of greeting. What met him, forcibly as a cold blast, was her inimical and chilling gaze. He stopped dead in the doorway. A feeling of dread, formless and heavy, settled on him, as if the vultures of fate clung to his shoulders, their claws digging into his flesh.

Then it cleared. He straightened. The weight was gone. The tower room was full of light, and facing him was a tall, arrow-straight woman in a grey robe, with dark hair bound back with silver, and cool grey eyes.

"Prince Mordred."

He bowed. "Madam."

"Forgive me for receiving you here. I was working. The King comes often, and takes things as he finds them. Will you sit?"

He pulled a stool towards him and sat. He glanced at the littered table. She was not, as he half expected, brewing some concoction over the brazier. The "work" consisted, rather, of a litter of tablets and papers. An instrument which he did not recognize stood in the window embrasure, its end tilted towards the sky.

Nimuë seated herself, turned to Mordred, and waited.

He said directly: "We have not met before, madam, but I have seen you."

She looked at him for a moment, then nodded. "The castle at Luguvallium? I knew you were nearby. You were hiding in the courtyard?"

"Yes." He added, wryly: "You cost me my liberty. I was trying to run away."

"Yes. You were afraid. But now you know that there was no reason for your fear."

He hesitated. Her tone was cold still, her look hostile. "Then why did you stop me? Did you hope then that the King would have me put to death?"

Her brows went up. "Why do you ask that?"

"Because of the prophecy."

"Who told you about it? Ah, yes, Morgause. No. I warned Urbgen to keep you close and see that you got to Camelot, because it is always better to keep a danger where one can

198

see it, than let it vanish, and then wonder from what direction it will strike."

"So you agree that I am a danger. You believe in the prophecy."

"I must."

"Then you have seen it, too? In the crystal, or the pool, or—" He glanced towards the instrument by the window. "—The stars?"

For the first time there was something other than hostility in her look. She was watching him with curiosity, and a hint of puzzlement. She said slowly: "Merlin saw, and he made the prophecy, and I am Merlin."

"Then you can tell me why, if Merlin believed his own prophetic voices, he let the King keep me alive in the first place? I know why Morgause did; she saved me because she thought I would be his bane. She told me so, and then when I was grown she tried to enlist me as his enemy. But why did Merlin even let her bear me?"

She was silent for a few moments. The grey eyes searched him, as if they would draw the secrets from the back of his brain. Then she spoke.

"Because he would not see Arthur stained with the wrong of murder, whatever the cause. Because he was wise enough to see that we cannot turn the gods aside, but must follow as best we can the paths they lay out for us. Because he knew that out of seeming evil can come great good, and out of welldoing may come bane and death. Because he saw also that in the moment of Arthur's death his glory would have reached and passed its fullness, but that by that death the glory would live on to be a light and a trumpet-call and a breath of life for men to come."

When she stopped speaking it seemed as if a faint echo of her voice, like a harp string thrumming, wound on and on in the air, to vibrate at last into silence.

At length Mordred spoke. "But you must know that I would not willingly bring evil to the King. I owe him much, and none of it evil. He knew this prophecy from the start, and, believing it, yet took me into his court and accepted me as his son. How, then, can you suppose that I would willingly harm him?"

She said, more gently: "It does not have to be by your will."

"Are you trying to tell me that I can do nothing to avert this fate that you speak of?"

"What will be, will be," she said.

"You cannot help me?"

"To avoid what is in the stars? No."

Mordred, with a movement of violent impatience, got to his feet. She did not move, even when he took a stride forward and towered over her, as if he would strike her.

"This is absurd! The stars! You talk as if men are sheep, and worse than sheep, to be driven by blind fate to do the will of some ill-wishing god! What of *my* will? Am I, despite anything I may wish or do, condemned to be the death or bane of a man I respect, a king I follow? Am I to be a sinner—more, the worst of sinners, a parricide? What gods are these?"

She did not reply. She tilted her head back, still watching him steadily.

He said, angrily: "Very well. You have said, and Merlin has said, and Queen Morgause, who like you was a witch" —her eyes flickered at that, perhaps with annoyance, and he felt a savage pleasure at getting through to her—"that through me the King will meet his doom. You say I cannot avoid this. So? How if I took my dagger—thus—and killed myself here and now? Would that not avert the fate that you say hangs in the stars?"

She had not stirred at the dagger's flash, but now she moved. She rose from her stool and crossed to the window. She stood there with her back to him, looking out. Beyond the open frame was a pear tree, where a blackbird sang.

She spoke without turning.

"Prince Mordred, I did not say that Arthur would meet his doom by your hand or even by your action. Through your existence is all. So kill yourself now if you will it, but through your death his fate might come on him all the sooner."

"But then—" he began desperately.

She turned. "Listen to me. Had Arthur slain you in infancy, it might have happened that men would have risen against him for his cruelty, and that in the uprising he would have been killed. If you kill yourself now, it might be that your brothers, blaming him, would bring him to ruin. Or even that Arthur himself, spurring here to Applegarth at the news, would take a fall from his horse and die, or lie a cripple while his kingdom crumbled round him." She lifted her hands.

"Now do you understand? Fate has more than one arrow. The gods wait behind cloud."

"Then they are cruel!"

"You know that already, do you not?"

He remembered the sickening smell of the burned cottage, the feel of the sea-washed bone in his hand, the lonely cry of the gulls over the beach.

He met the grey eyes, and saw compassion there. He said quietly: "So what can a man do?"

"All that we have," she said, "is to live what life brings. Die what death comes."

"That is black counsel."

"Is it?" she said. "You cannot know that."

"What do you mean?"

"I mean that you cannot know what life will bring. All I can tell you is this: that whatever years of life are left for you and for your father, they will see ambition realized, and will bring fulfillment and their meed of glory, both for him and for you."

He stood silent at that. It was more than he had imagined or expected, that she would give him not only a qualified hope, but the promise of a life fulfilled.

He said: "So it won't serve for me to leave court, and stay away from him?"

"No."

He smiled for the first time. "Because he wants me where he can see me? Because the arrow by daylight is better to face than the knife in the dark?"

There was a glimmer of a smile in reply. "You are like him," was all she said, but he felt the interview begin to lighten. A sombre lady, this one. She was beautiful, yes, but he would as soon, he thought, have touched a rousing falcon.

"You can't tell me any more? Anything?"

"I do not know more."

"Would Merlin know? And would he tell me?"

"What he knew, I know," she said again. "I told you, I am Merlin."

"You said this before. Is it some kind of riddling way of telling me that his power is gone, or just that I may not approach him?" He spoke with renewed impatience. "All my life I seem to have been listening to rumours of magical deaths and vanishings, and they are never true. Tell me straightly, if you will: if I go to Bryn Myrddin, will I find him?"

"If he wishes it, yes."

"Then he is still there?"

"He is where he always was, with all his fires and travelling glories round him."

As they talked the sun had moved round, and the light from the window touched her face. He saw faint lines on the smooth brow, the shadow of fatigue under the eyes, a dew of transparency on her skin.

He said abruptly: "I am sorry if I have wearied you."

She did not deny it. She said merely: "I am glad you came," and followed him to the tower doorway.

"Thank you for your patience," he said, and drew breath for a formal farewell, but a shout from the courtyard below startled him. He swung round and looked down. Nimuë came swiftly to his elbow.

"You'd better go down, and hurry! Your horse has slipped his tether, and I think he has eaten some of the new seedlings." Her face lit with mischief, young and alive, like that of a child who misbehaves in a shrine. "If Varro kills you with his spade, as seems likely, we shall see how the fates will deal with *that*!"

He kissed her hand and ran down to retrieve his horse. As he rode away she watched him with eyes that were once again sad, but no longer hostile.

7

Mordred was half afraid that the King would ask him what his business had been with Nimuë, but he did not. He sent for his son next day and spoke of the proposed visit to the Saxon king, Cerdic.

"I would have left you in charge at home, which would have been useful experience for you, but it will be even more useful for you to meet Cerdic and attend the talks, so as ever I am leaving Bedwyr. I might almost say as regent, since officially I am leaving my own kingdom for a foreign one. Have you ever met a Saxon, Mordred?"

"Never. Are they really all giants, who drink the blood of babies?"

The King laughed. "You will see. They are certainly most of them big men, and their customs are outlandish. But I am told, by those who know them and can speak their tongue, that their poets and artists are to be respected. Their fighting men certainly are. You will find it interesting."

"How many men will you take?"

"Under truce, only a hundred. A regal train, no more."

"You can trust a Saxon to keep a truce?"

"Cerdic, yes, though with most Saxons it's a case of trust only from strength, and keep the memory of Badon still green. But don't repeat that," said Arthur.

Agravain was also in the chosen hundred, but neither

Gawain nor Gareth. These two had gone north together soon after the council meeting. Gawain had spoken of travelling to Dunpeldyr and perhaps thence to Orkney, and, though suspecting that his nephew's real quest was far otherwise, Arthur could think of no good reason for preventing him. Hoping that Lamorak might have ridden westward to join his brother under Drustan's standard, he had to content himself with sending a courier into Dumnonia with a warning.

The King and his hundred set out on a fine and blowy day of June. Their way took them over the high downs. Small blue butterflies and dappled fritillaries fluttered in clouds over the flowery turf. Larks sang. Sunlight fell in great gold swaths over the ripening cropfields, and peasants, white with the blowing chalk dust, looked up from their work and saluted the party with smiles. The troop rode at ease, talking and laughing together, and the mood was light.

Except, apparently, for Agravain. He drew alongside Mordred where he was riding a little apart, some way behind the King, who was talking with Cei and Bors.

"Our first sally with the High King, and look at it. A carnival." He spoke with contempt. "All that talk of war, and kingdoms changing hands, and raising armies to defend our shores again, and this is all it comes to! He's getting old, that's what it is. We should drive these Saxons back into the sea first, and then it would be time enough to talk. . . . But no! What do we do? Here we ride with the duke of battles, and on a peace mission. To Saxons. Ally with Saxons? Pah!" He spat. "He should have let me go with Gawain."

"Did you ask to?"

"Of course."

"That was a peace mission, too," said Mordred, woodenly, looking straight between his horse's ears. "There was no trouble forecast in Dunpeldyr, only a little diplomatic talking with Tydwal, and Gareth along to keep it muted."

"Don't play the innocent with me!" said Agravain angrily. "You know why he's gone.

"I can guess. Anyone can guess. But if he does find Lamorak, or news of him, let us hope that Gareth can persuade him to show a little sense. Why else do you suppose Gareth asked to go?" Mordred turned and looked straight at Agravain. "And if he should come across Gaheris, you may hope the same thing yourself. I suppose you know where

Gaheris is? Well, if Gawain catches up with either of them, you'd best know nothing about it. And I want to know nothing."

"You? You're so deep in the King's counsels that I'm surprised you haven't warned him."

"There was no need. He must know as well as you do what Gawain hopes to do. But he can't mew him up for ever. What the King cannot prevent, he will not waste time over. All he can do is hope, probably in vain, that wise counsel will prevail."

"And if Gawain does run across Lamorak, which might happen, even by accident, what do you expect him to do then?"

"Lamorak must protect himself. He's quite capable of it." He added: "Live what life brings. Die what death comes."

Agravain stared. "What? What sort of talk is that?"

"Something I heard recently. So what about Gaheris? Are you content for Gawain to run across him, too?"

"He'll not find Gaheris," said Agravain confidently.

"Oh, so you do know where he is?"

"What do you think? He got word to me, of course. And the King doesn't know that, you may be sure! He's not as all-knowing as you think, brother." He slid a sideways look at Mordred, and his lowered voice was sly. "There's quite a lot that he doesn't see."

Mordred did not answer, but Agravain went on without prompting:

"Else he'd hardly go off on an unnecessary jaunt like this and leave Bedwyr in Camelot."

"Someone has to stay."

"With the Queen?"

Mordred turned to look at him again. The tone, the look, said what the bare words had not expressed. He spoke with contemptuous anger: "I'm no fool, nor am I deaf. I hear what the dirty tongues say. But you'd best keep yours clean, brother."

"Are you threatening me?"

"I don't need to. Let the King once hear—"

"If it's true they're lovers, he ought to hear."

"It cannot be true! Bedwyr is close to the King and Queen, yes, but—"

"And they do say the husband is always the last to guess."

Mordred felt a wave of fury so strong that it startled him. He began to speak, then, glancing towards the King's back and the riders to either side, said merely, in a low, suppressed voice: "Leave it. It's fool's talk anywhere, and here you might be overheard. And keep your tongue off it with me. I want no part of it."

"You were ready enough to listen when your own mother's virtue was questioned."

Mordred said, exasperated: "Questioned! I was there, my God! I saw her lying with him!"

"And cared so little that you let the man escape!"

"Let it go, Agravain! If Gaheris had killed Lamorak there, while the King was still negotiating with Drustan to leave Dumnonia and join the Companions—"

"You thought of *that? Then?* With her—them—*that* in front of your eyes?"

"Yes."

Agravain stared with bolting eyes. The blood flushed his cheeks and ran into his forehead. Then, with a sound of contempt and helpless fury, he reined his horse back so sharply that blood sprang on the bit. Mordred, relieved of his presence, rode on alone, until Arthur, turning, saw him there and beckoned him forward.

"See! There is the border. And we are awaited. The man in the center, the fair man in the blue mantle, that's Cerdic himself."

Cerdic was a big man, with silvery hair and beard, and blue eyes. He wore a long robe of grey, with over it a caped blue mantle. He was unarmed save for his dagger, but a page behind him bore his sword, the heavy Saxon broadsword, sheathed in leather bound with worked gold. On his long, carefully combed hair was a tall crown also of gold, elaborately chased, and in his left hand he held a staff which, from its golden finial and carved shaft, appeared to be a staff of royal office. Beside him waited an interpreter, an elderly man who, it transpired, had been son and grandson of federates, and had spent all his life within the bounds of the Saxon Shore.

Behind Cerdic stood his thegns, or warrior lords, dressed like their king save that where he wore a crown, they had tall caps of brightly coloured leather. Their horses, small beasts that showed almost like ponies beside Arthur's carefully bred cavalry mounts, were held in the background by their grooms.

Arthur and his party dismounted. The kings greeted one another, two tall men, richly dressed and glittering with jewels, dark and fair, eyeing one another over the unspoken truce like big dogs held back on leash. Then, as if some spark of liking had suddenly been kindled between them, they both smiled and, each at the same moment, held out a hand. They grasped one another's arms, and kissed.

It was the signal. The ranks of tall blond warriors broke, moving forward with shouts of welcome. The grooms came running forward with the horses, and the party remounted. Mordred, beckoned forward by the King, received Cerdic's ceremonial kiss, then found himself riding between the Saxon king and a red-haired thegn who was a cousin of Cerdic's queen.

It was not far to the Saxon capital, perhaps an hour's ride, and they took it slowly. The two kings seemed content to let their mounts pace gently, side by side, while they talked, with the interpreter craning to catch and relay what was said.

Mordred, on Cerdic's other side, could hear little, and after a while ceased trying to listen through the shouts and laughter of the troop, as Saxon and Briton tried to make themselves mutually understood. He and his neighbour, with gestures and grins, managed to exchange names: the red-haired thegn was called Bruning. A few of the Saxons — those who had spent all their lives in the federated territories of the Shore—knew enough of the others' language; these were mostly the older men; the younger men on both sides had to depend on goodwill and laughter to establish some sort of rapport. Agravain, scowling, rode apart with a small group of the younger Britons, who talked among themselves in low tones, and were ignored.

Mordred, looking about him, found plenty to interest him in the landscape that very soon began, even in the scant miles traversed, to look foreign. Lacking an interpreter, he and Bruning contented themselves with exchanging smiles from time to time, and occasionally pointing to some feature that they passed. The fields here were differently tilled; the instruments used by the working peasants were strange, some crude, some ingenious. Such buildings as they passed were very different from the stone-built structures he knew; here little stone was used, but the huts and shippons of the peasants showed great skill in the working of wood. The grazing cattle and flocks looked fat and well cared for.

A flock of geese, screaming, flapped across the road, sending the foremost of the horses rearing and plunging. The goosegirl, a flaxen child with round blue eyes and a lovely face aflame with blushes, scampered after them, waving her stick. Arthur, laughing, threw her a coin, and she called something in response, caught it, and ran off after her geese. The Saxons, it seemed, were not in awe of kings; indeed, the cavalcade that Agravain had angrily called a carnival now really began to bear that appearance. The younger men whistled and called after the running girl, who had kilted her long skirts up and was running as lightly as a boy, with a free display of long bare legs. Bruning, pointing, leaned across towards Mordred.

"Hwæt! Fæger mægden!"

Mordred nodded with a smile, then realized with surprise what had been slowly coming through to him now for some minutes. Through the shouting and laughter had come words here and there, and sometimes phrases, which, without consciously translating, he found himself understanding. "A fair maid! See!" The half-musical, half-guttural sounds were linked in his brain to images of his childhood: the smell of the sea, the tossing boats, the voices of fishermen, the beauty of the sharp-prowed ships that sometimes crossed the fishing grounds of the islanders; the big blond sailors who put into the Orcadian harbours in rough weather to shelter, or in fine weather to trade. He did not think they had been Saxons, but there must be many words and inflections common to Saxon and Norseman alike. He set himself to listen, and found sense coming back to him in snatches, as of poems learned in infancy.

But, being Mordred, he said nothing, and gave no sign. He rode on, listening.

Then they crossed the brow of a grassy hill, and the Saxon capital lay below them.

Mordred's first thought, on sighting Cerdic's capital, was that it was little more than a crudely built village. His second was amusement at the distance he, the fisherman's son, had travelled since the days when an even cruder village in the islands had struck him dumb with excitement and admiration.

The so-called capital of Cerdic was a large scattered collection of wooden buildings enclosed by a palisade. Within the palisade, centrally, stood the king's house, a big oblong structure, barnlike in size and made entirely of wood, with a steeply pitched roof of wattled thatch and a central vent for smoke. There was a door at either end of the hall, and windows, narrow and high, set at intervals along the walls. It was symmetrically built, and one would have said handsome, until memory recalled the gilded towers of Camelot and the great Roman-based stone structures of Caerleon or Aquae Sulis.

The other houses, also symmetrically built but much smaller, clustered around the king's house, apparently at random. Among them, beside them, even alongside their walls, stood the sheds for the beasts. The open spaces between the buildings swarmed with hens, pigs and geese, and children and dogs played in and out of the wheels of oxcarts, or among the scattered trees where the woodpiles stood. The air smelled of dung and freshly mown grass and wood-smoke.

The big gates stood wide open. The party rode through, under a cross-beam from which blew Cerdic's pennant, a slim, forked blue flag that cracked in the breeze like a whiplash. At the door of the hall stood Cerdic's queen, ready to receive the visitors into her house as her husband had received them into the kingdom's boundaries. She was almost as tall as her husband, crowned like him, and with her long flax-fair plaits bound with gold. She greeted Arthur, and after him Mordred and Cei, with the ceremonial kiss of welcome, and thereafter, to Mordred's surprise, accompanied the royal party into the hall. The rest of the troop stayed outside, where, in time, the distant shouting and the clash of metal and the hammering of hoofs indicated that the younger warriors, Saxons and British together, were competing in sport on the field outside the palisade.

The royal party, with the interpreter in attendance, seated themselves beside the central hearth, where the fire, freshly piled, was not yet lighted. Two girls, like fair copies of Cerdic, came carrying jugs of mead and ale. The queen herself, rising, took the jugs from her daughters' hands and poured for the guests. Then the maidens went, but the queen remained, seating herself again on her lord's left.

The talk, necessarily slowed by the need for translation, went on through the afternoon. For a beginning, the discussion kept mainly to home matters, trade and markets, and a possible revision, in the future, of the boundary between the kingdoms. Only as a corollary to this, the talk turned eventually on the possibility of mutual military aid. Cerdic was already conscious of the growing pressures being exerted against his countrymen in their ever-narrowing territory on the Continent. The East Saxons, more vulnerable than Cerdic's people, were already seeking alliances with the English between the Thames and the Humber. He himself had approached the Middle Saxons of Suthrige. When Arthur asked if he, Cerdic, had also explored an alliance with the South Saxons, whose kingdom, in the far southeast corner of Britain, was the nearest landfall for any ships from across the Narrow Sea, Cerdic was guarded. Since the death of the great leader of the South Saxons, Aelle, there had been no ruler of note. "*Nithings*" was the West Saxon king's expressive word. Arthur did not pursue the question, but turned to the news from the Continent. Cerdic had not heard of the death of Clodomir's children, and looked grave as he considered the probable changes that would ensue, and the increasingly hazardous position of Brittany, the only buffer state between the Shore territories of Britain and the threatened Frankish kingdoms. As the time wore on, it no longer seemed so outlandish an idea that at some time in the near future, Briton and Saxon might have to be at one in the defense of their country's shores.

At length the talk came to a close. In the doorway of the hall the sunlight slanted low and mellow. From the field outside, the sounds of sport had died down. Cattle were lowing as they were driven in for milking, and the smell of wood fires sharpened the air. The breeze had dropped. The queen rose and left the hall, and presently servants came running to set the boards up for supper, and to thrust a torch into the kindling for the fire.

Somewhere, a horn sounded. The warriors, Cerdic's and Arthur's together, came in still gay with their sport, and took their places, apparently at random, at the long tables, where, shouting as loudly as if still out on the open down, and hammering on the board with the handles of their daggers, they called for food and drink. The noise was tremendous. Arthur's Companions, after a few moments of deafened confusion, cheerfully joined in the tumult. Language ceased to matter. What was being said was more than clear to everyone. Then a fresh shouting arose as ale and mead were brought in, and after that the great trays of roasted meats, still smoking and sizzling from the ovens; and the Saxon thegns, who until then had been trying, with gestures and yells of laughter, to communicate, ceased abruptly and turned all their ferocious attention to eating and drinking. Someone handed Mordred a horn—it was polished like ivory and most beautifully mounted with gold—someone else filled it till it slopped over, then he in his turn had to give his full attention to his platter, which soon meant parrying his neighbours' efforts to pile his dish again and again with the best of the food.

The ale was strong and the mead stronger. Many of the warriors were soon drunk, and slept where they sat. Some, too, of Arthur's train succumbed to the overwhelming hospitality, and began to doze. Mordred, still sober, but knowing that he was only so by an effort, narrowed his eyes against the low sun from the open door, and looked to see how the kings were faring. Cerdic was flushed, and leaning back in his chair, but still talked; Arthur, though his platter was empty, looked as cool as might be in that heated hall. Mordred saw how he had done it: His big hound, Cabal, lay by his chair, licking his chops under the table.

The sun set, and presently torches were lit, filling the hall with smoky light. In the still evening the fire burned brightly, the smoke filtering up through the vent in the thatch, or drifting among the diners to make them cough and wipe their eyes. At length, when the platters were empty, and the drinking horns held out less frequently for filling, the entertainment began.

First came a troop of gleemen, who danced to the music of trumpets and horns, and with them a pair of jugglers who, first with coloured balls, then with daggers or with anything those lords still sober threw to them, made dazzling patterns in the smoky air. The two kings threw money down, and the gleemen, scooping it up, bowed and went, still jigging and dancing. Then the harper took his place. He was a thin dark man, in an embroidered robe that looked costly. He set his stool near the hearth, and bent his head to tune the strings. Mordred saw Arthur turn his head quickly at the sound, then sink back in his chair to listen, his face in shadow.

Gradually the noise in the hall sank to a silence qualified only by some drunken snoring, and an occasional snarling wrangle from the dogs fighting in the straw for scraps.

The harper began to sing. His voice was true, and, as such men are, he was learned in tongues. He sang first in the guests' language, a love song, and then a lament. Then, in his own tongue, he sang a song which, after the first half-dozen lines, held every man there who could hear it, whether he understood the words or not.

> *. . . Sad, sad the faithful man*
> *Who outlives his lord.*
> *He sees the world stand waste*
> *As a wall blown on by the wind,*
> *As an empty castle, where the snow*
> *Sifts through the window-frames,*
> *Drifts on the broken bed*
> *And the black hearthstone. . . .*

Bruning the redhead, who was opposite Mordred, was sitting as still as a mouse, with the tears running down his face. Mordred, moved at the touch of some long-forgotten grief, had to exert all his self-command not to show his own emotion. Suddenly, as if his name had been called, he turned to find his father watching him. The two men's eyes, so like, locked and held. In Arthur's was something of the look that he had seen in Nimuë's: a helpless sadness. In his own, he knew, were rebellion and a fierce will. Arthur smiled at him and looked away as the applause began. Mordred got swiftly to his feet and went out of the hall.

Throughout the long feasting men had gone out from time to time to relieve themselves, so no one queried his going, or even glanced after him.

The gates were shut, but within the palisade the place was clear. Beasts, poultry and children had all been herded in with sunset to supper and bed, and now the menfolk and their women were mostly withindoors. He paced slowly along in the shadow of the palisade, trying to think.

Nimuë and her stark message: *Your will is nothing, your existence is all.* The King, who many years back had had the same message, and had left it to those cruel, clouded gods . . .

But there would be ambition fulfilled, and his due of glory.

Not, of course, that a practical man believed in such soothsaying. Nor could he believe, by the same token, in the prophecies of doom. . . .

He pressed a palm to his forehead. The air felt cool and sweet after the smoky reek of the hall. Gradually his brain cleared. He knew how far he must be from realizing his ambitions, those secret ambitions and desires. It would be many years, surely, before he or the King need fear what the evil gods might have in store. What Arthur had done for him all those years ago, he could do for Arthur now. Forget "doom," and wait for the future to show itself.

A movement in the shadow of a tall woodpile caught his eye. A man, one of Arthur's followers. Two men; no, three. One of them moved across the glow of a distant cooking fire, and Mordred recognized Agravain. Not out here simply to relieve himself. He had seated himself on the shaft of a cart that stood empty by the woodpile, and his two companions stood by him, bending near and talking eagerly. One of them, Calum, he knew; the other he thought he recognized. Both were young Celts, close friends of Agravain and formerly of Gaheris. When Agravain had left Mordred's side in anger during the ride, he had re-joined the group where these two were riding, and snatches of their conversation had come from time to time to Mordred's ears.

Abruptly, all thought of Nimuë and her cloudy stars went from his head. The Young Celts; the phrase had recently taken on something of a political meaning, in the sense of a party of young fighting men drawn mostly from the outland Celtic kingdoms, who were impatient with "the High King's peace" and the centralization of lowland government, and bored with the role of peaceful law-enforcement created for his knights-errant. There had been little open opposition; the young men tended to sneer at the "old man's market-place" of the Round Hall; they talked among themselves, and some of the talk, it was rumoured, verged on sedition.

Such as the whispering, which in recent weeks had grown as if somehow carefully fostered, about Bedwyr and Queen Guinevere.

Mordred moved silently away until a barn interposed its

213

bulk between him and the little group of men. Pacing, head bent, brain working coolly now, he thought back.

It was true that in all his close dealings with them, he had never seen the Queen favour Bedwyr by word or look above other men, except as Arthur's chief friend, and in Arthur's presence. Her bearing towards him was, if anything, almost too ceremonious. Mordred had wondered, sometimes, at the air of constraint that could occasionally be felt between two people who had known one another for so long, and in such intimacy. No—he checked himself—not constraint. Rather, a distance carefully kept, where no distance seemed to be necessary. Where in fact distance seemed hardly to matter. Several times Mordred had noticed that Bedwyr seemed to know what the Queen meant without her having to put her thoughts into words.

He shook the thought away. This was poison, the poison Agravain had tried to distil. He would not even think this way. But there was one thing he could do. Like it or not, he was linked with the Orkney brothers, and lately most closely with Agravain. If Agravain approached him again, he would listen, and find out if the Young Celts' dissatisfaction was anything more than the natural rebellion of young men against the rule of their elders. As for the whispering campaign concerning Bedwyr and the Queen, that was surely only a matter of policy, too. A wedge driven in between Arthur and his oldest friend, the trusted regent who held his seal and acted as his other self, that would be the aim of any party seeking to weaken the High King's position and undermine his policies. There, too, he must listen; there, too, if he dared, he must warn the King. Of the slanders only; there were no facts; there was no truth in tales of Bedwyr and the Queen. . . .

He pushed the thought aside with a violence that was, he told himself, a tribute to his loyalty to his father, and his gratitude to the lovely lady who had shown such kindness to the lonely boy from the islands.

On the ride home he stayed away from Agravain.

8

He could not avoid him, though, once they were back in Camelot.

Some time after their return from Cerdic's capital the King sent again for Mordred, and asked him to stay close and watch his half-brother.

It transpired that word had come from Drustan, the famous fighting captain whom Arthur had hoped to attract to his standard, that, his term of service in Dumnonia being done, he himself, his northern stronghold and his troop of trained fighting men would soon be put at the High King's disposal. He was even now on his way north to his castle of Caer Mord, to put it in readiness, before coming on himself to Camelot.

"So far, good," said Arthur. "I need Caer Mord, and I had hoped for this. But Drustan, for some affair of honour in the past, is sworn blood-brother to Lamorak, and has, moreover, Lamorak's own brother, Drian, at present in his service. I believe you know this. Well, he has already made it clear that he will require me to invite Lamorak back to Camelot."

"And will you?"

"How can I avoid it? He did no wrong. Perhaps he chose his time badly, and perhaps he was deceived, but he was betrothed to her. And even if he had not been," said the

King wryly, "I am the last man living who would have the right to condemn him for what he did."

"And I the next."

The King sent him a glance that was half a smile, but his voice was sober. "You see what will happen. Lamorak will come back, and then, unless the three older brothers can be brought to see reason, we shall have a blood feud that will split the Companions straight through."

"So Lamorak is with Drustan?"

"No. Not yet. I have not told you the rest. I know now that he went to Brittany, and has been lodging there with Bedwyr's cousin, who keeps Benoic for him. I have had letters. They tell me that Lamorak has left Benoic, and it is believed that he has taken ship for Northumbria. It seems likely that he knows of Drustan's plans, and hopes to join him at Caer Mord. What is it?"

"Northumbria," said Mordred. "My lord, I believe—I know—that Agravain is in touch with Gaheris, and I also have reason to suspect that Gaheris is somewhere in Northumbria."

"Near Caer Mord?" asked Arthur sharply.

"I don't know. I doubt it. Northumbria is a big country, and Gaheris surely cannot know of Lamorak's movements."

"Unless he has news of Drustan's, and makes a guess, or Agravain has heard some rumour here at court, and got word to him," said Arthur. "Very well. There is only one thing to do: get your brothers back here to Camelot, where they may be watched and to some extent controlled. I shall send to Gawain with a strong warning, and summon him south again. Eventually, if I have to, and if Lamorak will agree, I shall let Gawain offer him combat, here, and publicly. That should surely suffice to cool this bad blood. How Gawain receives Gaheris is his own affair; there, I cannot interfere."

"You'd have Gaheris back?"

"If he is in Northumbria, and Lamorak is making for Caer Mord, I must."

"On the principle that it is better to watch the arrow flying, than leave it to strike unseen?"

For a moment Mordred thought he had made a mistake. The King flashed a quick glance at him, as if about to ask a question. Perhaps Nimuë had used the same image to him,

216

and about Mordred himself. But Arthur passed it by. He said: "I shall leave this to you, Mordred. You say that Agravain is in touch with his twin. I shall let it be known that the sentence on Gaheris is rescinded, and send Agravain to bring him back. I shall insist that you go with him. It's the best I can do; I distrust them, but beyond sending you I dare not show it. I can hardly send troops to make sure they come back. Do you think he will accept this?"

"I think so. I'll contrive it somehow."

"You realize that I am asking you to be a spy? To watch your own kinsmen? Is this something you can bring yourself to do?"

Mordred said, abruptly: "Have you ever watched a cuckoo in the nest?"

"No."

"They are all over the moors at home. Almost as soon as they are hatched, they throw their kin out of the nest, and remain—" He had been going to add "to rule," but stopped himself in time. He did not even know that he had thought the words. He finished, lamely: "I only meant that I shall be breaking no natural law, my lord."

The King smiled. "Well, I am the first to assert that my son would be better than any of Lot's. So watch Agravain for me, Mordred, and bring them both back here. Then perhaps," he finished a little wearily, "given time, the Orkney swords may go back into the sheath."

Soon after this, on a bright day at the beginning of October, Agravain followed Mordred as he walked through the market-place in Camelot, and overtook him near the fountain.

"I have the King's permission to ride north. But not alone, he says. And you are the only one of the knights he can spare. Will you come with me?"

Mordred stopped, and allowed a look of surprise to show. "To the islands? I think not."

"Not to the islands. D'you think I'd go there in October? No." Agravain lowered his voice, though no one was near except two children dabbling their hands in the fountain. "He tells me that he will revoke the ban on Gaheris. He'll let him come back to court. He asked me where he might send the courier, but I told him I was pledged, and couldn't break a pledge. So he says now that I may go myself to bring him back, if you go with me." A sneer, thinly veiled. "It seems he trusts you."

Mordred ignored the sneer. "This is good news. Very well, I'll go with you, and willingly. When?"

"As soon as may be."

"And where?"

Agravain laughed. "You'll find out when you get there. I told you I was pledged."

"You've been in touch all this time, then?"

"Of course. Wouldn't you expect it?"

"How? By letter?"

"How could he send letters? He has no scribe to read or write for him. No, from time to time I've had messages from traders, fellows like that merchant over there who is setting up his cloth stall. So get yourself ready, brother, and we'll go in the morning."

"A long journey? You'll have to tell me that, at least."

"Long enough."

The children, back at their play, sent a ball rolling past Mordred's feet. He reached a toe after it, flipped it up, caught it, and sent it back to them. He dusted his hands together, smiling.

"Very well. I'd like to go with you. It will be good to ride north again. You still won't tell me where we'll be bound for?"

"I'll show you when we get there," repeated Agravain.

They came at length, at the end of a dull and misty afternoon, to a small half-ruined turret on the Northumbrian moors.

The place was wild and desolate. Even the empty moors of mainland Orkney, with their lochs, and the light that spoke of the ever-present sea, seemed lively in comparison with this.

On every hand stretched the rolling fells, the heather dark purple in the misty light of evening. The sky was piled with clouds, and no glimmer of sun spilled through. The air was still, with no wind, no fresh breath from the sea. Here and there streams or small rivers, their courses marked with alders and pale rushes, divided the hills. The tower was set in a hollow near one such stream. The land was boggy, and boulders had been set as stepping-stones across a stretch of mire. The tower, thickly covered with ivy, and surrounded with stumps of mossy fruit trees and elderberries, seemed, once, to have been a pleasant dwelling; could be still, on a sunny day. But on this misty autumn evening it was a gloomy place. At one window of the tower a dim light showed.

They tethered their horses to a thorn tree, and rapped at the door. It was opened by Gaheris himself.

He had only been away from court for a few months, but already he looked as if he had never been in civilized company. His beard, carrot red, was half grown, his hair unkempt and hanging loose over his shoulders. The leather jerkin that he wore was greased and dirty. But his face lit with pleasure at seeing the two men, and the embrace he gave Mordred was the warmest that the latter had yet received from him.

"Welcome! Agravain, I'd hardly hoped that you'd get away, and come here to see me! And Mordred, too. Does the King know? But you'll have kept your word, I don't need to ask that. It seems a long time. Ah, well, come in and rest yourselves. You'll have plenty to tell me, that's for sure, so be welcome, and come in."

He led them to a smallish room in the curve of the tower wall, where a peat fire burned, and a lamp was lit. A girl sat by the hearth, stitching. She looked up, half shy, half scared at the sight of company. She had a longish pale face, not uncomely, and soft brown hair. She was poorly dressed in a gown of murrey homespun, whose clumsy folds did nothing to disguise the signs of pregnancy.

"My brothers," said Gaheris. "Get them something to eat and drink, then see to their horses."

He made no attempt to present her to them. She got to her feet, and, murmuring something, gave a quick, unpracticed curtsey. Then, laying aside her sewing, she trod heavily to a cupboard at the other side of the room, and took from it wine and meat.

Over the food, which the girl served to them, the three men spoke of general things: the turmoil in the Frankish kingdoms, Brittany's plight, the Saxon embassy, the comings and goings of Arthur's knights-errant, and the gossip of the court, though not as the latter touched the King and Queen. The way the girl loitered wide-eyed over her serving was warning enough against talk of that kind.

At last, at a brusque word from Gaheris about the care of the visitors' horses, she left them.

As the latch fell behind her, Agravain, who had been straining like a hound in the slips, said abruptly:

"It's good news, brother."

Gaheris set his goblet down. Mordred saw, with fastidious distaste, that his nails were rimmed with black. He leaned forward. "Tell me, then. Gawain wants to see me? He knows now that I had to do it? Or"—his eyes glinted in a quick sidelong look, very bright—"he's found where Lamorak is, and wants to join forces?"

"No, nothing like that. Gawain's still in Dunpeldyr, and there's been no word, nothing about Lamorak." Agravain, never subtle, was patently telling the truth as he knew it. "But good news, all the same. The King has sent me to take you back to court. You're free of it, Gaheris, as far as he's concerned. You're to go back to Camelot with Mordred and me."

A pause, then Gaheris, flushing to the eyebrows, let out a yell of glee, and tossed up his empty goblet and caught it again. With his other hand he reached for the wine jug, and poured again for all of them.

"Who's the girl?" asked Mordred.

"Brigit? Oh, her father was steward here. The place was under a siege of a sort from a couple of outlaw fellows, and I killed them. So I got the freedom of the place."

"Freedom indeed." Agravain grinned, drinking. "What does the father say to it? Or did you have to wed her?"

"He said the father was steward." Mordred's dry tone laid slight emphasis on the second verb.

Agravain stared, then nodded briefly. "Ah. Yes. No wedding, then?"

"None." Gaheris set his goblet down with a rap. "So forget that. No strings there. Come, let's have it all."

And, the girl dismissed, the twins plunged into talk of the King's pardon, his possible intentions and those of Gawain. Mordred, listening, sipping his wine, said very little. But he noticed that, surprisingly enough, Lamorak's name was not mentioned again.

Presently the girl came back, took her seat again, and picked up her sewing. It was a small, plain garment of some kind, probably, thought Mordred, for the coming child. She said nothing, but her eyes went from one twin to the other, watching and listening intently. There was anxiety in them now, even a trace of fear. Neither of the twins made any attempt to conceal the elation which both felt at Gaheris's recall to Camelot.

At length, with the lamp guttering and smoking, they prepared to sleep. Gaheris and the girl had a bed not far from the fire, and this, apparently, they were ready to share with Agravain. Mordred, to his relief and slight surprise, was taken outside into the cool fresh night and shown a flight of stone steps curving round the outside of the tower. This led to a small upper chamber, where the air, though chill, was fresh and clean, and a pile of heather and rugs made a bed better than many he had slept on. Tired from the ride, and the talk, he slipped off his clothes, and was soon fast asleep.

When he awoke it was morning. Cocks crowed outside, and a chill grey light filtered through the cobwebs of the slit window. There was no sound from the room below.

He threw back the covers and padded barefooted across to look out of the window. From here he could see the tumbledown shed that served as stable and henhouse combined. The girl Brigit was standing there, a basket of eggs on the ground beside her. She was scattering some remains of last night's food for the hens, which pecked and scratched, clucking, round her feet.

The stable was an open structure, back and side walls, a stone manger, and a sloping roof supported on pillars made from hewn pine trunks. From the window he could see the whole of the interior. And what he saw there sent him back to the bedplace, to snatch up his clothes and begin to dress with feverish haste.

There was only one horse standing in the stable. His own. The ropes that had tied his half-brothers' beasts trailed in the straw among the strutting hens.

He dressed quickly. No use cursing himself. Whatever had led his brothers to deceive him and to ride off without him, he could not have foreseen. He snatched up his sword belt, and, still buckling it on, ran down the stone steps. The girl heard him, and turned.

"Where have they gone?" he demanded.

"I don't know. Hunting, I think. They said not to wake

you, and they will come back soon for breakfast." But she looked scared.

"Don't fool with me, girl. This is urgent. You must have some idea where they've gone. What do you know?"

"I—no, sir. I don't know. Truly, sir. But they will come back. Perhaps tomorrow. Perhaps two days. I will look after you well—"

He was towering over her. He saw that she had begun to tremble. He took hold of himself, and spoke more gently.

"Listen—Brigit, isn't it? Don't be afraid of me. I shall not hurt you. But this is important. It's King's business. Yes, as important as that. To begin with, how long have they been gone?"

"About four hours, lord. They went even before dawn."

He bit his lip. Then, still gently: "Good girl. Now, there must be more that you can tell me. You must have heard them talking. What did they say? They were riding out to meet someone, is that it?"

"Y—yes. A knight."

"Did they mention a name? Was it Lamorak?"

She was trembling now, and her hands twisted together in front of her.

"Was it? Go on. Speak. You must tell me."

"Yes. Yes. That was the name. He was an evil knight who had dishonoured my lord's mother. He told me of it before."

"Where did they expect to meet this Lamorak?"

"There's a castle on the shore, many miles from here. When my lord went into the village yesterday, he heard— the traders pass through, and he goes for news—he heard that this knight Lamorak was expected there." The words were tumbling out now. "He was expected by sea, from Brittany, I think, and there is no harbour near the castle, no landing that is safe, with the weather we've been having, so they expected he would land half a day's ride to the south, and then, when he had found himself a horse, he would ride up the coast road. My lord Gaheris wanted to meet him there, before he got to the castle."

"Waylay him, you mean, and murder him!" said Mordred savagely. "That is, if Lamorak does not kill him first. And his brother, too. It's very possible. He is a veteran, one of

222

the King's Companions, and a good fighter. He is also a man dear to the King."

She stared, her face whitening. Her hands crept, shaking, to clasp one another below her breast, as if to protect the child who lay there.

"If you value your lord's life," said Mordred grimly, "you'll tell me everything. This castle. Is it Caer Mord?"

She nodded dumbly.

"Where is it, and how far?" He put out a hand. "No, wait. Get me some food, quickly, while I saddle my horse. Anything. You can tell me the rest later, while I eat. If you want to save your lord's life, help me to get on my way. Hurry now."

She caught up the basket of eggs, and ran. He dashed water over face and hands at the trough, then threw saddle and bridle on his horse, and, leaving it tethered, ran back into the tower. The girl had set bread and meat on the table by the cold ashes of the fire. She was crying as she poured wine for him.

He drank quickly, and chewed bread, washing it down with more of the wine.

"Now, quickly. What happened? What more did you hear?"

The threat to Gaheris had loosened her tongue. She told him readily: "After you'd gone up last night, sir, they were talking. I was in bed. I went to sleep, then when my lord did not come to bed, I woke, and I heard . . ."

"Well?"

"He was speaking of this Lamorak, who was coming to Caer Mord. My lord was full of joy because he has sworn to kill him, and now his brother had come, just at the right moment to go with him. He said—my lord said—that it was the work of the Goddess who had brought his brother to help him avenge his mother's death. He had sworn on his mother's blood . . ." She faltered and stopped.

"Yes? Did he tell you who shed his mother's blood?"

"Why, the evil knight! Was it not so, lord?"

"Go on."

"So he was overjoyed, and they planned to ride straight away, together, without telling you. They did not come to bed at all. They thought I was asleep, and they went out very quietly. I—I did not dare let them know I had heard what was said, but I was afraid, so I lied to you. My lord talked as if—" she gulped, "—as if he were mad."

"So he is," said Mordred. "All right. This is what I feared. Now tell me which way they have taken." Then, as she hesitated again: "This is an innocent man, Brigit. If your lord Gaheris kills him, he will have to answer to the High King Arthur. Now, don't weep, girl. The ship may not be in yet, nor Lamorak on the road. If you tell me the way, I may well catch them before the harm is done. My horse is rested, where Agravain's is not." He thought, with a thread of pity running through the desperate need for haste, that whatever happened the girl had probably seen the last of her lover, but there was nothing he could do about that. She was just another innocent to add to the toll that Morgause had taken through her life and death.

He poured some of the wine for her, and pushed the cup into her hand. "Come, drink. It will make you feel better. Quickly now. The way to Caer Mord."

Even this small act of kindness seemed to overset her. She drank, and gulped back her tears. "I am not sure, lord. But if you ride to the village—that way—and down to the river, you will find a forge there, and the smith will tell you. He knows all the ways." And then, sobbing afresh: "He will not come back, will he? He will be killed, or else he will leave me, and go south to the great court, and I have nothing, and how will I care for the child?"

Mordred laid three gold pieces on the table. "These will keep you. And as for the child—" He stopped. He did not add: "You will do well to drown it at birth." That went too close for comfort. He merely said goodbye, and went out into the grey dawning.

By the time he reached the village the sky was whitening, and here and there folk were stirring to their work. The tavern doors were shut, but a hundred paces on, where the roadway forded a shallow stream, the forge fires were lit, and the smith stretched himself, yawning, with a cup of ale in his hand.

"The road to Caer Mord? Why, this road, master. A matter of a day's ride. Go as far as the god-stone, then take the eastward track for the sea."

"Did you hear horsemen going this way in the night?"

"Nay, master. When I sleep, I sleep sound," said the smith.

"And the god-stone? How far?"

The smith ran his expert's eye over Mordred's horse.

"Yon's a good beast you've got there, master, but you've come a long ways, maybe? I thought so. Well, then, not pressing him, say by sunset? And from there, a short half hour to the sea. It is a good road. You'll be safe at Caer Mord, and no mishaps, well before dark."

"That I doubt," said Mordred, setting spurs to his horse, and leaving the smith staring.

9

To Mordred the Orkney man the god-stone, standing alone on the rolling moor, was a familiar sight. And yet not quite familiar. It was a tall standing stone, set in the lonely center of the moor. He had passed its mate many a time, single, or standing with others in a wide ring, on the Orkney moors; but there the stones were thinly slabbed and very high, toothed or jagged as they had been broken from the living cliff. This stone was massive, of some thick grey whinstone carefully shaped into a thick, tapering pillar. There was a flat altar-like slab at its base, with a dark mark on it that might be dried blood.

He reached it at dusk, as the sun, low and red, threw its long shadow across the black heather. He trotted the tired horse up to it. At its base the track forked, and he turned the beast's head to the south-east. From the pale wild look of the sky ahead, and something more than familiar in the air that met him, he knew that the sea could not be far away. Ahead, on the edge of the heather moor, was a thick belt of woodland.

Soon he was among the trees, and the horse's hoofs fell silently on the thick felt of pinedrift and dead leaves. Mordred allowed it to drop to a walk. He himself was weary, and the horse, which had gone bravely through the day, was close to exhaustion. But they had travelled fast, and there was a chance that he might still be in time.

Behind him the clouds, piling up, stifled the colours of sunset. With the approach of evening, a wind got up. The trees rustled and sighed. Sooner than he expected, the forest began to thin, and lighter sky showed beyond the trunks. There was a gap there; the gap, perhaps, where the road ran?

He was answered almost immediately. There must have been other sounds, of hoofs and clashing metal, but the wind had carried them away from him, and the sighing of the trees had drowned them. But now, from almost straight ahead, there came a cry. Not of warning, or of fear, or anger, but a cry of joy, followed by a shout of triumph, and then a yell of laughter, so wild as to sound half mad. The horse's ears pricked, then went flat back to its skull, and its eyes rolled whitely. Mordred struck the spurs in, and the tired beast lurched into a heavy canter.

In the forest's darkness he missed the narrow track. The horse was soon blundering through a thicket of undergrowth, bramble and hazel twined with honeysuckle, and fly-ridden ferns belly high. The canter slowed, became a trot, a walk, a thrusting progress, then stopped as Mordred sharply drew rein.

From here, hidden from sight in the deep shadow of the trees, he could see the level heath that stretched between the woodland and the sea, and, dividing it, the white line of the roadway. On this lay Lamorak, dead. Not far off his horse stood with heaving sides and drooping head. Beside the body, their arms flung round one another, laughing and pounding each other's shoulders, were Agravain and Gaheris. Their horses grazed nearby unheeded.

At that moment, in a lull of the wind, came the sound of horses. The brothers stiffened, loosed one another, ran for their own beasts and mounted hastily. For a moment Mordred thought they might ride for cover into the wood where he stood watching, but already it was too late.

Four horsemen appeared, approaching at a gallop from the north. The leader was a big man, armed, on a splendid horse. Straining his eyes in the twilight, Mordred recognized the leader's device: It was Drustan himself, come riding with a couple of troopers to meet the expected guest.

And beside him, of all men in the world, rode Gareth, youngest of Lot's sons.

Drustan had seen the body. With a ringing shout, he whipped his sword out and rode down upon the killers.

The two brothers whirled to face him, dressing themselves to fight, but Drustan, appearing suddenly to recognize the two assassins, dragged his horse to a halt and put up his sword. Mordred stayed still in shadow, waiting. The matter was out of his hands. He had failed, and if he rode forward now, nothing he could say would persuade the newcomers that he had had no part in Lamorak's murder, nor any knowledge of it. Arthur would know the truth, but Arthur and his justice were a long way away.

It seemed, though, that Arthur's justice ran even here.

Drustan, spurring forward with his troopers at his back, was questioning the brothers. Gareth had jumped from his horse and was kneeling in the dust beside Lamorak's body. Then he ran back to the group of horsemen, and grabbed Gaheris's rein, gesticulating wildly, trying to talk to him.

The brothers were shouting. Words and phrases could be heard above the intermittent rushing of the wind in the branches. Gaheris had shaken Gareth off, and he and Agravain were apparently challenging Drustan to fight. And Drustan was refusing. His voice rang out in snatches, clear and hard and high.

"I shall not fight you. You know the King's orders. Now I shall take this body to the castle yonder and give it burial.... Be assured that the next royal courier will take this news to Camelot.... As for you..."

"Coward! Afraid to fight us!" The yells of rage came back on the wind. "We are not afraid of the High King! He is our kinsman!"

"And shame it is that you come of such blood!" said Drustan, roundly. "Young though you are, you are already murderers, and destroyers of good men. This man that you have killed was a better knight than you could ever be. If I had been here—"

"Then you would have gone the same way!" shouted Gaheris. "Even with your men here to protect you—"

"Even without them, it would have taken more than you two younglings," said Drustan with contempt. He sheathed his sword and turned his back on the brothers. He signalled

228

to the men-at-arms, who took up Lamorak's body, and started back with it the way they had come. Then, hanging on the rein, Drustan spoke to Gareth, who, mounted once more, was hesitating, looking from Drustan to his brothers and back again. Even at that distance it could be seen that his body was rigid with distress. Drustan, nodding to him, and without another glance at Gaheris and Agravain, swung round to follow his men-at-arms.

Mordred turned his horse softly back into the wood. It was over. Agravain, seemingly sober now, had caught at his brother's arm and was holding him, apparently reasoning with him. The shadows were lengthening across the roadway. The men-at-arms were out of sight. Gareth was on Gaheris's other side, talking across him to Agravain.

Then, suddenly, Gaheris flung off his brother's hand, and spurred his horse. He galloped up the road after Drustan's retreating back. His over-ready sword gleamed in his hand. Agravain, after a second's hesitation, spurred after him, his sword, too, whipping from its sheath.

Gareth snatched for Agravain's bridle, and missed. He yelled a warning, high and clear:

"My lord, watch! My lord Drustan, your back!"

Before the words were done Drustan had wheeled his horse. He met the two of them together. Agravain struck first. The older knight smashed the blow to one side and cut him across the head. The sword's edge sliced deep into metal and leather, and bit into the neck between shoulder and throat. Agravain fell, blood spurting. Gaheris yelled and drove his horse in, his sword hacking down as Drustan stooped from the saddle to withdraw his blade. But Drustan's horse reared back. Its armed hoofs caught Gaheris's mount on the chest. It squealed and swerved, and the blow missed. Drustan drove his own horse in, striking straight at Gaheris's shield, and sent him, off-balance as he was, crashing to the ground, where he lay still.

Gareth was there at the gallop. Drustan, swinging to face him, saw that his sword was still in its sheath, and put his own weapon up.

Here the men-at-arms, having left their burden, came hastening back. At their master's orders, they roughly bound Agravain's wound, helped Gaheris, giddy but unharmed, to his feet, then caught the brothers' horses for them. Drustan, coldly formal, offered the hospitality of the castle "until your brother shall be healed of his hurt," but Gaheris, as ungracious as he had been treacherous, merely cursed and turned away. Drustan signed to the troopers, who closed in. Gaheris, shouting again about "my kinsman the High King," tried to resist, but was overpowered. The invitation had become an arrest. At length the troopers rode off at walking pace, with Gaheris between them, his brother's unconscious body propped against him.

Gareth watched them go, making no move to follow. He had not stirred a hand to help Gaheris.

"Gareth?" said Drustan. His sword was clean and sheathed. "Gareth, what choice have I?"

"None," said Gareth. He shook the reins and brought his horse round alongside Drustan's. They rode together towards Caer Mord.

The roadway was empty in the growing dusk. A thin moon rose over the sea. Mordred, emerging at last from the shadow, rode south.

That night he slept in the woods. It was chilly, but wrapped in his cloak he was warm enough, and for supper there was something left of the bread and meat the girl had given him. His horse, tethered on a long rein, grazed in the glade. Next day, early, he rode on, this time to the southwest. Arthur would be on his way to Caerleon, and he would meet him there. There was no haste. Drustan would already have sent a courier with the news of Lamorak's murder. Since Mordred had not appeared on the scene the King would no doubt assume the truth, that the brothers by some trick had managed to evade him. His assignment had not been Lamorak's safety; that was Lamorak's own concern, and he had paid for the risk he had taken; Mordred's task had been to find Gaheris and take him south. Now, once the twins' hurts were healed, Drustan would see to that. Mordred could still stay out of the affair, and this he was sure the King would approve. Even if the brothers did not survive the King's anger, the other trouble-makers among the Young Celts, assuming Mordred to be ambitious for whatever power he could grasp for himself, might turn to him and invite him to join their counsels. This, he suspected, the King would soon ask him to do. And if you do, murmured that other, ice-cold voice in his brain, and the campaign goes on that is to unseat Bedwyr and destroy him, who better to take his place in the King's confidence, and the Queen's love, than you, the King's own son?

It was a golden October, with chill nights and bright, crisp days. The mornings glittered with a dusting of bright frost, and in the evenings the sky was full of the sound of rooks going home. He took his time, sparing his horse, and, where he could, lodging in small, simple places and avoiding the towns. The loneliness, the falling melancholy of autumn, suited his mood. He went by smooth hills and grassy valleys, through golden woods and by steep rocky passes where, on the heights, the trees were already bare. His good bay horse was all the company he needed. Though the nights were cold, and grew colder, he always found shelter of a sort— a sheep-cote, a cave, even a wooded bank—and there was no rain. He would tether the bay to graze, eat the rations he carried, and roll himself in his cloak for the night, to wake in the grey, frost-glittering morning, wash in an icy stream, and ride on again.

Gradually the simplicity, the silence, the very hardships of the ride soothed him; he was Medraut the fisher-boy again, and life was simple and clean.

So he came at last to the Welsh hills, and Viroconium where the four roads meet. And there, at the crossways, like another welcome from home, was a standing stone with its altar at its foot.

He slept that night in a thicket of hazel and holly by the crossroads, in the lee of a fallen trunk. The night was warmer, with stars out. He slept, and dreamed that he was in the boat with Brude, netting mackerel for Sula to split and dry for winter. The nets came in laden with leaping silver, and across the hush of the waves he could hear Sula singing.

He woke to thick mist. The air was warmer; the sudden change in temperature overnight had brought the fog. He shook the crowded droplets from his cloak, ate his breakfast, then on a sudden impulse took the remains of the food and laid it on the altar at the foot of the standing stone. Then, moved by another impulse which he would not begin to recognize, he took a silver piece from his wallet and laid it beside the food. Only then did he realize that, as in his dream, someone was singing.

It was a woman's voice, high and sweet, and the song was one that Sula had sung. His flesh crept. He thought of magic, and waking dreams. Then out of the mist, no more than twelve paces away, came a man leading a mule with a girl mounted sideways on its back. He took them at first for a peasant with his wife going out to work, then saw that the man was dressed in a priest's robe, and the girl as simply, sackcloth and wimple, and the pretty feet dangling against the mule's ribs were bare. They were Christians, it appeared; a wooden cross hung from the man's waist, and a smaller one lay on the girl's bosom. There was a silver bell on the mule's collar, which rang as it moved.

The priest checked in his stride when he saw the armed man with the big horse, then, as Mordred gave him a greeting, smiled and came forward.

"Maridunum?" he repeated, in response to Mordred's query. He pointed to the road that led due west. "That way is best. It is rough, but passable everywhere, and it is shorter than the main road south by Caerleon. Have you come far, sir?"

Mordred answered him civilly, giving him what news he could. The man did not speak with a peasant's accent. He might have been someone gently bred, a courtier, even. The girl, Mordred saw now, was beautiful. Even the bare feet, dangling by the mule's ribs, were clean and white, fine-boned and veined with blue. She sat silently watching him, and listening, in no way discomposed by his look. Mordred caught the priest's glance at the altar stone where the silver coin gleamed beside the food. "Do you know whose altar this is? Or whose stone at the crossways?"

The man smiled. "Not mine, sir. That is all I know. That is your offering?"

"Yes."

"Then God knows who will receive it," said the man, gently, "but if you have need of blessing, sir, then my God can, through me, give it to you. Unless," he added, on a troubled afterthought, "there is blood on your hands?"

"No," said Mordred. "But there is a curse that says I shall have. How do I lift that?"

"A curse? Who laid it?"

"A witch," said Mordred, shortly, "but she is dead."

"Then the curse may well have died with her."

"But before her, a fate was spoken of, and by Merlin."

"What fate?"

"That I cannot tell you."

"Then ask him."

"Ah," said Mordred. "Then it is true he is still there?"

"They say so. He is there in his cave on the hill, for those who have the need or the fortune to find him. Well then, sir, I cannot help you, other than give you my Christian blessing, and send you on your way."

He raised a hand, and Mordred bowed his head, then thanked him, hesitated over a coin, decided against it, and rode on. He took the west road to Maridunum. Soon the mule's bell died out in the distance, and he was alone again.

He came to the hill called Bryn Myrddin at dusk, and slept again by a wood. When he woke there was mist again, with the sun rising behind it. The haze was tinged with rose, and a faint glimmer showed on the grey trunks of the beech trees.

He waited patiently, eating the hard biscuit and raisins that were his breakfast ration. The world was silent, no movement but the slow eddying of the mist between the trees, and the steady cropping of the horse. There was no haste. He had ceased to feel any curiosity about the old man whom he sought, the King's enchanter of a thousand legends who had been his enemy (and since Morgause had said so, he took it without question as a lie) since the day of his conception. Nor was there any apprehension. If the curse could be lifted, then no doubt Merlin would lift it. If not, then no doubt he would explain it.

Quite suddenly, the mist was gone. A slight breeze, warm for the time of year, rustled through the wood, swept the eddies aside and dispersed them down the hillside like smoke from a bonfire. The sun, climbing the hilltop across the valley, blazed scarlet and gold into his eyes. The landscape dazzled.

He mounted, turning towards the sun. Now he saw where he was. The travelling priest's directions had been accurate and vivid enough to guide anyone even through this rolling and featureless landscape.

"By the time you reach the wood, you will have gone past the upper slopes of Bryn Myrddin. Go down to the stream, cross it, and you will find a track. Turn uphill again and ride as far as a grove of thorn trees. There is a little cliff, with a path curling up beside it. At the head of the cliff is the holy well, and by it the enchanter's cave."

He came to the thicket of whitethorn. There, beside the cliff, he dismounted and tied the horse. He trod quickly up the path and came out on level ground and into mist again, thick and still and stained red gold by the sun, standing as still as lake water over the turf. He could see nothing. He felt his way forward. The turf was level and fine. At his feet, peering, he could just discern small late daisies, frost-nipped, and shut against the damp. Somewhere to his left was the trickle of water. The holy well? He groped forward, but could not find it. He trod on a stone, which rolled away, almost bringing him to his knees. The silence, broken only by the trickle of the spring, was eerie. In spite of himself, he felt the chill prickles of sweat creep down his spine.

He stopped. He stood squarely, and shouted aloud.

"Ho, there! Is anyone there?"

An echo, ringing from the wall of mist, rebounded again and again from the invisible depths of the valley, and died into silence.

"Is anyone there? This is Mordred, Prince of Britain, to speak with Merlin his kinsman. I come in peace. I seek peace."

Again the echo. Again the silence. He moved cautiously towards the sound of water, and his groping fingers touched the stone rim of the well. He stooped towards the water. Breaths of mist furred and fumed from the smooth glass of the surface. He bent nearer. Below that glass the clear depths, darkly shining, led the eye down, away from the mist. At the bottom of the well was the gleam of silver, the offerings to the god.

From nowhere came a memory: the pool below the ancient tomb where Morgause had bidden him watch the depths for visions. There he had seen nothing but what should rightly be there. Here, on the holy hilltop, the same.

He straightened. Mordred, the realist, did not know that a burden had dropped from him. He would have said only that Merlin's magic was no doubt as harmless as Morgause's.

What he had seen as a cursed fate, foreseen with grief by Merlin and twisted into evil by Morgause, dwindled in this world of clear water and lighted mist into its proper form. It was not even a curse. It was a fact, something due to happen in the future, that had been seen by an eye doomed to foresee, whatever the pain of that Seeing. It would come, yes, but only as, soon or late, all deaths came. He, Mordred, was not the instrument of a blind and brutal fate, but of whatever, whoever, made the pattern to which the world moved. *Live what life brings; die what death comes.* He did not see the comfort even as cold.

Nor did he, in fact, even know that he had been comforted. He reached for the cup that stood above the water, filled it and drank, and felt refreshed. He poured for the god, and as he returned the cup to its place said, in the tongue of his childhood, "Thank you," and turned to go.

The mist was thicker than ever, the silence as intense. The sun was right up now, but the light, instead of sweeping the air clear, blazed like a fire in the middle of a great cloud. The hillside was a swirl of flame and smoke, cool to the skin, clean to the nostrils, but blinding to the eye and filling the mind with confusion and wonder. The very air was crystal, was rainbow, was flowing diamond. "*He is where he always was,*" Nimuë had said, "*with all his fires and travelling glories round him.*" And "*If he wishes it, you may find him.*"

He had found, and been answered. He began to feel his way back towards the head of the cliff. Behind him, invisible, the falling drops of the spring sounded for all the world like the sweet, faint notes of a harp. Above him was the swirl of light where the sun stood. Guided by these he felt his way forward until his foot found the drop to the path.

When he reached the base of the hill he turned east and rode straight and fast for Caerleon and his father.

10

By the time Mordred reached Caerleon matters had begun to settle themselves. The King had been very angry over Lamorak's murder, and it was certainly to Agravain's advantage that his wound would keep him, and Gaheris with him, in the north until it was healed. Drustan duly sent an account of the incident to Arthur, but its bearer was not a royal courier, it was Gareth; and Gareth, though far from trying to excuse his brothers, pleaded successfully with the King for their pardon. For Gaheris he pleaded madness; Gaheris, who had loved Morgause and had killed her. Gareth, out of his own grief, could make a guess at what had passed in his brother's bruised mind as he knelt there in his mother's blood. And Agravain, as ever, had acted as the shield and dagger alongside his twin's sword. Now that Lamorak was dead, urged Gareth, it was surely possible that Gaheris could put the bloody past behind him, and take his place again as a loyal man. And Drustan, though sorely provoked, had held his hand, so it might well be that now the swinging pendulum of revenge could be stilled.

Unexpectedly enough, the main opposition to Gareth's pleading came from Bedwyr. Bedwyr, deploring the blood tie that linked Arthur to the Orkney brothers, disliked and distrusted them, and lost no chance to set the King on guard against them. He was known throughout the court to be using all his considerable influence to prevent the twins from being recalled. And where, Bedwyr insisted, with growing suspicion, was Mordred? Had he, too, perhaps, assisted in the murder, and fled before Drustan and Gareth came on the scene? Mordred himself arrived in Caerleon in time to save confusion about his part in the affair, and eventually, in spite of Bedwyr, Gareth was sent north again, to bring his brothers back to court when they were both, in mind and body, whole once more.

Gawain came back, briefly, soon after the court returned to Camelot, while Agravain and Gaheris were still in the north. He had a long interview with Arthur, and after it another with Mordred, who told him what he had seen of Lamorak's murder and its aftermath, and finished by urging Gawain to listen to the King's pleas and show the same restraint as Drustan, and to refrain from adding another stone to the bloody cairn of revenge.

"Lamorak leaves a young brother, Drian, who rides with Drustan's men. By the kind of logic that you use, he has the right now to kill either of your brothers, or you yourself. Even Gareth," said Mordred, "though I doubt if that is likely. Drustan will have seen to it that Drian knows what happened, and that—the Goddess be thanked!—Gareth kept his head and acted like a sensible man. He could see —as indeed any man could who was there—that Gaheris was crazed in his wits. If we make much of that circumstance, it is possible that when he comes back healed, no one will attempt to strike at him." He added, meaningly: "I believe that neither of the twins will ever be trusted again by the King, but if you can bring yourself to forgive Gaheris for our mother's murder, or at any rate not to take action against him, then you may, with Gareth and myself, stay within the edges of the King's favour. There may yet be a noble future for you and for me. Do you ever want to rule your northern kingdom, Gawain?"

Mordred knew his man. Gawain was anxious that nothing should interfere with his title to the Orkneys, or eventually to the kingdom of Lothian. Neither title would be worth anything without Arthur's continued support. So the matter was settled, but when the time came for the twins' return, the King saw to it that their elder brother was away from Camelot. Queen Morgan, at Castell Aur in Wales, provided him with just the excuse he needed. Gawain was dispatched there, ostensibly to investigate complaints from the peasants about abuses of authority by Morgan's guardians, and carefully kept there out of the way until the dust on the Lamorak murder should settle.

It was apparent, though, to Mordred, that Bedwyr's doubts about him were not quite resolved. In place of the guarded friendliness that Arthur's chief marshal had lately shown, Mordred was to observe a return to the wary watchfulness that Bedwyr also accorded Agravain and certain other of the Young Celts.

The phrase "Young Celts," used lightly enough at first to denote the young outlanders who tended to stick together, had by this time taken on the ring of a sobriquet, a title as clearly defined as that of the High King's companion knights. And here and there the two lines crossed; Agravain was in both, and Gaheris, and so, eventually, was Mordred. Arthur, as Mordred had anticipated, sent for him and asked him, once his half-brothers were back at court, to keep watch on them, and on the others of the Young Celts' party. A little to Mordred's surprise he found that, though there was still discontent with some of Arthur's home policies, there was no talk that could be called seditious. Loyalty to Arthur's name and fame still held them; he was duke of battles still, and enough of glory and authority hung about him to keep them loyal. His talk of wars to come, moreover, bound them to him. But there was enmity for Bedwyr. The men from Orkney who had come south to join Lot's sons in Arthur's train, and others from Lothian who hoped for Gawain's succession there (and who had some small grievances, real or imagined, against the Northumbrian lord of Benoic), knew that Bedwyr distrusted them, and that he had done his best to block the return of Agravain and Gaheris to court; had advocated, rather, their banishment back to their island home. So when, as was inevitable among the young men, the talk turned to the gossip about Bedwyr and the Queen, Mordred soon realized that this was prompted mainly by hatred of Bedwyr, and the desire to shut him out of the King's favour. When Mordred, moving carefully, let it be known that he might be persuaded to take their part, the Young Celts assumed his motive to be the natural jealousy of a King's son who might, if Bedwyr could be discredited, become his father's deputy. As such, Mordred would be a notable acquisition to the party.

So he was accepted, and in time regarded as one of the party's leaders, even by Agravain and Gaheris.

Mordred had his own rooms within the royal palace at Camelot, but he had also, for the last year or so, owned a pleasant little house in the town. A girl of the town kept house for him, and made him welcome whenever he could spare the time for her. Here, from time to time, came the Young Celts, ostensibly to supper, or for a day's fowling in the marshes, but in reality to talk, and for Mordred to listen.

The purchase of the house had in fact been the King's suggestion. If Mordred was to share the party's activities, this was not likely to happen in his rooms within the royal palace. In the easier atmosphere of his leman's house Mordred could more readily keep in touch with the currents of thought that moved the younger men.

To his house one evening came Agravain, with Colles, and Mador, and others of the Young Celts. After supper, when the woman had placed the wine near them and then withdrawn, Agravain brought the talk abruptly round to the subject that, of late, had obsessed him.

"Bedwyr! No man in the kingdom can get anywhere, become anybody, without that man's approval! The King's besotted. Boyhood friends, indeed! Boyhood lovers, more like! And still he has to listen whenever my lord high and mighty Bedwyr chooses to speak! What d'ye say, Colles? We know, eh? Eh?"

Agravain, as was usual these days, was three parts drunken, early as it was in the night. This was plain speaking, even for him. Colles, usually a hopeful sycophant, tried an uneasy withdrawal. "Well, but everyone knows they fought together since years back. Brothers-in-arms, and all that. It's only natural—"

"Too natural by half." Agravain gave a hiccup of laughter. "Brothers-in-arms, how right you are! In the Queen's arms, too. . . . Haven't you heard the latest? Last time the King was from court, there was my lord Bedwyr, snugged down right and tight in the Queen's bed before Arthur's horse was well out of the King's Gate."

"Where did you get that?" This, sharply, from Mador.

And from Colles, beginning to look scared: "You told me. But it's only talk, and it can't be true. For one thing the King's not that kind of a fool, and if he trusts Bedwyr—and trusts her, come to that—"

"Not a fool? It's a fool's part to trust. Mordred would agree. Wouldn't you, brother?"

Mordred, with his back to the company, pouring wine, was heard to assent, shortly.

"If it were true," began someone, longingly, but Mador cut across him.

"You're a fool yourself to talk like that without proof. It can't be true. Even if they wanted to, how would they dare? The Queen's ladies are always there with her, and even at night—"

Agravain gave a shout of laughter, and Gaheris, lounging back beside him, said, grinning: "My poor innocent. You're beginning to sound like my saintly brother Gareth. Don't you ever listen to the dirt? Agravain's been laying one of Guinevere's maids for nigh on a month now. If anyone hears the gossip, he should."

"And you mean that she says he's been in there at night? Bedwyr?"

Agravain nodded into his wine, and Gaheris gave a crow of triumph. "Then we've got him!"

But Colles insisted: "She saw him? Herself?"

"No." Agravain looked round defiantly. "But we all know the talk that's been going round for long enough, and we also know that there's no fire without smoke. Let us look past the smoke, and put out the fire. If I do get proof, will you all act with me?"

"Act? How?"

"Do the King a service, and get rid of Bedwyr, from the King's bed *and* the King's counsels!"

Calum said doubtfully: "You mean just tell the King?"

"How else? He'll be furious, who wouldn't, but afterwards he's got to be grateful. Any man would want to know—"

"But the Queen?" This was a young man called Cian, who came from the Queen's own country of North Wales. "He'll kill her. Any man, finding out . . . " He flushed, and fell silent. It was to be noticed that he avoided looking at Gaheris.

Agravain was confident and scornful. "He would never hurt the Queen. Have you never heard what happened when

240

Melwas of the Summer Country took her and held her for a day and a night in his lodge on one of the Lake islands? You can't tell me that that lecher never had his way with her, but the King took her back without a word, and gave her his promise that, for that or even for her barrenness, he would never put her aside. No, he'd never harm her. Mordred, you know him better than most, and you're with the Queen half your time as well. What do you say?"

"About the King's tenderness towards her, I agree." Mordred set the wine jug down again, and leaned back against the table's edge, surveying them. "But all this is moonshine, surely? There is talk, I've heard it, but it seems to me that it comes mostly from here, and without proof. Without any kind of proof. Until proof is found, the talk must remain only talk, concocted from wishes and ambitions, not from facts."

"He's right, you know," said one Melion, who was Cian's brother. "It is only talk, the sort that always happens when a lady is as lovely as the Queen, and her man's away from her bed as often and for as long as the King has to be."

"It's bedroom door gossip," Cian put in. "Do you ask us to kneel down in the dirt and peer through chamber key-holes?"

Since this was in fact exactly what Agravain had been doing, he denied it with great indignation. He was not too drunk to ignore the hardening of the meeting against any idea of harming the Queen. He said virtuously: "You've got me wrong, gentlemen. Nothing would persuade me to injure that lovely lady. But if we could contrive a way to bring Bedwyr down without hurt to her—"

"You mean swear that he forced his way in? Raped her?"

"Why not? It might be possible. My wench would say anything we paid her for, and—"

"What about Gareth's?" asked someone. It was known that Gareth was courting Linet, one of the Queen's ladies, a gentle girl and as incorruptible as Gareth himself.

"All right, all right!" Agravain, a dark flush in his face, swung round to Mordred. "There's plenty to be thought about, but by the dark Goddess herself, we've made a start, and we know who's with us and who isn't! Mordred, what about it? If we can think of some way that doesn't implicate the Queen, then you're with us? You, of all men, can hardly stand Bedwyr's friend."

"I?" Mordred gave that cool little smile that was all that remained in him of Morgause. "Friend to Bedwyr, chief marshal, best of the knights, the King's right hand in battle and the council chamber? Regent in Arthur's absence, with all Arthur's power?" He paused. "Bring Bedwyr down? What should I say, gentlemen? That I reject the notion utterly?" There was laughter and the drumming of cups on the table, and shouts of "Mordred for regent!" "Well, why not? Who else?" "Valerius? No, too old." "Well, Drustan then? Or Gawain?" And then in a kind of ragged unanimity: "Mordred for regent! Who else? One of us! Mordred!"

Then the woman came in, and the shouting died, and the talk veered away to the harmless subject of tomorrow's hunt.

When they had gone, and the girl was clearing away the debris of scattered food and spilled wine, Mordred went out into the air.

In spite of himself, the talk and the final accolade had shaken him. Bedwyr gone? Himself the undisputed right hand of the King, and, in the King's absence, unquestioned regent? Once he were there, and once proved as fighter and administrator, what was more likely than that Arthur would also make him his heir? He was still not that: The King's heir was still Constantine of Cornwall, son of that Duke Cador whom Arthur, in default of a legitimate prince, had declared heir to the kingdoms. But that was before he knew that a son of his body would be—was already—begotten. Legitimate? What did that matter, when Arthur himself had been begotten in adultery?

Behind him the girl called him softly. He looked round. She was leaning from the bedchamber window, the warm lamplight falling on the long golden hair and on one bared shoulder and breast. He smiled and said, "Presently," but he hardly saw her. In his mind's eye, against the darkness, he saw only the Queen.

Guinevere. The lady of the golden hair, still lovely, of the great grey-blue eyes, of the pretty voice and the ready smile, and with it all the gentle wit and gaiety that lighted her presence-chamber with pleasure. Guinevere, who so patently loved her lord, but who understood fear and loneliness and who, out of that knowledge, had befriended an insecure and lonely boy, had helped to lift him out of the murk of his childhood memories, and shown him how to love with a light heart. Whose hands, touching his in friendship, had blown to blaze a flame that Morgause's corrupt mouth could not even kindle.

He loved her. Not in the same way, in the same breath even, as he had loved other women. There had been many in his life, from the girl in the islands whom at fourteen he had bedded in a hollow of the heather, to the woman who waited for him now. But his thoughts of Guinevere were not even in this context. He only knew that he loved her, and if the tale were true, then by Hecate, he would like to see Bedwyr brought down! The King would not harm her, he was sure of that, but he might, he just might, for his honour's sake, put her aside....

He went no further. It is doubtful if he even knew he had gone as far. Oddly for Mordred, the cool thinker, the thoughts were hardly formulated. He was conscious only of anger at the vile whispers, the stain on the Queen's name, and of his own renewed distrust of the twins and their irresponsible friends. He recognized, with misgiving, where his duty lay as King's watcher (King's spy, he told himself sourly) among the Young Celts. He would have to warn Arthur of the danger to Bedwyr and the Queen. The King would soon get to the truth of the matter, and if action had to be taken, he was the one who must take it. Duty lay that way, and the King's trust.

And Bedwyr, if it were proved that he had forfeited that trust?

Mordred thrust the thought aside, and on an impulse that, even if he recognized it, he would not admit, he went back into the house and took his pleasure with a violence that was as foreign to him as his mental turmoil had been, and that was to cost him a gold necklace in appeasement next day.

I I

Later that night, when town and palace were quiet, he went to see the King.

Arthur, as was his wont these days, was working late in his business room. His white hound Cabal lay at his feet. It was the same puppy that he had chosen on the day Mordred was first brought to him. It was old now, and scarred with the mementoes of some memorable hunts. It lifted its head as Mordred was shown in, and its tail beat the floor.

The servant withdrew, and the King nodded his secretary out of the room.

"How is it with you, Mordred? I am glad you came. I was planning to send for you in the morning, but tonight is even better. You know I have to go to Brittany soon?"

"It has been rumoured. So it's true?"

"Yes. It's time I had a meeting with my cousin King Hoel. I'd also like to see for myself how things are shaping over there."

"When do you leave, sir?"

"In a week's time. The weather should be fair then."

Mordred glanced at the window curtains, where a fitful wind plucked at them. "Your prophets tell you so?"

The King laughed. "I go to surer sources than the altars, or even Nimuë at Applegarth. I ask the shepherds on the high downs. They are never wrong. But I forgot, my fisher-boy. Perhaps I should have asked you, too?"

Mordred shook his head, smiling. "I might have ventured a prophecy in the islands, though even the old men there were often out of reckoning; but here, no. It's a different world. A different sky."

"You don't hanker for the other now?"

"No. I have all I want." He added: "I would like to see Brittany."

"Then I am sorry. What I wanted to tell you is that I plan to leave you here in Camelot."

In spite of himself his heart gave a jump. He waited, not looking at Arthur in case the latter read his thought.

As if he had—which, with Arthur, was even possible—the King went on: "Bedwyr will be here, of course. But this time I want you to do more than observe how things go; you will be Bedwyr's deputy, as he mine."

There was a pause. Arthur saw with interest, but without understanding, that Mordred, who had lost colour, was hesitating, as if not knowing what to say. At length Mordred asked: "And my—the other Orkney princes? Do they go with you, or stay here?"

Arthur, misunderstanding him, was surprised. He had not thought that Mordred was jealous of his half-brothers. If his mission had been a military one, he might have taken Agravain and Gaheris with him, and so drawn off some of their energy and discontent, but as it was he said, quickly and definitely: "No. Gawain is in Wales, as you know, and likely to be there for some time. Gareth would not thank me for abstracting him from Camelot, with his wedding so near. The other two can hardly expect favour of me. They stay here."

Mordred was silent. The King began to talk about his forthcoming journey and the discussions he would hold with King Hoel, then about the role Mordred would assume at home as deputy to the regent. The hound woke once, and scratched for fleas. The fire dwindled, and Mordred, obedient to a nod from his father, fed it with a log from the basket. At length the King had done. He looked at the younger man.

"You are very silent. Come, Mordred, there will be another time. Or even a time when Bedwyr will be the one to go with me, and you the one to remain as temporary king. Does the prospect dismay you so much?"

"No. No. It is—I am honoured."

"Then what is it?"

"If I ask that Bedwyr should go with you this time and leave me here, you will think that I outrun even the ambition of a prince. But I do ask it, my lord King."

Arthur stared at him. "What is this?"

"I came tonight to report to you what is being said among the Young Celts. They met at my house this evening. Most of the talk tonight was of Bedwyr. He has enemies, bitter enemies, who will plot to bring him down." He hesitated. He had known this would be hard, but he had not known how hard. "Sir, I beg you not to leave Bedwyr here while you go abroad. This is not because I myself covet the regency. It is because there is talk about him and—" He stopped. He licked his lips. He said lamely: "He has enemies. There is talk."

Arthur's eyes were black ice. He stood. Mordred got to his feet. To his fury he found that he was trembling. He was not to know that every man who hitherto had met that hard cold stare was dead.

The King said, in a flat voice that seemed to come from a great distance:

"There is always talk. There are those who talk, and there are those who listen. Neither are men of mine. No, Mordred, I understand you very well. I am not deaf; and neither am I blind. There is nothing in this talk. There is nothing to be said."

Mordred swallowed. "I said nothing, my lord."

"And I heard nothing. Go now."

He nodded a dismissal curter than the one the servant had had. Mordred bowed and went.

He had a hand on the door when the King's voice halted him.

"Mordred."

He turned. "My lord."

"This changes nothing. You remain with the regent as his deputy."

"My lord."

The King said, in a different voice: "I should have remembered that it was I who asked you to listen, and that I have no right to blame you for doing so, or for reporting to me. As for Bedwyr, he is aware of his enemies' ambitions." He looked down, resting his finger-tips on the table in front of him. There was a pause. Mordred waited. Without looking up, the King added: "Mordred. There are some matters better not spoken of; better not even known. Do you understand me?"

"I think so," said Mordred. And indeed, misjudging Arthur as the King had misjudged him, he thought so. It was apparent that Arthur knew what was being said about Bedwyr and the Queen. He knew, and chose to ignore it. Which meant simply one thing: Whether there was any truth in it or not, Arthur wanted no action taken. He wanted to avoid the kind of upheaval that must result from an open accusation levelled at the King's deputy and the Queen. So far, Mordred was right. But not in his final conclusion, which was that of a man and not of a prince: that Arthur was indifferent to the matter, and chose to ignore it out of pride as well as policy. "I think so, sir," he said again.

Arthur looked up and smiled. The bleak look was gone, but he looked very weary. "Then stay watchful for me, my son, and serve the Queen. And know Bedwyr for your friend, and my faithful servant. And now, good night."

Soon after this the King left Camelot. Mordred found that his work as deputy regent meant a series of day-long sessions in the Round Hall listening to petitions, alternating with days watching troop exercises, and finishing each evening after the public supper in hall (when further petitions were often brought to the high table) with the stacked tablets and papers in the King's business room.

In public Bedwyr, as before, took the King's place beside the Queen, but as far as Mordred, casually watchful, could ascertain, he made no opportunities for private talk with her, and neither he nor Guinevere ever attempted to dispense with Mordred's company. When the regent spoke with the Queen, as he did each morning, Mordred was there beside him; Mordred sat on her left at supper time; Mordred walked on her left hand when she took the air in her garden with Bedwyr for company and her ladies round her.

He found Bedwyr surprisingly easy to work with. The older man went out of his way to allow his deputy some scope. Soon he was passing almost three out of five judgments across to Mordred, only stipulating that the verdicts might be privately agreed before they were given. There was very little disagreement, and as the days went by Mordred found that more and more the decisions were his. It was also noticeable that as the day of Arthur's return drew near, the work awaiting him was appreciably less than it had been after previous absences.

It was also to be noticed that, in spite of the lightened burden on him, Bedwyr grew quieter and more nervy. There were lines in his face and his eyes were shadowed. At supper, leaning to listen, a smile fixed on his lips, to the Queen's soft voice beside him, he ate little, but drank deeply. Afterwards in the business room he would sit silently for long periods staring at the fire, until Mordred, or one of the secretaries, would with some query bring him back to the matter in hand.

All this Mordred noticed, watching. For him, the nearness to Guinevere was at once a joy and a torment. If there had been a look, a touch, a gesture of understanding between her and Bedwyr, Mordred was sure he would have seen or even sensed it. But there was none, only Bedwyr's silence and the sense of strain that hung about him, and perhaps an extra gaiety in the Queen's chatter and laughter when she and her ladies graced some function of the court. In either case this could be attributed to the cares of office, and the strain imposed by Arthur's absence. In the end Mordred, mindful of the King's last interview with him, put the recollection of the Young Celts' gossip out of his mind.

Then one evening, long after supper, when the King's seal was used for the last time and the secretary returned it to its box, bade the two men good night, and took himself away, there was a tap at the door and the servant came in to announce a caller.

This was Bors, one of the older knights, a Companion who had fought with Arthur and Bedwyr through the great campaign, and had been with them at Badon Hill. He was a simple man, devoted to the King, but was known to be fretting almost as fiercely as the Young Celts for action. No courtier, he was impatient of ceremony, and longed for the simplicities and movement of the field.

He gave Bedwyr the salute of the camp, and said with

his usual abruptness: "You are to go to the Queen. There's a letter she wants to show you."

There was a short, blank silence. Then Bedwyr got to his feet. "It's very late. Surely she has retired? It must be urgent."

"She said so. Or she'd not have sent me."

Mordred had risen when Bedwyr did. "A letter? It came with the courier?"

"I suppose so. Well, you know how late he was. You got the rest yourself not long ago."

This was true. The man, who had been due at sundown, had been delayed on the road by a flash flood, and had ridden in not long before. Hence the late working-hours they had been keeping.

"He mentioned no letter for the Queen," said Mordred.

Bedwyr said sharply: "Why should he? If it is the Queen's it is not our concern, except as she chooses to talk about it with me. Very well, Bors. I'll go now."

"I'll tell her you will come?"

"No need. I'll send Ulfin. You get to bed, and Mordred, too. Good night."

As he spoke he began to buckle on the belt he had cast aside when the men settled down to the evening's work. The servant brought his cloak. From the side of his eye he saw Mordred hesitating, and repeated, with some abruptness: "Good night."

There was nothing for it. Mordred followed Bors out of the room.

Bors went off down the corridor with his long outdoor stride. Mordred, hurrying to catch him up, did not hear Bedwyr's quick words to the servant:

"Go and tell the Queen I'll be with her shortly. Tell her... No doubt her ladies retired when she did. You will see to it that she is attended when I come. No matter if her waiting-women are asleep. Wake them. Do you understand?"

Ulfin had been the King's chief chamberlain for many years. He said briefly, "Yes, my lord," and went.

Mordred and Bors, walking together across the outer garden court, saw him hurrying towards the Queen's rooms.

Bors said abruptly: "I don't like it."

"But there was a letter?"

"I didn't see one. And I saw the man ride in. If it's true he carried a letter for the Queen, why does she need to talk with him now? It's near midnight. Surely it could wait till morning? I tell you, I don't like it."

Mordred shot him a glance. Was it possible that the whispers had come even to the ears of this faithful veteran? Then Bors added: "If anything has happened to the King, then surely the tidings should have gone straight to Bedwyr as well. What can they have to discuss that needs privacy and midnight?"

"What indeed?" said Mordred. Bors gave him a sharp glance, but all he said was, gruffly:

"Well, well, we'd best get to bed, and mind our business."

When they reached the hall where most of the young bachelors slept, they found some of them still awake. Gaheris was sober, but only just, Agravain was drunk as usual, and talkative. Gareth sat at tables with Colles, and a couple of others lounged over dice by the dying fire.

Bors said good night, and turned away, and Mordred, who in the King's absence lived and slept within the palace, started through the hall towards the stairway that led to his rooms. Before he reached it one of the young knights, the man from Wales called Cian, came swiftly in from the outer court, pushing past Bors in the doorway. He stood there for a moment, blinking, while his dark-dazzled eyes adjusted themselves to the light. Gaheris, guessing where he had been, called out some pleasantry, and Colles, with a coarse laugh, pointed out that his clothes were still unbraced.

He took no notice. He came with his swift stride into the middle of the hall and said, urgently:

"Bedwyr's gone to the Queen. I saw him. Straight in through the private doorway, and there's a lamp lit in her chamber window."

Agravain was on his feet. "Has he, by God!"

Gaheris, lurching, got himself upright. His hand was on his sword. "So, it was true. We all knew it! Now let us see what the King will say when he hears that his wife lies with a lover!"

"Why wait for that?" This was Mador. "Let us make sure of them both now!"

Mordred, from the foot of the stairs, raised his voice urgently above the hubbub: "She sent for him. A letter came

250

by the courier. It could be from the King. There was something in it she had to discuss with Bedwyr. Bors brought the message. Tell them, Bors!"

"It's true," said the old man, but worry still sounded in his voice, and Mador said shrewdly: "You don't like it either, do you? You've heard the stories, too? Well, if they are having a council over the King's letter, let us join it! What objection can there be to that?"

Mordred shouted: "Stop, you fools! I tell you, I was there! This is true! Are you all mad? Think of the King! Whatever we find—"

"Aye, whatever we find," said Agravain thickly. "If it is a council, then we join it as loyal King's men—"

"And if it's a tryst for lusty lovers," put in Gaheris, "then we can serve the King in other ways."

"You'd not dare touch her!" Mordred, sharp with fear, pushed his way through the crowd and gripped Gaheris's arm.

"Her? Not this time." Gaheris, drunk, but perfectly steady, laughed through ghost-haunted eyes. "But Bedwyr, ah, if Bedwyr's where I think he is, what will the King do but thank us for this night's work?"

Bors was shouting, and being shouted down. Mordred, still holding Gaheris's arm, was talking swiftly, reasonably, trying to contain the mood of the crowd. But they had drunk too much, they were ripe for action, and they hated Bedwyr. There was no stopping them now. Still clutching Gaheris's sleeve, Mordred found himself being swept along with them— there were a dozen of them now, Bors hustled along with them, and even Gareth, white-faced, bringing up the rear— through the shadowed arcades that edged the garden court, and in through the doorway that gave on the Queen's private stair. The servant there, sleepy but alert enough, came upright from the wall with his lips parting for a challenge. Then he saw Mordred, and in the moment of hesitation that this gave him, he was silenced with a blow from the butt of Colles's dagger.

The act of violence was like the twang that looses the taut bowstring. With shouts the young men surged through the door and up the stairway to the Queen's private chambers. Colles, leading, hammered on the wood with his sword hilt, shouting:

"Open! Open! In the King's name!"

Locked in the press on the stairway, struggling to get through, Mordred heard from within the room a woman's cry of alarm. Then other voices, shrill and urgent, drowned by the renewed shouting from the stairway.

"Open this door! There's treachery! Treachery to the King!"

Then suddenly, so quickly that it was obvious it had not been locked, the door opened wide.

A girl was holding it. The room was lighted only by the night-lamps. Three or four women were there, their voluminous wraps indicating that they had been in their night robes and had been roused hastily from their beds. One of them, an elderly lady with grey hair loose about her face as if she had recently been startled from sleep, ran to the door of the inner room where the Queen slept, and turned to bar the way.

"What is this? What has happened? Colles, this unseemly —And you, Prince Agravain? If it's the lord Bedwyr that you want to see—"

"Stand aside, Mother," said someone breathlessly, and the woman was thrust to one side as Colles and Agravain, shouting, "Treachery, treachery to the King!" hurled themselves, with swords out and ready, at the Queen's door.

Through the tumult, the hammering, the women's now frightened screaming, Mordred heard Gareth's breathless voice:

"Linet? Don't be afraid. Bors has gone for the guard. Stand over there, and keep back. Nothing will happen—"

Then, between one hammer-blow and the next, the Queen's door opened suddenly, and Bedwyr was standing there.

The Queen's bedchamber was well lighted, by a swinging silver lamp shaped like a dragon. To the attackers, taken by surprise, everything in the room was visible in one swift impression.

The great bed stood against the far wall. The covers were tumbled, but then the Queen had already been abed when the letter—if there had been a letter—had come. She, like her women, was wrapped from throat to feet in a warm loose robe of white wool, girdled with blue. Her slippers were of white ermine fur. The golden hair was braided with blue, and hung forward over her shoulders. She looked like a girl. She also looked very frightened. She had half risen from the cross-stool where she had been sitting, and was holding the hands of the scared waiting-woman who crouched on a tuffet at her feet.

Bedwyr, holding the door, was dressed as Mordred had seen him a short time ago, but with neither sword nor dagger. Fully dressed as he was, facing the swords at the chamber door, he was, in the parlance of the fighting man, naked. And, with the lightning action of a fighting man, he moved. As Colles, still in the van, lunged towards him with his sword, Bedwyr, sweeping the blade aside with a swirl of his heavy cloak, struck his attacker in the throat. As the man staggered back, Bedwyr wrenched the sword out of his grip, and ran him through.

"Lecher! Murderer!" yelled Agravain. His voice was still thick with drink, or passion, but his sword was steady. Mordred, shouting something, caught at him, but Agravain struck the hand aside and jumped, murderous blade shortened, straight for Bedwyr. Colles's body blocked half the doorway, and for a moment Agravain was alone, facing Bedwyr's sword. In that moment, Bedwyr, veteran of a thousand combats, struck Agravain's flashing blade almost idly aside and ran his attacker through the heart.

Even this killing did not give the attacking mob pause. Mador, hard on Agravain's heels, got half in under Bedwyr's guard before he could withdraw his blade. Gareth, his young voice cracking with distress, was shouting: "He was drunk! For God's sake—" And then, shrilly, in agonized panic: "Gaheris, no!"

For Gaheris, murderer of women, had leaped straight over Agravain's fallen body, past the whirling swords where Bedwyr fought, and was advancing, sword levelled, on the Queen.

She had not moved. The whole mêlée had lasted only seconds. She stood frozen, her terrified woman crouched at her knees, her eyes on the deadly flash of metal round Bedwyr. If she was aware of Gaheris and his threat she gave no sign. She did not even raise a hand to ward off the blade.

"Whore!" shouted Gaheris, and thrust at her.

His blade was struck up. Mordred was hard behind him. Gaheris turned, cursing. Mordred's sword ran up Gaheris's blade and the hilts locked. Body to body the two men swayed, fighting. Gaheris, pressed back, lurched against the Queen's stool, and sent it flying. The waiting-woman screamed, and the Queen, with a cry, moved at last, backing away towards the wall. Gaheris, swearing, lashed out with his dagger. Mordred snatched out his with his left hand and brought the hilt down as hard as he could on his half-brother's temple. Gaheris dropped like a stone. Mordred turned, gasping, to the Queen, and found himself facing Bedwyr's blade, and Bedwyr's murderous eyes.

Bedwyr, hotly engaged, had seen, through the haze of blood dripping from a shallow cut on his forehead, the sudden thrust towards the Queen, and the struggle near her chair. He started to cut his way towards her with a fury and desperation that gave him barely time for thought. Gareth, exposed by Agravain's fall, and still reiterating wildly, "He was drunk!" was cut down and died in his blood almost at the Queen's feet. Then the deadly sword, red to the hilt, engaged Mordred's, and Mordred, with no time for words or for retreat, was fighting for his life.

Dimly he was aware of fresh hubbub. One of the women, regardless of danger, had run into the room, and was on her knees by Gareth's body, wailing his name over and over again. A screaming was audible along the corridor where others had run for help. Bedwyr, as he cut and thrust, shouted out some sort of command, and Mordred knew then that the guard had been called, and was there. Gaheris heaved on the floor, trying to rise. His hand slipped in Gareth's blood. Mador had been seized by the guard and dragged away, shouting. The others, some still resisting, were one by one overpowered, and hustled away. The Queen was calling something, but through the uproar she could not be heard.

Mordred was conscious mainly of two things, Bedwyr's eyes of cold fury, and the knowledge that, even through that fury, the King's marshal was deliberately refraining from killing or maiming the King's son. A chance came, was ignored; another came and was turned; Bedwyr's sword ran in over Mordred's blade, and he took the younger man neatly through the upper part of his sword arm. As Mordred staggered back, Bedwyr, following him, struck him with his dagger's hilt, a heavy blow on the temple.

Mordred fell. He fell across Gareth's outstretched arm,

and the girl's tears, as she wept for her lover, fell on his face.

There was no pain yet, only dimness, and the sense of the turmoil coming and going like the waves of the sea. The fighting was over. His head was within a foot of Guinevere's hem. He was dimly conscious of Bedwyr stepping over his body to take the Queen's hands. He heard him speak, low and urgently: "They did not come to you? Is all well?" And her shaken reply, in that soft voice filled with distress and fear: "You're hurt? Oh, my dear—" And his swift: "No. A cut only. It's over. I must leave you with your ladies. Calm yourself, madam, it is over."

Gaheris, back on his feet, but bleeding from a deep cut on the arm, was being dragged away, dazed and unresisting, by the guards. Bors was there, with a face of tragedy, speaking urgently, but the words came and went, like the surge of the sea waves, with the beat of Mordred's pulse. The pain was beginning now. One of the guards said, "Lady—" and tried to lift Linet from Gareth's body. Then the Queen was there, near, kneeling beside Mordred. He could smell her scent, feel the soft wool of the white robe. His blood smeared the wool, but she took no notice. He tried to say, "Lady," but no sound came.

In any case she was not concerned with him. Her arms were round Linet, her voice speaking comfort shot with grief. At length the girl let herself be raised and led aside, and the guards took up Gareth's body to carry it away. Just before he lost consciousness Mordred saw, beside him on the floor, a crumpled paper that had fallen from the Queen's robe as she knelt beside him.

He saw the writing, elegant and regular, the hand of an expert scribe. And at the foot of the message, a seal. He knew that seal. It was Arthur's.

The story of the letter had, after all, been the truth.

Mordred, waking from the first deep swoon, swam up into
consciousness to find himself in his own house, with his
mistress beside the bed, and Gaheris bending over him.

His head ached fiercely, and he was very weak. His wound
had been hurriedly cleaned and bandaged, but blood still
oozed, and the whole arm and side seemed to be one throb
of pain. He could remember nothing of how he had come
here. He did not know that, as he was carried from the
Queen's bedchamber, Bedwyr had shouted to the guards to
see him safe and to tend his hurts. Bedwyr, indeed, was
thinking only of keeping the King's son safely until the King
himself should arrive, but the guards, who had not seen the
fight, assumed in the haste and chaos that Mordred had been
there to help the regent, so bore him straight to his own
house and the care of his mistress. Here Gaheris (having
contrived, by feigning to be worse hurt than he was, to elude
the guards) had fled under cover of that same chaos, with
only one thought in his mind, to get out of Camelot before
Arthur's arrival, and to use Mordred to that end.

For Arthur was on his way home, far sooner than he had
been looked for. The fateful letter, hurriedly dispatched by
a king already on the road, was to warn Guinevere of his
imminent arrival, and to ask her to tell Bedwyr immediately.
Word had gone round already among the guards; Gaheris

ad heard them talking. The courier's delay would mean that the King must be only a few short hours behind him.

So Gaheris leaned urgently over the man in the bed.

"Come, brother, before they remember you! The guards brought you here in error. They will soon know that you were with us, and then they will come back. Quickly now! We've got to go. Come with me, and I'll see you safe."

Mordred blinked up at him, vaguely. His face was drained of blood, and his eyes looked unfocused. Gaheris seized a flask of cordial and splashed some of it into a cup. "Drink this. Hurry, man. My servant's here with me. We'll manage you between us."

The cordial stung Mordred's lips. Some of the painful fog lifted, and memory came back....

It was good of Gaheris, he thought hazily. Good of Gaheris. He had hit Gaheris, and Gaheris had fallen. Then Bedwyr had tried to kill him, Mordred, and the Queen had said no word. Not then, and apparently not since, if the guards were coming back to take him as one of the traitors.... The Queen. She wanted him to die, even though he had saved her life. And he knew why. The reason came to him, through the swimming clouds, like clear and cold logic. She knew of Merlin's prophecy, and so she wanted him to die. Bedwyr, too. So they would lie, and no one would know that he had tried to stop the traitors, had in fact saved her from Gaheris, murderer of women. When the King came, he, Mordred, Arthur's son, would be branded traitor in the sight of all men....

"Hurry," said Gaheris, with urgency.

No guards came. After all, it was easy. With his half-brother's arm round him and his mistress at his other side he walked, no, floated out into the dark street where, tense and silent, Gaheris's servant waited with the horses. Somehow they got Mordred to the saddle, somehow held him between them, then they were out of the town and riding down the road to the King's Gate.

Here they were challenged. Gaheris, pulling back slightly, with his face muffled against the cold, said nothing. The servant, forward with Mordred, spoke impatiently.

"It's Prince Mordred. He's hurt, as you know. We've to take him to Applegarth. Make haste."

The guards knew the story, which had gone round with

the dawn wind. The gates were opened, the riders were through, and free. Gaheris said exultantly: "We did it! We're out! Now let us lose this burden as soon as we may!"

Mordred remembered nothing of the ride. He had a vague recollection of falling, of being caught and pulled across onto the servant's horse, while the dreadful jolting ride went on. He felt the warmth of blood breaking through the bandages, then after what seemed an age the welcome stillness as the horses were pulled up.

Rain drove down on his face. It was cool and refreshing. The rest of his body, closely wrapped as it was, was clothed in hot water. He was floating again. Sounds came and went in beats, like the pulse of the blood that was seeping from the wound. Someone—it was Gaheris—was saying:

"This will do. Don't be afraid, man. The brothers will care for him. Yes, the horse, too. Tie it there. Now leave him."

He laid his cheek on wet stone. His whole body burned and throbbed. It was strange how, when the horses had stopped, the hoofbeats still thudded through his veins.

The servant reached across him and tugged at a rope. Somewhere in the distance a bell jangled. Before the sound had died away the horses were gone. There was no sound in the world but the rain driving steadily down on the stone step where they had left him.

Arthur, arriving almost on the heels of the courier, rode next morning into a city still buzzing like a stirred hive. His regent was sent for before the King had even taken off the dirt of the journey.

When Bedwyr was announced, Arthur was sitting behind the table in his business room, his man at his feet pulling off the scuffed and muddy riding boots. The servant, without a glance at either man, took the boots and withdrew. Ulfin had been Arthur's man throughout his whole reign. He had heard rather more gossip than the next man, and had said a good deal less about it than anyone. But even he, the silent and the trusted, went out with relief. Some things were better not said, or even known.

The same thought was in both men's minds. In Arthur's eyes might even be read the plea to his friend: Do not force me into asking questions. Let us in some way, in any way get past this ambush and back into the open rides of trust. More than friendship, more than love, depends on this silence. My kingdom would even now seem to hang on it.

It would doubtless have surprised the Orkney princes, and some of their faction, if they could have heard his first words. But both King and regent knew that, if the first and greatest trouble could not be spoken of, the second would have to be dealt with soon: Gawain of Orkney.

The King shoved his feet into his furred slippers, swung round in the great chair, and said with furious exasperation: "By all the gods below, did you have to kill them?"

Bedwyr's gesture had the quality of despair.

"What was I to do? Colles I could not avoid killing. I was naked, and he was on me with his sword. I had to take it. I had neither time nor choice, if he was not to kill me. For Gareth I am sincerely sorry. I am to blame. I cannot think that he was there in treachery, but only because he was among the pack when the cry went up, and he may have been anxious for Linet. I confess I hardly saw him in the press. I did cross swords with Gaheris, but only for a moment. I think he took a cut—no more than a scratch—from me, but then he vanished. And after Agravain fell, all my thought was for the Queen. Gaheris had been loudest of all throughout, and he was still shouting insults at her. I remembered how he had dealt with his own mother." He hesitated. "That part was nightmare-like. The swords, the yelled insults, the pack near the Queen, and she, poor lady, struck dumb and shocked all in the few seconds it had taken from peace to bloody war. Have you seen her yet, Arthur? How does she do?"

"I am told she is well, but still shaken. She was with Linet when I sent to inquire. I shall go to her as soon as I've cleaned up. Now tell me the rest of it. What of Mordred? They tell me he was hurt, and that he has gone—fled—with Gaheris. This is something that I fail to understand. He was only with the Young Celts at my request—in fact, he came to me shortly before I left Camelot, to give me some word of warning about what they might be planning to do.... You could not have known that. It was my fault; perhaps I should have told you, but there were aspects of it..." He left it at that, and Bedwyr merely nodded: this was the debatable ground that each man could tread without a word spoken.

Arthur frowned down, then raised troubled eyes to the other man's. "You cannot be blamed for turning your sword on him; how could you guess? But the Queen? He is devoted to her—we used to call it boy's love, and smile at it, and so did she—so why on earth should he have tried to harm the Queen?"

"It is not certain that he did. I'm not sure what happened there. When I crossed swords with Mordred, the affair was almost over. I had the Queen safe at my back, and by that time the guards were there. I would have disarmed him and then spoken with him, or else waited for your coming, but he is too good a fighter. I had to wound him, to get the sword from his hand."

"Well," said Arthur heavily, "he is gone. But why? And especially, why with Gaheris, unless indeed Mordred is still spying for me? You know where they will have gone, of course."

"To Gawain?"

"Exactly. And what," said Arthur, his voice warming into a kind of desperation, "are we going to do about Gawain?"

Bedwyr said, grim-mouthed: "Let me take what comes."

"And kill him? If you do not, he will kill you. You must know that. And I will not have it either way. Troublesome though he is, I need Gawain."

"I am in your hands. You'll send me away, I suppose. You can hardly send Gawain, I see that. So, when, and where?"

"As for when, not immediately." Arthur hesitated, then looked straight at the other man. "I must first of all give some public evidence of trust in you."

As if without thinking, his hand had strayed across the surface of the table. This was of veined green marble, edged with wrought gold. The King, on coming in, had flung his gloves down there, and Ulfin, in his haste to be gone, had left them. Now Arthur picked one of them up, and ran it through his fingers. It was a glove of softest calf-skin, worked as supple as velvet, its cuff embroidered with silken threads in rainbow colours, and with small river-pearls. The Queen herself had done the work, not letting her women set even one of the stitches. The pearls had come from the rivers of her native land.

Bedwyr met the King's eyes. His own, the dark poet's

eyes, were profoundly unhappy. The King's were as somber, but held kindness.

"As for where, will your cousin make you welcome in your family's castle in Brittany? I should like you to be there. Go first, if you will, to King Hoel at Kerrec. I think he will be glad to know that you are so near. These are anxious times for him, and he is old, and ailing a little lately. But we'll talk about this before you go. Now I must see the Queen."

From Guinevere, to his great relief, Arthur learned the truth. Far from attacking her, Mordred had prevented Gaheris from getting to her with his sword. He had, indeed, struck Gaheris down, before himself being attacked by Bedwyr. His subsequent flight, then, must have been through fear of being identified (as Bedwyr had apparently identified him) with the disloyal faction of Young Celts. This was puzzling enough, since Bors, as well as the Queen, could obviously swear to his loyalty, but the greater puzzle lay behind: why should he have fled with, of all men, Gaheris? To this Mordred's mistress, on being questioned, provided the first clue. Gaheris, himself bleeding and obviously distraught, had managed to convince her of her lover's danger; how easy, then, it had been for him to persuade the half-conscious and weakened prince that his only hope lay in flight. She had added her own pleas to Gaheris's urging, had helped them to the horses, and seen them go.

The gate guards finished the tale, and the truth was plain. Gaheris had taken the wounded man as his own shield and pass to freedom. Arthur, now seriously concerned for his son's health and safety, sent the royal couriers out immediately to find Mordred and bring him home. When it was reported that neither Mordred nor Gaheris had been to Gawain, the King ordered a country-wide search for his son. Gaheris they had orders to secure. He would be held until the King had spoken with Gawain, who was already on his way to Camelot.

Gareth, alone of the dead, lay in the royal chapel. After his burial Linet would take her grief back to her father's house. The affair was over, but about Camelot hung still a murmur of disaster, as if the bright gold of its towers, the vivid scarlet and green and blue of its flags, was smeared over with the grey of a coming sadness. The Queen wore mourning; it was for Gareth, and for the other deaths and spilled blood of what was noised abroad as a mistaken loyalty; but there were those who said that it was mourning for the departure of her lover into Brittany. But they whispered it more softly than before, and as often as not the rumour was hotly denied. There had been smoke, and fire, but now the fire was out, and the smoke was gone.

It was to be seen that the Queen kissed the departing marshal on both cheeks; then, after her, the King did the same. And Bedwyr, apparently unmoved after the Queen's embrace, had tears in his eyes as he turned from the King.

The court saw him off, then turned with anticipation to greet Gawain.

The doorstep where Mordred had been abandoned belonged, not to one of the King's protected foundations, but to a small community living remote from any town or road, and vowed to silence and poverty. The track that led through their little valley was used only by shepherds, or strayed travellers looking for a short cut, or, as in Gaheris's case, by fugitives. No messenger came there, no news, even, of the recent stirring scenes enacted in Arthur's capital. The good brothers nursed Mordred with dutifully Christian care, and even with some skill, for one of their number was a herbalist. They had no way of guessing who the stranger was who had been left on their doorstep during the storm. He was well dressed, but carried neither weapon nor money. Some traveller, no doubt, who had been robbed, and who owed his life to the fear—even perhaps the piety—of the thieves. So the brothers nursed the stranger, fed him from their plain rations, and were thankful when, the fever gone, he insisted on leaving their roof. His horse was there, an undistinguished beast. They packed a saddle-bag for him of black bread, wine in a leather flask, and a handful of raisins, and sent him on his way with a blessing and, it must be admitted, a private Te Deum afterwards. There had been something about the grim and silent man that had frightened them, and the brother who had watched his sleep had told them with fear of words spoken in grief and dread where the names of the High King and his Queen recurred. Nothing more could be understood: Mordred, deep in fever, had raved in the language of his childhood, where Sula and Guinevere and Queen Morgause came and went in the hot shadows, and all looks were alien, all words hurtful.

The wound was healed, but some residue of weakness remained. He rode barely eight miles on the first day, thankful for the plodding steadiness of the beast he bestrode. By instinct he went northward. That night he spent in a deserted woodcutter's hut deep in the forest; he had no money for an inn, nor had the brothers been able to spare him any. He would have to live, as they did (he thought hazily, as he huddled for warmth in his cloak and waited for sleep), on charity. Or else on work.

The thought, strange for so many years, aroused him to a sort of bitter amusement. Work? A knight's work was fighting. A weaponless man on a poor horse would be taken on only by the pettiest and poorest of rulers. And any ruler would ask questions. So, what work?

Out of the advancing clouds of sleep the answer came, with amusement still gone awry, but with something about it of an old longing. Sail. Fish. Dig peats. Grow a thin crop of grain and harvest it.

An owl sweeping low over the woodcutter's thatch gave its high, tearing cry. Half asleep, and already in vision on the edge of the northern sea, Mordred heard it as the cry of a gull, and it seemed like part of a decision already made. He would go home. He had been hidden there once before. He would hide there again. And even if they came looking for him amongst the islands, they would be hard put to it to find him. It did not occur to him to do anything but hide, so fixed in his poisoned delirium had Gaheris's lies and his own delusions become.

He turned over and slept, with cold air on his face and the cry of the gull still in his dream. Next day he turned westward. Two successive nights he spent in the open, avoiding the monastery houses where he might have heard of Arthur's search for him. The third was passed in a peasant's hut, where he shared the last of the brothers' hard bread and wine, and chopped firewood for his lodging-fee.

On the fourth day he reached the sea. He sold the horse, and with the money paid his passage northward on a small and barely seaworthy trader which was the last to leave port for the islands before winter closed the way.

Meanwhile Gawain came back to Camelot. Arthur sent Bors to meet him, to give him a full account of the tragedy, and also to temper as far as he might Gawain's grief over Gareth and Agravain and his anger with their killer. Bors did his best, but all his talk, his assertion of the Queen's innocence, his tale of Agravain's drunkenness and habitual (in these days) violence, of Gaheris's murderous intentions, of the attack on the unarmed Bedwyr, and the half-lit chaos of the fighting in the Queen's bedchamber... say what he might, nothing moved Gawain. Gareth's undeserved death was all he spoke of, and, Bors began to think, all he slept, ate and dreamed with.

"I'll meet him, and when I do, I shall kill him," was all he would say.

"He's been sent away from court. The King has banished him. Not for anything that stains the Queen, but—"

"To keep him out of my reach. Yes. Well," said Gawain stonily, "I can wait."

"If you do kill Bedwyr," said Bors, desperately, "be sure Arthur will kill you."

The hot, blood-veined Orkney eyes turned to him. "So?" Then the eyes turned away. Gawain's head went up. They were just in sight of the golden towers, and the sound of a bell tolling slowly came floating, echoing from the water that edged the roadway. They would be there for Gareth's burial.

Bors saw the tears on Gawain's cheeks, and, drawing his horse back, said no more.

What passed between Gawain and his uncle the High King no one else ever knew. They were closeted together in the King's private rooms for the best part of a day, from the moment the funeral was over, right into the night and towards the next morning. Afterwards, without a word to any man, Gawain went to his rooms and slept for sixteen hours, then rose, armed himself, and rode to the practice field. That evening he ate at a tavern in the city, and stayed through the night with a girl there, reappearing next day in the field.

For eight days and nights he did this, talking with no one except as business required. On the ninth day he left Camelot, escorted, and rode the few miles to Ynys Witrin, where the King's ship, the latest *Sea Dragon*, lay.

She set her golden sail, raised her crimson dragon to the autumn winds, and weighed anchor promptly for the north.

It was Arthur's bid for two things: to get a trouble-maker as far out of the way as possible, and into the cooling winds of distance and time; and to give Gawain's hurt and angry spirit some work to do.

He had done the obvious thing, the one thing Mordred had not even thought of. Gawain, King of the Orkneys, had gone back to take up the rule of his islands.

BOOK III

The
Wicked Day

SAXONIA

AUSTRASIA

• METZ

NEUSTRIA

PARIS

BRITTANY

BENOIC

• KERREC

• ORLEANS

R. LOIRE

• AUTUN

BURGUNDY

AQUITAINIA

R. RHONE

BORDEAUX

PROVENCE

SEPTIMANIA

TOULOUSE

• MARSEILLES

VISIGOTHIC
KINGDOM

I

Winter passed, and March came in with its roaring winds and spasmodic storms, then softened towards the sweetness of an early spring. Sea-pinks covered the cliffs with rose, white flowers danced along the arched bramble boughs, red campion and wild hyacinth shone in the grass. Nesting birds called over the lochs, and the moors echoed to the curlew's bubbling note. On every skerry, and every grassy bank near the water, swans had built their weedy castles, and on each one slept a great white bird, head under wing, while the watchful mate cruised nearby, head up and wings set like sails. The water's surface echoed with the screaming of the oystercatchers and the gulls, and the upper sky quivered with lark-song.

A man and a boy were working on the stretch of moorland heather that covers the rolling center of Orkney's main island. At this time of year the heather was dark and dead-looking, but along the edges of the trodden roadway, and by every bank, crowded the pale, scented primroses. At the foot of the rolling moorland lay a thin strip of grazing, golden with dandelions. Beyond this a great loch stretched, and beyond that again, another, lying almost parallel, the two great waters separated at their southern extremities only by a narrow causeway and a strip of land well trodden by hoofs and feet, for this was a holy place in the islands. Here stood the great circles of stone, brooding, enigmatic, huge, and to be feared even by those who knew nothing of their purpose or their building. It was well known that no horse could be made to cross the causeway between dusk and dawning, and no deer had ever been seen to feed there. Only the goats, unchancy creatures always, would graze between the stones, keeping the grass smooth and short for the ceremonies still practiced there at the right seasons.

The two workers were busy on a level piece of moorland not far above these lochs with their guarded causeway. The man was tall, lean, hard, and though dressed as a peasant he did not move like one; his were the swift economical movements of a trained body. His face, young still, but engraved with bitter lines, was restless, in spite of the country tasks and the tranquil day. Beside him the boy, dark-eyed like his father, helped him peg together a board for one of the hives that would be carried to the moor when the heather bloomed, and set on the neat row of platforms that awaited them.

To them, with no warning but the soft pace of hoofs in the heather, and a shadow falling across the man's preoccupation, came Orkney's king, Gawain.

The man looked up. Gawain, starting a casual greeting, checked his horse sharply and stared.

"Mordred!"

Mordred let fall the mallet he had been using, and got slowly to his feet as a group of riders, a dozen or so with footmen and hounds, followed the king over the brow of the hill. The boy stopped his task and straightened to stare, openmouthed.

Mordred laid a reassuring hand on his son's shoulder. "Why, Gawain! Greetings."

"You?" said Gawain. "Here? Since when? And who is this?" His look measured the boy. "No, I don't need to ask that! He's more like Arthur—" He checked himself.

Mordred said dryly: "Don't trouble. He speaks only the island tongue."

"By the gods," said Gawain, diverted in spite of himself, "if you got that one before you left here you must have been up earlier than any of us!"

The other riders had come up with them. Gawain, with a gesture, sent them back to wait out of earshot. He slipped

270

from the saddle, and a groom ran forward to lead his horse aside. Gawain seated himself on one of the wooden platforms. Mordred, after a moment's hesitation, sat down on another. The boy, at a gesture from his father, began to gather up the tools they had been using. He did it slowly, stealing glances all the while at the king and his followers.

"Now," said Gawain, "tell me. How and why, all of it. The tale went out that you were dead, or you'd have been discovered long since, but I never believed that, somehow. What happened?"

"Do you need to ask? Gaheris must have told you. I assumed he was riding to join you."

"You didn't know? But I'm a fool, how could you? Gaheris is dead."

"Dead? How? Did the King catch up with him? I'd hardly have thought, even so—"

"Nothing to do with the King. Gaheris was wounded that night, nothing much, but he neglected it, and it went bad. If he had come to me—but he didn't. He must have known how little welcome he would be. He went north to his leman, and by the time they got to him there, there was no help for him. Another," said Gawain bitterly, "to Bedwyr's account."

Mordred was silent. He himself could mourn none of them but Gareth, but to Gawain, the only survivor now of that busy and close Orkney clan, the loss was heavy. He said as much, and for a while they spoke of the past, memories made more vivid by the familiar landscape stretching around them. Then Mordred, choosing his words, began to feel his way.

"You spoke of Bedwyr with bitterness. I understand this, believe me, but Bedwyr was hardly to blame for Gaheris's own folly. Or, in fact, for anything that happened that night. I don't plan to hold him accountable even for this." He touched his shoulder, briefly. "You must see that, Gawain, now that you have had time to come to terms with your grief. Agravain was the leader that night, and Gaheris with him. They were determined to destroy Bedwyr, even if it meant destroying the Queen as well. Nothing anyone could say—"

"I know. I knew them. Agravain was a fool, and Gaheris a mad fool, and still carrying the blood-guilt for a worse crime than any done that night. But I was not thinking of them. I was thinking of Gareth. He deserved better of life than to be murdered by a man he trusted, a man whom he had served."

"For the gods' sake, that was no murder!" Mordred spoke explosively, and his son looked up quickly, alarmed. Mordred spoke quietly in the local tongue. "Take the tools back to the house. We'll do no more work here today. Tell your mother I'll come down before long. Don't worry, all is well."

The boy ran off. The two men watched, not speaking, while the slight figure dwindled downhill in the distance. There was a cottage set in a hollow near the loch-side, its thatch barely visible against the heather. The boy vanished through the low doorway.

Mordred turned back to Gawain. He spoke earnestly. "Gawain, don't think I have not grieved for Gareth as much as any man could. But believe me, his death was an accident, as far as a killing in hot blood in a crazy mêlée can be an accident. And Gareth was armed. Bedwyr was not when he was attacked. I doubt if for the first minutes he even knew who was at the edge of his blade."

"Ah, yes." The bitterness was still in Gawain's voice. "Everyone knows you were on his side."

Mordred's head went up. He spoke incredulously. "You know *what*?"

"Well, even if you weren't for Bedwyr, at least it's known you were against the attack. Which was sense, I suppose. Even if they had been caught in bed together, twined naked, the King would have punished the attackers even before he dealt with Bedwyr and the Queen."

"I don't understand you. And this is beside the point. There never was any question of adultery." Mordred spoke with stiff anger, a royal rebuke that came incongruously from the shabby workmanlike peasant to the splendidly dressed king. "The King had sent a letter to the Queen, which she wished to show Bedwyr. I suppose it was to tell them he was on his way home. I saw it there, in her chamber. And when we broke in they were both fully clad—warmly wrapped, even—and her women were awake in the ante-room. One of them was in the bedchamber with Bedwyr and the Queen. Not an easy setting for adultery."

"Yes, yes." Gawain spoke impatiently. "I know all this. I spoke with my uncle the High King." Some echo in the

272

ords, in that place, brought memory back. His glance
lifted. He said quickly: "The King told me what had hap-
ened. It seems you tried to stop the fool Agravain, and you
d prevent Gaheris from harming the Queen. If he had even
uched her—"

"Wait. This is what I don't understand. How do you know
is? Bedwyr could not have seen what happened, or he
ould not have attacked me as he did. And I think Bors had
ready gone for the guard. So how did the King hear the
uth of the matter?"

"The Queen told him, of course."

Mordred was silent. The air round him was filled with the
nging of the moorland birds, but what he heard was silence,
e haunted silence of those long dreaming nights. She had
en. She knew. She had not hunted him away.

He said slowly: "I begin to see. Gaheris told me the guards
ere coming for me, and I must leave Camelot to save my-
lf. He would take me away to safety, he said, in spite of
e risk to himself. Even at the time, astray though I was in
y wits, I thought it strange. I had struck him down myself,
save the Queen."

"Gaheris, my dear Mordred, was saving no one's skin but
s own. Did it not occur to you to wonder why the guards
t him out of the gates, when they must have known of the
fray? Gaheris alone they would have stopped. But Prince
lordred, when Bedwyr himself had given orders that he
as to be cared for . . . ?"

"I barely remember anything about it. The ride is like a
ad dream. Part of a bad dream."

"Then think of it now. That is what happened. Gaheris
ot out, and away, and as soon as he could he left you, to
e or to recover, as God and the good brothers might con-
ive."

"You know of that, too?"

"Arthur found the monastery after a time, but you had
one. He had riders out searching for you, the length and
readth of the land. In the end they counted you lost, or
ead." A smile without mirth in it. "A grim jest of the gods,
rother. It was Gaheris who died, and you who were mourned.
ou would have been flattered. When the next Council was
eld—"

Mordred did not hear the rest. He got suddenly to his

feet, and took a few paces away. The sun was setting, an
westward the water of the great loch shimmered and shone
Beyond it, between it and the blaze of the sunset, loome
the hills of the High Island. He drew a long breath. It wa
like a slow coming alive again. Once, long ago, a boy ha
stood like this, on the shore not far from here, with his hear
reaching out across the hills and the water to the remote an
coloured kingdoms. Now a man stood gazing the same way
seeing the same visions, with the hard bitterness breakin
in his brain. He had not been hunted. He had not bee
traduced. His name was still bright silver. His father sough
for him in peace. And the Queen...

Gawain said: "A courier will be here within the sennight
You'll let me send a message?"

"No need. I'll go myself."

Gawain, regarding his lighted face, nodded. "And those?
A gesture towards the distant cottage.

"Will stay here. The boy will soon be able to take m
place and do the man's work."

"Your wife, is she?"

"So she calls herself. There was some local rite, cake
and a fire. It pleased her." He turned the subject. "Tell me
Gawain, how long will you be here?"

"I don't know. The courier may bring news."

"Do you expect to be summoned back again? I hardl
need to ask," said Mordred bluntly, "why you are here i
the islands. If you do go back, what then of Bedwyr?"

Gawain's face hardened, setting in the familiar obstinat
cast. "Bedwyr will tread warily. And so, I suppose, will I.

His gaze went past Mordred. A woman had come out c
the distant cottage, and, with the boy beside her, stood gaz
ing towards them. The breeze moulded her gown agains
her, and her long hair blew free in a flurry of gold.

"Yes, well, I see," said Gawain. "What is the boy's name?
"Medraut."

"Grandson to the High King," said Gawain, musing. "Doe
he know?"

"No," said Mordred sharply. "Nor will he. He does nc
even know he is mine. She was wedded after I left the is
lands, and she bore three other children before her man wa
drowned. He was a fisherman. I knew him when we wer
boys. Her parents live still, and help her care for the childrer

274

They made me welcome, and were glad to get us handfasted after so long, but I could see they never expected me to stay for long, and she, certainly, has said she will never leave the islands. I have promised to see them all provided for. To the children—to all four of them—I am their stepfather. Some day Medraut may get to know that he is the bastard of 'King Lot's bastard,' but that is all, until perhaps one day I send for him. And saving your presence, brother, there are a few of those around. What need to whet ambition further?"

"What indeed?" Gawain got to his feet. "Well, will you stay with them, or come with me now to await the ship? The palace will give you more comfort than your hidingplace."

"Give me a day or so to make my peace, and I'll come." Mordred laughed suddenly. "It will be interesting to see how its luxury strikes me this time, after these months back at my old tasks! I haven't lost the taste for fishing, but I confess I was not looking forward to digging the peats!"

The King's relief and pleasure, and the Queen's obvious happiness at seeing him again, were, to Mordred, like the breaking of summer after a long winter of near-starvation. Not much was said about the events of that grim night; it was something that neither Arthur nor the Queen wished to dwell on; instead they asked for news of Mordred's months in exile, and soon, as he told of his attempts to get back into the hard-working rhythms of his childhood, they all three lost the memories of the "dreadful night" in laughter.

They spoke then of Gawain, and Mordred handed his half-brother's letter to the King. Arthur read it, then looked up.

"You know what's in this?"

"The main of it, yes, sir. He said he would petition you to let him come south again."

Arthur nodded. His next remark answered the question Mordred had not asked. "Bedwyr is still in Brittany, at his castle of Benoic, north of the great forest that they call Perlous. Indeed, to our loss, he looks to be settled there. He married during the winter."

Mordred, back in the stronghold of courtiers, betrayed no surprise except with a slight lift of the brows. Before he could speak, Guinevere, rising, brought both men to their feet. Her face was pale, and for the first time Mordred saw, in its lively beauty, the signs of strain and sleeplessness. Her mouth had lost some of its gentle fullness, as if it had been set over too many silences.

"I will go now, by your leave, my lords. You will have much still to say to one another, after so long." Her hand went out again to Mordred. "Come soon to talk with me again. I long to hear more of your strange islands. Meanwhile be welcome here, back in your home."

Arthur waited until the door shut behind her. He was silent for a space, and his look was heavy and brooding. Mordred wondered if he was thinking back to the events of that night, but all he said was:

"I tried to warn you, Mordred. But how could you have read my warning? Or reading it, what could you have done, more than you did? Well, it's done with. Again I thank you, and now let us speak no more of it.... But we must needs discuss the result. When you spoke with Gawain, what did he say of Bedwyr?"

"That he would contain himself as best he could. If tolerance of Bedwyr is the price for coming back into service with the Companions, then I think he will pay it."

"He says as much in this letter. Do you think he will keep to this?"

Mordred moved his shoulders in a shrug. "As far as he can, I suppose. He is loyal to you, sir, be sure of that. But you know his temper, and whether he can control it..." He shrugged again. "Will you recall him?"

"He is not banished. He is free to come, and if he does so of his own will, all should be well enough. Bedwyr is settled in Brittany, and he has written to me that his wife goes with child. So for all our sakes, and for my cousin Hoel's, too, it is best that he stay there. There is trouble coming in Brittany, Mordred, and Bedwyr's sword may be needed there, along with mine."

"Already? You spoke of this before."

"No. Not the matter that we discussed before. There is a totally new situation. While you were away in your islands there has been news from abroad, which will bring great changes both in the eastern and western empires."

He went on to explain. News had come of the death of Theodoric, king of Rome and ruler of the western empire. He had reigned for thirty years, and his death would bring changes as great as they were sudden. Though a Goth, and

276

erefore by definition a barbarian, Theodoric, like many of is race, had admired and respected Rome even as he fought conquer her and make a place for his own people in the indly climate of Italy. He had embraced what he saw to be est in Roman culture, and had attempted to restore, or shore p, the structures of Roman law and the Roman peace. Uner him Goths and Romans continued to be separate nations, ound by their own laws and answerable to their own triunals. The king, from his capital in Ravenna, ruled with istice and even with gentleness, welding together a loyal gislature both in Ravenna and Rome, where the ancient tles of procurator, consul, legate, were still conferred and pheld.

Theodoric was succeeded by his daughter, acting as reent for her ten-year-old son, Athalaric. But it was not thought at the boy had any chance of the succession. In Byzantium, o, there had been a change. The ageing emperor Justin ad abdicated in favour of his nephew Justinian, and had laced upon his head the diadem of the East.

The new emperor Justinian, wealthy, ambitious, and erved by brilliant commanders, was reputed to be eager to estore the lost glories of the Roman Empire. It was ruioured that he had already cast his eyes towards the land f the Vandals, on the southern fringe of the Mediterranean; ut it seemed likely that he would first seek to extend his mpire westward. The Franks of Childebert and his brothers ept a watch always for any movement from the east, but ow to the perennial threat of the Burgundians and the Aleians might be added the larger menace of Rome. Behind e barrier of Frankish Gaul, and dependent on her goodwill, ly the tiny land of Brittany.

Bordered on three sides by the sea, on the fourth Brittany as defended only by land nominally Frankish, but in fact alf deserted, a dense forest peopled by wary tribesmen or lk displaced by war, who huddled together in makeshift illages, and with their half-savage leaders led an existence wing allegiance to no man.

Recently, King Hoel had written, there had been disuieting reports from some of these forest enclaves to the orth-east of his capital. Reports had filtered in of raids, bbery, violent attacks on householders, and, the most reent, a horrifying case of wholesale slaughter where a farmstead had been deliberately fired, and its inmates—eight people with some half-dozen children—burned to death, and their goods and animals stolen. Fear had spread in the forest, and it was being murmured that the raiders were Franks. There was no confirmation of this, but anger was rising, and Hoel feared blind reprisals and a *casus belli*, at the very moment when friendship with his Frankish neighbours was most necessary.

"Hoel's own men could doubtless deal with it," said Arthur, "but he suggests that my presence, with some of the Companions, and a show of strength, might be an advantage, not just in this, but in the graver matter that he writes of. But see for yourself."

He handed Hoel's letter to Mordred. The latter, alone of the Orkney brothers, had, under the tuition of the priest who had taught them the mainland speech, taken the trouble to learn to read. Now he frowned his way slowly through the beautifully penned Latin of Hoel's scribe.

It seemed that King Hoel had recently received a message sent, not by the new emperor, but by an officer purporting to represent him. This was one Lucius Quintilianus, called Hiberus, "the Spaniard," one of the recently styled consuls. Writing with a truly imperial arrogance, and quoting Rome as if she still bristled with eagles and legions, he had sent to Hoel demanding gold and a levy of troops—far more than he could ever raise—to "help Rome protect Brittany from the Burgundians." He did not state what the penalty would be for refusal; he did not need to.

"But the Franks? King Childebert?" asked Mordred.

"Like his brothers, a mere shadow of their father. Hoel believes they must have had the same demand, so it looks as if Rome must have strength enough to enforce it. Mordred, I am afraid of this emperor. The Celtic lands have not weathered Rome's desertion, and the threat of barbarian domination, to accept once again the collar and chain of Rome, whatever 'protection' she brings with her."

The situation, Mordred reflected, was not without its ironies. Arthur, blamed at home by the Young Celts for his adherence to Roman forms of law and centralized government, was nevertheless prepared to resist a possible attempt to bring Celtic territories back within Rome's fold.

"Under her yoke, rather!" said Arthur, in reply to his

son's wry comment. "The times are long past when, in return for tribute, a king and his people were protected. Britain was taken by force, and thereafter forced to pay tribute to Rome. In return she enjoyed, after the settlement, a period of peace. Then Rome, self-seeking as always, lifted her shield, and left her weakened dependencies open to the barbarians. We in these islands, and our cousins in their near-isle of Brittany, alone kept our nationhood and remained stable. We have achieved our own peace. Rome cannot expect now to reimpose debts we do not owe. We have as much right to demand tribute from her for Roman territories which are now British again!"

Mordred said, startled: "Are you saying that this new emperor—Justinian?—has demanded tribute of *us*?"

"No. Not yet. But if he has asked it of Brittany, then sooner or later he will ask it of me."

"When do you go, sir?"

"Preparations are already well forward. We go as soon as we may. Yes, I said 'we.' I want you with me."

"But with Bedwyr away in Brittany—or will you leave Duke Constantine in charge here?"

Arthur shook his head. "No need. It should not be a long visit. The immediate business is this trouble in the Perilous Forest, and that should not take us long to clear up." He smiled. "If we do see action there, you can call it re-training after your holiday in the Orkney isles! If the other matter becomes serious, then I shall send you home as my regent. Meanwhile I shall leave the Council in charge, with the Queen, and send a sop to Duke Constantine in the form of a letter charging him with the guardianship of the west."

"A sop?"

"A comfort and a drug, maybe, for a violent and ambitious gentleman." Arthur nodded at Mordred's quick lift of the brows. "Yes, Too violent, I have long thought, for the country's need. His father Cador, to whom I promised the kingdoms in default of an heir of my body, was of different metal. This man is as good a fighter as his father, but I mislike some of the tales I have heard about him. So I give him a little favour, and when I return from Brittany, I will send for him here and come to an understanding."

They were interrupted then by an urgent message relayed

from the harbour on Ynys Witrin where the *Sea Dragon* lay. She was equipped, provisioned, and ready to sail. So the King said no more, and he and Mordred parted to make ready for the journey into Brittany.

2

As so often happens, one trouble breeds another. While Arthur and his Companions were still on the Narrow Sea, tragedy, this time real and immediate, struck at Brittany's royal house.

King Hoel's niece Elen, sixteen years old and a beauty, set out one day from her father's home towards Hoel's castle at Kerrec. The party never arrived. Her guards and servants were attacked and killed, and the girl and one of her women, her old nurse, Clemency, were carried off. The other woman in the party, though unhurt, was too shocked to give a coherent account of what had happened. The attack had taken place at dusk, almost within sight of the place where the party had proposed to lodge for the night, and she had not noticed what badge the attackers wore, or indeed anything about them, except that their leader, he who had dragged Elen up before him on his horse and spurred off into the forest, had been "a giant of a man, with eyes like a wolf and a shock of hair like a bear's pelt, and an arm like an oak tree."

Hoel, not unnaturally discounting most of this, jumped to the conclusion that the outrage was the work of the ruffians who had been terrorizing the Forest. Whether they were Bretons or Franks, his hand was forced. The women must be rescued, and the attackers punished. Even King

Childebert would not blame the Breton king for avenging such an outrage. Arthur and his party sailed into Kerrec's harbour to find the place in a turmoil, and themselves just in time to lead the hastily mounted punitive expedition into the Forest. Hoel's chief captain, a trusted veteran, with a troop of Breton cavalry, accompanied Arthur and his Companions.

The party rode fast, and more or less in silence. According to what information could be gathered from the princess's surviving waiting-woman, the attack had taken place on a lonely stretch of road just where the way left the Forest and bordered a brackish lake. This was one of the shore lagoons, not quite an inlet of the sea, but moved by the tides, and in spring and autumn washed through by the sea itself.

They reached the lake shore soon after dusk, and halted short of the site of the abduction, to wait for daylight, and for Bedwyr to join them. There had been no rain for several days, so Arthur was hopeful that there would still be traces of the struggle, and tracks to show which way the marauders had gone. Hoel's messenger had gone ahead already to Benoic, and now, just as orders were given for the night's halt, Bedwyr arrived out of the dark with a troop of men at his back.

Arthur greeted his friend with joy, and over supper they fell at once to talk and planning for the next move. No shadow of the past seemed to touch them; the only reference, and that oblique, to the events that had banished Bedwyr to Less Britain was when he greeted Mordred.

This was after supper, when the latter was on his way to the pickets to see that his horse had been properly cared for. Bedwyr fell in beside him, apparently bent on the same errand.

"They tell me that you, too, have been sojourning in the outer dark, Mordred. I am glad to see you back with the King. You are fully recovered now, I trust?"

"Small thanks to you, yes," said Mordred, but smiling. He added: "On second thoughts, all thanks to you. You could have killed me, and we both know it."

"Not quite so easy. The decisions were not all mine, and I think we both know that, too. You're a bonny fighter, Mordred. Some day perhaps we may meet again . . . and in rather less earnest?"

"Why not? Meantime I am told I am to wish you happy. I gather you are lately wedded? Who is she?"

"Her father is Pelles, a king in Neustria whose land borders mine. Her name is Elen, too."

The name jolted them back to the urgencies of the moment. As they inspected their horses Mordred said: "You must know the ground hereabouts?"

"I know it well. It's barely a day's ride from my family's castle of Benoic. We used to hunt here, and fish the lake. Many's the time my cousins and I—"

He broke off, straightening.

"Look yonder, Mordred! What's that?"

"That" was a point of light, red, flickering with shadows. Another wavered below it.

"It's a fire. On the shore, or near it. You can see the reflection."

"Not on the shore," said Bedwyr. "The shore is farther away. There's an island there, though. We used to land and make fire to cook the fish. It must be there."

"No one lives there?"

"No. There's nothing there. That side of the lake is wild land, and the island itself nothing but a pile of rock with ferns and heather, and on the summit a grove of pine trees. If someone is there now it's worth our while to find out who it is."

"An island?" said Mordred. "It might well be. A good choice, one would think, for a night or so of undisturbed rape."

"It has been known," said the other, very dryly. He turned with the words, and the two men went swiftly back to Arthur.

The King had already seen the fire. He was giving orders, and men were hurrying to saddle up again. He turned quickly to Bedwyr.

"You saw? Well, it could be. It's worth looking at, anyway. How do we best get there? And without alarming them?"

"You can't surprise them with horses. It's an island." Bedwyr repeated what he had told Mordred. "There's a spit of land, rock and gravel, running out from the shore on the far side of the lake. That's about three miles from here. You can get half that distance by the shore road, then you must leave it and enter the forest. There's no path there along the shore; you would have to make a wide detour to skirt the thick trees. Bad going, and quite impossible in the dark. And the forest goes all the way to the sea."

"Then it hardly seems likely that their horses are round there. If that's our rapist still on the island, then he got there by boat, and his horse will still be on the shore road. Right. We'll take a look, then picket the road in case he tries to make a break. Meanwhile we need a boat ourselves. Bedwyr?"

"There should be one not far away. This is oyster water. The beds are only a short way from here, and there may be a boat there—unless, of course, that's the one he took."

But the oyster-fisher's boat was there, lying beached on the shingle near a pier of rough stones. The boat was a crude, shallow-draught affair with an almost flat bottom. Normally she would be poled out slowly over the oysterbeds, but there were paddles, too, tied together and stuck up in the ground like flagstaffs.

Willing hands seized her and shoved her down the shingle. The men moved quietly and quickly, without talking.

Arthur, looking out towards the distant glimmer, spoke softly. "I'll take the shore road. Bedwyr"—a smile sounded in his voice—"you're the expert on expeditions of this kind. The island's yours. Who do you want with you?"

"These craft won't hold more than two, and they're hard to handle if you're to go farther than pole depth. I'll take the other expert. The fisherman's son, if he'll come."

"Mordred?"

"Willingly." He added, dryly: "Re-training after my sojourn in the islands?" and heard Arthur laugh under his breath.

"Go, then, and God go with you. Let us pray the girl still lives."

The boat went smoothly down the bank, met the water, and rode rocking there. Bedwyr took his seat cautiously in the stern, with the pole overside to act as rudder, and Mordred, stepping lightly in after him, gripped the paddles, and settled down to row. With a last shove from the men on shore, they were afloat, and drifting into darkness. They could just hear, above the lapping of the lake, the muffled sounds as the troop moved off, their horses keeping to the soft edges of the roadway.

Mordred rowed steadily, pushing the clumsy craft through

the water at a fair speed. Bedwyr, motionless in the stern, watched for the guiding glimmer from the island.

"The fire must be almost dead. I've lost the light. . . . Ah, it's all right, I can see the island shore now. By your left a little. That's it. Keep as you are."

Soon the island was quite clear to their night-sight. It was small, peaked, black against dark, floating dimly on the faint luminescence of the lagoon. A slight breeze ruffled the water, and concealed the sound of the paddles. Now that the fitful and somehow baleful light of the fire had vanished, the night seemed empty, and very peaceful. There were stars, and the breeze smelled of the sea.

They both heard it at the same moment. Over the water, in a lull of the breeze, came a sound, soft and dreadful, that dispelled the illusory peace of the night. A long, keening ululation of grief and fear. On the island. A woman crying.

Bedwyr cursed under his breath. Mordred drove the paddles in hard, and the clumsy boat jumped and lurched, swinging broadside onto the rock of the shore. He shipped the paddles and grabbed at the rock in one spare, expert movement. Bedwyr jumped past him, his sword ready in his hand.

He paused for a moment, winding his cloak round his left arm. "Beach her. Find his boat and sink it. If he dodges me, stay here and kill him."

Mordred was already out, and busy with the rope. From the black wooded bank above them the sounds came again, hopeless, terrified. The night was filled with weeping. Bedwyr, treading from shingle to pine needles, vanished in silence.

Mordred made the boat fast, drew his own weapon, and moved quietly along the shingle, looking for the other boat.

The island was tiny. In a very few minutes he was back at his starting-point. There was no boat. Whoever he was, whatever he had done, he was gone. Mordred, his sword at the ready, climbed fast after Bedwyr towards the noise of weeping.

The fire was not quite out. A pile of ashes still showed a residual glow. Beside it, in its faint red light, the woman sat, hunched and wailing. Her hair, straggling unbound over a torn robe of some dark colour, showed pale. The fire had been kindled on the island's summit, where a stand of pine trees, clinging to what seemed to be bare rock, had laid down

285

a carpet of needles, and where a cairn, built long ago and fallen apart with time and weather, made some sort of crude shelter. The grove appeared to be empty but for the crouched and mourning figure of the woman.

Mordred, many years younger than the other man, was close behind him as he reached the grove. The two men paused there.

She heard them, and looked up. The starlight, and the faint glimmer from the fire, showed that this was no girl, but an old woman, grey-haired, her face a mask of fear and grief. The wailing stopped as if she had been struck in the throat. Her body stiffened. Her mouth gaped wider, as if for a scream.

Bedwyr put out a hand and spoke quickly:

"Madam—Mother—don't be afraid. We are friends. Friends. We have come to help."

The scream was choked back on a strangled gasp. They heard her breathing, short and ragged, as she strained white-eyed to see them.

They moved forward slowly. "Be calm, Mother," said Bedwyr. "We are from the King—"

"From which king? Who are you?"

Her voice was breathless and shaking, but now with the exhaustion of grief, not fear. Bedwyr had spoken in the local tongue, and she answered in the same. Her accent was broader than Bedwyr's, but the language of Less Britain was close enough to that of the mother kingdom for Mordred to understand it easily.

"I am Bedwyr of Benoic, and this is Mordred, son of King Arthur. We are King's men, seeking for the lady Elen. She has been here? You were with her?"

Mordred, while Bedwyr was speaking, had stooped to pick up a handful of pinedrift, and a broken spar of wood. He scattered the stuff on the ashes, and a flame spurted, caught and held. Light flickered up redly, and showed the woman more clearly.

She was well, though plainly, dressed, and was perhaps sixty years old. Her clothing was dirtied and torn, as if in some sort of struggle. Her face, grimed and distorted with weeping, showed a big discoloured patch of bruising over one cheek, and her lips were split and crusty with dried blood.

"You come too late," she said.

286

"Where has he gone? Where has he taken her?"

"I mean too late for the Princess Elen." She pointed towards the tumbled cairn of stones. They looked that way. Now in the strengthening light of the fire they could see that something—someone—had been scrabbling in the thickly heaped pine needles. Some of the smaller stones from the cairn had been pulled down, and pine cones and needles scattered over them.

"It was all I could do," said the woman. She held out her hands. They were shaking. The men looked at them, stirred by horror and pity. The hands were torn and bruised and bloody.

The two knights went across to the cairn where the body lay. It was imperfectly hidden. Beneath the scattered stones and pine needles the girl's face could be seen, streaked with dirt and agonized with death. Her eyes had been closed, but the mouth gaped still, and the neck, with the death marks on the throat, hung crookedly.

Bedwyr, still with the gentleness that Mordred would never have suspected in him, said, half to himself: "She has a lovely face. God give her rest." Then, turning: "Don't grieve, Mother. She shall go home to her own people, and lie in royal fashion, at peace with her gods. And this foul beast shall die, and go to his, for his just reward."

He took a flask from his belt and knelt beside her, holding it to her lips. She drank, sighed, and in a while grew calmer. Soon she was able to tell them what had happened.

She did not know who the ravisher was. He was not, she affirmed to their relief, a foreigner. He had spoken but little, and that mostly curses, but he and his followers were unmistakably Bretons. The reports of a "giant" were not so very far wrong: He was a man huge in every way, stature, girth, strength, with a loud voice and a bellowing laugh. A bull of a man, who had burst out of cover with three companions—roughly clad fellows, like common thieves—and slain four of the princess's escort with his own hands before they had well had time to recover from their surprise. The remaining three fought valiantly but were all killed. Herself and the princess were dragged away. Elen's other woman ("a poor thing, who wailed and screamed so, if I had been one of those beasts I would have killed her on the spot," said the nurse trenchantly) had been left alone, but the at-

tackers, riding off, took the party's horses with them, so ha
little fear of pursuit.

"They brought us to this place, at the water's edge. I
was still dark, so it was hard to make out the way. One o
them stayed with the horses on shore, and the others rowe
us across to this rock. My lady was half fainting, and I trie
to tend her. I had no other thoughts. We could not hav
escaped. The big man—the bull—carried her up the rock
to this place. The other fellows would have dragged me after
but I dodged them and ran, and when they saw that I ha
no intention of trying to leave my lady, they let me be."

She coughed, and licked her cut lips. Bedwyr held ou
the flask again, but she shook her head and presently con
tinued:

"The rest I cannot speak of, but you can guess at it. Th
two fellows held me while he—the bull—raped her. Sh
was never strong. A pretty girl, but pale always, and ofte
ill during the cold winters."

She stopped again, and bent her head. Her fingers twiste
together.

After a while Bedwyr asked gently: "He killed her?"

"Yes. Or rather, what he did with her killed her. She died
He cursed, and left her yonder by the stones, and then cam
back to me. I had made no outcry—they shut my mout
with their stinking hands—but I was afraid that now the
would kill me also. For what they did then . . . I had hardl
thought . . . I am past my sixtieth year, and then one shoul
be . . . Well, no more of that. What is done is done, and no
you are here, and will slay this animal while he lies sleepin
off his lust."

"Lady," said Bedwyr forcefully, "he shall die this night
if he is to be found. Where did they go?"

"I do not know. They spoke of an island, and a tower
That's all I can tell you. They had no thought of pursuit, o
they would have killed me, too. Or perhaps, being animals
they did not think. They threw me down beside my lady
and left me. After a while I heard horses going. I think the
went towards the coast. When I could move, I gave my lad
what burial I could. I found a place in the stones of the cair
where someone, fishermen perhaps, had left flint and iron
and so made a fire. Had I not been able to do that I shoul
have died here. There is neither fresh water nor food, an

288

I cannot swim. If they had seen the fire and come back themselves, then I should have died sooner, that is all." She looked up. "But you—two young men like you against that monster and his fellows...No, no, you must not seek him yourselves. Take me with you, I beg of you, but do not seek him out. I would see no more deaths. Take my story back to King Hoel, and he—"

"Lady, we come from King Hoel. We were sent to find you and your lady, and punish the ravishers. Do not fear for us: I am Bedwyr of Benoic, and this is Mordred, son of Arthur of Britian."

She stared in the dimming light. It was apparent that she had either not heard before, or had not understood. She repeated, still only half believing: "Bedwyr of Benoic? Himself? Arthur of Britain?"

"Arthur is here, not far away, with a troop of soldiers. King Hoel is sick, but he sent us to find you. Come now, Lady. Our boat is small, and none too seaworthy, but if you will come with us now to safety, we will return later and carry your lady back for a seemly burial."

So it was done. Two litters were improvised from pine boughs, and on them the girl's body, decently shrouded in a cloak, and the old nurse, collapsed into a feverish sleep, were sent to Kerrec under guard. The remainder of Arthur's force, guided by Bedwyr, rode for the sea shore.

It was low tide. The sand stretched wide and flat and grey, shining faintly under the darkness. They splashed across the river mouth where the lake water and the tide mingled, and then, away ahead of them to seaward in the breaking dawn, they saw the steep cone of the sea-islet which, by Bedwyr's reckoning, must be the "island tower" of which the ruffians had spoken.

Since the old woman had been abandoned to die on the lake island, the tide had flowed and ebbed again, so there were no guiding marks on the sand, but inland on the flats where the river wound its way through its delta of salt turf to the sea, the tracks of horses were plain to be seen making straight for the shore and the rough causeway that led across, at low tide, to the island. Its high rocks, cloudy with trees, loomed out of a calm sea, the tide, just on the turn, creaming along the island's base and between the stones of the causeway. No light showed anywhere, but they could just see, guided by Bedwyr's pointing finger, the outlines of a tower at the summit.

The King regarded this, sitting his horse at the sea's edge, motionless but for the knuckle that tapped thoughtfully at his lip. He might have been contemplating the making of a rose-bed in the Queen's garden at Camelot. He looked no more warlike than he had done on that "peace mission" to Cerdic, when Agravain had inveighed so bitterly against the apparent tameness of the "duke of battles." But Mordred, at his side, watching with interest and a rising excitement that he found hard to conceal, knew that he was seeing for the first time, at last, the Arthur of the legends; this was a professional, an expert at his trade, the man who alone had saved Britain from the Saxon Terror, deciding how best to set about a very minor matter.

The King spoke at last.

"The place looks half ruined. The fellow is a brigand, holed up here like a badger. This is not a case for siege, or even attack. By rights we should take hounds and bay him out like a boar."

There was a murmur from the others, like a growl. They had all seen the girl Elen's body as it was carried ashore. Bedwyr's horse reared suddenly, as if sharing its rider's tension. Bedwyr's hand was already at his sword, and behind, among the Companions, metal gleamed in the chill dawn light.

"Put up your swords." Arthur neither glanced aside, nor raised his voice. He sat relaxed and quiet, knuckle to lip. "I was about to say that this was a matter for one man only. Myself. Do not forget that the Princess Elen was kin to me, and I am here for King Hoel, whose niece and subject she was. This beast's blood is for me." He turned then, stilling the renewed murmur. "If he kills me, then you, Mordred will take him. After you, if it becomes necessary, then Bedwyr and the others will do as they wish. Understood?"

There were assenting noises, some of them obviously reluctant. Mordred saw Arthur smile as he went on:

"Now listen to me, before we scale the island. There are apparently at least three other men with him. There may be more. They are your meat; tackle them how you will. Now they may have seen our approach; they will surely suspect it. They may come out to face us, or they may try to barricade

hemselves in the tower. In that case it will be your task to
pay or burn them out, and bring their leader to face me."
He shook the reins, and his horse moved forward, fetlock
deep in the sea. "We must cross now. If we delay longer the
tide will be over the causeway, and they will come down to
take us at a loss as we swim our beasts ashore."

In this he proved wrong. The gang, secure in their knowledge of the rising tide, and, with the stupidity of their brutish
natures, unheeding of pursuit, were all within the tower's
walls, and had set no watch. Round the remains of their
supper fire they slept, four of them, in a litter of gnawed
bones and greasy remnants of food. The leader was still
awake, nearest the fire, turning over in filthy hands a pair
of golden bangles and the jewelled charm that he had torn
from Elen's pretty neck. Then some sound must have caught
his ear. He looked up, to see Arthur in the moonlight beyond
the tower doorway.

The roar he gave was indeed like a bayed boar. And he
was as swift, a giant of a man, with thews like a smith, and
eyes blazing red as a wild beast's. The King would not have
scrupled to kill him unarmed—this was no fight, as he had
said, but the slaughter of mad brutes—but no sword could
have been wielded within the tower's walls, so Arthur perforce stayed where he was, and let the man snatch up his
weapon, a massive club which outreached the shorter man's
weapon by inches, and rush out on him. His fellows, slower
with sleep and surprise, tumbled out in his wake, to be seized
by the knights who waited to either side of the tower door,
and killed forthwith. Mordred, hand to hand with a burly
fellow who stank, and whose breath reeked like an open
drain, found himself forgetting all the knightly practice that
the years had taught him, and reverting to the tricks that
had once served the fisherman's son in the rough tussles of
his boyhood. And it was two to one in the end. As Mordred,
tripping, went down under the other man's weight, Bedwyr,
joining him almost casually, spitted the fellow like a fowl,
then stooping, cleaned his sword on the grass. The dead
man's clothes were too dirty for the office.

The gang were all dead within seconds of emerging from
the tower. Then the Companions stood back to watch the
execution of the leader.

To their trained eyes it seemed obvious that he had himself had some kind of training in the past. A brute he was, but a brave brute. He rushed on Arthur, club against sword, and with the first tremendous swipe of the club outreached the shorter man's sword with a blow that sent the King reeling, and dinted the metal of his shield. The heavy club, sliding across the metal, took the giant for a moment with its impetus, and in that moment Arthur, recovering his balance, cut past club and arm, straight for the unprotected throat above the thick leather jerkin. The giant, for all his size, was quick on his feet. He jumped back, the club beating upward again and striking the sword out of line. But Arthur's arm and body went with the thrust, taking the blow higher, over the club and straight at the giant's face. The point just scraped his forehead, a short cut but a deep one, right above the eyes. The man yelled, and Arthur jumped back as the great club flailed round again. Blood spurted and flowed down the giant's face. It blinded him, but the very blindness almost proved Arthur's undoing, for the man, maddened by the sting of the wound, hurled himself straight at the King, ignoring the ready sword, and with the surprise of his rashness getting past it so that he came breast to breast with his opponent, and with his great weight and wrestling grip began to bear Arthur backward to the ground.

Perhaps Mordred was the only one there to appreciate the swift and very foul blow with which the King extricated himself. He wrenched out of the monster's grip, dodged the club again with apparent ease, and cut the man across the back of the knees. Yelling, the giant fell with a crash like a tree, thrashing about him as he went. The King waited, poised like a dancer, till the club's head thudded into the turf, then cut the wrist that held it. The club lay where it had struck. Before the giant could even feel the pain of the fresh wound the King stepped past through the gush of blood and stabbed him cleanly through the throat.

They recovered the princess's jewels from the tower, threw the bodies into it, and set fire to it. Then the troop rode back to catch up with their companions, and carry their heavy news to King Hoel.

3

One positive good came out of the tragedy of the Princess Elen. It was certain that Hoel's Frankish neighbours had had nothing to do with the rape, and, when it was known that the "giant" and his ruffianly companions were dead, the villagers and the forest folk who had suffered from the robbers' depredations dared speak out at last, making it quickly apparent that the recent raids and harassments had all been the work of the same robber band.

Accordingly, as soon as the funeral was done with, but before the time of mourning was past, Hoel and Arthur were able to sit down and discuss the demand made by the consul Quintilianus Hiberus. They decided to send an embassy to him, ostensibly to discuss the Roman emperor's proposals, but in reality to see for themselves what his strength was. Hoel had already sent to King Childebert and his brothers to find out if they had encountered the same demands, and if so, what stand they were prepared to take.

"It will take a little time," said Hoel, stretching his feet nearer the fire, and rubbing a hand over an arthritic knee, "but you'll stay, I trust, cousin?"

"To deploy my troops with yours in full sight, while your embassy goes to nose out Hiberus' intentions? Willingly," said Arthur.

"I'd hoped that you might lend some weight to the embassy, too," said Hoel. "I'm sending Guerin. He's as wily an old fox as ever wasted a council's time. They'll never understand half he says, let alone what his proposals mean. He'll make time for us, and meanwhile we'll get an answer from the Franks. Well, cousin?"

"Of course. For me, then, Bors. He has no wiles at all, but his honesty is patent, and therefore disarming. We can instruct him to leave the politics to Guerin. I'd like Valerius to command the escort."

Hoel nodded approvingly. They were in his private apartments in the palace at Kerrec. The old king was now free of his bedchamber, but spent the days sitting, wrapped in furs, over a blazing fire. His muscular bulk had run, with age, to overweight, and this had brought with it the usual attendant ills; his bones, as he put it, creaked in the draughts of his old-fashioned and relatively comfortless stronghold.

Arthur, with Mordred, and two or three of Hoel's own lords, had supped with the king, and now sat over a bowl of mulled and spicy wine. Bedwyr was not with them. He had gone back at his own request to his lands in the north of Brittany. The reason he gave was his young bride's health. He had confided to Mordred, on the ride south with the body of the murdered princess, that his own Elen, being subject to the fears of her condition, had dreamed of death, and could not rest until her husband returned to her in safety. So, the funeral once over, Bedwyr had ridden north, leaving those of the Young Celts' faction who were present with Arthur's forces to whisper that he had gone sooner than come face to face with Gawain.

For Gawain was on his way to Brittany. Arthur had judged it wise to invite his nephew, now back in the ranks of the Companions, to follow him and share such action as might ensue. The expected fighting had proved to be merely a punitive skirmish with a robber gang, and for this Gawain had sailed too late. So now, discussing with Hoel the composition of the joint embassy, Arthur suggested that Gawain should be part of it. Since Hoel could not go, and Arthur judged it better that he himself should not, some representative of the royal house ought to be present to lend the right dignity to the occasion.

Hoel, humming and huffing in his beard, cast a look at Mordred, misinterpreted the frown he saw there, and cleared his throat to speak, but Arthur, catching the exchange of glances, said quickly:

"Not Mordred, no. He is the obvious choice, but I need him elsewhere. If I am to stay here till this is settled then he must go back to Greater Britain in my place. The Queen and Council make a stopgap government, but that is all it is, and there are matters outstanding that must be dealt with, with more authority than I have left with them."

He turned to his son. "After all my talk, eh? Re-training, indeed! Rowing a boat on a lagoon, and killing a robber or two. I'm sorry, Mordred, but a dispatch I had today makes it necessary. Will you go?"

"Whatever you bid me, sir. Of course."

"Then we'll talk later," said the King, and turned back to the discussion.

Mordred, half disappointed and half elated, was nevertheless wholly puzzled. What could be the urgent business that was forcing the King to change his plans? Only yesterday he had spoken of sending Mordred with the embassy. Now it was to be Gawain. And Mordred doubted the wisdom of that choice. His half-brother would be sailing over with the hope of some sort of action; he would be disappointed, not to say angry, to find himself taking part in a peaceable deputation. But Arthur seemed sure. Speaking now in answer to some question of Hoel's, he was declaring that recently, over the affair of Queen Morgan, and during the past months in Orkney, and finally in the moderate tone he was now taking over Gareth's killer, Bedwyr, Gawain had shown himself to have acquired a certain steadiness, and would find the adventure on foreign soil, though it might prove merely to be a diplomatic mission, a rewarding experience.

In which Arthur, as seemed his fate whenever he had to deal with Morgause's brood and blood, was mistaken. Even as he spoke, Gawain and his young cronies, while their ship neared the Breton coast, were busily burnishing up their war weapons, and talking eagerly of the fighting to come.

Later Arthur, having bidden Hoel good night, bore Mordred off with him to his own apartments for the promised talk.

It was a long talk, lasting well into the night. The King spoke first of the message that had caused his change of plan. It was a letter from the Queen. She gave no details, but confessed herself far from happy in her increasingly precarious role. She reported that Duke Constantine, having removed to Caerleon with his train of knights, had announced his intention of proceeding to Camelot "as more fitting for one ruling the High Kingdom." The Queen had sent begging him to hold to what Arthur had bidden, but his reply had been "eager and intemperate."

"I fear what may happen," she had written. "Already I have had reports that in Caerleon, far from holding his force there at the disposal of the Council, he acts and speaks like one already ruling in his own right, or as sole and rightful deputy of the High King. My lord Arthur, I look daily for your return. And I live in fear of what may come if some ill should befall you or your son."

Reading the letter, Mordred was eager to go. He did not pause, did not want, to analyze his feelings towards Duke Constantine. Enough that the man still acted as if Arthur had no son of his body, let alone the blood-kin of his half-sister's son Gawain. And as Arthur had said, the stories of some of Constantine's doings augured ill for the kingdom. He was a stark ruler and a cruel man, and the note of fear in Guinevere's letter was easy to interpret.

Any regret Mordred might have felt at leaving the King's side vanished. This regency, brief though it might be, was the time he had wanted, a trial period when he would rule alone with full authority. He had no fear that Constantine, once he, Mordred, was back in Camelot and at the head of the royal bodyguard there, would persist in his arrogant pretensions. Mordred's return, with the King's authority and the King's seal, should be enough. "And you will find there," said the King, touching the pouch of letters that bore his seal, "my mandate to raise whatever force you may think needful, to keep the peace at home, and to make ready in case of trouble here."

So, in mutual trust, they talked, while the night wore away, and the future seemed set as fair behind the clouded present as the dawn that slowly gilded the sea's edge beyond the windows. If Morgause's ghost had drifted across the chamber in the hazy light and whispered to them of the doom foretold so many years ago, they would have laughed, and watched for the phantasm to blow away on their laughter.

But it was the last time that they would ever meet, except as enemies.

At length the King came back to the subject of the coming embassy. Hoel had high hopes of its success, but Arthur, though he had concealed it from his cousin, was less sanguine.

"It may come to a fight yet," he said. "Quintilianus is serving a new master, and is himself on trial, and though I know little enough about those surrounding him, I have a suspicion that he will be afraid to lose credit with that master by treating with us. He, too, needs to make a show of strength."

"A dangerous situation. Why do you not go yourself, sir?"

Arthur smiled. "You might say that that, too, is a question of credit. If I go as an ambassador I cannot take my troops, and if the embassy should fail, then I am seen to fail. I am here in Brittany as a deterrent, not as a weapon. . . . I dare not be seen to lose, Mordred."

"You cannot lose."

"That is the belief that will subdue Quintilianus and the hopefuls of the new Rome."

Mordred hesitated, then said frankly: "Forgive me, but there's something else. Let me speak now as your deputy, if not your son. Can you trust Gawain and the young men on a mission of this kind? If they go with Valerius and Bors, I think there may be fighting."

"You may be right. But we shall lose little by it. Sooner or later there must be fighting, and I would rather fight here, against an enemy not yet fully prepared, than on my own borders the other side of the Narrow Sea. If the Franks hold the line with us, then we may well succeed in deterring this emperor. If they do not, then for the present the worst that can happen is that we lose Brittany. In that case we take our people, those who are left, back to their homeland, and find ourselves once again embattled behind our blessed seas." He looked away, staring into the heart of the fire, and his eyes were grave. "But in the end it will all come again, Mordred. Not in my time, nor, please God, in yours, but before your sons are old men it will come. It will not be an easy task, whoever attempts it. First the Narrow Sea, and then the ramparts of the Saxon and English kingdoms, manned by men fighting for their own lands. Why do you think I have been determined to let the Saxons own their settled lands? Men fight for what is theirs. And by the time our shores are seriously threatened, I shall have Cerdic on my side."

"I see. I wondered why you did not seem more worried about the embassy."

"We need the time it may buy for us. If it fails we fight now. As simple as that. Now it grows late, so to finish our business." He reached a hand towards the table where a letter lay, sealed with the dragon seal. "Invincible or not, I have given thought to the chance of my death. Here is a letter, which in that event you are to use. In it I have informed the Council that you are my heir. Duke Constantine knows well that my oath to his father was only valid in default of a son of my body. Like it or not, he must accept it. I have written to him, too, a letter that he cannot gainsay. With it comes a grant of land; his dukedom will include the lands that came to me with my first wife, Guenever of Cornwall. I hope he will be content. If he is not"—a glint in the King's eyes as he glanced up at his son—"then that will be your affair, not mine. Watch him, Mordred. If I live, then I myself will call the Council as soon as I return to Camelot, and all this will be settled publicly once and for all."

It is never easy to receive a bequest from one still living. Mordred, for once at a loss for words, began to speak, haltingly, but the King waved him into silence, coming at last to the subject that, to Mordred, would have been first.

"The Queen," said Arthur, his gaze on the fire. "She will be under your protection. You will love and care for her as her own son, and you will see to it that for the rest of her days she lives safely, with the honour and comfort due to her. I do not ask you to swear this, Mordred, knowing that I need not."

"I do swear it!" Mordred, on his knees by his father's chair, spoke for once with uncontrolled emotion. "I swear by all the gods there are, by the God of the kingdom's churches, and the Goddess of the isles, and the spirits that live in the air, that I will hold the kingdoms for the Queen, and love and care for her and secure her honour as you would do were you still High King."

Arthur reached to take the younger man's hands between his own, and raising him, kissed him. Then he smiled.

"So now we will stop talking about my death, which will not come yet awhile, I assure you! But when it does, I give my kingdoms and my Queen into your hands with a quiet spirit, and with my blessing and God's."

Next day Mordred sailed for home. A few days after he had gone, the embassy, gay with coloured pennants and tossing plumes, set out for Quintilianus Hiberus' encampment.

Gawain and his friends rode at ease. Though the talk was of the sort that Mordred would have recognized—the young men looking to Gawain for reckless leadership and excitement—they did contain themselves with decorum on the ride. But none of the younger faction made any attempt to conceal their hope that the peaceful overtures would fail, and that they would see action.

"They say Quintilianus is a hot man, and a clever soldier. Why should he listen to an old man giving another old man's message?" Such was Mador's description of King Hoel's embassy. Others chimed in: "If we don't get fighting, at least they're sure to show us sport—games, hunting—and it will go hard if we cannot show these foreigners what we can do!" Or again: "They say the horses in Gaul are beauties. We might get some trading done, if the worst comes to the worst."

But it seemed they were doomed to disappointment on all counts. Quintilianus' headquarters was a temporary camp built on a bleak stretch of moorland. The party arrived towards evening of a dull day with a chilly wind carrying rain. The dead springtime heather stretched black and wet on every hand, the only colour in the moorland being the livid green of the boggy stretches, or the metallic gleam of water. The camp itself was laid out on the Roman pattern. It was well built with turfs and stout timber, and was impressive enough as a temporary stance, but the young Britons, ignorant of warfare and accustomed to the great Roman-based permanent structures of Caerleon and Segontium, looked about them with disappointment and contempt.

It was hard to say whether caution or care for his guests' comfort had impelled Quintilianus Hiberus to house the British outside the walls of the camp. Tents had been erected some hundred paces outside the surrounding ditch, with their own horse lines and a pavilion which would serve as a hall.

There they were invited to dismount, while their own grooms took their horses to the lines. Then on foot they were led up the main way towards the camp's center, where the commander's headquarters stood.

There Quintilianus Hiberus and Marcellus, his second in command, received the embassy with chilly courtesy. Speeches, previously prepared and learned by rote, were exchanged. They were long, and so over-careful as to be almost incomprehensible. No mention was made either of the emperor's message or of Hoel's intentions. Rather, a rambling account of the old king's health was produced in answer to their host's indifferent query, with details, delicately touched on, of his cousin Arthur's anxiety, which had provoked that warrior to visit Brittany's king. That he had brought a sizeable force with him was not stated, but the Roman consul knew it, and they knew that he knew. . . .

Only when the polite sharpening of blades had been going on for some time did Guerin and Bors allow themselves to approach a statement—still far from direct—of Hoel's position and its backing by Arthur of Britain.

The young men, waiting formally behind their ambassadors, chafing after the decorous inaction of the ride, and thinking of food and recreation, had time to grow bored, to eye their surroundings curiously, and to exchange stares with the warriors of the opposite faction who waited in equal boredom behind their own leaders.

These leaders, after a lengthy and dragging parley, made more tedious than need be by the fact that Bors spoke little or no Latin, and Marcellus spoke nothing else, came at length to a stalemate pause. There would be, said Quintilianus, drawing his mantle about him and rising, further parley tomorrow. Meanwhile the visitors would no doubt care to rest and refresh themselves. They would be shown now to the tents prepared for them.

The ambassadors bowed gravely and withdrew. Their hosts came forward, and the party was escorted back through the camp.

"No doubt," said the youth escorting Gawain, with rather threadbare politeness, "you are weary after your journey? You will find the lodgings rough, I am afraid, but we ourselves have become accustomed to living in the field—"

He yawned as he spoke. This meant no more than that

he was as weary of the talks as the other young men, but Gawain, bored, contemptuous, and beginning to see his hopes of glory fading, chose to take it otherwise.

"Why should you think we are not used to rough quarters? Because we have come with a peaceful embassy, it doesn't mean that we are not fighters, and as ready in the field as any rabble on this side of the Narrow Sea!"

The youth, surprised, and then as quickly angry as the other, flushed scarlet to his fair hair. "And what field of battle have you ever been on, Sir Braggart? It's a long time since Agned and Badon! Even the fabled Arthur, that your fellows were boasting about in there, would be hard put to it to wage a war nowadays, with men who are only good for talking!"

Before Gawain could even draw breath, "And not even too good at that," put in someone else, with a cruel imitation of Bors's thick Latin.

There was laughter, and through it a quick attempt by cooler spirits to pass the exchange off with jesting, but Gawain's brow was dark, and hot words still flew. The fair youth, who seemed to be someone of consequence, bore through the talk with a ringing shout of anger:

"So? Didn't you come all this way to beg us *not* to fight you? And now you boast and brag about what *your* leaders can do! What do you expect us to think of such empty braggarts?"

Here Gawain drew his sword and ran him through.

The stunned minutes that followed, of unbelief, then of horror and confusion, as the fallen man's companions ran to raise him and find if life remained in him, gave the British just enough time to escape. Gawain, shouting, "Get to the horses!" was already half-way to the picket lines, followed closely by his friends who, from the moment the bitter words began to pass, had seen the violent end coming. The ambassadors, dismayed, hesitated only for a moment before following. If the assailant had been any other than Arthur's nephew, they might have given him over to the punishment due to one who broke a truce, but as it was, the leaders knew that the embassy, never hopeful, was now irretrievably shattered, and all their party, as truce-breakers, were in great danger. Valerius, an old soldier used to instant decisions, took swift command, and had his whole party mounted and

301

out of the lines at the gallop before their hosts had wel
grasped what had occurred.

Gawain, wildly galloping with the rest, struggled to pu
his horse out of the troop and wheel back.

"This is shameful! To run away, after what they said
Shame on you, shame! They called us cowards before, wha
will they call us now?"

"Dead men, you fool!" Valerius, furiously angry, was i
no mood to mince words, prince or no prince. His han
came hard down on Gawain's rein, and dragged the hors
into the rapid gallop alongside his own. "It's shame on you
prince! You knew what the kings wanted from this embassy
If we come alive out of this, which is doubtful, then we shal
see what Arthur will have to say to you!"

Gawain, still rebellious and unrepentant, would have re
plied, but at that moment the troop came to a river, and the
spread out to force their horses through it. They could hav
forded it had there been time, but at that moment the pur
suing party came in sight, and there was nothing for it bu
to fight. Valerius, furious and desperate, turned and gav
orders for the attack.

The engagement, with tempers high on both sides, wa
short, ferocious and very bloody. The fight was a runnin
one, and ended only when half the embassy, and rather mor
of the pursuing force, were dead. Then the Romans, gathere
for a few minutes' respite at the edge of a little wood, seeme
to be taking counsel, and presently two of their numbe
turned and made off towards the east.

Valerius, unwounded, but exhausted and liberally staine
with other men's blood, watched them go. Then he said
grimly:

"Gone for reinforcements. Right. There's nothing we ca
do here. We leave. Now. Bring the loose horses and pic
up that man yonder. He's alive. The rest we'll have to leave.

This time there was no argument. The British turned an
rode off. The Romans made no attempt to stop them, no
were any taunts exchanged. Gawain had had his way, an
proved what had not needed to be proved. And both side
knew what must happen now.

4

Mordred sat at the window of the King's business room in Camelot. The scents from the garden below eddied on the warm breeze in sudden gusts of sweetness. The apple blossom was gone, but there were cherries still in bloom, standing deep among bluebells and the grey spears of iris. The air was full of the sound of bees, and birds singing, while down in the town bells rang for some Christian service.

The royal secretaries had gone, and he was alone. He sat, still thinking over some of the work that had been done that day, but gradually, in the scented warmth, his thoughts drifted into dreaming. So little time ago, it seemed, he had been in the islands, living as he had lived in boyhood, thinking in bitterness that he had lost everything in that one night when the Orkney brothers had risked all for themselves and their friends on that mad, vicious attempt to finish Bedwyr. Thinking, too, of the summer's tasks ahead of him: harvesting and drying fish, cutting peats, rebuilding walls and repairing thatch against the dreadful Orkney winter. And now?

His hand, resting on the table, touched the royal seal. He smiled.

A movement outside the window caught his eye. Guinevere the Queen was walking in the garden. She wore a gown of soft dove-grey, that shimmered as she moved. Her two little dogs, silver-white greyhounds, frisked round her.

From time to time she threw a gilded ball and they bounded after it, yelping and wrangling as the winner carried it back to lay it at her feet. Two of her women, both young and pretty girls, one in primrose yellow and the other in blue, walked behind. Guinevere, still lovely, and secure in her loveliness, was not one of those who seek to set her beauty off by surrounding herself with plain women. The three lovely creatures, with the dainty little dogs at their skirts, moved with grace through the garden, and the flowers of that sweet May were no fairer.

Or so thought Mordred, who was rarely a poet. He gazed after the Queen, while his hand once more, but quite unconsciously, reached out and touched the dragon of the royal seal. Again he drifted into dream, but this time it was not a dream of the islands.

He was brought sharply to himself by the sounds, urgent and unmistakable, of a King's messenger being ushered through the royal apartments. A chamberlain opened the door to announce a courier, and even as he spoke the man hurried by him and knelt at the regent's feet.

One glance told Mordred that here was news from Brittany, and that it was not good. He sat back in the great chair and said, coolly:

"Take your time. But first—the King is well?"

"Yes, my lord. God be thanked for it! But the news is ill enough." The man reached into his pouch, and Mordred put out a hand.

"You have letters? Then while I read them, compose yourself and take a cup of wine."

The chamberlain, who missed nothing, came in unbidden with the wine, and while the man drank gratefully, Mordred broke the seal of the single letter he had brought, and read it.

It was bad, but, to one remembering that last conversation with the King, not yet tragic news. Once again, thought Mordred, the evil fates summoned by Morgause were at their work. To put it more practically, the Orkney rashness had yet again brought the promise of disaster close. But possibly something could be saved from near-disaster; it was to be hoped that all Gawain had done was to bring matters to a head too soon.

The King's letter, hastily dictated, gave the facts merely

of the disastrous embassy and the running fight that had followed. Under Mordred's questioning the courier supplied the details. He told of the rash exchange between Gawain and the Roman youth, of the murder, and of the flight of the embassy and the subsequent skirmish by the river's bank. His story confirmed what Arthur's letter indicated, that all hope even of a temporary peace had vanished. It was possible that Hoel might be able to take the field, but if not, Arthur must command Hoel's army, together with such force as he had brought with him. Bedwyr had been recalled from Benoic. Arthur had already sent to Urbgen, to Maelgon of Gwynedd, to Tydwal and the King of Elmet. Mordred was to send what force he could, under the command of Cei. He would then be well advised to put forward his own meeting with Cerdic, when he could apprise him of the situation. The letter closed briefly, with urgency:

"See Cerdic. Warn him and his neighbours to watch the coast. Raise what force you can meanwhile. And guard the Queen's safety."

Mordred dismissed the man at length to rest. He knew that there was no need to enjoin discretion; the royal couriers were well chosen and highly trained. But he knew that the man's coming would have been noted, and rumour would have run through Camelot within minutes of the tired horse's coming up through the King's Gate.

He walked over to the window. The sun had slanted some way towards the west, and shadows were lengthening. A late thrush sang in a lime tree.

The Queen was still in the garden. She had been cutting lilac. The girl in the blue dress walked beside her, carrying a flat willow basket filled with the white and purple blooms. The other girl, with the two little dogs leaping and barking round her, was stooping, with her skirt kilted up in one hand, over a border of ferns. She straightened with the gilded ball in her hand and threw it, laughing, for the greyhounds. They raced after it, both reaching it at the same moment, and fell into a yelping, rolling tangle, while the ball flew free.

Keep the Queen safe. How long could this serene and flower-filled garden peace be kept? The battle might already have started. Might be over. With enough bloodletting, thought Mordred, to content even Gawain.

His thoughts went further; were checked. Even now he himself might be High King in fact, if not yet in name . . .

As if his thought had been the shadow of a flying cloud that touched her, he saw the Queen start, then lift her head as if listening to some sound beyond the garden walls. The spray of lilac which she loosed sprang back into its own scented bank of blossom. Without looking she dropped the silver knife into the basket which the girl held beside her. She stood still, except for her hands, which seemed to rise of their own will to clasp themselves at her breast. Slowly, after a moment, she turned to look up towards the window.

Mordred drew back. He spoke to the chamberlain.

"Send down to the garden to ask if I may speak with the Queen."

There was an arbour, pretty as a silk picture, facing south. It was embowered with early roses, showers of small pale-pink blossoms, with coral-coloured buds among them, and falling flowers fading to white. The Queen sat there, on a stone bench warm from the sun, waiting to receive the regent. The girl in yellow had taken the greyhounds away; the other remained, but she had withdrawn to the far side of the garden, where she sat on a bench below one of the palace windows. She had brought some sewing out of the pouch at her girdle, and busied herself with it, but Mordred knew how carefully he was watched, and how quickly the rumours would spread through the palace: "He looked grave; the news must be bad. . . ." Or, "He seemed cheerful enough: the courier brought a letter and he showed it to the Queen. . . ."

Guinevere, too, had some work by her. A half-embroidered napkin lay beside her on the stone bench. Suddenly a sharp memory assailed him: Morgan's garden in the north, the dying flowers and the ghosts of the imprisoned birds, with the angry voices of the two witches at the window above. And the solitary, frightened boy who hid below, believing that he, too, was trapped, and facing an ignominious death. Like the wildcat in its narrow cage; the wildcat, dead presumably these many years, but, because of him, dead in freedom with its own wild home and its kittens sired at will. With the lightning-flicker with which such thoughts come between breath and breath, he thought of his "wife" in the islands, of his mistress now gone from Camelot and comrtably settled in Strathclyde, of his sons of those unions rowing up in safety—for the children of that solitary boy uld now incur, how readily, the sting of envy and hatred. e, like the wildcat, had found the window to freedom. ore, to power. Of those scheming witches, one was dead; e other, for all her boasted magic, still shut away in her astle prison, and subject, now, to his will as ruler of the igh Kingdom.

He knelt before the Queen and took her hand to kiss. He lt its faint tremor. She withdrew it and let it fall to her lap, here the other clasped and held it tightly. She said, with a almness forced over drawn breath:

"They tell me a courier has come in. From Brittany?"

"Yes, madam." At her nod he rose, then hesitated. She estured to the seat, and he sat beside her. The sun was hot, nd the scent of the roses filled the air. Bees were loud in e racemes of pink blossom. A little breeze moved the flow- rs, and the shadows of the roses swayed and flickered over e Queen's grey gown and fair skin. Mordred swallowed, leared his throat and spoke.

"You need have no fear, madam. There have been grave oings, but the news is not altogether bad."

"My lord is well, then?"

"Indeed yes. The letter was from him."

"And for me? Is there a message for me?"

"No, madam, I'm sorry. He sent in great haste. You shall ee the letter, of course, but let me give you the gist of it rst. You know that an embassy was sent, jointly from King oel and King Arthur, to talk with the consul Lucius Quin- lianus."

"Yes. A fact-finding mission only, he said, to gain time r the kingdoms of the west to band together against the ossible new alliance of Byzantium and Rome with the Ger- ans of Alamannia and Burgundy." She sighed. "So, it went rong? I guessed it. How?"

"By your leave, the good news first. There were other act-finding missions on their way at the same time. Mes- engers were sent to sound out the Frankish kings. They et with encouraging success. One and all, the Franks will esist any attempt by Justinian's armies to reimpose Roman omination. They are arming now."

She looked away, past the boles of the lime trees now

lighted from behind by the low sun, and gilded with red gold.
The young leaves, wafers of beaten gold, shone with their
own light, and the tops of the trees, cloudy with shadow,
hummed with bees.

Mordred's "good news" did not appear to have given her
any pleasure. He thought her eyes were filled with tears.

Still regarding those glowing tree-trunks with their mosaic
of golden leaves, she said: "And our embassy? What happened there?"

"There had to be, for courtesy, a representative of the
royal house. It was Gawain."

Her gaze came back to him sharply. Her eyes were dry.
"And he made trouble." It was not a question.

"He did. There was some foolish talk and bragging that
led to insults and a quarrel, and the young men fell to fighting."

She moved her hands, almost as if she would throw them
up in a classic gesture of despair. But she sounded angry
rather than grieved. "Again!"

"Madam?"

"Gawain! The Orkney fools again! Always that cold north
wind, like a blighting frost that blasts everything that is good
and growing!" She checked herself, took in her breath, and
said, with a visible effort: "Your pardon, Mordred. You are
so different, I was forgetting. But Lot's sons, your half-
brothers—"

"Madam, I know. I agree. Hot fools always, and this time
worse than fools. Gawain killed one of the Roman youths,
and it turned out that the man was a nephew of Lucius
Quintilianus himself. The embassy was forced to flee, and
Quintilianus sent Marcellus himself after them. They had to
turn and fight, and there were deaths."

"Not Valerius? Not that good old man?"

"No, no. They got back in good order—indeed, with a
kind of victory. But not before there had been several running engagements. Marcellus was killed in the first of these,
and later Petreius Cotta, who took command after him, was
taken prisoner and brought back to Kerrec in chains. I said
it was a victory of a kind. But you see what it means. Now
the High King himself must take the field."

"Ah, I knew it! I knew it! And what force has he?"

"He leads Hoel's army, and with them the troops he took
with him, and Bedwyr is called down from Benoic with his

308

en." Coolly he noted the slightest reaction to the name: he had not dared ask if Bedwyr, too, were safe; but now had told her, and watched her colour come back. He went : "The King does not yet know what numbers the Frankish ngs will bring to the field, but they will not be small. From itain he has called on Rheged and Gwynedd, with Elmet, d Tydwal from Dunpeldyr. Here I shall raise what rein-rcements I can in haste. They will sail under Cei's com-and. All will be well, madam, you will see. You know the igh King."

"And so do they," she said. "They will only meet him if ey outnumber him three to one, and that, surely, they can . Then even he will be in danger of defeat."

"He will not give them time. I spoke of haste. This whole ing has blown up like a summer storm, and Arthur intends attack in the wake of it, rather than wait for events. He already marching for Autun, to meet the Burgundians on eir own ground, before Justinian's troops are gathered. He pects the Franks to join him before he reaches the border. t you had better read his letter for yourself. It will calm ur fears. The High King shows no doubts of the outcome, d why should he? He is Arthur."

She thanked him with a smile, but he saw how her hand embled as she held it out for the letter. He stood up and epped down from the arbour, leaving her alone to read. ere was a fluted stone column with a carefully contrived oken capital overhung with the yellow tassels of laburnum. e leaned against this and waited, watching her surrepti-usly from time to time under lowered lids.

She read in silence. He saw when she reached the end of e letter, then read it through again. She let it sink to her p and sat for a while with bent head. He thought she was ading the thing for the third time, then he saw that her es were shut. She was very pale.

His shoulder came away from the pillar. Almost in spite himself he took a step towards her. "What is it? What do u fear?"

She gave a start, and her eyes opened. It was as if she d been miles away in thought, recalled abruptly. She shook r head, with an attempt at a smile. "Nothing. Really, noth-g. A dream."

"A dream? Of defeat for the High King?"

"No. No." She gave a little laugh, which sounded genuin
enough. "Women's folly, Mordred. You would call it so,
am sure! No, don't look so worried, I'll tell you, even if yc
laugh at me. Men do not understand such things, but w
women, we who have nothing to do but wait and watch an
hope, our minds are too active. Let us but once think. Wha
will come to me when my lord is dead? and then all in
moment, in our imagination, he is laid in sad pomp on h
bier, and the grave is dug in the center of the Hanging Stone
the mourning feast is over, the new king is come to Camelo
his young wife is here in the garden with her maidens, an
the cast-off queen, still in the white of mourning, is questin
about the kingdoms to see where she may with honour an
with safety be taken in."

"But, madam," said Mordred, the realist, "surely my—
the High King has already told you what dispositions hav
been made against that day?"

"I knew you would call it folly!" With an obvious attemp
at lightness, she turned the subject. "But believe me,
is something that every wife does. What of your ow
Mordred?"

"My—?"

She looked confused. "Am I mistaken? I thought you wer
married. I am sure someone spoke of a son of yours
Gwarthegydd's court of Dumbarton."

"I am not married." Mordred's reply was rather too quick
and rather too emphatic. She looked surprised, and he thre
a hand out, adding: "But you heard correctly, madam. I hav
two sons." A smile and a shrug. "Who am I, after all, t
insist on wedlock? The two boys are by different mother:
Melehan is the younger, who is with Gwarthegydd. The oth
is still in the islands."

"And their mothers?"

"Melehan's mother is dead." The lie came smoothly. Sinc
the Queen apparently had known nothing about his illic
household in Camelot, he would not confess it to her now
"The other is satisfied with the bond between herself an
me. She is an Orkney woman, and they have different cus
toms in the islands."

"Then married or not," said Guinevere, still with tha
forced lightness, "she is still a woman, and she, like me
must live through the same dreams of the wicked day whe

310

a messenger comes with worse news than this you have brought to me."

Mordred smiled. If he thought that his woman had too much to occupy her than to sit and dream about his death and burial, he did not say so. Women's folly, indeed. But as he held his hand for the letter, and she put the roll into it, he saw again how her hand shook. It changed his thoughts about her. To him she had been the Queen, the lovely consort of his King, the elusive vision, too, of his desires, a creature of gaiety and wealth and power and happiness. It was a shock to see her now, suddenly, as a lonely woman who lived with fear. "We have nothing to do but wait and watch and hope," she had said.

It was something he had never thought about. He was not an imaginative man, and in his dealings with women—Morgause apart—he followed in the main his peasant upbringing. He would not wittingly have hurt a woman, but it would not have occurred to him to go out of his way to help or serve one. On the contrary, they were there to help and serve him.

With an effort of imagination that was foreign to him he cast his mind forward, trying to think as a woman might, to fear fate as it would affect the Queen. When Arthur did meet death, what could she expect of the future? A year ago the answer would have been simple: Bedwyr would have taken the widow to Benoic, or to his lands in Northumbria. But now Bedwyr was married, and his wife was with child. More than that: Bedwyr, in sober fact, was not likely to survive any action in which Arthur was killed. Even now, as Mordred and the Queen talked together in this scented garden, the battle might already be joined that would bring to reality her dream of the wicked day. He recalled her letter to Arthur, with its unmistakable note of fear. Fear not only of Arthur's danger, but of his own. "You or your son," she had written. Now, with a sudden flash of truth as painful as a cut, he knew why. Duke Constantine. Duke Constantine, still officially next in line for the throne and already casting his eyes towards Camelot, whose title would be greatly strengthened if, first, he could claim the Queen-regent...

He became conscious of her strained and questioning gaze. He answered it, forcefully.

"Madam, for your dreams and fears, let me only say this.

I am certain that the King's own skill, and your prayers, wil keep him safe for many years to come, but if it should hap pen, then have no fear for yourself. I know that Constantine of Cornwall may try to dispute the King's latest disposi tion—"

"Mordred—"

"With your leave, madam. Let us speak directly. He ha ambitions for the High Kingdom, and you fear him. Let me say this. You know my father's wish, and you know that i will be carried out. When I succeed him as High King, then you need fear nothing. While I live you will be safe, and honoured."

The red flew up into her cheeks, and her look thanked him, but all she said was, trying still to smile: "No cast-of queen?"

"Never that," said Mordred, and took his leave.

In the shadow of the garden gateway, out of sight of the arbour, he stopped. His pulse was racing, his flesh burned He stood there motionless while the heat and the hammering slowly subsided. Coldly he crushed back the lighted pictur in his mind: the roses, the grey-blue eyes, the smile, the touch of the tremulous hands. This was folly. Moreover, i was useless folly. Arthur, Bedwyr... whatever Mordred wa or might be, until both Arthur and Bedwyr were dead, with that lovely lady he could come only a poor and halting third

He had been too long without a woman. To tell the truth he had been too busy to think about them. Till now. He would find time tonight, and quench these hot imaginings.

But all the same, he knew that today his ambition ha taken a different turn. There were precedents, undisputed He had no wife. She was barren, but he had two sons. I Constantine could think about it, then so could he. And by all the gods in heaven and hell, Constantine should not have her.

With the King's letter crumpled fiercely in his hand, he strode back to the royal chamber, shouting for the secre taries.

5

t was some time before Mordred saw the Queen again. He
was plunged immediately into the whirlwind business of
quipping and embarking the troops Arthur had asked for.
In a commendably short time the expeditionary force sailed,
under the command of Cei, the King's foster brother, with
reasonable hope of coming up with Arthur's army before
the clash came. The courier who returned from this voyage
brought news that was, on the whole, cheering: Arthur, with
Bedwyr and Gawain, had already set out on the march eastward, and King Hoel, finding himself miraculously recovered at the prospect of action, had gone with them. The
Frankish kings, with a considerable army, were also reported
to be converging on Autun, where Arthur would set up his
camp.

After this, news came only spasmodically. None of it was
bad, but, coming as it did long after the events reported, it
could not be satisfactory. Cei and the British kings had joined
Arthur; that much was known; and so had the Franks. The
weather was good, the men were in high heart, and no trouble
had been met with on the march.

So far, that was all. What the Queen was feeling Mordred
did not know, nor did he have time to care. He was setting
about the second of Arthur's commissions, raising and training men to bring the standing army up to strength after the

departure of the expeditionary force. He sent letters to al
the petty kings and leaders in the north and west, and himsel
followed where persuasion was needed. The response wa
good: Mordred had laid openly on the table the reasons fo
his demand, and the response from the Celtic kingdoms wa
immediate and generous. The one leader who made no repl
at all was Duke Constantine. Mordred, keeping the promise
eye on the Cornish dukedom, said nothing, set spies, an
doubled the garrison at Caerleon. Then, once the tally o
kings and the arrangements for receiving and training th
new army were complete, he sent at last to Cerdic the Saxo
king, to propose the meeting Arthur had suggested.

It was late July when Cerdic's answer came, and tha
same day, on an afternoon of misty rain, a courier arrive
from the Burgundian battlefront, bearing with him a singl
brief dispatch, with other tokens which, when the man spille
them on the table in front of Mordred, told a dreadful tale

As was usual, most of his news would be given verbally
learned by rote. He began to recite it now to the still-face
regent.

"My lord, the battle is over, and the day was ours. Th
Romans and the Burgundians were put to flight, and th
emperor himself recalled what force was left. The Frank
fought nobly alongside us, and on all sides some marvellou
deeds were done. But—"

The man hesitated, wetting his lips. It was apparent tha
he had given the good news first, in the hope of cushionin
what was to follow. Mordred neither moved nor spoke. H
was conscious of a fast-beating heart, a constricted throat
and the necessity for keeping steady the hand that lay besid
the spilled tokens on the table. They lay in a jumbled an
glittering pile, proof that a tragic story was still to come
Seals, rings, badges of office, campaign medals, all the me
mentoes that, stripped from the dead, would be sent hom
to the widows. Cei's badge was there, the royal seneschal'
gilded brooch. And a medal from Kaerconan, rubbed thi
and bright; that could only be Valerius'. No royal ring; n
great ruby carved with the Dragon, but—

But the man, the veteran of a hundred reports, both goo
and evil, was hesitating. Then, meeting Mordred's eye, h
swallowed and cleared his throat. It was a long time sinc
the bearers of bad news had had, as in some barbarous lands

to fear ill-treatment and even death at the hands of their masters; nevertheless his voice was hoarse with something like fear as he spoke again. This time he was direct to the point of brutality.

"My lord, the King is dead."

Silence. Mordred could not trust himself with word or movement. The scene took on the shifting and misted edges of unreality. Thought was suspended, as random and weightless as a drop of the fine rain that drifted past the windows.

"It happened near the end of the day's fighting. Many had fallen, Cei among them, and Gugein, Valerius, Mador and many others. Prince Gawain fought nobly; he is safe, but Prince Bedwyr fell wounded on the left. It is feared that he, too, will die...."

His voice went on, naming the dead and wounded, but it was doubtful if Mordred heard a word of it. He moved at last, interrupting the recital. His hand went out to the parchment lying on the table.

"It is all here?"

"The news, my lord, but not the details. The dispatch was sent by Prince Bedwyr himself. While he could still speak he had them write it. The list of casualties will follow as soon as they are known and checked, but this, my lord, could not be delayed."

"Yes. Wait, then."

He took the letter across to a window, and with his back to the man, spread the page out on the sill. The careful script danced under his eyes. The drifting curtain of the rain seemed to have come between him and the letter. He dashed the back of his hand impatiently across his face and bent nearer.

In the end, and after three careful readings, the sense of it went right into his brain and lodged there, thrumming like the arrow that lodges deep in the flesh, spreading, not pain, but a numbing poison.

Arthur was dead. The news that followed, of complete and annihilating victory over the Romans and Burgundians, came as an irrelevance. Arthur was dead. The dispatch, dictated hastily in a field dressing station, gave few details. The High King's body had not yet been recovered from the field. Parties were still searching among the piled and pillaged dead. But if the King were still living, said Bedwyr tersely, he would by this time have made himself known. The regent must assume his death, and act accordingly.

The parchment slipped from Mordred's hand and floated to the floor. He did not notice. Through the window beside him, washed and sweet on the damp air, floated the scents of the Queen's garden. He looked out at the rain-heavy roses, the glittering leaves that quivered under the drifting drops, the misted grass. No one was there today. Wherever she was, she would know of the courier's coming, and she would be waiting for him. He would have to go to her and tell her. Arthur. And Bedwyr. Arthur and Bedwyr both. That was enough for her, and too much. But he must hear the rest first. He turned back to the courier.

"Go on."

The man talked eagerly now, his fear forgotten. The regent was alive again, not composed exactly, but in command, his questions quick and direct.

"Yes, my lord, I was there myself. I left the field at full dark, as soon as the news was sure. The King was seen fighting still towards sunset, though by that time the main resistance was over, and Quintilianus himself had fallen. Everywhere was chaos, and already men were robbing the bodies of the dead and killing the dying for their weapons and their clothes. Our men were not merciful, but the Franks... My lord, these are barbarians. They fight like mad wolves, and they can no more be controlled than wolves. The enemy broke and fled in several directions, and were pursued. Some of them threw down their arms and held their hands out for chains, begging their lives. It was—"

"The King. What of the King?"

"He was seen to fall. His standard had been cut down, and in the growing dark it could not be observed just where he was fighting, or what had happened. Bedwyr, wounded as he was, struggled to that part of the field and searched for him, and others with him, calling. But the King was not found. Many of the bodies were stripped already, and if the King had been among them—"

"You are telling me that his body had still not been recovered?"

"Yes, my lord. At least, not when I left the field. I was sent as soon as it became too dark to search further. It may

316

well be that by this time another dispatch is on its way. But it was thought that the news should be brought to you before other rumours reached the country."

"So this is why no token, neither sword nor ring, has been brought back to me?"

"Yes, my lord."

Mordred was silent for a while. Then he spoke with difficulty. "Is there still thought to be hope for the High King?"

"My lord, if you had seen the field . . . But yes, there is hope. Even in naked death, the High King's body would surely have been known—"

Under Mordred's gaze, he stopped. "My lord."

After a few more questions Mordred sent him away, and sat alone, thinking.

There was still a chance that Arthur was not dead. But his duty was plain. Before the news reached these shores—and with the coming of the courier's ship the rumours must already be spreading like heath fires—he must take control of the country. His immediate moves were easily mapped: an emergency meeting of the Council; a public reading of Arthur's declaration of succession, with its ratification of his, Mordred's authority; a copy of this to be made and sent to each of the kings; a speech made to the army leaders.

Meanwhile the Queen waited, and while she waited, suffered. He would go to her, and take what comfort he could.

And what love he might.

Before he had taken three steps into the room she was on her feet. Afterwards he realized that he had not known to whom her first query related.

She said it, hands to throat. "He is dead?"

"Alas, madam, yes. That is the message as it came to me. He was seen to fall in the moment of victory, but, when the messenger was sent to me, they had not yet found his body."

She was so white that he thought she might fall. He went close quickly, and put out his hands. Hers flew out and held them tightly. He said urgently: "Madam, there is hope. And Bedwyr is alive, though wounded. He was well enough to order the search for the King's body before darkness fell."

She shut her eyes. Her lips, thin and gaping round a black O, drew air in as if she were drowning. Her lids fluttered. Then as if some ghostly hand had slid under her chin and drawn her up, she stiffened and grew taller, then her eyes opened and her white face composed itself. She removed her hands quietly from Mordred's grasp, but let him lead her to a chair. Her women would have clustered near with hands and words of comfort, but she waved them back.

"Tell me all that you know."

"I know very little, madam. The letter was brief. But the messenger gave me a report." He recounted what the man had told him. She listened without interruption; indeed, a casual observer might have thought without attention; she seemed to be watching the raindrops following one another down the drooping stem of a rose that hung beyond the window-frame.

Mordred stopped speaking at last. The raindrops ran, gathered, swelled on a thorn, dropped splashing to the sill.

The Queen said quietly, in a calm, dead voice:

"If there is indeed hope of the King's life, then surely a second courier will be following hard on the first. Meantime we must do as my lord commanded."

"Assuming his death," said Mordred.

"Assuming that." Then, with a sudden break of grief and terror: "Mordred, what will become of Britain now? What will come to us? So short a while ago we spoke of this, you and I—and now—now the day is upon us...."

He made an involuntary move towards her, only a slight one, but it sufficed. She was still again, controlled, queenly. But her eyes betrayed her. She could not have spoken again without weeping. And that must not happen until she was alone.

He said, in as flat and matter-of-fact a tone as he could manage: "Two things must be done immediately. I must see Cerdic. A meeting has already been arranged. And I have convened the Council. They meet tonight. Until tidings come that either confirm or deny this news, it is vital that men should see there is still a central power in Britain, with a ruler appointed by the King's command, and carrying out his wishes."

He added, gently: "For you, madam, I do not think anyone will wonder at it if you are not present at the Council meeting."

"I shall be present."

"If you so wish—"

"I do wish it. Mordred, the High King's body has not been found. You have his seal, which you and I, as co-regents here in Camelot, have been empowered to use. But his ring and his sword, the true symbols of kingship, cannot be brought to you except from his dead body."

"That is so, madam."

"So I shall attend the Council. With Arthur's Queen at your side to support you, there will be no man in the kingdoms who will not have to accept Arthur's son as his rightful ruler."

He found nothing to say. She put out a hand, and he bent his head and kissed it. Then he left her. She would have time for her mourning before she took her place in the Round Hall beside the new King of Britain.

In a pine wood at the foot of the hills east of Autun, Arthur stirred and woke.

He lay wrapped in his war cloak, his sword to his hand. His shoulder and side were stiff with bruising from the blow that had felled him during the battle, and his head ached abominably, but he was otherwise unhurt. His tethered horse grazed near him. His companions, some forty men, were, like him, rousing to the first misty light of the new day. Three of the men were busy already relighting the blackened remains of the night fire. Others brought water, carefully cradled in their leather helmets, from the river that slid over its sparkling boulders some fifty paces away. They were cheerful, and laughed and jested, but under their breath, for fear of rousing the sleeping King.

Birds were singing in the alders by the river, and from the steep valley side beyond came the bleating of sheep, where some herdboy watched his flock. A harsher sound turned Arthur's eyes to a place beyond the ridge of woodland where big black birds swung and called in the misty morning. There lay the enemy they had pursued from the field. A few survivors, bound, lay nearby under the trees, but thirty or so men lay still unburied, their stiffened bodies exposed with the waxing day to the crows and kites.

It was well after noon before the burial party had done its work, and the King headed back with the troop towards Autun.

A mile or so short of the battlefield, he came across two

bodies. The messenger he had sent back to Bedwyr and Hoel to tell them that he was safe, and would return with the daylight, had fallen in with two stragglers from Quintilianus' army. One he had killed; the other, though wounded and now near dead with exposure and loss of blood, had killed him.

Arthur killed the man himself, and spurred his horse into a gallop back to his headquarters.

6

"The treaty is void," said Cerdic.

He and Mordred sat face to face. They had met on a high
shelf of the downs. It was a fine morning, and larks sang
wildly in the blue. To southward the smoke of a Saxon village
could be seen hanging in the still air. Here and there, in
cleared spaces between the thickets of ash and thorn, the
golden green of ripening barley showed among the white
flints where some Saxon peasant had scratched a living from
the bony land.

Mordred had come in kingly state. The Council, apprised
of Arthur's wishes before he left for Brittany, had raised no
slightest objection to Mordred's assumption of leadership; on
the contrary; those councillors who were left after the departure of Arthur and his Companions into Brittany were most of
them greybeards, and in their grief and fear at the news from
the battlefield they acclaimed Mordred with outspoken relief.
Mordred, wise in the ways of councils, moved with care. He
emphasized the doubtful nature of the news, spoke of his still-
held hope of his father's life, disclaimed any title but that of
regent, and renewed his vows of faith to the Council, and liege
homage to his father's Queen. After him Guinevere, speaking
briefly and with obviously fragile composure in her husband's
name, affirmed her belief that Mordred must now be invested
with power to act as he saw fit, and, herself resigning, pro-

posed him as sole regent. The Council, moved to a man, accepted her withdrawal and decided then and there to send a message to Constantine of Cornwall asking him to affirm his loyalty to the High King's successor.

Finally Mordred spoke again of urgency, and made clear his intention of riding south next day to the interview with Cerdic. He would take with him a detachment of the newly raised troops; it was never wise to approach their good Saxon neighbours without some show of strength. This, too, the Council voted him. So, escorted like a king, he faced Cerdic on the downs.

The Saxons, too, kept state. Cerdic's thegns crowded behind his chair, and an awning of brightly coloured cloth woven with gold and silver thread made a regal background to the thrones set for him and the regent. Mordred regarded Cerdic with interest. It was barely a year since he had last met the Saxon king, but in that time the latter had aged perceptibly and appeared not to be in robust health. Beside his chair stood his grandson Ceawlin, a young copy of the old fighter, who was said to have already fathered a brood of sturdy boys.

"The treaty is void."

The old king said it like a challenge. He was watching Mordred closely.

"Why else am I here?" Nothing could be gathered from the regent's smooth tone. "If it is true that the High King is dead, then the treaty—the same, or one revised as we may agree—must be ratified between myself and you."

"Until we know for certain, there is little point in talking," said Cerdic bluntly.

"On the contrary. When I last spoke with my father he gave me a mandate to make a new agreement with you, though I agree that there is little point in discussing that until another matter is cleared up. I doubt if I need to tell you what that is?"

"It would be best to come to the point," said Cerdic.

"Very well. It has lately come to my ears that Cynric, your son, and others of your thegns are even now back in your old lands beyond the Narrow Sea, and that more men daily flock to their standards. The bays fill with their longships. Now with the treaty between our peoples made void

322

by the High King's death—supposing this to be true—what am I to think of this?"

"Not that we prepare war again. Until proof comes of Arthur's death this would not only be ignoble, but folly." There was a gleam in the old king's eyes as he looked at the younger man. "I should perhaps make it clear that in no case are we contemplating war. Not with you, prince."

"Then what?"

"Only that with the advance of the Franks and the westward spread of people who are not our friends, we in our turn must move westward. Your King has halted this emperor's first sally, but there will be another, and after that another. My people want a safe frontier. They are gathering to embark for these shores, but in peace. We shall receive them."

"I see." Mordred was remembering what Arthur had said to him in their last discussion at Kerrec. "*First the Narrow Sea, and then the ramparts of the Saxon and English kingdoms.... Men fight for what is theirs.*" So might Vortigern have reasoned when he first called Hengist and Horsa to these shores. Arthur was no Vortigern, and so far he had been right not to doubt Cerdic: Men fight for what is theirs, and the more men manning the ramparts of the Shore, the more safely could the Celtic kingdoms lie behind them.

The old king was watching him closely, as if guessing what thoughts raced behind the smooth brow and unexpressive eyes. Mordred met his look.

"You are a man of honour, king, and also a man of wisdom and experience. You know that neither Saxon nor Briton wants another Badon Hill."

Cerdic smiled. "Now you have flashed your weapon at me, Prince Mordred, and I mine at you. That is done. I said they would come in peace. But they will come, and many of them. So, let us talk." He sat back in his chair, shifting a fold of the blue robe over his arm. "For the present I believe we must assume the High King's death?"

"I think so. If we make plans for that assumption they can be revised if necessary."

"Then I say this. I am willing, and Cynric with me, who will reign here when I am too old to fight, to remake the treaty with you that I made with your uncle." A sharp, twinkling look from under the shaggy brows. "It was your uncle last time we met. Now your father, it seems?"

"Father, yes. And in return?"

"More land."

"That was easily guessed." Mordred smiled in his turn. "More men need more land. But you are already too close for some men's peace of mind. How can you move forward? Between your lands and ours there lies this stretch of high downland. You see it." He gestured to the thin patch of barley shoots. "No ploughs, not even yours, King Cerdic, can make these stony uplands into rich fields of grain. And I am told that your neighbours, the South Saxons, no longer grant you free movement there."

Cerdic made no immediate reply. He reached behind him, and a guard put a spear into his hand. Behind Mordred a rustle and a whisper of metal betrayed quick movement among his own fighting men. He gestured with a hand, palm down, and the movement stilled. Cerdic reversed the spear and, leaning forward in his chair, began to draw in the chalky dust.

"Here we are, the men of Wessex. Here, in the rich corner lands, the South Saxons. And here stand you and I, now. The lands I am thinking of would be no nearer to your capital than our present borders. Here. And here."

The spear moved gently northward, then, just as Mordred would have protested, veered to the east and across the downland towards the upper Thames valley. "This way. This part is thick forest, and here is marshland, thinly peopled and poor. Both can be made good."

"Surely much of that is already Saxon land? Where your spear is now, that is the southern region, as they call it, of the Middle Saxons?"

"The Suthrige. Yes. I told you that we would take nothing that need trouble you."

"Would these settlers accept your people?"

"It is agreed." The old king slanted a bright glance up at the other man. "They are not a strong people, and it is rumored that the South Saxons are casting their eyes in that direction. They will welcome us. And we will make the land good for ourselves and for them."

He went on to talk about his plans, and Mordred questioned, and they talked for some time. Later Mordred said:

"Tell me, king. My information is not always correct." (This was not true, and he knew that Cerdic knew it, but the gambit brought a subject under discussion that neither had liked to broach openly.) "Since Aelle died, has there been a leader of note among the South Saxons? The land there is the best in the south, and it has long seemed to me that the king who held Rutupiae and the lands behind it held a key in his hand. The key to the mainland of the Continent and its trade."

There was a gleam of appreciation in the old king's eyes. He did not say in so many words that Aelle's descendants had no such grasp of the situation, but again, the two men understood one another. He merely said, thoughtfully: "I am told—though of course my information is not always correct—that the harbour at Rutupiae is beginning to silt up, and no attempt is being made to keep it clear."

Mordred, who, too, had heard this, expressed surprise, and the two men talked for a while longer to their mutual satisfaction, with at the end a very clear idea that, should Cerdic decide that the gateway to the Continent would be worth a foray by the West Saxons, Mordred with the British would at the very least refrain from pushing in through the back door, and at the most would throw his weight in beside the West Saxon king.

"With eventual free access for British traders to the port, of course," he said.

"Of course," said Cerdic.

So, with a good deal of satisfaction on both sides, the conference ended. The old king set off southward with the elder thegns, while his younger warriors escorted Mordred and his troops part of the way north, with a joyous accompaniment of shouting and weapon-play. Mordred rode alone for most of the way, ahead of the troops. He was dimly conscious of the noise behind him, where Saxon and Briton alike seemed to be celebrating what was now an alliance, rather than a mere treaty of non-aggression. He knew, as Cerdic had known without saying it, that such an agreement could not so readily have been reached with the victor of Badon and its forerunning battles. A new start had been made. The day of the young men had begun. Change was in the air. Plans, long stifled, buzzed in his brain, and the blood he shared with Ambrosius and Arthur and Merlin the vanished statesman ran free at last with the power to do and to make.

It is certain that if, on his return to Camelot, he had found awaiting him the royal courier with the news of Arthur's safety and imminent return, there would have been a perceptible weight of disappointment among the relief and joy.

No courier was there. For days now the wind had blown steadily eastward across the Narrow Sea, keeping the British ships sealed in the Breton harbours. But it carried a ship from Cornwall to Brittany with letters from Constantine the duke. They were identical, addressed the one to King Hoel, and the other to Bedwyr, and the latter was carried straight to Arthur, where he lay still at Autun.

> Mordred has shown himself in his true colours. He has given out through the kingdoms that King Arthur is slain, and he has assumed the kingship. The Queen has resigned her regency, and letters have come bidding me to resign my rights as Arthur's heir, and accept Mordred as High King. He treats now with Cerdic, who is to hold the ports of the Saxon Shore against all comers, and whose son is in Saxony raising his thousands, all of whom swear allegiance to Mordred.
>
> Meanwhile Mordred the King talks with the kings of Dyfed and Guent, and men from Mona and Powys, and is riding even now to meet the leaders from the north who have long spoken against Arthur the High King, wanting freedom for every man to rule as he wills, without reference to the Round Hall and the Council. Mordred, perjurer that he is, promises them self-rule and a change of the law. So he makes allies.
>
> Finally, with the High King gone, he plans to take Queen Guinevere to wife. He has lodged her at Caerleon, and consorts with her there.

Though the interpretation of Mordred's actions was Constantine's, the main facts as set out in the letter were true.

As soon as he returned from his meeting with Cerdic, Mordred had persuaded the Queen to go to Caerleon. Until the truth of Arthur's death was known, and the country—at present in the inevitable panic and turmoil following the sudden death of a powerful ruler—was more settled, and the new chain of command set up and working smoothly, he wanted, as he had promised, to ensure her safety. Camelot was as strong a city as Caerleon, but it was too far east; and ny trouble that was coming, as Mordred judged, would ome that way. The west was safe. (Except, he reminded imself, from Duke Constantine, that silently resentful exeir of Arthur's, who had sent no answer to the courteous avitations of the Council to discuss the matter at the round able. But Caerleon, armed and defended, was as safe from im as from any other disaffected man.)

It was too near for Guinevere's liking to her own homend of Northgalis, where a cousin now ruled who had wanted nce to marry her, and who said so rather too often to the vife he eventually had to take. But the alternatives were ven less comfortable. Guinevere would have preferred to ake refuge in a convent, but of the two best sanctuaries, ne nearer—the Lake convent on Ynys Witrin —was in the ummer Country, and the Queen would on no account put erself under the protection of its king, Melwas. The other, t Amesbury, Arthur's own township, which would have velcomed her, had failed signally to protect the last queen had housed. Morgause's murder still haunted the place.

So Mordred, making necessity a pleasure, chose Caer-con, where he had already convened meetings with those ings from the west and north with whom he had not already ad the chance to talk. He escorted the Queen there himself, mbarking with her at Ynys Witrin, and setting sail for the sca's mouth on the shore of the Severn Sea.

The voyage was calm, the sea gentle, the breezes light nd fresh. It was a golden interval in the turmoil of that iolent summer. The Queen kept apart with her ladies, but n the morning and evening of the two days' voyage Mordred isited her and they talked. On one of these occasions she old him, briefly and without detail, why she had been so eluctant to take refuge with King Melwas. It appeared that nany years ago, in the hot spring of youth, Melwas had bducted the Queen by force and stratagem, and carried her ff to a remote island in the water-logged fens of the Summer Country. There, by his magic, Merlin had discovered her, nd had led Bedwyr to a timely rescue. Later, Arthur and Melwas had fought, a notable combat, at the end of which he King, being the victor, had spared Melwas's life.

"After that?" said Mordred, shocked for once into bluntness. "I would have dragged him to your feet and killed him here, slowly."

"And had every man and woman in the kingdoms sure of his guilt and my shame?" She spoke calmly, but her cheek had reddened, whether at the memory of that shame or at the young man's fervour it was impossible to guess.

Mordred bit his lip. He recalled the story that Agravain had once told at a meeting of the Young Celts, and that he, Mordred, had not believed. So it was true; and now the cryptic references made by Bedwyr and Arthur at the site of the Princess Elen's rape became clear. He remembered further: the girl's violated body lying under its scrambled covering of pine needles.

He said thickly: "Later, then. But policy or no policy, would not have let him live."

He took his leave then. After he had gone the Queen sat for a long while without moving, looking out across the deck-rail at the shining water, and the distant shore sliding by, with its trees like clouds, and the clouds above them like towers.

Having installed Guinevere in comfort in the Queen's palace at Caerleon, Mordred plunged into the round of meetings with the leaders and petty kings assembled in the fortress to meet him. What he had not expected, and what Constantine, that western duke, knew well, was the dissatisfaction, even hostility, he found there for some of Arthur's policies. In the remoter highlands, the silver-age Romanization so dear to Ambrosius and Arthur had never been acceptable. It was not only the young men who wanted change; the older kings, too, were chafing against what they saw as the restrictive policies of a remote and lowland center of government. Arthur, in attempting to restore the territorial integrity of Roman Britain, had remodelled his federation of kingdoms in a way that to many of the rulers seemed outdated. To these men Mordred, outlander and Young Celt, was the leader they hoped for. That Arthur had just stood against actual Roman domination in defense of the Celtic lands would do much to bring him nearer their hearts again, but Arthur was presumed dead, and it became increasingly apparent that in the Celtic Highlands his return would not be altogether welcome.

Mordred trod carefully, talked sparingly, counted the allies sworn to his banner, and went every evening to see the Queen.

It was perhaps a little sad to see how Guinevere lighted up at his visits, and how eagerly she plied him with questions.

e answered her readily, keeping her more fully informed an Arthur had found time to do, of every move of state. he did not guess that he was simply taking every chance seeing her, and every means of prolonging his meetings ith her, letting her grow easier with him, become used to m in his role of ruler and protector. She thought merely at he was trying to bring her comfort and distraction, and as grateful accordingly, and her gratitude, in that time of ncertainty, grief and fear, brought her (as Mordred had oped) within touching distance of tenderness, and sighting stance of love. At any rate, when he held her hand to kiss , or, greatly daring, laid his own over it by way of comfort, e no longer hurried to withdraw from his touch.

As for Mordred, with his new authority, the uncertainty, e brilliant starting of long-held plans, the closeness of the ng-desired and lovely Guinevere, he was swept forward om day to day on a full tide of sovereignty and power, and is doubtful if at this stage he could have gone back. In ve, as in other things, there comes a time when the will signs and franks the desire, and then not even Orpheus, rning back, could cause his love to vanish. He had had at one glimpse of her, the real Guinevere, a lonely woman raid of life, a leaf to be blown into a safe corner by any rong wind. He would be—was—her safety. He was subtle ough to see that she recognized it, and used her gently. e could wait.

So the days went by, and the wind still closed the Narrow ea, and each of them, constantly, watched the road and e harbour for the messenger from Brittany. And each spent ours of the night watching the dark and thinking, thinking, d when they finally slept it was not of each other they reamed, but of Arthur.

Of Duke Constantine, brooding in his Cornish castle, they d not think at all.

7

Constantine's letter was brought to Arthur at his camp nea
Autun. King Hoel, feeling his years and his ailments now
that the battle was over, had withdrawn towards home. Bu
for Gawain, who in these days was always at his elbow
Arthur was alone.

He was also very tired. He had returned from the brie
punitive foray into the mountains to find near-panic among
the troops who, though still searching among the heape
dead for his body, believed themselves kingless. Even hi
return permitted little rejoicing, for Bedwyr, worse hurt tha
he had admitted, or that anyone had judged, was now se
riously ill, and the surgeons shook their heads over the palle
where he lay unconscious in an annex of the royal pavilion

So Arthur was alone in more ways than one. Bedwyr wa
dying. Cei, the elder foster-brother with whom he had bee
brought up, was dead. Caius Valerius, too, the ageing war
rior, veteran of Ambrosius' wars, and friend to Uther Pen
dragon and Merlin... The list seemed endless, the names
roll culled from the tale of Arthur's past glories, or even
simple tally of his friends. Of those close to him Gawai
alone was unwounded, and he, flown with the joy of his firs
great fight and resounding victory, had proved himself
strong support. To him Arthur, feeling his age for the firs

me (though he was by many years King Hoel's junior),
urned in gratitude and affection.

He started to read the duke's letter. Through the skins of
he tent wall he could hear the groaning and muttering where
Bedwyr tossed on his sickbed. He would die before morning
hey said, if the fever did not break.

The letter again. Mordred... making himself High King,
alking with Cerdic, gathering the kings of Wales and the
orth...

"Well," said Arthur, frowning; his head ached and the
orchlight made the words swim. "Well, all this is to be
xpected. If news of my supposed death was taken to
Mordred, he would take exactly these steps. We spoke of it
efore he left Kerrec. He was to meet with Cerdic to ratify
he treaty and talk over a possible new settlement in the
uture. Now, if my death was reported to him, he may well
ave thought it expedient to negotiate new terms, since the
ld treaty would then be invalid."

"New terms! An alliance that sounds like folly at its best,
nd at its worst a deadly peril! This about Cynric, raising
resh Saxon levies over here. Did you know, uncle?"

On the other side of the tent wall the sick man cried out,
hen was silent. Someone spoke hurriedly, there was mut-
ering, quick footsteps, the swish of robes. The King was
alf on his feet, the parchment falling to the floor, forgotten,
vhen the muttering began again. Not death yet, then; not
quite yet. Arthur sank back in his chair.

"Did you know about Cynric?" persisted Gawain.

"Cynric? Oh, calling men to his standard in Saxony. No,
ut if it is true—"

"I'm pretty sure it's true," said Gawain. "I've already
eard rumours going about the camp. Men massing by the
Neustrian shore. Longships lying in the harbours like arrows
ammed in a quiver. And for what? Cynric sails, and Cerdic
noves towards the south-east ports to meet him, then the
South Saxons are caught between the two, and the whole
outh-east will be Cerdic's, with freedom to invite whom-
soever he pleases to come over and swell his army. The
South Saxons have been the other wall that contained him,
nd who is to contain him now?"

His angry eyes glared into the King's, as if the latter's
omposure chafed him. If he heard the sounds from beyond

the wall, he gave no sign of it. He had not attempted to lowe
his voice.

"No doubt the next courier will bring me a report of Cyn
ric's doings." Arthur sounded weary but relatively unwor
ried. "But for the rest of this letter, Gawain, remember whe
writes. Duke Constantine did not take kindly to Mordred's
nomination as regent: He will have taken even less kindly
to his appointment as my sole heir. Everything he say
there—" He gestured to the letter on the floor, and Gawain
stooped to pick it up. "Everything he says that Mordred ha
done, Mordred and I agreed should be done. We only have
Constantine's word, which is hardly the word of a friend
for the way it is being done."

"But surely Mordred himself should have sent a report
If Constantine's man could get through—"

"If he believed the report of my death," said Arthur, "to
whom would he send it?"

Gawain, with an impatient shrug, started to hand the lette
back to his uncle. Then he checked. "There's more here
On the other side, see?"

Arthur took it from him, saw the last sentences on the
back, and began to read them aloud.

"'Finally, with the High King gone, he plans to take Quee
Guinevere to wife. He has lodged her at Caerleon, and—''

He did not finish it, but Gawain did, on a rising note where
genuine anger was shot with a kind of triumph.

"'And consorts with her there'!" He swung away, the
back to the King. "Uncle, whether or not he believes yo
dead, this is the act of a traitor! He has no proof as yet, no
shadow of reason for hauling the Queen off to Caerleon, an
paying his court to her! You say the rest of this letter coul
be true.... If it is, in whatever fashion, then this must b
true also!"

"Gawain—" began the King, in a warning voice, but Ga
wain, burning, swept on:

"No, you must hear me! I'm your kin. You'll hear truth
from me. I can tell you this, uncle, Mordred wanted the
kingdom always. I know how ambitious he was, even a
home in the islands, even before he knew he was your son
Your son, yes! But still a fisher-brat, a peasant with a peas
ant's guile and greed, and a huckster's honour! He's take
the first chance to turn traitor and get what he wants. Wit

he Saxons and the Welsh at his back, and the Queen at his
ide . . . 'consorts' indeed! He wasted no time! I've seen the
vay he looked at her—"

Something in Arthur's face stopped him there. It was hard
o say what it was, for the King looked like a dead man
arved in grey stone. Something about him suggested a man
vho sees at his feet a deadly pitfall lined with spears, and
vho with sheer stubborn faith holds to the one frail sapling
hat may stop him from falling. There was silence now from
he next room.

Arthur's voice was still steady, still reasonable, but with-
ut life or tone. "Gawain. The last thing I enjoined on my
on was, in the event of my death, to care for and protect
he Queen. He stands to her also as a son. What has been
aid, we shall forget."

Gawain bowed his head and muttered something that might
ave been an apology. Arthur handed him the letter.

"Burn this letter. Now. That's it," as Gawain held the
archment up to a torch and watched it blacken and curl
nto crow's feathers. "Now I must go to Bedwyr. In the
norning—"

He did not finish. He began to get to his feet, moving
lowly, putting weight on the arms of his chair like an old
nan, or a sick one. Gawain, who was fond of him, was seized
vith sudden compunction, and spoke more gently:

"I'm sorry, uncle, believe me, I am. I know you don't
vant to believe this of Mordred, so let us hope there is news
oon. Meanwhile, is there anything I can do for you?"

"Yes. You can go and give the orders for our return home.
Whatever the truth of the matter, I shall have to go back.
Either I must deal with Mordred, or with Constantine. This
s not the time to pursue our victory further, or even to call
or talks with the emperor. Instead, I shall send him a mes-
age."

"Yes?" queried Gawain, as the King paused.

Arthur's look was cryptic. "A task that will please you.
See that Lucius Quintilianus' body is disinterred and sent to
he emperor, with this message: that this is the tribute that
he British pay to Rome. Now leave me. I must go to Bed-
vyr."

* * *

333

Bedwyr did not die. The silence that had frightened the King was not death, or coma, but sleep, and the sick man woke from it with his fever gone and his wounds cool. Arthur, in spite of what might lie ahead of him, could set out for Britain with a free mind and a lighter heart.

The King set sail at last on a cloudy day with white spume blowing back from the wave-tops and the far sky leaning low over the heaving grey. The sea witch, it seemed, held sway over the Channel waters. Though the wind had changed its quarter at last, sea and sky alike still seemed to conspire against Arthur, her old enemy. Even the gulls, flakes ripped from the white waves, drove to and fro in the wind with shrieks of uncanny laughter, like a mockery. A gloomy, driving sea, without glitter, without light, heaved northward in the sudden turn of the wind. A gust took the *Sea Dragon's* standard and shredded it into streamers that whirled down wind. "An omen," men whispered, but Arthur, looking up, laughed, and said:

"He has gone ahead of us. If we seize the weather, we shall fly as fast as he."

And fly they did. What they could not know was that Cynric's Saxons had seized the same chance of wind, and that the longboats were also on their way across the Narrow Sea. Long and low, in those heaving seas the British caught no sight of them until, in the final gleams of a late and clouded afternoon, as they scudded along with the line of the Saxon Shore like a white wall on the horizon, the *Sea Dragon's* lookout saw what looked like Saxon longships riding in nearer the coast.

But when the King, with the heavy slowness that he showed these days, clambered up to a viewpoint by the mast, the longships—or their shadows—were gone.

"South Saxon ships, caught by the change of wind," said the master, at Arthur's elbow. "Shallow draught. They're lucky. They'll be back at anchor now, and no trouble to us. If we—"

He did not finish. A shout from the masthead made them all look round.

Low over the sea, its rain tearing out like a witch's hair, came a squall. Its shadow fled on before like a doom. The

334

master shouted. The seamen ran to their places. King, knights, sailors gripped the nearest stay.

The squall struck. In an instant all was screaming wind and rain. The air was black. Water cascaded down, whipping their faces so that they covered their eyes. The little ship shook and shuddered, stopped as if struck on a rock, then keeled over, reared and bucked like a frightened horse, groaned. Somewhere a crack of timber gave warning.

The squall blew for perhaps ten minutes. When, as suddenly as it had come, it blew away, fleeing over the sea above its shadow, the fleet, scattered and damaged, found itself driven almost within hailing distance of the coast. But the coast was the West Saxon shore, and there was no way that they could beat farther westward against a capriciously veering wind, to make the Dumnonian harbours, or even the bated shelter of Potters' Bay.

The King, with water licking the lower deck of the *Sea Dragon*, and two of her sister ships wallowing badly alongside, gave the order.

And so the sea witch drove Arthur ashore in Saxon territory where Cerdic's son Cynric, watching for the stragglers of his own immigrant fleet, rested with a band of his men after their stormy voyage. To him, from the ruins of the Roman lighthouse, came the watchman, running. Ships— three ships, and others heading shorewards behind them— were coming into the deep harbour to westward. There was no standard, no device. But by their lines and rig they were British ships, and they were setting inshore where they surely had no right to be. He had had, in the rapidly worsening light, no hint of their beaten condition.

Cynric did not know that the proposed immigration was known to and approved by the British; nor could he know that, by Mordred's new treaty with Cerdic, the incoming British ships were welcome to land. He drew his own conclusions. His landing had been observed, and was now, perhaps, to be opposed. He sent a messenger urgently inland to report his arrival and summon Cerdic's help, then gathered his men together to oppose the British landing.

If the two forces could have held apart long enough for the leaders to recognize one another or dispatch and receive

a message, all might have been well. But they met in th
growing dusk of that murky day, each side bent on its ow
desperate course and blind to all else.

The Saxons were tired after a stormy voyage, and mos
of them strange to the country and therefore alive to appre
hension. They also had with them their women and children
Primed with legends about the wars fought for each hide o
land since Hengist's time, and seeing the incoming troop
at a disadvantage as their craft ran inshore, they seized thei
weapons and raced down to the attack.

Arthur was indeed at a sad disadvantage. His men wer
highly trained and seasoned troops, but they had had littl
rest, and were some of them still suffering badly from th
effects of the voyage. He did have one stroke of luck: th
horse carriers, seeking a flat beach, had ventured farthe
along the coast to land, so those of the cavalry mounts which
had survived the crossing uninjured were safely got to shor
some distance off. But they—Arthur's best troops —coul
be no help against Cynric's men. Arthur and those of hi
knights who were with him, met by armed Saxons as they
struggled up the steep and streaming pebbles of the shore
fought on foot and in no sort of order. The struggle wa
disorganized, bloody and, on both sides, disastrous.

Just before dark a panting messenger on a lathered pon
came to Cynric's side. The message passed. Cerdic was on hi
way and Britain's new king with him. Cynric was to withdraw

Cynric, thankfully, withdrew as best he could, his mer
streaming off inland into the gathering darkness, guided by
the messenger towards the oncoming army of the West Sax
ons.

Arthur, exhausted but unhurt, listened in silence to the
report of someone who had heard the Saxon's shouted mes
sage.

"It was Cynric himself, my lord, who led this attack. Now
he has sent to his father for help, and Cerdic is coming. With
Britain's new king, I heard them say so, marching against
you to help Cynric and these invaders."

Arthur, weary to death and grieving over his losses, which
were even now being assessed, leaned heavily on his spear
confused, and, what was strange to him, irresolute. Tha
"Britain's new king" must be Mordred was obvious. Ever

if Mordred believed him, Arthur, dead, he would hardly march with Saxons to intercept British troopships obviously bringing home Arthur's battle-weary troops, unless Constantine had been right, and he coveted the kingdom to the point of treachery.

Someone was approaching, his feet sliding in the grinding pebbles. As Arthur turned, half expecting the angry Orkney voice at his elbow, triumphant over this evidence of treachery, a man came up.

"My lord, my lord! Prince Gawain is hurt. His boat was wrecked as it drove ashore, and he was wounded even before he could come to land. It is thought that he is dying."

"Take me there," said the King.

Gawain had been carried ashore on a stretcher of smashed planking from the wrecked boat. The remains of this, splintered and gaping, lay tilted on the shingle in the edge of the tide. Bodies of the dead and wounded lay about on the beach, looking like heaps of sodden clothing.

Gawain was conscious, but it was plain that he had received his death wound. His face was waxen, and his breathing shallow and sparse.

Arthur bent over him. "How is it with you, nephew?"

The pale lips gaped. In a while Gawain whispered: "My evil luck. Just as the war starts."

The war he had wanted, had almost worked for. The King put the thought aside, and stooping lower, moistened the dying man's lips from his wine flask.

The lips moved again.

"What's that? I didn't hear."

"Bedwyr," said Gawain.

"Yes," said the King, wondering. "Bedwyr is well enough. They say he is recovering fast."

"Bedwyr..."

"Gawain, I know that you have much to forgive Bedwyr for, but if you are asking me to take any message other than one of forgiveness and friendship, you ask in vain, dying or no."

"Not that. Bring Bedwyr back now. Needed. Help you kill...the traitor...Mordred."

Arthur made no reply to that. But in a few moments he could see that none was needed.

So, still counselling murder and strife, died the fourth of Morgause's sons. Leaving only the one, Mordred, his own son. *Mordred, the traitor?*

8

Mordred was back in Camelot when the news reached him of fighting on the south coast. No details were given. Mindful of his commitment to Cerdic, he gathered what troops were available and hastened southward, falling in with the West Saxon army just as a second messenger came panting with a fuller but strange-sounding version of what had happened.

His story was this: King Arthur's troopships had been sighted by the Saxon shore-dwellers, appearing soon after the longships, unable to reach the harbour at the mouth of the Itchen, had discharged their cargo of immigrants in the shallow, sheltered water behind Seal Island. Then a flying scud of cloud and mist had blotted out the fleet. The Saxon incomers, nervous, and not knowing what to expect from the approaching ships, had hurried their women and children inland away from the shore, and gathered in a defensive crowd within reach of signals from the lighthouse. The shore-folk who had come down to receive them gave them quick reassurance. They were safe now. The High King's ships, whether or no the King himself was on board, would not come into the shore ports, which were by treaty ceded to the Saxons these many years.

But hard on the reassurance came the runner from the lighthouse, gasping. The ships had turned under cover of the squall, had come inshore, and were even now landing armed men on the beaches only a short way to the west. It was apparent that, having been warned of this fresh influx of Saxon immigrants, Arthur had hoped to stop them by sea, but having failed, had sent his troops ashore to kill them or take them prisoner. To those who expressed doubt of this— these were the citizens of long standing, and Cynric himself was among them—the newcomers would not listen. The risk was too great. If the British meant business, and were allowed time to get their horses ashore . . . Everyone knew the reputation of Arthur's cavalry. . . .

So the Saxons, unorganized and weary as they were, had charged to the beaches and closed with Arthur's men. There they had met slaughter and defeat, and now, exhausted, were straggling inland with the frightened inhabitants of the shore villages, with Arthur and his cavalry in pursuit. And, the messenger concluded, with a sidelong glance of mistrust at Mordred, the Saxons—men, women, and little children— cried to their king for help against Arthur the breaker of treaties, the invader of their rightful kingdom, the slayer of lawful and peaceful incomers.

The distressful tale came pelting out, in the rough tongue of the Saxon peasant. It is doubtful if Mordred understood more than one word in three. But he grasped the central fact, and, rigid at Cerdic's side, felt the cold creep over him as if the blood drained from his body down into the chalky earth. The man stopped speaking, Cerdic began a question, but across it Mordred, for once heedless of courtesy, demanded harshly:

"The High King? Is that what he is saying? That Arthur himself is there?"

"Yes. It seems," said Cerdic, with fierce self-control, "that we have moved too soon, Prince Mordred!"

"This is certain?"

"Certain."

"This changes everything." Mordred, with an effort, made the understatement calmly, but his mind was whirling. What had happened could lead—had already led—to complete disaster: for himself, for the Queen, for the future of Britain.

Cerdic, watching him closely under those fierce brows merely nodded.

"Tell me exactly what has happened," said Mordred

quickly. "I hardly understood. If there could be any possibility of error . . . ?"

"As we go," said Cerdic. "Ride beside me. There is no time to waste. It seems that Arthur is not content with taking the shore villages, but he has driven their people inland, and is gathering his cavalry for pursuit. We must go to defend them." He spurred his pony, and as Mordred brought his own mount alongside, the old king repeated the rest of the messenger's tale.

Almost before he had done, Mordred, who had been biting his lips with impatient fury, exploded.

"This is absurd! Room for doubt, indeed! It is simply not to be believed! The High King break his own treaty? Is it not patent that his ships were driven ashore by the storm, and made landfall where they could? For one thing only, if he had intended to attack, he would have landed his cavalry first. It sounds to me as if he had been forced to go ashore, and that Cynric's people attacked on suspicion, without even an attempt at parley."

"That much is certainly true. But according to this man they knew only that the ships were British; the royal ship flew no standard. This in itself was suspicious—"

Mordred felt a sudden leap of the heart: shame and hope together; the chance that all, still, could be well. (Well? He did not pause, in that shame and hope, to examine the thought.) "Then it is possible that Arthur himself was not there? Was Arthur seen? Recognized? If his standard was not flying—"

"Once the British gained the beach, the Dragon was raised. He was there. This man saw him himself. Gawain as well. Gawain, incidentally, is dead."

The horses' hoofs beat softly on the sodden ground. Rain drove in their faces. After a long silence Mordred said, his voice once more cool and steady:

"Then if Arthur lives, his treaty with you still stands. It cancels the new alliance, which was made on the assumption of his death. What's more, it is certain that he would not break that treaty. What could he stand to gain? He fought only because he was attacked. King Cerdic, you cannot make his a cause for war."

"For whatever reason, the treaty has been broken," said Cerdic. "He has advanced, armed, into my country, and has killed my people. And others have been driven from their homes. They have called to me for help, and I have to answer their call. I shall get the truth from Cynric when we meet. If you do not wish to ride with us—"

"I shall ride with you. If the King is indeed bringing his troops ashore through Saxon territory, then it is of necessity. He does not want war. This I know. There has been a tragic error. I know Arthur, and so, king, should you. He favours the council chamber, not the sword."

Cerdic's smile was grim. "Lately, perhaps. After he got his way."

"Why not?" retorted Mordred. "Well, ride to join Cynric if you must, but talk with Arthur, too, before any further follies are committed. If you will not, then you must give me leave to talk with him myself. We can come out of this storm yet, king, into calm weather."

"Very well," said the old king heavily, after a pause. "You know what you must do. But if it does come to fighting—"

"It must not."

"If Arthur fights, then I shall fight him. But you—what of you, Prince Mordred? You are no longer bound to me. And will your men obey you? They were his."

"And are now mine," said Mordred shortly. "But with your leave, I shall not put their loyalty to the test on this field. If parley fails, then we shall see."

Cerdic nodded, and the two men rode on side by side in silence.

Mordred, as events were to prove, was right in his judgment of his army. The main body of his troops were men who had trained and served under him, and who had accepted him willingly as king. If a new Saxon war was to be started, the people—the townspeople, the merchants, the now thriving farmers in their lands made safe by the old treaties—wanted none of it. Mordred's recent announcement of his decision to ratify the treaty and, more, close an alliance with the powerful West Saxon king had been welcomed loudly in the halls and market-places. His officers and men followed him loyally.

Whether they would take arms against Arthur himself, for whatever reason, was another matter. But of course it would not come to that....

Arthur, leaving a picked force of men to guard the beaches

ships while the storm damage was repaired, led the remainder of his army fast inland, hoping to avoid the Saxon stragglers, and reach the border without further trouble. But soon his scouts returned with the news that Cerdic himself, marching to his son's rescue, was between the British and home. And presently, through a gap of the high downland, they could see the spears and tossing horsehair of Cerdic's warband, with in the rear, dimly glimpsed through the rain, the glitter of cavalry massed and orderly under what looked like the Dragon of Arthur's own standard. Less mistakable was Mordred himself, riding beside Cerdic at the head of the Saxons.

The troops recognized him first. *Mordred, the traitor.* The mutter went through the ranks. There were men there who had heard Gawain's dying words, and now at the sight of Mordred himself, approaching with the Saxon army, conspicuous on the glossy black horse that had been Arthur's gift, a growl went round, like a wind-borne echo of Gawain's final breath.

"Mordred! Traitor!"

It was as if the cry had burst in Arthur's own brain. The doubts, the accumulation of exhaustion and grief, the accusations levelled by Gawain, whom in spite of his faults Arthur had loved, weighed on the King and numbed his powers of thought. Caught in his unguarded confusion, in the aftermath of so much grief and loss, he recalled at last, as if the winds had blown that, too, out of the past, the doom foretold by Merlin and echoed by Nimuë. Mordred, born to be his bane. Mordred, the death-dealer. Mordred, here on this dark battlefield, riding against him at the head of the Saxons, his ancient enemies . . .

The canker of suspicion, biting with sudden pain, became certainty. Against all belief, against all hope of error, it must be true. *Mordred, the traitor.*

Cerdic's army was moving, massing. The Saxon king, his arm thrown up in command, was speaking to Mordred. In the throng behind the two leaders there was an ominous shouting and clash of shields.

Arthur was never one to wait for surprise. Before Cerdic could form his war-band for battle, his cavalry charged.

Mordred, shouting, spurred forward, but Cerdic's hand came down on his rein.

343

"Too late. There'll be no talking today. Get back to your men. And keep them off my back. Do you hear me?"

"Trust me," said Mordred, and, wheeling his horse, lashed the reins down on its neck and sent it back through the Saxon ranks at a gallop.

His men, some way to the rear of the Saxons, had not yet seen what was happening. The regent's orders were curt and urgent. "Flight" was not the word he used, but that was the essence of the order. To his officers he was brief:

"The High King is here, and joins battle with Cerdic. We have no part in this. I will not lead you against Arthur, but nor can I take Arthur's part against a man whose hand I have taken in treaty. Let this day come to an end and we will sort things out like reasonable men. Get the troops back towards Camelot."

So, with unbloodied swords and fresh horses, the regent's army retreated fast towards its base, leaving the field to the two ageing kings.

Arthur's star still held steady. He was, as Merlin had foretold, the victor in every field he took. The Saxons broke and yielded the field, and the High King, pausing only to gather the wounded and bury his dead, set off towards Camelot, in pursuit of Mordred's apparently fleeing troops.

Of the battle at Cerdices-leaga it can only be said that no one celebrated a victory. Arthur won the fighting, but left the lands open again to their Saxon owners. The Saxons, gathering their dead and counting their losses, saw their old borders still intact. But Cerdic, looking after the British force as, collected now and orderly, it left the field, made a vow.

"There will be another day, even for you, Arthur. Another day."

9

The day came.

It came with the hope of truce and the time to achieve sense and moderation.

Mordred was the first to show sense. He made no attempt to enter Camelot, much less to hold it against its King. He halted his troops short of the citadel, on the flat fields along the little River Camel. These were their practice grounds, and an encampment was there, furnished ready with supplies. This was as well, for already the warnings of war had gone out. The villagers, obedient it seemed to words carried on the wind, had withdrawn into the citadel, their women, children and cattle housed in the common land to the north-east within the walls. Mordred, going the rounds that night, found his men puzzled, beginning to be angry, but loyal. The main opinion seemed to be that the High King, in his age, was failing in judgment. He had wronged the Saxon king; that was one thing, and soon forgiven; but also he had wronged his son, the regent Mordred, who had been a faithful guardian of the kingdom and of the King's wife. So they said to Mordred; and they were visibly cheered when Mordred assured them that the next move would be a parley; there would soon, he said, be daylight on these dark doings.

"No sword will be drawn against the High King," he told

them, "except we be forced to defend ourselves from him through calumny."

"He asked for a parley," said Arthur to Bors.

"You'll grant it?"

The King's force was drawn up at some distance from the regent's. Between the two armies the Camel, a small stream, flowed glittering among its reeds and kingcups. The stormy skies had cleared, and the sun shone again in his summer splendour. Beyond Mordred's tents and standards rose the great flat-topped hill of Caer Camel, with the towers of Camelot gold-crowned against the sky.

"Yes. For three reasons. The first is that my men are weary and need rest; they are within sight of the homes they have not seen these many weeks, and will be all the more eager to get there. The second is that I need time, and reinforcements."

"And the third?"

"Well, it may even be that Mordred has something to say. Not only does he lie between my men and their homes and wives, but between me and mine. That needs more explaining than even a sword can do."

The two armies settled watchfully down, and messengers, duly honoured and escorted, passed between them. Three other messengers went secretly and swiftly from Arthur's camp: one to Caerleon, with a letter to the Queen; one to Cornwall, bidding Constantine to his side; and the third to Brittany, asking for Bedwyr's help, and, when he could, his presence.

Sooner than expected, the looked-for herald came. Bedwyr, though still not fully recovered from his sick-bed, was on his way, and with his splendid cavalry would be at the King's side within a few days.

And none too soon. It had come to the King's ears that certain of the petty kings from the north were marching with the intention of joining Mordred. And the Saxons along the whole length of the Shore were reported to be massing for a drive inland.

For neither of these things was Mordred responsible, and indeed, he would have prevented them if at this stage it had been possible; but Mordred, like Arthur, was, without the wish for it, without the reason, being thrust closer hour by

hour to a brink from which neither man could take a backward step.

In a castle far to the north, beside a window where the
birds of morning sang in the birch trees, Nimuë the enchantress threw back the coverlets and rose from her bed.

"I must go to Applegarth."

Pelleas, her husband, stretched a lazy hand out and pulled
her to him where he still lay in bed.

"Within raven's stoop of the battlefield?"

"Who said it would be a battlefield?"

"You, my dear. In your sleep last night."

She lifted herself from him, with her robe half round her,
staring down. Her eyes were wide, blurred still with sleep,
and tragic.

He said gently: "Come, love, it's a hard gift to have, but
you have grown used to it now. You've spoken of this, and
looked for it, for a long time. There is nothing you can do."

"Only warn, and warn again."

"You have warned them both. And before you Merlin
gave the same warning. Mordred will be Arthur's bane. Now
it is coming, and though you say Mordred is no traitor in his
heart, he has been led to act in ways that must appear treacherous to all men, and certainly to the King."

"But I know the gods. I speak with them. I walk with
them. They do not mean us to cease to act, just because we
believe that action is dangerous. They have always hidden
threats with smiles, and grace lurks behind every cloud. We
may hear their words, but who is to interpret them beyond
doubt?"

"But Mordred—"

"Merlin would have wished him dead at birth, and so
would the King. But from him already much good has come.
If even now they might be brought to talk together, the
kingdom might be saved. I will not sit idly by and assume
the gods' doom. I will go to Applegarth."

"To do what?"

"Tell Arthur that there is no treachery here, only ambition
and desire. Two things he himself showed in abundance in
youth. He will listen to me, and believe me. They must talk
together, or between them they will break our Britain in two,

347

and let her enemies into the breach that they have made. And who, this time, will repair it?"

In the Queen's palace at Caerleon the courier brought the letter to Guinevere. She knew the man; he had gone many times between herself and Mordred.

She turned the letter over in her hand, saw the seal, and went as white as chalk.

"This is not the regent's seal. It is from the King's ring, that was on his hand. They have found him, then? My lord is truly dead?"

The man, who was still on his knee, caught the roll as it fell from her hand, and rising, backed a step, staring.

"Why, no, madam. The King lives and is well. You have had no news, then? There have been sore happenings, lady, and all is far from well. But the King is safely back in Britain."

"He lives? Arthur lives? Then the letter—give me the letter!—it is from the King himself?"

"Why, yes, madam." The man gave it again into her hand. The colour was back in her cheeks, but the hand shook with which she tried to break the seal. A confusion of feelings played across her face like shadows driving over moving water. At the other end of the room her ladies, in a whispering cluster, watched anxiously, and the man, obedient to a gesture from the chief of them, went softly from the room. The ladies, avid for his news, went rustling after him.

The Queen did not even notice their going. She had begun to read.

When the mistress of the ladies returned, she found Guinevere alone and in visible distress.

"What, my lady, weeping? When the High King is alive?"

All Guinevere would say was "I am lost. They are at war and whatever comes of it, I am lost."

Later she rose. "I cannot stay here. I must go back."

"To Camelot, madam? The armies are there."

"No, not to Camelot. I will go to Amesbury. None of you need come with me unless you wish it. I shall need nothing there. Tell them for me, please. And help me make ready. I shall go now. Yes, now, tonight."

Mordred's messenger, arriving as the morning market carts rumbled over the Isca bridge, found the palace in turmoil, and the Queen gone.

10

It was a bright day, the last of summer. Early in the morning the heralds of the two hosts led the leaders to the long-awaited parley.

Mordred had not slept. All night long he had lain, thinking. What to say. How to say it. What words to use that would be straightforward enough to permit of no misinterpretation, but not so blunt as to antagonize. How to explain to a man as tired, as suspicious and full of grief as the ageing King, his, Mordred's, own dichotomy: the joy in command that could be, and was, unswervingly loyal, but that could never again be secondary. (Co-rulers, perhaps? Kings of North and South? Would Arthur even consider it?) At the truce table tomorrow he and his father would be meeting for the first time as equal leaders, rather than as before, King and deputy. But two very different leaders. Mordred knew that when his time came he would be not a copy of his father, but a different thing. Arthur was of his own generation; by nature his son had his thoughts and ambitions channelled otherwise. Even without the difference in their upbringing this would have been so. Mordred's hard necessity was not Arthur's, but each man's commitment was the same: total. Whether the old King could ever be brought to accept the new ways that Mordred could foresee, ways that had been embodied (though in the end discreditably) in the phrase "Young Celts," without seeing them as treachery, he could not guess. And then there was the Queen. That was one thing he could not say. "Even were you dead, with Bedwyr still living, what chance had I?"

He groaned and turned on the pillow, then bit his lip in case the guards had heard him. Omens bred too fast when the armies were out.

He knew himself a leader. Even now, with the High King's standard flying over his encampment by the Lake, Mordred's men were loyal. And with them, encamped beyond the hill, were the Saxons. Between himself and Cerdic, even now, there might be the possibility of a fruitful alliance; a concourse of farmers, he had called it, and the old Saxon had laughed.... But not between Cerdic and Arthur; not now, not ever.... Dangerous ground; dangerous words. Even to think such thoughts was folly now. Was he, at this most hazardous of moments, seeing himself as a better king than Arthur? Different, yes. Better, perhaps, for the times, at any rate the times to come? But this was worse than folly. He turned again, seeking a cool place on the pillow, trying to think himself back into the mind of Arthur's son, dutiful, admiring, ready to conform and to obey.

Somewhere a cock crew. From the scrambled edges of sleep, he saw the hens come running down the salt grass to the pebbled shore. Sula was scattering the food. Overhead the gulls swept and screamed, some of them daring to swoop for it. Sula, laughing, waved an arm to beat them aside.

Shrill as a gull's scream, the trumpet sounded for the day of parley.

Half a mile away, in his tent near the Lake shore, Arthur slept, but his sleep was an uneasy one, and in it came a dream.

He dreamed that he was riding by the Lake shore, and there, standing in a boat, poling it through the shallow water stood Nimuë; only it was not Nimuë, it was a boy, with Merlin's eyes. The boy looked at him gravely, and repeated in Merlin's voice, what Nimuë had said to him yesterday when, arriving at the convent on Ynys Witrin among her maidens, she had sent to beg speech with him.

"You and I, Emrys," she had said, giving him the boyhood name Merlin had used for him, "have let ourselves be blinded by prophecy. We have lived under the edge of doom, and feel ourselves now facing the long-threatened fate. But hear this, Emrys: fate is made by men, not gods. Our own follies, not the gods, foredoom us. The gods are spirits; they work by men's hands, and there are men who are brave enough to stand up and say: '*I am a man; I will not.*'

"Listen to me, Arthur. The gods have said that Mordred will be your bane. If he is so, it will not be through his own act. Do not force him to that act. . . . I will tell you now what should have remained a secret between Mordred and myself. He came to me some time ago, to Applegarth, to seek my help against the fate predicted for him. He swore to kill himself sooner than harm you. If I had not prevented him, he would have died then. So who is guilty, he or I? And he came to me again, on Bryn Myrddin, seeking what comfort I, Merlin, could give him. If he could seek to defy the gods, then so, Arthur, can you. Lay by your sword, and listen to him. Take no other counsel, but talk with him, listen, and learn. Yes, learn. For you grow old, Arthur-Emrys, and the time will come, is coming, has come, when you and your son may hold Britain safe between your clasped hands, like a jewel cradled in wool. But loose your clasp, and you drop her, to shatter, perhaps for ever."

In his dream Arthur knew that he had accepted her advice; he had called the parley, resolving to listen to anything his son had to say; but still Nimuë-Merlin had wept, standing in the boat as it floated away on the glassy Lake and vanished into the mist. And then, suddenly, as he turned his horse to ride up towards the meeting-place, the beast stumbled, sending him headlong into deep water. Weighted by his armour—why was he full-armed for a peaceful parley?—he sank, deep and ever deeper, into a pit of black water where fish swam around him, and watersnakes like weeds and weeds like snakes wrapped his limbs so that he could not move them. . . .

He cried out and woke, drenched in sweat as if he had indeed been drowning, but when his servants and guards came running, he laughed and made light of it, and sent them away, and presently fell again into an uneasy sleep.

This time it was Gawain who came to him, a Gawain bloody and dead, but imbued somehow with a grotesque energy, a ghost of the old, fighting Gawain. He, too, came floating on the Lake water, but he passed from its surface right into the King's tent and, pausing beside the bed, drew a dagger from his blood-encrusted side, and held it out to the King.

"Bedwyr," he said, not in the hollow whisper in which ghosts should speak, but in a high metallic squeaking like the tent poles shifting in the breeze. "Wait for Bedwyr. Promise anything to the traitor, land, lordship, the High Kingdom after you. And with it, even, the Queen. Anything to hold him off until Bedwyr comes with his host. And then, when you have the certainty of victory, attack and kill him."

"But this would be treachery."

"Nothing is treachery if it destroys a traitor." This time Gawain's ghost spoke, strangely, in Arthur's own voice. "This way you will make certain." The blood-stained knife dropped to the bed. "Crush him for ever, Arthur, make certain, make certain, certain. . . ."

"*Sir?*"

The servant at his bedside, touching the King's shoulder to wake him, started back as the King, jerking upright in the bed, glared round as if in anger, but all he said was, abruptly: "Tell them to see to the fastenings of the tent. How am I expected to sleep when the whole thing shifts about as if a storm was blowing?"

It had been agreed, in the exchange between the heralds, that fourteen officers from each side should meet at a spot half-way between the hosts.

There was a strip of dry moorland not far from the Lake shore where a pair of small pavilions had been pitched, with between them a wooden table, where the two leaders' swords were laid. Should the parley fail, the formal declaration of battle would be the raising, or drawing of a sword. Over one pavilion flew the King's standard, the Dragon on gold. To this device, Mordred, as regent, had also been entitled. He, his mind set on the necessity of being received into grace, and not putting in the way of grace the smallest rub, had given orders that his royal device should be folded away, and until the day was spent and he was declared once more as Arthur's heir, a plain standard should be carried for him.

This flew now on the other pavilion. As the two men took their places at the table, Mordred saw his father eyeing it. What he cannot have known was that Arthur himself, as a young man, had borne a plain white banner. "White is my colour," he had said, "until I have written on it my own device. And write it, come in the way what will, I shall."

To Nimuë in her convent of maidens on the island in the Lake came Arthur's sister Queen Morgan. This was a Morgan subdued and anxious, knowing well what might be her fate if Arthur should be defeated or die in battle. She had been her brother's enemy, but without him she was, and would be, nothing. She could be trusted now to use all her skill and vaunted magic on his behalf.

So Nimuë accepted her. As Lady of the Lake convent, Nimuë stood in no awe of Morgan, either as sorceress or queen. Among her maidens were other royal ladies; one of them a cousin of Guinevere's from North Wales, another from Manau Guotodin. With them she set Morgan to prepare medicines and to make ready the barges that would be used to ferry the wounded across to the island for healing.

She had seen Arthur and delivered her warning, and he had promised to call the parley and let the regent have his say. But Nimuë, for all her words to Pelleas, knew what the gods withheld behind the thunder-clouds that even now were building up beyond the shining Lake. Small from the island, the two pavilions could be seen, with the small space between.

For all the massed clouds on the far horizon, it promised to be a beautiful day.

The day wore on. Those officers who had accompanied their leaders to the truce table showed ill at ease at first, eyeing friends or former comrades on the other side with distrust, but after a while, relaxing, they began to talk among themselves, and fell into groups behind their respective leaders' pavilions.

Out of earshot of them, Arthur stood with Mordred. Occasionally they moved, as if by consent, and paced a few steps and back. Sometimes one spoke, sometimes the other. The watchers, focused on them even while they spoke of other things, tried to read what was happening. But they could not. The King, still looking tired, and frowning heavily, did nevertheless listen with calm courtesy to what the younger man was, with emphasis, saying.

Farther away, unable to see clearly or to hear anything at all, the armies watched and waited. The sun climbed the sky. The heat increased, brightness flashing back from the glassy surface of the Lake. Horses stamped and blew and switched their tails, impatient of heat and flies, and in the ranks the slight fretting of suspense changed to restlessness. The officers, themselves on the fidget, checked it where they could, and watched the truce table and the sky with steadily growing tension. Somewhere in the distance the first dull roll of thunder sounded. The air weighed heavy, and men's skins tightened with the coming storm. It was to be guessed that neither side wanted the fight, but, by the irony that governs affairs of violence, the longer the truce talks went on, the more the tension grew, till the slightest spark would start such a fire as only death could quench.

None of those watching was ever destined to know what Arthur and Mordred spoke of. Some said later—those who lived to speak—that in the end the King smiled. Certain it is that he was seen to put out a hand to his son's arm, turning back with him towards the table where the two swords lay side by side, unsheathed, and beside them two goblets and a golden jug of wine. Those nearest heard a few words:

"...To be High King after my death," said Arthur, "and meanwhile to take lands of your own."

Mordred answered him, but in a voice too low to overhear. The King, gesturing to his servant to pour the wine, spoke again. "Cornwall," they could hear, and later, "Kent," and then, "It may well prove that you are right."

Here he stopped and glanced round as if some sound had interrupted him. A sudden stray current of air, thunder-heavy, had stirred the silk of his pavilion, so that the ropes creaked. Arthur shifted his shoulders as if against a cold draught, and looked sideways at his son, a strange look (it was the servant who, afterwards, told this part of the story), a look which was mirrored in a sudden flash of doubt in Mordred's face, as if, with the smile and the smooth words and the proffered wine, there might still be trickery there. Then in his turn the regent shrugged, smiled, and took the goblet from his father's hand.

A movement went through the waiting ranks, like a ruffle of wind across a cornfield.

The King raised his goblet, and the sun flashed in the gold.

An answering flash, from the group beside his pavilion, caught his eyes. He whipped round, shouting. But too late.

An adder, a speckled snake no more than two handspans long, had crept from its hiding to bask on the hot ground. One of Arthur's officers, intent on the scene at the truce table, stepped back unseeingly onto the creature's tail. Whipping round, the adder struck. At the pain the man, whirling, saw the snake on the recoil. His own reflex, that of a trained fighting man, was almost as fast. He snatched his sword out and slashed down at the snake, killing it.

The sun struck the metal. The sword's flash, the King's raised arm, his sudden movement and shout of command, came to the watching hosts as the long-awaited signal. The inaction, the nerve-stretching tension, made almost unbearable by the thundery heat and the sweating uncertainty of that long vigil, suddenly snapped, in a wild shout from both sides of the field.

It was war. This was the day. This was the wicked day of destiny.

A dozen flashes answered as the officers on both sides drew their swords. The trumpets screamed, drowning the shouts of the knights who, trapped between the armies, seized their horses from the grooms and turned furiously to hold back the converging ranks. They could not be heard; their gestures, misinterpreted as incitements to attack, were wasted. It was a matter only of seconds, seconds of furious noise and confusion, before the front ranks of the two armies met in a roaring clash. The King and his son were swept apart, each to his proper station, Arthur under the great Dragon, Mordred no longer regent and King's son, but for all time branded traitor, under the blank standard that, now, would never be written on. And then over the bar of the field, called by the trumpets, like a sea of tossing manes, came the spears and horsehair of the Saxons, and the black banners of the northern fighters who, like the ravens, could hardly wait to take the pickings from the dead.

Soon, too late to dull those flashing signals, the thunderheads came slowly massing across the hot sky. The air darkened, and in the distance came the first flicker of lightning, the herald of the storm.

The King and his son were to meet again.

Towards the end of the day, with his friends and long Companions dead or dying round him, and the hundreds of wasted deaths reeking to the now dark and threatening sky, it is doubtful if Arthur even remembered that Mordred was anything but a traitor and an adulterer. The straight speaking, the truths laid down during that talk by the truce table, the faith and trust so nearly reaffirmed, all had vanished in the first stress and storm of the attack. It was Arthur, duke of battles, who once more took the field. Mordred was the enemy, the Saxon allies his savage helpers; this battle had been fought before, and many times. This was Glein and Agned, Caerleon and Linnuis, Cit Coit Caledon and Badon Hill. On all these fields the young Arthur had triumphed; for all of them his prophet and adviser, Merlin, had promised him the victory and the glory. Here, too, on the Camel field, it was victory.

At the end of the day, with the thunder overhead and the lightning flaming white from the sky and the water of the Lake, Arthur and Mordred came once again face to face.

There were no words. What words could there have been? For Mordred, as for his father, the other man was now the enemy. The past was past, and there was no future to be seen beyond the need to get to the end of this moment that would bring with it the end of the day.

It was said afterwards, no one knows by whom, that at the moment of meeting, as the two men, on foot now, and white with the sweat and dust of the battlefield, knew one another, Mordred checked in his stride and stroke. Arthur, the veteran, did not. His spear took his son straight and clean beneath the rib-cage.

Blood gushed down the spear shaft in a hot stream over Arthur's hand. He loosed the shaft, and reached for his sword. Mordred lurched forward like a spitted boar. The butt of the shaft struck the ground. He leaned on it, and, still carried forward by the weight of the half-checked stroke, came within sword's length of his father. Arthur's hand slippery with blood, fumbled momentarily on Caliburn's grip and in that moment Mordred's sword swung, even as he fel dying, in a hard and deadly blow to the side of the King's head.

Mordred pitched down then into the pool of his own blood. Arthur stood for a few seconds still, his sword dropping from his bloodied hand, his other hand moving numbly as if in an attempt to ward off some slight and trivial blow; then slowly his body bent and buckled, and he, too, fell, and his blood joined with Mordred's on the ground.

The clouds broke, and like a waterfall the rain came down.

EPILOGUE

The cool stream on his face brought Mordred back for a moment into the dark. It was quiet, too, all sounds hushed and far, like distant water lapping on a pebbled shore.

A cry somewhere nearby. *"The King! The King!"*

A bird calling. The hens were coming down the shingle for food. A gull screaming, but in words now: *"The King! The King!"*

Then, and this made him sure it was a dream, the voices of women. He could see nothing, feel nothing, but near him was the rustle of a gown and a gust of women's scent. Voices eddied across him, but no one touched him. A woman's voice said:

"Lift him carefully. Here. Yes, yes, my lord, lie still. All will be well."

And the King's voice, too faint to hear, followed—surely?—by Bedwyr's:

"It is here. I have it safely. The Lady will keep it for you till you need it again."

Again the voices of women, and the first voice, strongly: "I shall take him to Applegarth, where we shall see to the healing of his wounds."

Then the rain, and the creak of rowlocks, and the sound of women's weeping fading into the lapping of the lake water and the hiss of the rain falling.

His cheek was on a cushion of thyme. The rain had washed the blood away, and the thyme smelled sweetly of summer.

The waves lapped. The oars creaked. The seabirds cried. A porpoise rolled, sleek in the sun. Away on the horizon he could see the golden edge of the kingdom where, since he was a small child, he had always longed to go.

THE LEGEND

I have used fragments from two sources, the "history" written by Geoffrey of Monmouth in the twelfth century, and the romance of Malory's *Le Morte d'Arthur*, written in the fifteenth.

Geoffrey of Monmouth's
History of the Kings of Britain

In the time of the emperor Leo, Lucius Hiberius, procurator of the Roman republic, sent a message to King Arthur demanding that he pay tribute to Rome, and commanding him to appear before the Senate to answer for his failure to do so. Refusal would mean that the Romans would attack Britain, and restore her to the Roman republic.

Arthur's reply was to gather together an army and sail to Brittany, where, with his cousin King Hoel, he sent word around asking his allies to join him. Meanwhile he sent ambassadors to Lucius Hiberius informing him that he would not pay the tribute, but would fight. "Thereupon the ambassadors depart, the Kings depart, the barons depart, nor are they slow to perform what they had been bidden to do."

Meanwhile ill news was brought to Arthur and Hoel. Hoel's niece, the Princess Helena, had been seized by a monstrous giant, who had fled with her to the top of St. Michael's

Mount. Arthur himself, with Kay and Bedivere, set out to deal with the monster. They saw a fire of wood blazing on the Mount, and another on a smaller island nearby. Bedivere, sent to spy things out, found a small boat and rowed across to the islet, where, as he landed, he heard the ullaloo of a woman wailing, and found, by the fire, an old woman weeping beside a new grave-mound. The giant had killed the princess, and gone back to his lair on St. Michael's Mount. Bedivere reported to Arthur, who thereupon tackled the monster in his hilltop lair, and killed him in single combat.

King Arthur then gathered his army and marched with his allies to Autun in Burgundy to meet the army of the Romans. He sent an embassy ahead to Lucius Hiberius to bid him withdraw, or he, Arthur, would give battle as he had sworn. Gawain was with the embassy, and the younger knights, spoiling for a fight, egged Gawain on to start a quarrel. Which he did, and after some high words killed one Gaius Quintilianus, nephew of Hiberius himself. So battle was joined. Bedivere and Kay were killed, but Arthur was victorious, and pressed on eastward, intending to go on to Rome and make himself emperor.

But at this point he heard that his nephew Mordred, to whom he had committed the charge of his kingdom during his absence, had set the crown on his own head, and taken Queen Guinevere to wife, in spite of her former marriage.

Mordred had also sent Cheldric, duke of the Saxons, into Germany, to enlist others of his countrymen and take them back to Britain to swell Mordred's army. For this, more land was to be granted to the Saxons. Mordred had also gathered together the Scots, Picts and Irish and was preparing to resist Arthur's return to Britain.

Arthur, hastening back, landed at Richborough, and there defeated Mordred's troops, but in the fighting Gawain was killed. Mordred fled, but took his stand again at Winchester, where he had lodged the Queen. She fled in fear to a convent near Caerleon, and there took the veil. Arthur and Mordred fought again near Winchester, and again Mordred broke and fled towards Cornwall, where, in the final battle on the River Camel, both he and Arthur fell.

Arthur, who was carried to the island of Avilion for the healing of his hurts, left his kingdom to Constantine of Cornwall. One of Constantine's first acts was to seek out both of Mordred's sons and murder them "by a cruel death" at the sanctuary altar.

Sir Thomas Malory's
Le Morte D'Arthur

1. When Arthur heard of Mordred's birth, he sent for all the children born in the same month, in the hope of finding Mordred and destroying him. The ship in which the children were placed foundered, but Mordred was cast up, and taken in by a good man, who nourished him till he was fourteen, then took him to the court.

2. When Queen Morgause's sons knew that she had taken Sir Lamorak for her lover, Gawain and his brothers sent for her to a castle near Camelot, intending there to trap and kill Lamorak. One night, while Lamorak was with the queen, Gaheris seized his chance, and, creeping fully armed to their bedside, seized his mother by the hair and struck off her head. Because Lamorak was unarmed Gaheris could not kill him. Lamorak had no choice but to flee, but eventually the Orkney brothers, with Mordred, tracked him down and killed him.

3. Some time later Sir Tristram, challenged by Agravain and Gaheris, refused to fight them, recognizing them by their device as Arthur's nephews. "It is shame," he said, "that Sir Gawain and ye be come of so great a blood that ye four brethren be named as ye be, for ye be called the greatest destroyers and murderers of good knights that be now in this realm." The brothers shouted insults at the Cornish knight, on which he turned to ride away. Agravain and Gaheris promptly attacked him from behind. Tristram, forced to fight, struck Agravain on the head, causing a grievous wound, and also knocked Gaheris out of the saddle. Gareth speaking later with Tristram, declared himself at odds with his brothers: "I meddle not of their matters, therefore there is none of them that loveth me. And for I understand that they be murderers of good knights I left their company."

4. Agravain and Mordred hated Guinevere the Queen and Lancelot. Agravain insisted that the King be told of what he

swore (and Lancelot later denied on oath) was their adultery. Agravain went to Arthur to tell him that Lancelot and the Queen were betraying him, and must be brought to trial, as the law demanded. He offered to bring proof to Arthur. The King, wanting only to ignore the charge, and loving both Lancelot and the Queen, was forced to accede. He agreed to go hunting and to tell Guinevere that he would be away all night. Agravain and Mordred got twelve knights together—all apparently their own countrymen from Orkney—and hid near the Queen's bedchamber to await events. When Lancelot told Sir Bors that he was bidden that night to speak with the Queen, Sir Bors, uneasy but ignorant of what was afoot, tried to stop him. Lancelot refused to listen to him, and went to see the Queen. At a given moment the twelve knights rushed Guinevere's door, shouting: "Now thou art taken!" and smashed the door open with a bench. Lancelot, who was unarmed, wound his mantle round his arm, let the first man in, then killed him. The Queen's ladies helped him don the dead man's armour. In the subsequent mêlée Agravain was killed, and Gareth, and Mordred was wounded, but managed to flee. He rode straight to the King and told him of the affray, and Arthur grieved bitterly, because he foresaw the end of the fellowship of the Round Table, and also because, by law, he must now put Guinevere to trial by fire.

(Here follows the inevitable last-minute rescue of Guinevere by Lancelot, and the flight of the lovers to Lancelot's castle of Joyous Gard.) Arthur pursued him, and defeated him in battle, whereupon Lancelot returned the Queen ceremoniously to her husband, and fled overseas. Lancelot, who ruled all France," went to his castle in Burgundy, and gathered another army to withstand King Arthur. Arthur, leaving Mordred as regent, or "ruler of all England," went with Gawain, and a great host at his back, to attack Lancelot in Burgundy. There was a great battle, with dreadful losses on both sides.

But then it was reported to Arthur that Mordred had had letters forged, purporting to come from overseas with the news of his, Arthur's, death. Mordred had called a parliament, which pronounced him king, whereupon he declared his intention of taking Guinevere to be his queen. But she, being unwilling, fled to the Tower of London, and held it against him. While Mordred pleaded with her he heard that King Arthur was returning at the head of an army to reclaim his kingdom. Mordred thereupon sent around the kingdom to seek support, which he got in good measure, because "then was the common voice among them that with Arthur was none other life but war and strife, and with Sir Mordred was great joy and bliss. . . . And so fared the people at that time, that they were better pleased with Sir Mordred than they were with King Arthur." So Mordred led a great host to Dover to face his father on landing. A terrible fight ensued. Gawain was found dying in a half-beached boat, and with his last breath he advised Arthur to forgive Lancelot and invite him back to help crush Mordred. Then Gawain died, and Arthur pursued Mordred and his fleeing host and gave battle once more on the downs, where again Mordred was put to flight.

Eventually the two hosts took their stand "westward towards Salisbury, and not far from the seaside." In Mordred's host were the men "of Kent, Southsex, and Surrey, Estsex, and of Southfolk, and of Northfolk." But during the night King Arthur dreamed evil dreams, and into them came Gawain, warning the King that if he should fight on the morrow he would be killed. Once more Gawain advised him to send for Lancelot, and to hold Mordred off with promises, in order to delay the battle till help should come, and Mordred could be destroyed.

So in the morning the King sent messengers to Mordred to promise him "lands and goods as much as ye think best . . . and at the last Sir Mordred was agreed for to have Cornwall and Kent, by Arthur's days; after, all England after the days of King Arthur."

Next a meeting was arranged between Mordred and the King. Each took with him fourteen knights, and they met at a place between the two armies. Both leaders had warned their armies that, should the talks fail, the signal for attack would be the drawing of a sword. "And so they met as the appointment was, and so they were agreed and accorded thoroughly; and wine was fetched, and they drank." But a adder crept out of a little heath bush, and stung a knight on the foot. The man drew his sword to slay the adder, and at that the watching hosts attacked one another. Towards the end of the day of carnage Arthur sought out Mordred, wh alone of his host still lived. Of Arthur's army only Sir Lucan, Sir Bedivere and the King survived. Sir Lucan tried to dissuade Arthur from seeking Mordred out, for "we have won the field, for here we be three on live, and with Sir Mordred none is on live, and if ye leave off now this wicked day of destiny is past."

But Arthur, unheeding, attacked and killed Mordred, and in so doing received his own death wound. Sir Bedivere carried him to the shore, where a barge awaited him; in it were three queens—his sister Queen Morgan, the Queen of Northgalis, and the Queen of the Waste Lands, with Nimuë, the chief Lady of the Lake. The barge took sail for the vale of Avilion, where the King might be healed of his grievous wound.

AUTHOR'S NOTE

"The wicked day of destiny," as Malory calls it, is the day when Arthur's final battle was fought at Camlann. In this battle, we are told, "Arthur and Medraut fell."

This reference, from the *Annales Cambriae*, which was compiled three or possibly four centuries after Camlann, is all we know of Mordred. When he reappears some centuries later, in the romances of Malory and the French poets, he has taken on the role of villain necessary to the convention of romance. Mordred the traitor, perjurer and adulterer is as much an invention as the lover and great knights Sir Lancelot, and the roles played by both in the tales of "King Arthur and his Noble Knights" are filled with the absurdities inevitable in a long-drawn series of stories.

In the fragments of those stories that have been used in this book, the absurdities speak for themselves. Throughout the final debacle Arthur, that wise and experienced ruler, shows neither sense nor moderation; worse, he is tainted with the same treachery for which he condemns his son. Arthur had had any reason at all to distrust Mordred (for instance over the murder of Lamorak or the exposure of Lancelot and the Queen) he would hardly have left him as "ruler of all England" and guardian of the Queen, while he himself went on an expedition from which it was possible he might never return. Even granted that he did appoint Mordred his regent, it is hard to see why Mordred, with every hope of becoming his father's heir, should have forged a letter purporting to tell of Arthur's death, and on the strength of that seized both kingdom and Queen. Knowing that Arthur was still alive, and with a vast army at his back, Mordred could be sure that the King would come straight home to punish his son and repossess kingdom and Queen. More, the final battle between King and "traitor" was brought about by accident, in the very moment when the King was about to seal a truce with the villainous Mordred, and grant him lands to rule. (It is another, though minor, absurdity that the lands are Cornwall and Kent, at opposite sides of the country, the one already held by the Saxons, the other by Arthur's declared heir, Constantine.)

For none of the "Mordred story," then, is there any evidence at all. It is to be noticed that the *Annales Cambriae* does not even state that he and Arthur fought on opposite sides. It would have been possible—and very tempting—to have rewritten the story completely, and set Arthur, with Mordred at his side, against the Saxons, who (as recorded in the *Anglo-Saxon Chronicle*) fought a battle against the Britons in A.D. 527, and presumably won it, since the *Chronicle* does not emphasize Saxon defeats. The battle, at the right date, might even have been the battle of Camlann, the last stand of the British against the Saxons.

But the temptations had to be resisted. Until I came to study in detail the fragments that make up Mordred's story, I had accepted him without question as the villain of the piece, an evil man who brought about the tragedy of Arthur's final downfall. Hence, in my earlier books, I had made Merlin foresee that doom, and warn against it. So I could not rewrite the Camlann battle. Instead I tried to iron out the absurdities in the old story, and add some saving greys to the portrait of a black villain. I have not made a "hero" out of Mordred, but in my tale he is at least a man who is consistent in his faults and virtues, and has some kind of reason for the actions with which legend has credited him.

Perhaps the most exciting thing about the tale of the final years of Arthur's reign is the way which the actual historical events can be made to fit with the legend. Arthur most certainly existed, and so may Mordred have done, but since the traitor of romance was a figment of the story-teller's imagination, then I would suggest that the Mordred of my story is just as valid, since I, too, have perhaps earned a place among those of whom Gibbon writes with such urbane contempt:

> The declamations of Gildas, the fragments and fables of Nennius, the obscure hints of the Saxon laws and chronicles, and the ecclesiastical tales of the venerable Bede have been illustrated by the diligence, and sometimes embellished by the fancy, of succeeding writers, whose works I am not ambitious either to censure or transcribe.

> *—Decline and Fall of the Roman Empire*

Some other brief notes

Camlann. The site of Arthur's last battle cannot be identified with any certainty. Some scholars have suggested Birdoswald in Northumbria (the Roman Camboglanna), others the Roman Camulodonum (Colchester). The most usually accepted site is in Cornwall, on the River Camel; this because of Arthur's strong connection with West Country legend. I have set the battle beside the River Camel near South Cadbury in Wiltshire. The hill at South Cadbury has, owing to recent excavations, a strong claim to being an Arthurian strong point, possibly "Camelot" itself. Hence there seemed no need to look further for the site of the final battle. I do not know when the local stream was called the Camel, but the long ridge nearby was in antiquity known as "Camel Hill."

At that date, also, there would be lake and fenland stretching right inland from the estuary of the River Brue almost as far as South Cadbury. The hills of modern Glastonbury would then be islands—Ynys Witrin, or the Glass Isle—and Caer Camel "not far from the seaside." The barge that carried the wounded Arthur to be healed at Avilion would have only a brief journey to the legendary place of healing.

The date of Camlann. Scholars place the date of the battle somewhere between A.D. 515 and 539—a wide choice, but a date somewhere about 522 to 527 seems reasonable. One date given for Badon Hill is A.D. 506, and we are told (in the *Annales Cambriae*) that Camlann was twenty-one years later.

The following is a table of the "real" (as opposed to guess-work) dates:

A.D.

524. Clodomir, son of Clovis and ruler of the central part of the Frankish kingdom, was killed at Vézeronce in battle with the Burgundians. Two of his sons, aged ten and seven, were put in charge of Clovis's widow, Clothild, in Paris, but were murdered by their uncles. The third son fled into a monastery.

526. Theodoric, King of Rome and "emperor of the West," died at Ravenna.

527. Justin, ageing "emperor of the East," abdicated in favour of his nephew Justinian.

527. According to the *Anglo-Saxon Chronicle*, "in this year Cerdic and Cynric fought against the Britons at the place which is called *Cerdicesleag*" (Cerdic's field or woodland).

Neustria. This was the name given to the western portion of the Frankish empire after its division at Clovis's death in 511.

Drustan. Drust or Drystan, son of Talorc, is an eighth-century warrior who later was absorbed into the Arthurian legend as Tristram.

Linet. In one version of the Gareth legend he marries Liones, in another her sister Linet.

Arthur's sons. We have the names of two, Amr and Llacheu.

Convent. The word did not always, as now, imply a religious house for women only. It was used interchangeably

369

with "monastery." Many of the foundations had communities of both women and men.

The harper's song. This is a free translation of an Anglo-Saxon poem, "The Wanderer," which in *The Last Enchantment* I attributed to Merlin.

Seal Island: Selsey. *Suthrige:* Surrey.

Edinburgh and Lochawe,
1980–1983

ABOUT THE AUTHOR

LADY MARY STEWART's career as a novelist began in 1954, with the publication of MADAM, WILL YOU TALK? Since that time, she has written seventeen more novels, including three children's books. THE WICKED DAY follows three previous novels based on Arthurian legend: THE CRYSTAL CAVE, THE HOLLOW HILLS, and THE LAST ENCHANTMENT. In 1971, the Scottish chapter of the International PEN Association awarded her the Frederick Niven Prize for THE CRYSTAL CAVE.

Lady Mary lives in Edinburgh, Scotland, with her husband, Sir Frederick Stewart, who has recently retired from the chairmanship of the Geology Department of Edinburgh University.